The
Troll
Circle

The Troll Circle

(Trollringen)

Translated,
with an afterword
and notes, by
Sverre Lyngstad

Sigurd Hoel

University of Nebraska Press, Lincoln and London

Originally
published as *Trollringen*,
© Gyldendal
Norsk Forlag A/S 1958
© 1991 by the
University of Nebraska Press
Manufactured in the United
States of America
The paper in this book
meets the
minimum requirements of
American National
Standard for Information
Sciences –
Permanence of Paper for
Printed Library Materials,
ANSI Z39.48–1984.
Translation of this
book has been
assisted by a grant
from the Norwegian
Cultural Council.
Library of
Congress Cataloging-
in-Publication Data
Hoel, Sigurd, 1890–1960.
[Trollringen. English]
The troll circle / by Sigurd
Hoel ; translated and with
an afterword and notes by
Sverre Lyngstad. p. cm. –
(Modern Scandinavian
literature in
translation) Translation of:
Trollringen. Includes biblio-
graphical references.
ISBN 0-8032-2359-5
(alk. paper)
I. Lyngstad, Sverre.
II. Title. III. Series.
PT8950.H58T713 1991
839.8'2374 – dc20
91-17820 CIP

Translator's dedication:

*T*o Gerd Brændstrup,
in recognition of her commitment
to the legacy of Sigurd Hoel and
of her concern that his work reach
a wider audience.

Contents

Translator's Note

*T*he text of *The Troll Circle* exhibits many features of oral narrative, including use of dialect, most extensively in the inserted tales such as Mari's account of the Berg family and the 'bellyful' of local lore related by Jon. Folk figures, Mari and Jon have distinctive narrative styles, Mari's alternately earthy and biblical, Jon's racy and sardonic. I have not attempted to find a dialectal counterpart in English, lest all too specific – and misleading – signals be given as to the story's setting. Instead, the tonal and other effects of dialect have been sought through a replica of simple, 'common,' folksy speech.

Everyday language and folk narrative tend to be repetitious. Therefore I have occasionally replaced a verbatim rendition with a synonym for the sake of readability – except where motifs are involved. Such motifs abound in *The Troll Circle*, with its extensive use of structural imagery. I have tried to reproduce these motifs as faithfully as possible. Finally, words and phrases with no counterparts in English have been translated by near equivalents. To comment on a word has always seemed to me a betrayal of the very end of translation. Still, some words in *The Troll Circle* have no English equivalents, near or remote, and in such instances a note of explanation has been supplied.

I would like to thank Karin Lyngstad and Eléonore Zimmermann for reading the entire manuscript and offering helpful criticism and suggestions.

Part *I*

Way Up North in the Woods

The Parish

Nordbygda, as it was called, lay all by itself way up north in the woods.

They didn't have a proper road in the parish – they had never had such a road, nor would they ever have any. Other places had such roads – they had probably always been there. But this parish wasn't made for such things. In other places though, somebody said, they were building new roads. Oh well, people would dream up all sorts of things. If you were to go by everything you saw and believe all you heard these days, doomsday couldn't be far off. Many of Hauge's friends, as they called themselves, were of the opinion that doomsday was near.[1]

Make a road up here, why? The Lord must surely have meant something when he laid this parish in such an out-of-the-way place, with forests for miles and miles all around and only a narrow bridle path, over the hill and along the little stream, leading to the outside world. And that was just fine. You'd get to the graveyard fast enough using the road they had.

The impatient ones – for such people were to be found here too – would hint every now and then that they could build a road. But what good would a road be to this parish, where people didn't have any vehicles with wheels? For that matter, what good would wheeled vehicles be to them? They didn't have a road, after all.

In summertime people walked when they had an errand somewhere. Or they went on horseback, if it was far, or rowed across the lake. If something was to be transported, you used a horse and packsaddle; that was the way the Lord had ordered things. But there wasn't much that needed transporting. Every now and then a body had to be buried in summer, and the horse would sometimes get a bit sweaty from pulling the summer sledge with the coffin, that was so.

In the winter it was different, for then they had sledges, here as elsewhere. What needed to be hauled had to wait until winter.

---

1. 'Hauge's friends' were followers of Hans Nielsen Hauge (1771–1824), the most influential Norwegian revivalist. In the eighteenth century official Christianity in Norway, as in many other European countries, was marked by the rationalism of the Enlightenment. Hauge and his disciples, the Haugians (*Haugianerne*), preached the necessity of conversion and emphasized the importance of personal religious experience. The movement started by Hauge has had a lasting influence on Norwegian religious life.

A beaten path wound its way around the hamlet, with many twists and turns, hitting most of the big farms, where it passed through the yard, and sending offshoots over crags and through thickets up to cotter country and the more remote farms. And between the farms, between the cotter's plots, from farm to cotter's plot and from one cotter's plot to another, there were other paths. Some well beaten and well used, others narrow and little used, with grass growing in the middle of the path. There were many reasons for such things. A word might have been dropped someplace, about someone or something in some other place. It might have been spoken in anger and spite, in a state of drunkenness, or in thoughtlessness pure and simple. Or it didn't need to have been spoken at all but had sprung up by itself, as it were, out of thin air or old women's chatter, between one place and another. Such a word, once dropped, would somehow grow, sprout, and strike root, and in due course it would stand tall, with blossoms and barbs. Not very much happened in such a parish, and people had few opportunities of forgetting anything. So when the time was ripe — years might have passed in between — the injured party would usually play a little prank in return. The target of the prank had long since forgotten the word; but he remembered the prank. In this way the path between two farms or two cotter's plots could get overgrown.

Ordinarily there was little traffic on the parish road. A person would walk by occasionally — often some old pauper who dragged herself along, stick in hand, from one farm to another, or a cotter's wife with a beggar's scrip on her back. Now and then a man with a packhorse on his way to or from the summer dairy. Once in a blue moon a man on horseback.

Then people in the fields alongside the road would straighten their backs and stare — stare a good long time, and then talk. You took note of such things, they lifted your day out of the humdrum. Who it was, where he was going. Those far away would shade their eyes to see better. They could recognize the horse any time, even at a distance of six to seven hundred yards. The man was sometimes harder to pin down. People talked it over among themselves until they agreed.

In this way the parish kept track of who trekked along the road.

What was happening on each farm, they had other ways of finding out. The cotters told tales, the maids did likewise, and some things you could see through the windowpanes for yourself and pass on. In a pinch you could lie in hiding behind the fence or make scouting excursions at night, if the neighborhood was right for it.

4

When something important happened, it became known all over the parish in a day or two. Then the paths were used late and early, those which weren't too overgrown, and the women would take their knitting and walk, house by house, from one end of the hamlet to another. Seldom any farther. On the border there usually sat some house or other, with people who could convey the news from there on.

It was mostly reports of misfortune which traveled all around the parish this way. Or it could be some breach of common decency or local custom. But that was more seldom. In actual fact, it was very seldom. The parish maintained strict discipline on this score. All people knew, from their tenderest years, what was required by custom and common decency. And a hundred pairs of eyes followed each and everyone late and early – around the clock, one might say – seeing to it that the good old rules were observed. Few people wanted to rebel against them, and even fewer had the courage to do so.

But it happened, of course. There were oddballs here as in other parishes – people who wouldn't or couldn't behave like everybody else. These caused the tongues to wag even more than usual. If they could make you laugh, it wasn't so bad. People like to laugh and will forgive almost anything as long as they can laugh. It was worse if it wasn't a laughing matter – if someone was different in dead earnest. Such behavior wasn't seemly – it was a sign of pridefulness and anything but good. Such people mostly ended up alone. And lo and behold, very often their strangeness, the thing which had made them different, went from bad to worse, till one day they were crazy as a loon and had to be hauled to Kerstaffer Berg's basement – unless the farm where the lunatic came from was such that they chose to keep him at home.

It must be said the parish was blessed in having someone like Kerstaffer. Earlier, these nuts used to loaf about at home, on the farm, where they messed around with their food, screamed and hollered, frightening both young and old, and dreamed up unmentionable things. Now they were all gathered in one place, at least. That was what people called progress, no doubt. And Kerstaffer made money from the whole mess.

But Kerstaffer, well, he made money from everything.

This parish had had a good many lunatics for ages. For ages? Well, perhaps not, but for several generations anyway. Really old people, who treasured what they had heard from still older people, could tell that at one time there were no more lunatics here than other places. Indeed, that was so even now; but at one time there weren't as many as now. So it was clear as daylight there must be something or other about *the new* which caused the misfortune. Whatever it might be. Some thought it was because of the big, dark forest. No wonder there are so many lunatics at Oppi, they said. The farm sits right below the Svartlia woods.

But then, the forest had always been there.

Others thought it was because of the constant intermarriage among kin. It was said to be prohibited by law. In the old days it really *was* prohibited by law. But what was the use if something was prohibited nowadays? If two kinfolk happened to cast sinful eyes upon each other, they merely applied to the king for permission to get hitched. They paid a couple of dollars, and then the illegal had become legal. Could you expect anything but misfortune from such things? In the old days such people, who did exactly what they pleased, were put in the stocks – or they were made to ride the wooden horse. But those things were now all gone, and neither stocks nor other gear was to be found on the church green anymore.

That was what some of the old people said. Others, who might be just as old and just as wise, said something else. In spite of everything, they said, there was still reason to rejoice that some things didn't change quite as fast in this parish as they did out there in the world at large – out there the end was nigh at hand all the time.

Other people were heard to say that things were as they had always been in this parish, and as they would always be. The young were thoughtless, but grew older and wiser as time passed. The poor were poor and would remain so. The big farms had always belonged to those who owned them now, or to their family.

That many of the big farms had passed from one family to another, more than once, didn't change any of this.

It was a sinful world we were living in, and people were weak. Therefore, certain things had to be impressed on people over and over again, until they would remember them even in their sleep:

It was shameful for a good man to have a child with a cotter's daughter. But it could be forgotten. If he married her, it could never be forgotten.

It was shameful to earn money in a dishonest manner. But once the money had been stashed away in your coffer, it was yours.

Other things were a bit more difficult.

One of the most important things was to be of good family.

When the younger son of a farmer got himself a cotter's plot on the family farm, people would remember that those who lived there were of good lineage, for a while – one or two generations. Then it required some effort to remember it.

6

The years passed over this parish as over other parishes but didn't produce any big changes. The parish lay where it lay and was the way it was. At one time, though, it must have been different. The area had once been cleared, after all. Had it been done by outlaws? Or had the parish served as summer-dairy country for the large parish farther out? Which farms had been cleared first?

Nobody knew. Once upon a time it had happened, but it was awfully long ago. Perhaps even before the country adopted Christianity. Yes, before that time, surely. For in the attic at Nordby there stood a pair of strange figures, no doubt the relics of crass paganism. You could still see 'St. Halvard' carved on one of them.[2]

Few went out into the world, even fewer came here from the outside world. This parish had become a world apart. And its breed of people had become a breed apart – through constant intermarriage with one another, generation after generation, as far back as the parish had existed. It had become a special race, easily recognizable by any outsider who had once set eyes on people from this parish.

How? There seemed to be a special trait – something about the eyebrows? Or was it the cheekbones? Or the mouth? It wasn't easy to say exactly what it was, but it was something. A sort of heaviness, or heavyheartedness? No, not really, it couldn't be – for they liked to laugh in this parish and did so quite often. Still, perhaps there was a certain heaviness, which merely retreated briefly when they laughed, especially when they laughed gloatingly at others' folly or thoughtlessness. Then their heavyheartedness returned again; it sat brooding, just as the forest sat brooding. Or like a brooding gray sky in the fall, day after day, just before the dark, cold winter set in.

What was one to do during those long winter evenings? What was there to think about, dream about, talk about? Oh – what other people were doing. Something good? But there wasn't very much good. Evil? There was plenty of evil, Lord help us.

Nothing much happened. Or – those who had spent some time outside the parish felt that nothing much happened. On the other hand, whatever did happen was carefully noted, turned around time and again, and not soon forgotten. That might be the reason why affronts, or things which could be perceived as affronts, were so long remembered and could seldom be reme-

2. Often spelled Hallvard – Norwegian saint and the patron saint of the city of Oslo.

died. That might be the reason why so many of the paths between the farms were getting overgrown.

Let people from the outside go on about how backward the parish was. Sure it was backward, the way they figured it – in terms of roads and that sort of thing. On the other hand, it escaped much of the corruption, if that was the right word, which roads brought along with them. No taverns, no houses with card playing and girls along the road. Anyone who wanted to procure that kind of pleasure here had to work hard for it and look for it in out-of-the-way places.

So. Few people moved out. Even fewer moved in. It had happened only three or four times in living memory that someone from this parish got himself a wife from the outside. And even those three or four times might just as well have been left undone. Well, Rønnau Olstad was turning out all right – or so one hoped. In any case, the master at Olstad, good old Ola, said nothing to the contrary during the years he lived. But then, Ola Olstad didn't say much about anything.

And no sooner had his grave had time to get properly green than she married a second time. This time an out-and-out stranger! That was the end of that.

Hans Nordby and His Cronies

*I*t was on April 22, 1818, that the honorable widow Rønnau Larsdaughter Olstad, from Nordbygda, married bachelor Håvard Gjermundsen Viland, farm steward to Peder Laurentius Thurmann, the rector. Many made a note of that day. The wedding was held at Olstad, lasted for three days, and was the biggest celebration the parish had seen in many years. Such a wedding was often remembered for ever so long, like a sort of landmark on a drab thoroughfare – oh yes, such and such happened the year after the wedding at Olstad.

But here there was something more than that. Many of the women in the parish figured that from now on they had to start counting on their fingers and to keep doing so for some time ahead. When a well-to-do widow like Rønnau married an outsider, one without a farm at that, she had to have a *reason*, after all.

These women were sitting quietly on chairs and benches along the walls. They were so quiet, their quick eyes alert and taking note of everything.

There had been considerable talk about this wedding during the previous days and weeks. All kinds of talk.

That Rønnau had found herself a husband from outside the parish had been less of a surprise to these women than to their stupid husbands. For when everything was said and done, Rønnau was an outsider herself, though she came from no farther away than the home parish.

Her new husband was an outsider, all right. From far away *he* was. But there was an old adage which said that the mountains were never so far apart that the mountain trolls couldn't get together.

Anyway, Ola Olstad had come to grief when he put on airs and looked for a wife outside the parish. He had to content himself with the used goods of the mill owner, people said; but that was another matter. The male heir he had hoped for in marrying the stuck-up hen didn't come. For all his bluster, Ola may not have had what it takes – or so people said. Anyway, he died by accident in his prime – got his chest crushed by a pine trunk way up in the woods, so that he had to be hauled back to the village with a horse and summer sledge, like a log. And you couldn't be sure it would end any better this time. Now there would be *two* outsiders at Olstad, and this new fellow that Rønnau had gotten herself couldn't be regarded as much more than a tramp, however much he had served at the parsonage. Nobody even knew where he came from, nobody knew anything about his family. Telemark, they said.[3] That was supposed to be somewhere far, far westward, they said, over by England apparently. And this brother of his, who was roaming around at this wedding – *was* he really his brother? The only proof of that was that both of them spoke the same strange language, almost as though they sang when you asked them something. Was it decent to talk like that? No, if this ended well, then everything would. Though you probably couldn't expect anything else from someone like Rønnau, who had let herself be used by the mill owner for many years, until he grew tired of her and dropped her. But she didn't waste any time, and soon she had gotten that arrogant fellow Ola Olstad for herself. . . .

Their eyes followed Rønnau and Håvard as they danced past.

Nothing showed on Rønnau yet. Not yet, no. But from now on one had better start counting on one's fingers, you bet.

The men said, Hm! and Well, well and To be sure . . . This Håvard fel-

3. While considered part of the East Country (*Østlandet*), the county of Telemark forms a transition to south and west Norway in respect to topography as well as language and culture. Telemark is notable for its picturesque landscape and its folk art and music.

low was a nimble one, no doubt about it. That handspring of his on the dance floor the first evening of the wedding – there weren't many who could match that. And Rønnau was a splendid woman, no doubt about it. But she might just as well have found herself a husband from the neighborhood – there were several unattached widowers around, with farm and timberland and all.

It takes time to break up from a three-day wedding. The first to leave after the big wedding at Olstad – as was to be expected, those who lived farthest away – cleared the yard by ten o'clock in the evening. The wife climbed onto the horse's back, the husband walked alongside leading the horse.

The last ones were the immediate neighbors along the road south, the folks at Nordby, Flateby, Strøm, and Nordset. They were all on foot, the distance being quite short, and they didn't get away until around two o'clock in the morning.

The newlyweds, Rønnau Olstad and her new husband, this stranger Håvard Gjermundsen, stood on the porch saying good-bye almost without interruption.

One had to admit he had made a good deal, this head servant to the new parson – or, well, steward. The handsomest woman in the entire parish, and one of the best farms into the bargain. Well, he was supposed to be a farmer's son where he came from. And, be it said in all fairness, he did look nifty.

These last guests were six altogether, groping their way south in the dark of night. Four men and two women. Anne Nordby had been bedridden for over ten years, and Goro Strøm was expecting almost any day, so she had stayed home.

When they crossed the yard at Nordby and stopped to say good night, Nordby asked the three men if they wouldn't come in for an ever-so-little nightcap.

Nordby was peculiar in one respect: once he'd gotten well started on a spree, he found it difficult to stop.

The women grumbled a bit; they knew all about these nightcaps of Hans Nordby.

But they didn't grumble for long; for they knew Nordby as well. He was one of the wealthiest and most powerful men in the parish. Perhaps the wealthiest and the most powerful of all – and a man who forgot nothing and was known for toughness in all his dealings.

The men accepted at once. He had good liquor, Nordby did. And he had whispered beforehand to two of them, Ola Nordset and Anders Flateby, that, just wait, and they might see him hook a fish tonight. They thought they had a pretty good idea what it was about – Nordby was a buyer of timberland for Baron Rosenkrantz in these parts, and the third man, Sjønne Strøm, had lots of excellent timberland.[4] Strange that Nordby hadn't managed to cheat him out of it before, innocent and stupid as Sjønne was – walking around at home picking at that fiddle of his and otherwise having very little to say for himself.

All Nordby said to him was, 'Come inside and try out the fiddle!' But it sufficed. Sjønne's eyes at once took on an eager look, and he followed Nordby like a dog.

Nordby was one of those who had been lucky. He wasn't born to the farm, being only the next eldest son. But the eldest fell on evil days. Once, at Nes,[5] he'd heard this preacher, Hans Nielsen Hauge. Afterward he went around saying that all people were brothers. And that was not all: he behaved as if he believed it himself. He built new servants' quarters where the cotters and the servants could spend their leisure hours; he even bought an expensive new stove for the place. He used to walk around in the fields singing hymns. And he would pray with his own servants. Oh well, that could be tolerated; other Haugian friends did the same, and many thought it paid off. But Erik Nordby offered up his prayers during working hours! Such things wouldn't do in the long run. Then he got engaged to a cotter's daughter, and right afterward he increased the daily wages for his cotters by two shillings. Then it became obvious to everybody that he had lost his wits, and Hans got his mother to sign a note that Erik wasn't in his right mind. He was hauled north to Kerstaffer Berg, who took in such people. He had stayed in the basement at Berg ever since.

And so Hans got the farm – for his mother took to her bed as soon as she had signed that piece of paper. She never got up again and died shortly afterward.

The following year Hans got himself another farm. He married the only child on the neighboring farm, Haug, a girl named Anne. Haug was a good

4. The Rosenkrantz family, one of the best-known among the Norwegian nobility, stemmed from North Jutland in Denmark. The person here referred to is most likely Marcus Gjøe Rosenkrantz (1762–1838), who owned estates in Østfold County (near Oslo) and elsewhere and held many important political appointments.
5. A township in Akershus County bordering on Nord-Odal Township, which corresponds to Hoel's Nordbygda.

farm, with fishing rights in the lake and mining up the hill. This daughter wasn't much to look at – one hip was somewhat skewed and her face was slightly crooked – but she was a good, gentle soul. One year after the wedding she had a daughter and almost gave up the ghost. The old midwife warned them that one more child would kill her. But in that she was mistaken, for the following year Anne had a son and she didn't die from it, only became bedridden from then on. As Hans told the angry midwife – if she didn't get well again, she would just have to stay flat on her back; the farm could surely afford to feed her, now that she had accomplished what she was supposed to and had given the farm a male heir.

A couple of years later Anne's parents died, so now Nordby was the owner of two of the best farms in the parish. And as is written, unto him who has shall be given: not long afterward he became a buyer for Baron Rosenkrantz himself, who owned immense tracts of timberland, plenty of mines and sawmills, and more farms than anybody could name – the wealthiest man in the whole country, in the opinion of many. He didn't become any poorer on account of Hans Nordby. Nor did Hans Nordby on account of the Baron.

He loved his children, as he loved all his property. Most of all his son, naturally. Many were of the opinion he loved that boy even more than the writing desk where he kept all his dollars. The boy was now about ten years of age and gave promise of becoming the spit and image of his father. The cotters noticed this and sighed.

As mentioned before, this strong man had this one weakness: once he had gotten started on a spree – whether at a wedding, a funeral, or some other celebration – he found it difficult to stop. It was as though some other man awakened inside him, and this other man didn't want to go to bed. He could go on day after day, needing little sleep but all the more liquor and company. He somehow couldn't give up – couldn't stop and admit that the party was over and that the drab workaday world was back again. When he had these attacks, he would wear out one set of companions after another. In fact, more than once this wealthy freeholder had ended up by begging his own cotters to enter the parlor and drink expensive liquor with him.

The spell lasted every time until he had to be carried to bed, stiff as a board. Sometimes it would take a whole week before things got that far. Afterward he usually stayed in bed for several days.

When he eventually got out of bed again, he was so gruff and mad that he could have eaten nails. Then people had better stay out of his way. His cotters especially had better keep well out of his way, bend their backs and make themselves small, not dare to utter a sound, forget that they had ever sat at his table, toasted him – perhaps even with French brandy – and listened to fulsome praise and handsome promises, his arms around their necks.

But he found them – even if they hid in the farthest corner of the lower hayloft. He found them and made them regret the day they'd been born, the day they became cotters at Nordby, and the day they'd sat in the parlor drinking with their master.

Add to this the fact that the cotters didn't at all feel comfortable in the big gloomy parlor in the middle of the night. Was it haunted? Perhaps no more than other places. Nearly everyone could have heard the old lady, his mother or whoever it was, wandering in the hallways, sighing and weeping. And some had experienced what was worse – that Nordby himself sat talking endlessly to someone nobody else could even catch a glimpse of. Had heard him curse and cry, beg and pray. Listening to his master as he sat there bargaining with the devil himself about his own soul could make the chills run down a poor cotter's spine.

It was cold and dark in the parlor when the four men entered. But Nordby went out into the kitchen and woke up the maid who slept there – there was always a maid sleeping there, to be at hand should his sick wife in the bedroom show a change for the worse. Anne wouldn't last much longer now, as they all knew.

The maid came, pale and scared, put a candle on the table, lighted the fire, and fetched beer from the cellar. Nordby himself walked up and down, fetched liquor and glasses, and got out tobacco and long-stemmed pipes. Meanwhile his three friends had sat down, each in his own log chair, around the big deal table.

Anders Flateby, small and lightfooted, red-haired and sharp-nosed, sat at one end of the table. People in the parish called him the Fox. He knew about this and put up with it, even liked it. He thought it couldn't do any harm. Now, as he snuggled in his chair, he looked more than ever like a curled-up fox.

He followed Nordby with his eyes as he got glasses and bottles from the big brown corner cabinet. It made him think about that other cabinet – the brown writing desk in the bedroom, and the paper lying there.

Anders Flateby owed Nordby a hundred dollars. He had owed the money for more than four years now and could see no possibility of repaying it this year either.

It weighed heavily upon him, that debt of a hundred dollars.

Not that Nordby had put much pressure on him. This last year he hadn't asked for payment even once.

But he couldn't help thinking about it. He was constantly thinking about it. He thought, as so often before: Thank heaven, Nordby is a friend. A good friend. He doesn't want to hurt me.

But the next moment he couldn't help thinking how much he would have liked to see this piece of paper in the writing desk, which he had signed when he was drunk. Would have liked to see with his own eyes that it contained nothing which Nordby could use to squeeze him out of his farm.

He had never meant to ask for a hundred dollars. He needed twenty-five. Even so, he walked around mute and anxious for weeks before going to Nordby. But there he got yes at the very first word. At that moment such a load was taken off his mind that when Nordby brought a bottle and offered him a drink, he had a little more than was good for him. When Nordby suggested that twenty-five dollars was no sum for a man like him, that he would let him have a hundred, he agreed. But he couldn't for the life of him remember what it said on the paper that he signed late that night. Oh, yes. It did say a hundred dollars, in letters and numbers. But it said something more. If he only knew what it was.

'The rest doesn't mean anything,' Nordby said. 'It's just a form we use, the Baron and I.'

The Baron and I. The Baron and I. It was always the Baron and I. He was a proper fool that way, Nordby was. Made himself a laughingstock to the parish.

Why hadn't he let the sheriff take it all, horses and cows and goats!

What if he dared to ask if he could see that piece of paper? But it couldn't be done. Not until he had the money in his hand.

He knew one thing – that he wouldn't have a single carefree day, not really carefree, until he could slap that money down on Nordby's table. But when that would be, well . . .

At the other end of the table sat Ola Nordset, big and heavy, with darker hair and beard than most people in these parts.

He sat there, heavy with food, beer, and brandy, following Nordby with his eyes and wondering vaguely why he always seemed to feel ill at ease when he entered this room. He certainly didn't have any reason to. A nice room, to be sure, but the parlor at Nordset wasn't much poorer. Not quite as big, but still. This parlor was really oversized; now at night you could barely make out the soot-covered walls – you could almost become afraid of the dark from sitting here.

But Nordby obviously wasn't. There he paced up and down, round as a tub and so well satisfied he gave the impression of owning every last bit here. And so, of course, he did. Like his father before him, and *his* father before *him*, as far back as anyone could remember. And all of them made of the same stuff. He himself had heard old people say: Hans Nordby, well, he's the spitting image of his grandfather. I can remember Old Hans, for sure, a round, sturdy fellow, just like Nordby now. And just as tough in all his dealings. And his grandfather, in turn, was of the same sort.

A thought occurred to Nordset which he pushed aside, with his hand as it were, stroking his face. Ola Nordset's grandfather was a cotter's son – and an outsider at that. He came to this parish as a blacksmith and got himself a worthless cotter's plot at Nordset, but he knew a thing or two. At any rate he got the farmer's daughter with child, and the upshot was that he took over the whole caboodle – farm and timberland, wife and child.

But that was some time ago. Long since dead and buried.

People in this parish had a good memory though – especially for things that might just as well be forgotten.

'Welcome, fellows! And skoal!' Nordby said. He had taken his place in the high seat.

'You too, Sjønne, have a drink, won't you!'

For Sjønne, who sat directly opposite Hans Nordby, had gotten hold of the fiddle, and so he forgot about everything else. His hair in his eyes, he sat there picking at the fiddle, put his ear against it and listened, then picked at it again. This fiddle left by Erik was quite extraordinary. Erik had been so careful with it, as though it were his child. Many a fine dance tune had been played on this fiddle – in the years before Erik turned devout and went mad.

They all drank. Afterward they coughed, as was meet and proper, and said, as custom required, that this was good strong liquor indeed.

And that was that. Nordby served good, powerful stuff.

The next moment it grew sort of quiet in the room. And then they heard, through the door leading to the bedroom, his wife, Anne, give a couple of loud groans; it sounded as though she was choking – she had gotten into the habit of losing her breath lately, they had heard. Outside, an owl hooted three times: whoo-hoo, whoo-hoo, whoo-hoo-hoo! The three men started and looked about them. But Nordby said in a loud voice:

'We must drink, fellows, if there's going to be any cheer!'

They picked up their glasses again. And as soon as they had emptied them, Nordby filled them afresh. He was a good host that way.

Anders Flateby was thinking that this evening he wouldn't try to ingratiate himself with Nordby. He had gotten into the habit of doing that. Whatever the reason might be. Actually he knew what the reason was. It was supposed to be a small installment, sort of. But it was stupid. He knew it was stupid. Nordby despised him for it, and sooner or later the others were bound to realize that something was up between him and Nordby.

It had become a habit, all right. His lips spoke fawning, flattering words to Nordby against his will, without his being able to stop it. He behaved like a cotter and a slave. Yes, that was it, a slave! He felt his jaw getting hot from anger and shame.

Never again! he thought. But he thought so in the same heavy, resigned manner a drunkard does after a binge. He thought, Never again! But at the back of his mind he suspected that he would do it over again at the first opportunity. He didn't dare not to. For though Nordby no doubt despised him for this toadying, he had become accustomed to getting it. And in a way he needed it. He would miss it if it wasn't forthcoming, look in surprise at Anders Flateby and think, Well? And then he would remember that piece of paper in the writing desk.

Therefore Flateby didn't dare but flatter and curry favor – knowing full well it would remind Nordby of that piece of paper in the writing desk.

Never again! Anders Flateby thought. And he heard himself say, 'Boy, this is a mighty big parlor. Or what do you say, Nordset?'

He regretted it bitterly the moment he'd said it. He had been here before, many times, and every time he'd said the same thing. But now that he had begun, he must continue:

'How big is it really, Hans?'

The same moment he regretted it even more. For he had asked this so often – so often that it was almost an outright insult to ask it once more.

'Twenty-five feet square!' Nordby said, looking at him with a faint, sort of weary smile. It said something like, Oh, Anders!

Then followed another toast and 'Why, this liquor is certainly . . .' And 'Damn it, Sjønne, you must drink too!'

For Sjønne had gotten hold of the fiddle again and sat there plucking at the strings and tuning it.

Ola Nordset drank and was silent. He always needed a bit of time to warm up in a new place, even if he was a little tipsy from before. He sat looking about him in the large, dark room, thinking about his grandfather.

16

Strange that such a small thing – far removed in time and all – could somehow make you feel insecure. He himself was probably the only one who remembered it.

Anders Flateby felt he had to make up for his remark about the parlor as quickly as possible.

He slapped his thighs.

'I say, Hans, that quip at Olstad this evening, when you got back at Kerstaffer Berg, was a real knock-out!'

True enough, Nordby had had the laughter on his side there.

Flateby explained, eager and laughing:

'You, Nordset, had gone behind the house for a moment – it was an hour or so before we left. And you, Sjønne, stood over by the fiddler. Then Kerstaffer comes along, half-drunk and cantankerous, and says to Nordby, just to pick a fight, you know:

' "Now, tell me honestly, Hans," he said, "when do you plan on taking that brother of yours, Erik, back home again?" he said. "The time should be ripe for it fairly soon now," he said, "so he could take back Nordby by allodial right," he said.[6]

' "We don't collect crazy people at Nordby," Hans said.

'Then Kerstaffer got mad:

' "Erik crazy? He is no more crazy than I am," he said.

' "Then, by God, he's crazy enough!" Nordby said.'

Flateby laughed uproariously but soon noticed he was the only one who did. Glancing over at the others, he saw they were looking in the direction of Nordby. When he looked at Nordby himself, he knew right away that this was something he should never, never have brought up. For there was nothing Hans Nordby disliked more than being reminded of that crazy brother of his.

Hans Nordby made a slight grimace. 'Leave Kerstaffer alone. He is a good farmer at least,' he said.

Anders Flateby curled up tighter in his chair. Coiling himself in a sort of circle in the oversized chair, he resembled a trapped fox which had struggled as best he could and settled down, dead tired, to take whatever was coming.

6. According to allodial privilege or law (*odelsrett*), which still prevails in Norway and is protected by the Constitution, landed property belongs to the extended family (*slekten*). Therefore, to prevent property from falling into strange hands, family members have certain rights, such as the right of pre-emption and the right of redemption at its appraised value. Allodial tenure is established after twenty years of continuous ownership by the same person or his offspring. A farm can be redeemed within a period of three years from the date of transfer out of the family, as long as the nonfamily buyer has not, in turn, acquired allodial rights.

But nothing came – not aimed at him anyway. Nordby started talking about something he used to bring up repeatedly – about the honest, trusting freeholder who was exploited and plundered by everybody, by tax collector and judge and sheriff, by parson, parish clerk, bishop, and county governor, and by townspeople who wore fine clothes all year round and never did a day's honest work but just sat on their asses, stuffed with *privileges*, conning the honest freeholder out of his hard-earned shillings.

The others fell back in their chairs – this was Hans's pet peeve in a way, and they had heard it many times before. Strange that such a man would put himself at the disposal of the Baron. Otherwise they agreed with every word of it, that was clear.

Suddenly Ola Nordset said, 'It is these outsiders, you see! It's getting almost impossible to make a living for a freeholder – who has done nothing wrong other than to sit on his farm like his father before him, and his father before him again, for hundreds of years . . .'

He fell silent all at once, wrinkling his brows. What had he said this time?

He meant it. In fact, he meant it more sincerely than most. Even so, he sometimes felt like biting his tongue after making just this remark, because he could tell from the others' eyes, or thought he could, that now he had clearly reminded them once again of what he wanted them most of all to forget. Sometimes he would say to himself, Don't ever say that again! Shut up, don't ever say a word! But the next time occasion offered, he blurted it out again. It was like a compulsion.

He had seen it in the eyes of Nordby more than once. Cotter's son! it said.

Nordset wondered what he could say or do to remove that 'cotter's son' from Nordby's eyes once and for all. At any rate he, Nordset, had never invited his cotters into the parlor for a drink!

This time, though, it seemed as though Nordby hadn't even heard what he said. He only kept harping on that honest freeholder of his. Leaning forward on the table, hot and eager, he said, 'Just listen to this!'

Then he turned toward Sjønne, who sat there plunking and bowing the fiddle, and said, 'You too listen, Sjønne. For what I'm going to tell you now is something that concerns us all.'

They pricked up their ears. Sjønne put away the fiddle and moved up to the table; he pushed the hair out of his eyes and sort of moved them up closer. Then Nordby started off, telling them about what he called *the new plot against the freeholder*.

To be sure, it couldn't be called anything but a rumor, though it was certainly more than a rumor. It was a plan, as they called it. Which hadn't *yet* become law; but it *would* become law. Nordby had it all from the Baron himself. The Baron, no doubt, as each and everyone knew, could be hard and stubborn when it came to standing up for his rights. But otherwise he wished the freeholder well. A prosperous class of freeholders meant a wealthy landowner class and a happy nation, whereas a poor freeholder class meant an impoverished and unhappy nation, the Baron said. Enough of that. This plan, the Baron thought, went too far.

Well. They had heard, no doubt, that what was called the 'state finances' were in poor condition. What that really meant was that the bigwigs in the city had played fast and loose with them for so long that now there wasn't any more money left but only bills and debts. The silver tax hadn't done the job.[7] And now all the big shots sat in the city scratching their heads, without the faintest idea where to get the money from. For naturally the biggest and wealthiest had stowed away their silver, now as before. Nobody would get their hands on that.

Then they figured out they had to begin *confiscations*. And what did they mean to confiscate? But of course – the miserable timberland of the freeholder. The honest, trusting freeholder would have to foot the bill, now as always.

Every freeholder who owned more than five hundred hectares of timberland would have to give up the excess over five hundred. Without compensation. And if several farms owned timberland jointly, with each owning more than five hundred hectares, then the farms were jointly to hand over the excess. Without compensation. It was to be declared crown land and would belong to the state. But the state couldn't engage in lumbering, so it had to offer all this timberland for sale to those who were able to pay. But the prospective buyer had to pay in silver! It wasn't a stupid idea, for this way the silver was pretty sure to turn up. And if the freeholder perished in the process, what did the big shots in the city care about that?

The eyes of the three listeners were popping now. This was the worst . . .

Anders Flateby owned part of the vast Flateby forest, six hundred hectares. Nordset owned seven hundred. They sat there figuring as well as they could.

7. At the time of Norway's separation from Denmark in 1814, the government finances were in a shambles. In 1816 the government felt obliged to levy the so-called silver tax on the wealthy to secure the necessary capital stock for the newly founded Bank of Norway. The forced contributions were to be paid in gold or silver. Between one-fourth and one-third was paid in the form of unminted metal. It has been hypothesized that this tax, and the consequent melting down of silver articles for minting into coins, entailed a considerable cultural loss to Norway.

But Sjønne was the most pop-eyed of all. He was one of those who took it badly when he thought he'd suffered an injustice, Sjønne was. And then he was so poor at defending himself.

Nordby continued.

At this point there weren't many who knew about what was brewing. But wait till the rumor started spreading! Then you would see some race among freeholders with over five hundred hectares of timberland – a race to find landowners and mill owners and proprietors so they could sell while there was still time; for the big wheels sat there with their privileges and weren't touched by the law – had you ever heard that one raven picked out the eyes of another?

Then you would see some pleading – dear, kind mill owner, would you please be so kind as to buy a bit of timberland from me? Just three hundred hectares, two hundred – you can have it all for practically nothing!

Practically nothing, sure! Prices would come tumbling down toward zero. Still, the freeholders had to sell – for otherwise they wouldn't get anything! And the price of lumber would drop, for the mill owners could manage for a long time with the lumber from their own forests! Had the freeholder been forced to his knees before, now he would be thrown flat on his back.

Nordby stopped to catch his breath and filled the glasses at the same time. From the bedroom there came a couple of moans, and they could hear Anne's throat wheezing and rattling. A chair crashed, and they heard the voice of the maid: 'So – is it better now?' Flateby and Nordset stirred uneasily in their chairs. Sjønne, who didn't seem to have heard anything, was just staring at Nordby, staring with open mouth, as though he saw the devil or hell itself in front of him. But Hans Nordby, who was probably used to hearing such sounds from his wife, went on as before.

He himself had pondered, time and again, what he ought to do. For he owned nine hundred hectares of timberland. But luckily about five hundred belonged to Nordby and four hundred to Haug. So if he deeded Haug to little Pål – the Baron thought it would be all right . . .

He gave a quick glance at Flateby and Nordset. Then he got up. 'Hm. Might as well step out into the yard for a moment,' he said.

They followed him, the two of them. Sjønne stayed behind – made as if to get up too, but remained seated. His knees felt too wobbly, it seemed. Well, Nordby had been filling his glass pretty steadily.

Day was breaking in the east. Flateby and Nordset leaned up against the wall of the house. Their legs weren't quite steady. The cold air did them good. Nordby stood right beside them, without support. Liquor didn't affect him the way it did other mortals. But he wiped his forehead with his hand, he was perspiring.

Ola Nordset staggered over to him, grabbed his shoulder and leaned against him: 'But can all this be really true?'

Nordby again passed his hand over his face, as though he wanted to brush away something. Expelling his breath, he said, quite dryly, 'True and true. I said it was a rumor.'

He smiled his narrow smile. And suddenly Nordset seemed to have a revelation, as he later told Flateby. He recalled what Hans had said to him before they entered the house this evening. 'I mean to hook a fish here tonight!' he had said.

That was it! Sjønne! Sjønne who sat there with seven hundred hectares of timberland, which he didn't have the brains either to work or to sell. It was those two hundred hectares Nordby was after, and no mistake – he was buying up timberland for the Baron all over the place!

'Hans, you are something!' was all Nordset could say. And Flateby, who had had the same revelation as Nordset, said, like an echo rebounding from the wall, 'Hans, you are something!'

What a relief! So at any rate Nordby wasn't out to get *them* tonight, with his tricks. Then they could just watch and relish the way he went about softening up Sjønne. Nobody came even close to Nordby at that sort of thing, softening up the seller.

In their joy they went completely wild, both Nordset and Flateby. They rushed at Nordby from opposite sides.

'Hans, you are something!'

They flung their arms around his neck. They slapped his back – you are something, Hans!

And in his excessive joy Nordset didn't notice that he was urinating on Nordby's trouser leg, swaying to and fro and gesticulating wildly with one hand: 'You are something, Hans!'

Nordby must have been a bit drunk as well, though he stood there as firm as a tree stump. At any rate he didn't notice that one of his shoes was getting wet.

Then they went in again.

Sjønne was already sufficiently soft, it seemed. His eyes seemed about to pop out of his head, and he swallowed every word of Nordby's as though it were Scripture. Which wasn't so strange, or so Nordset and Flateby thought. For when Nordby lied in order to bring off a business deal, he lied so hard that he believed it himself. Honest to god, Flateby and Nordset themselves were within an ace of believing it.

It was from this moment that the fun really started. To sit there quiet as a mouse and watch as Nordby hooked Sjønne – now giving out a bit of line, now hauling in again. No one could touch Nordby at that.

Afterward they often told each other that this was one of the most entertaining nights they had spent in all their lives.

Sjønne didn't have any understanding of land or timber. He knew it himself and didn't let it prey on his mind, ordinarily. Things are working out somehow, bumping along, he would say. My father wasn't much smarter, and yet he managed. And it was true. But occasionally when he got frightened, like now, he got so excessively frightened, because he was well aware he didn't know anything – apart from playing the fiddle. But nobody could run a farm with a fiddle, and he was smart enough to know it.

In the end Sjønne was in such a state that he began to entreat and beg. 'You straighten it out for me, Hans, won't you,' he begged. 'You are the only one I can trust. You're the best friend I have,' he said.

Nordby pretended to edge away. 'Hm,' he said. 'Maybe,' he said. He twisted and turned and edged away, and Sjønne jumped after. People used to say that by lying still the adder could make the wagtail jump straight into its open mouth. It was a bit like that.

'You know, it's just a rumor, Sjønne,' Nordby said. But rumor or no rumor, Sjønne wanted to sell timberland.

'All right,' Nordby said, 'but I can't exactly offer you top price, you know. I'm doing this on my own responsibility, without a commission from the Baron. And that fellow, you know, doesn't like to throw his money around.'

The other two sat watching it all. The worse for liquor, they didn't quite agree afterward about everything that happened.

But they agreed about one thing: just before sunrise Nordby and Sjønne wrote a contract concerning sale of timberland, situated between Clay Slide Brook and North Twin River and belonging to Sjønne Tostensen Strøm, to wit, 200 – two hundred – hectares, to Hans Pavelsen Nordby for the sum of 200 – two hundred – rix-dollars,[8] the first half to be paid in cash, the second half within a year from this day.

They had signed their names, neatly and evenly, and Nordby had handed Sjønne the hundred dollars – when the maid came rushing in, her face all white.

'It's Anne!' she said, with difficulty. 'I think she's dying!'

---

8. Silver coin worth about one American dollar (four Norwegian kroner). The rix-dollar, which was divided into 120 shillings, was official currency until 1873.

Nordby quickly got up from the bench and followed the maid out. He stayed away for quite a while, and they heard wheezing noises, sighs, and moans from the bedroom. Something fell on the floor in there. The same moment the sun rose – it shone through the two windows on the east wall and lighted up the table with bottles and glasses, puddles of beer, tobacco ashes strewn everywhere, and the fiddle in the midst of it all. Both Flateby and Nordset felt dizzy and sort of fagged out. An ugly little gnome, Nordset thought, watching Anders Flateby with his red stubble glinting in the sunlight and his red, lifeless eyes. Black as a gypsy, Flateby thought, watching Nordset's dark hair and wiry bristle.

Sjønne sat with non-seeing eyes, as if in a world all his own, mumbling something the others couldn't make out, staring into vacancy and fiddling with the dollar bills he was holding in his hand.

Nordby returned, looking just as sober as the previous evening, though he had been drinking steadily with them all night.

'That was Anne. She was having a choking fit,' he said. Then he turned in the doorway and called the maid. Now they would drink a toast to seal the bargain. And they would put some more logs on the fire. When the maid brought the wood, he shouted, 'Put on the coffeepot. We're going to have *coffee* this morning. And set the table for a proper breakfast. We'll have some herring! And cured meat! And fried bacon! And be quick about it – meanwhile Anne will have to take care of herself.'

After breakfast they began playing cards. It was Flateby who suggested it – the hundred dollars in Sjønne's pocket made his fingers itch.

If Sjønne had had the least bit of brains, he would have taken himself home now. It might be tricky enough as it was to explain to his wife what he had done. But it looked as though he'd taken leave of his last remnant of common sense. He stayed where he was and did what they asked him to do.

When they had played cards a couple of hours and won their first fifty dollars off Sjønne, Nordby said it would have to suffice awhile. The other two understood he didn't want them to clean out Sjønne completely either. And they had done all right as it was. Anders Flateby, who was always such a clever rogue with the cards, sat there with forty dollars in his pocket, which he didn't have when he came, and he started counting on his fingers – those hundred dollars he owed didn't seem such an impossible sum anymore. He was suddenly overcome by a heartfelt desire to tell Nordby a couple of home truths.

Sjønne sat hunched in his chair – his hair in his eyes, lines of weariness in his face, his eyes only two slits in his swollen eyelids. Perhaps he was beginning to realize what he had come up against tonight. Two hundred hectares of timberland – and two hundred dollars, no, one hundred and fifty.

Hans Nordby stepped out into the yard – just for a moment, he said. Meanwhile the three men took an ever-so-tiny wink – Flateby in the log chair, Nordset at the other end of the table, and Sjønne lying at full length on the bed in the corner.

Nordby only went to check that the hired men were at work and that they didn't slacken off any; but nobody did – they knew the master, and Nordby could see it and liked what he saw.

He, too, had become a little red-eyed. A bit unwashed and with a yellow, bristling stubble. Not exactly a sight for sore eyes. But he was alert and hearty and cheerful. A spree didn't affect him at all until the fifth or sixth day.

When he returned he could relate that he had seen the bridegroom, this fellow from Telemark, Håvard, ride past with his brother, Gjermund, or whatever he was called. He was probably going to show him the way south through the woods to the home parish and the royal road.

Anders Flateby roused in his log chair. He had dreamed that he told Nordby *the truth* and immediately got scared – he hadn't talked in his sleep, had he? No, Nordby looked kindly enough. Anyway, he was just stepping through the doorway.

But Håvard, this new big shot – suddenly he got furiously angry with this stranger who had come and forced his way in among them.

'He's supposed to be such a smart farmer, this Håvard fellow,' he said. 'Has gone to school and learned things, they say. The parson said at the wedding that as far as farming was concerned, Håvard would be like a kind of *missionary* up our way!'

He snorted with contempt.

'They say he's supposed to have such a knack for plowing. With an *iron plow*, which cuts straight through the topsoil and right down into the clay! But what he's best at is plowing his way between women's thighs, most likely. Or he would never have gotten hold of Rønnau!'

'Such strangers . . . ,' Nordset said, but stopped short.

Suddenly it didn't suit Hans Nordby to talk dirt about the man whose hospitality he had enjoyed – not with a man like Anders Flateby in any case.

'He's certainly a good farmer,' Nordby said. 'I have talked both with the parson and with this horse dealer, Bruflaten, who dropped by at the wedding, about the matter. He has served an apprenticeship with Principal Sverdrup at Kongsberg – and he could have done worse than that.[9] The

9. Jacob Liv Borch Sverdrup (1775–1841) was the principal of the Agricultural Seminary at

mill owner says that this fellow Sverdrup is among the best we have in this country, so we might all have something to learn from him.'

Anders Flateby shrank in his chair, until he was the size of a very small fox. What the hell – now he had said too much again. Nordby, who could talk more dirt about people than anybody else when he was in the mood for it, would take a holier-than-thou attitude when he felt like it – but then he disliked the person he was talking to!

Oh! If only one could smash the fat head of that pig, so he wouldn't know his face from his ass!

But that day, he knew, would never come. It was a long, long way from the forty dollars he had in his pocket to the hundred – with interest! – that he owed Nordby.

He answered humbly that, no doubt, Nordby was right, as usual. But he felt so wretched that he saw no way out except to doze off again in his chair right away.

Sjønne lay snoring over in the bed. Nordset sat quietly asleep at the end of the table, his face against the tabletop.

Hans Nordby looked at his three guests. They made anything but a pretty picture – grimy and unkempt, and with a stubble several days old.

Oh well, he was a bit unwashed himself, and with a stubble which felt raspy to the touch. He could certainly do with an hour's nap or so, he too. He went over to the bed and lay down beside Sjønne.

The shafts of sunlight entered at a slant, cutting bright slices in the dense air.

Håvard Gjermundsen Has a Vision in the Woods

lowly, step by step, Håvard Gjermundsen rode north through the forest, back to the strange parish where he was to spend the rest of his life.

In the gap to the south, he had said good-bye to Gjermund, his brother. That, too, for life.

His mount, a dun-colored fjord horse which Gjermund had brought from Telemark, picked its way carefully on the poor road.

Nedre Sem in the township of Borre, Vestfold County. This county has a common border with Håvard's native Telemark, as does Buskerud County, where the town of Kongsberg is situated. J. L. B. S. was brother to the distinguished classicist and politician Georg Sverdrup (1770–1850) and father of Johan Sverdrup (1816–92), who was prime minister when parliamentarism was introduced in Norway in 1884.

Håvard was so deep in thought that he scarcely noticed where the horse was going.

He thought about Gjermund, his brother, to whom he'd said good-bye an hour ago. It was quite strange to part from your only brother, knowing you'd never see him again.

He thought about his father and mother waiting at home, whom he wouldn't see anymore either. He thought about Tonè, who had jumped into the waterfall for his sake.

He had burned his bridges, all right – no way back for him, he thought, no more than for that man from Morgedal who stood at the edge of the cliff looking down on his farm, where wife and children, cattle and traps had been lost in a fire.[10] He had to turn his back on it all, as the man from Morgedal had done, and find himself a new place, a new parish. And to say, as he did – if he had the strength to – that the old place, the old parish, didn't exist, had never existed.

He had, in fact, found a new place and a new parish. Wife too, and a farm.

He pondered how it had happened, going over it step by step; he would like to know if *he* had wanted it or someone else, or if it had just turned out that way. He had thought about it before, many times, all too many. But he didn't get anywhere – it was like running your head into a stone wall. He didn't get anywhere this time either. Sure, he could have acted differently, any number of times – if he were someone else. And the same was probably true for the others too, above all for Rønnau and Tonè.

Then it must have been fate, as they called it, which had brought him here.

People talked so much about fate. And many thought it had some meaning. *He* had never been able to see any particular meaning in what happened to him – not in what happened to people he knew, either. Fate, well – if fate were to mean something, if what happened to you were to have a meaning, it was up to you to control it, often by putting your back to what most people called fate and turning it where it really didn't want to go. . . .

He could see Gjermund before him the moment he got home – in a week or so. Could both see and hear him. He had to laugh as he rode along. He might not know very much about the way of the world, but he knew nearly all there was to know about Gjermund.

His mother stood in the doorway. His father didn't move from his bench

---

10. The Morgedal valley is located in the township of Kviteseid in central Telemark. The valley is the home of modern skiing. The uppermost farms in this area are located at 2,000 feet above sea level.

– he wasn't going to get up to welcome somebody returning from such an errand.

Mother – well, she did. Couldn't help herself. But even she couldn't bring herself to ask any questions right away. First, Gjermund had to see to the horse, get inside, change, and have a bite to eat. Then, while stirring the embers in the fireplace perhaps, she asked, her back turned, 'And how is Håvard?'

For he was still her son, the one she loved the best – even more now when he'd lost his honor in his native parish.

Gjermund answered, dryly and indifferently, between two pulls at his pipe, 'Oh, there's no need to worry about Håvard. He's got himself a nice big farm, and a fine woman.'

Another couple of pulls at his pipe. Then, sullenly, as though he'd been wronged, 'Håvard always lands on his feet, you bet.'

Another couple of pulls at his pipe. Then, 'The farm is three times the size of Viland. And seven hundred hectares of timberland.'

At that the old man, too, turned his head a bit. Mother had long since straightened her back. She said, softly, a little scared, 'So perhaps we can hope it was all for the best, then.'

The others didn't even bother to answer. They were smarting from shame – Gjermund, the brother, from other things as well. But, ever so gingerly, Mother began to ask him about Rønnau. . . .

Håvard drew himself up in the saddle.

Rønnau . . .

Whether what had happened was for the best or not, he didn't know. Whether he liked this new farm or not – or how he would make out in this new parish – he didn't know that either. But one thing he knew for sure: now that he'd gotten to know Rønnau, he didn't wish for any other fate – even if Old Nick were to greet him with a pair of red-hot tongs when the journey was over.

Gotten to know Rønnau?

For the best or not? No, he didn't know. But he did know something else – that people didn't always want what was best for them. They did what they *had to*. And from the day he met Rønnau, he had to.

When *she* wanted it! The thought flashed through his mind before he knew it. He felt a slight shudder, then quickly resumed his thoughts.

I'll never see my family again, he thought. I'll never see Telemark again. Once here, willy-nilly I've got to stay here.

Lost in thought, he didn't notice where he was going.

Dobbin picked his way on his own, nimbly and carefully, in the manner of fjord horses. Light and sure-footed, taking small steps, he skipped along like a young girl. He walked around the biggest puddles, stepped over the large roots, and closely watched the road with his intelligent eyes, nodding his head as though talking to himself.

They passed an old tumbledown shack sitting at the edge of the road in the thick of the forest. A beggar with a child on her arm stood before the door. She was holding out her hand without a word. Roused from his thoughts, Håvard looked at the woman.

He saw a pale face, sallow from hunger, unkempt, wasted, spent, without hope. Stretching behind her as she stood there were weeks, months, years, of toil and poverty. When he looked into her eyes he met a glance as black as a pit, and empty, like a deep, dried-out well, and yet with an expression which reminded him of something . . . it was like . . . All in rags, she stood there motionless, her arm held stiffly in front of her without any hope of a handout, or even the strength to let it fall.

A cotter's wife, it was plain to see. She was probably on her way south to the home parish, begging from door to door for a few days. In the meantime there would be one mouth less around the gruel bowl at home, and perhaps she managed to keep the child alive too, at least for the time being.

The child, equally gray and sallow and almost without any signs of life, hung in the crook of her elbow. It had the face of a withered old woman. It could be a year or two – impossible to tell the exact age of little ones like that, who hadn't had enough to eat from the moment they were born. There was just sufficient life in the child to make it fret and whimper a bit; its voice had no real kick anymore.

Through the small window of the shack behind her (one of the two panes was broken and a rag had been stuck into the hole) he could make out a moving shadow. Somebody was watching them in there – most likely some-one who'd heard the sound of a horse's hoofs and had sent this specter onto the road.

Håvard unbuckled his saddlebag, took out his food pack and gave it to the woman, quickly, with trembling hands; he seemed in a terrible hurry.

Her hand accepted it, her fingers closing on the food like claws, and a semblance of life flickered in her black eyes. Suddenly she dropped the child, which hit the ground with a thud, hunched her back and threw herself upon the food, ripping and tearing at meat and cheese and *lefse*,[11] while the child lay forgotten beside the road, fretting a little louder than before.

11. Thin pastry of rolled dough, usually folded and eaten with butter, sugar, and – sometimes – cinnamon between the layers.

Håvard rode on. He heard a door slam behind him, and an angry woman's voice started buzzing.

But he knew now what this beggar had reminded him of. It was not of Tonè – not directly anyway – but of a dream he'd had about Tonè one night during the wedding. He'd forgotten the dream till now.

He had dreamed about Tonè, but it was not Tonè – yet it was she. It was a wounded reindeer up in the mountains he'd been dreaming about. The reindeer, Tonè – they merged into one – lay on the ground, her spine broken by a bullet, and couldn't move. Layers of flies and horseflies had infested the wound and were eating their way into the flesh. Tonè didn't say a word in the dream, just looked at him with her black eyes – eyes like those you sometimes see in a hunted animal when it has given up the fight and abandoned all hope long ago.

She didn't say anything in the dream, but just looked at him and took his knife – the family dagger he'd given her as a pledge – took it and cut her throat with a long slash, so that her head fell backward and the blood gushed out.

A curious dream. Because this was not how Tonè had ended her life. She jumped into the waterfall. Jumped into the waterfall one cold evening at the end of March, the day after she had received his letter. Down into the green icy water – ugh! But she had remembered to return the dagger, bringing it to Jon, the old schoolmaster.

'Make sure this thing gets back to Håvard, will you.'

Then up the hill she went and straight into the waterfall.

Håvard felt his side. There hung the dagger, in its worn leather sheath.

It was the same dagger he'd used when cutting the throat of the wounded reindeer. Many years ago now.

Rønnau wakened him when he had dreamed that dream. She said, 'You're moaning so terribly in your sleep – you're having a bad dream, aren't you?'

He mumbled something to the effect that he'd been uncomfortable – had probably gone to sleep on the wrong side. This happened toward morning the second wedding night, with dawn about to break outside. He felt Rønnau's eyes on him, restless, searching. But she didn't say any more.

He forced these thoughts aside and instead turned his mind to the beggar. He knew there were scores of them on the road right now, during the spring shortage. Wives from numerous cotter's plots, where full meals were few and far between summer and winter. Often the husband would distill a spot of liquor from the bit of barley they had – there was a little cheer while it lasted anyhow. Perhaps he managed to sell a few pots too, at sixpence a pot, and bring home a few shillings. But as time wore on, there was neither seed grain nor flour for food. And then the wife had to take to the road, and the cotter dragged himself to the master, on bended knees and with bowed head, begging food and seed.

He might be lucky and get it, after a proper volley of abuse and admonitions. Or he might get nothing, except the abuse. Because sometimes the master, too, had made himself some liquor and used up his barley.

They got accustomed to hitting the bottle regularly, both cotter and freeholder, working in the cold every single winter hauling charcoal and ore to the Mill. . . .

Suddenly he knew, as in a vision, that this was where his task lay.

Whether fate had meant something with what had happened to him, he didn't know. But he did know that, if the worst came to the worst, he could put his back to it and turn it around – or at least try to.

And now I know where I'll put my strength, he thought.

Vision after vision, plan after plan, streamed into his mind, as if they had long been drifting on a slow current someplace inside him but had been blocked by a dam, meanwhile rising higher and higher, very quietly, until this very moment, when the dam suddenly gave way and a swirling mass of dreams, visions, and plans gushed forth.

This parish . . .

Hungry cotters with bent backs and hard, smug freeholders, proud enough but not very far from the poverty line themselves.

He had only been in this parish for a short while and knew little or nothing about it. Still, he suddenly felt as he rode along that he knew it inside out – that nobody knew it as well as he did.

There it lay, out-of-the-way and isolated, surrounded by one forest behind another, miles upon miles, and gradually slipping into the hands of the big shots in Christiania.[12] The farmers couldn't do anything about it, they didn't even understand it.

In the capital lived the big proprietors who already owned half the timberland around here – soon it would be three-quarters. They were the only ones who were entitled to saw the timber into boards; they bought up the forests from the farmers at their own price, and timber from those who still had any trees left – that too, roughly, at their own price. The farmers weren't allowed to build sawmills – not even on their own land, not for their own use even – without committing themselves to saw poor boards with a wane. Squared-off beams and planks and boards were off-limits for the farmers. Because there was money in that.

12. Christiania was the name of Oslo from 1624 to 1924.

30

It was a damn shame. But it was the law. The law had been made by the wealthy, so they could heap up even more wealth.

In the home parish was the Mill. It smelted iron, brewed beer, made stoves, grindstones, scythes, and axes and sold them all over; but it needed coal and ore. The farmers up here were duty-bound to deliver ore and charcoal. They dug ore in the little mines all over the ridge, hauled it to the Mill, and received a few pennies – just enough to make them feel it was worthwhile. The pennies mostly went for drink on the job, the horses got worn out, and the manure was left behind on the road; and the forests were thinned out.

Maybe there was nothing one could do about it: the Mill had privileges and money and authority, and the farmers had the sheriff over them.

But there was one thing that neither the law nor authority or privileges could block – they couldn't keep the farmers from learning how to use the land properly.

And that he could teach them.

Suddenly his entire past life acquired coherence and meaning. Everything he'd thought was confused and accidental got straightened out, fell into place, became meaningful. That year when he strayed down into Drangedal valley,[13] found a girl there, and managed the farm for her father, a bedridden farmer who had spelled his way through the *Norwegian Board of Agriculture Collections* in bed. The three years he spent at Parson Thurmann's and those six months at Principal Sverdrup's in Kongsberg – just a waste of time, he had sometimes thought: Was he supposed to get stuck there and go to seed? He hadn't gathered much in the way of riches, but he'd learned something, really learned what agriculture was all about and what it could become. Those six months he worked as a carpenter at Strong-Kristian's forge in Nedre Eiker[14] – they would come in handy now; even the summers spent in the mountains as a herdsman and his turns as a drover with Mons Bruflaten, the horse dealer – everything fell into place: he had become a fully qualified farmer, with an understanding of the land and the woods, of buildings and tools, of feeding and care of horses and cattle. There wasn't a doubt in his mind: in these parts there was nobody, not even Parson Thurmann himself, who was so well versed in these matters, point by point and overall, as he was.

That a new age had begun worldwide for everything called agriculture,

13. A township about twenty miles southwest of the town of Skien in southeastern Telemark.
14. A township in Buskerud County situated on both sides of the Drammen River, west of Oslo.

that a few here at home had picked up some of the new know-how, that he was one of the few who had, in turn, learned a thing or two from these few – all this rushed through his head, quick, quick, more as visions than as thoughts.

And now he'd come to this place.

There must be some meaning to it! he thought.

It was strange to frame that thought in so many words. He looked about him, a bit jittery, almost frightened. But all was quiet, not a soul to be seen.

He had seen enough of the farming up here to know one thing: with the correct use of the land the yield could be doubled, or more than doubled. At the moment this parish was on the verge of poverty, putting wealth into the hands of others while the farmers were in debt and the cotters were starving and the cotters' wives went begging far and wide. It could become a prosperous place, where nobody suffered want.

All this could be done by the farmers themselves – and they didn't even know it.

Everything was backward here, run according to customs a hundred years old – two or three hundred, more likely. They picked at the ground with a wooden plow and sowed the same wretched oats and the same impure barley in the same field year after year, until it was scarcely worthwhile throwing the seed into the ground. But they eked out a living, somehow. Then, every third year, there would be a crop failure and every ninth year a famine, and so they starved; some died – in fact, many died – while the rest pulled through somehow, a little scrawnier than before, with a little more in the pockets of the proprietors and the mill owners, and things went on just as before.

Every sixth week the parson stood in the pulpit trying to teach them something better – he spoke about potatoes and winter rye more often than about heaven and hell. They went to sleep and didn't listen, nor did they understand his Danish.[15] Everything remained the same.

Anyway, they didn't want to understand him. It was like talking to a stone wall. Certainly, they said. Certainly. The parson has a good point there, no doubt about it.

Behind his back they sneered and exchanged a joke or two.

15. When Norway was separated from Denmark in 1814, it had been part of the kingdom of Denmark-Norway for over four hundred years. Since Norway did not have a university of its own until 1811, Norwegians used to obtain their higher education in Copenhagen. Moreover, Norway did not yet have a national language; the written language was Danish. The majority of the population, particularly in the countryside, spoke a variety of dialects derived from Old Norse. The parson here referred to, the Reverend Mr. Thurmann, is fairly representative of the so-called 'potato parsons' of the Enlightenment period.

They were good at that up here, killing with little jokes.

He would put his back to it, all right. Push and pull. Coax, not threaten, not frighten. Above all, not frighten.

Those farmers up here, he didn't know any of them. Haw! He knew them like his own pocket. There wasn't a dark corner in their souls he didn't know – better than they knew it themselves.

They were proud, self-willed, and stubborn. But scared. And slow. Oh, so slow.

They were scared of anything unfamiliar, anything new, as scared as they were of the devil – more in fact; for the devil they sort of knew.

It was just the same as in other parishes – perhaps a little worse, because this parish was so out of the way and backward. And the people half knew but didn't want to know; and so, being unsure of themselves, they made themselves doubly sure.

Oh no, he wasn't going to talk to them.

They would gloat over him at first. Sneer and drop their little jokes. Old neighbors, so near that they'd let the path between their houses get overgrown, would find each other again in shared merriment over this stranger, who had learned in the city how to use the land and imagined that things could be done differently from the way they had been done a thousand times before.

They would skip many a work period to share their merriment over this. Many overgrown paths would be opened up again, you bet!

But they would wonder, too. They would go around peeping and spying. Many overgrown paths up to Olstad would be opened up again – but not all the way, only up to the fence.

They would lean over the fence and *look* and afterward feel their way with little questions – to others, naturally, not to him. God forbid! Then, at home, they would pace the floor and ponder – they were only human. And after a couple of years had gone by and the crops at Olstad got bigger and bigger, while theirs remained the same as before, nature would have its way and they'd begin to fret.

They fretted. They laughed and dropped their little jokes, but they fretted more and more, because that nut really did grow bigger and bigger crops, could afford to improve the lot of his cotters and chopped down fewer trees in his woods, and he did it all without stinting himself – indeed, with a full storehouse and with more and more cash stashed away, judging by common talk.

But to go to him? Make inquiries? *Learn*? No way – not as long as Per and Pål and Ola and Hans considered themselves too good for that sort of thing.

Until the firstcomer wound his way across the fields and into the parlor at Olstad one evening, cocked his head, and began asking questions. Cautiously, to be sure, very cautiously, like Nicodemus at night. But not cautiously enough. Some fellow had seen him, somebody else had heard about him, a third had both seen and heard, a fourth became so deadly afraid of being left behind in the race that he came puffing and panting in broad daylight.

Ask questions? Learn? Well, why not? When Per and Pål and Ola and Hans didn't consider themselves too good for that sort of thing . . .

Håvard chuckled in the saddle. It would probably take some five to six years, if people around here were much the same as in other parishes.

Still, he would remain a stranger here to his dying day. And he would hardly have any friends during his lifetime. His son might, if it turned out to be a son. . . .

Drawing a sigh of relief, he seemed to wake up and looked about him. What a fine day. Sparkling spring, bright as silver.

He was approaching a big puddle, which mirrored the sky and the trees, but with a tinge of yellow due to the mud on the bottom. Dobbin looked at the puddle for a moment, then waded into it – he saw it was quite shallow. The horse's legs shattered the reflection, leaving only a yellow puddle.

Yes, he thought, we'll do this more often – stir up still puddles. But don't be scared, Dobbin, it's not as deep as it looks.

They startled a wood grouse, which rose and flew away through the evergreens. You could hear how heavy it was as it crashed through the small branches, which were left trembling in its wake. A squirrel, making a sputtering noise, watched him carefully from behind a spruce. Then, realizing there was danger, it sputtered again and shot up like an arrow, high in the air, made a jump, and rode on its tail onto the next spruce.

You're scared, he thought, scared like I won't say who. But I don't carry arms and I wish you all well – idiots.

He felt in a better and better mood. Everything seemed so simple, simple and obvious. Did he say five to six years? A little less ought to do the trick. Four to five? Because, well, people up here weren't exactly stupid, once you got them interested in something.

The path wound north along a broad shelf on the ridge. Then it turned east and up the crest of the hill – and suddenly a wide view opened before him. Here, at the outermost edge, you could take in all of Nordbygda, with open country far and wide.

He had meant to take a rest here. True, he didn't have his snack anymore, but Dobbin could use a bit of oats. He dismounted, got out the oats and put on the nosebag. Then he sat down at the edge of the road, where the first coltsfoots were starting to peep out, and let his eyes wander around the countryside before him.

It was a clear day toward the end of April. Spring came late up here in the woodland settlements, but now it was under way. The air was thin and transparent, the light so sharp it hurt your eyes. He saw the entire hamlet more clearly than he ever had.

In the forest it had been calm and cozy; only the organ tones from the treetops had told him it was a windy day. Out here in the open there blew a cold, damp north wind, which pierced your clothes like a knife. Håvard shuddered as he sat there. And suddenly it struck him, hard and hurtfully, as though somebody had hammered an awl clean through his head:

You'll never make it!

It came so suddenly that he gave a start. And it hit him so hard that he had to ask himself, Where did it come from? But he sort of knew the answer beforehand. It was the hamlet itself which had spoken up.

There it was, stretched out before him in the nippy weather – pale yellow and black in the bright sunlight, with dirty strips of snow on the north slopes and with poor fields, where people were carting manure by sledge over the bare ground. It should have been done earlier, before the snow went away, but . . . there were so many other things.

There lay the hamlet, wide and open like a huge, shallow pot, with the forest like a black crust around the upper edge and the lake with the melting spring ice like a dull, grayish blue spot down at the bottom. The pot had chinks and cracks, where brooks and little streams flowed into the lake, and alongside these cracks appeared black spruce thickets, reddish brown birches and yellow aspens. All around sat farms and clusters of houses, like blotches in the wall of the pot. Everything was so clear in the thin, nippy air, everything was so distinct and so close up that it seemed to eat its way into his eyes.

It struck him that the entire hamlet was standing at bay in the cold wind. The spruce thickets stirred a bit but braced themselves and stood where they stood. The farmsteads sat there, warped and sagging, iron-gray with age; squat and dumpy, they turned their broad bottoms against the north wind, grappled the earth and refused to budge. They seemed to say to the wind, So, you think you can move us, do you? Oh no, you are a stranger, a footloose tramp, not worth worrying about. We stand where we stand, sit where we sit. Before us there were other houses here, the same as us; they stood here until they rotted into the ground. And before them still others. We've been here on the same spot for a thousand years. So, get out of here. Nothing but trash and tricks has ever come from the outside. Nobody can budge *us*!

And between the houses walked the people. He could see them distinctly hundreds of yards away, could see them bending their knees and slowly turning, doing their work with the same slow strokes they had used all their lives, from the very moment they picked them up from the old folks, who had acquired them from still older folks. And sometime in the future they would themselves pass them on to the young ones, who would grow old in turn and hand down the same strokes once more. Changes? Our ways were good enough for my father and my grandfather, and for his father and grandfather before that; and I reckon they will be good enough for my son and grandson, too!

Slow, steady, and unshakable, with suspicion toward all and everything, they went about their business – their ways were as familiar as they were old, and backed by tradition.

In this pot they were still cooking the same old porridge, all right – nothing but, in fact.

Oh, well, we'll see! Håvard thought. He stood up, took care of the nose-bag, got into the saddle and rode down toward the homesteads. He waved aside his sad thoughts again – they had probably presented themselves only because he'd been shivering with cold. But as he rode on, crossing one farmyard after another and seeing again the terribly old-fashioned methods they used everywhere, quite against his will he was overcome by despondency. They had a long way to go here. A long, long way.

At that moment – he couldn't help it – his innermost heart was touched by something that reminded him of what he'd felt the first time he rode alone through this countryside, last fall that was. It was as though an inner voice told him: Now you're riding into the mountain, into the mountain. Deeper and deeper and never back. In and in and never out. Into the mountain, into the mountain, joining the dwarfs and the giants . . .

These were the thoughts that occupied him as he rode through the big yard at Nordby. Conditions were a little better there than on most farms, and he thought, The master at Nordby is supposed to be such a progressive fellow, perhaps I can find some help there.

As he was leaving the yard, he heard somebody calling his name. Hans Nordby himself stood on the steps inviting him in.

Death at Nordby

*H*ans Nordby looked awful. Unwashed and unkempt, with a bristling, ginger-colored stubble that made his chin look like a pin-
cushion. His eyes were red and swollen, and anyone could see he
had been drinking nonstop since he got home last night.

From inside came laughter and shouting – he hadn't been drinking alone.

Strangely enough, Nordby somehow appeared sober as he stood there.
His eyes were keen and alert, perhaps a bit suspicious.

'I saw you riding by,' he said, snuffling a little when he talked. 'And so I
thought you had to join us for a drink. You see, we're having a nightcap after
the wedding party.'

Håvard was about to reply that he was expected at home. But he checked
himself – he was new in this parish and had better take things as they came
at the beginning.

He accepted the invitation, tied up Dobbin, and followed him in.

He recoiled momentarily on entering the parlor. The air was dense and
heavy, as though packed with a foul man's smell several days old. One of the
fellows had even vomited on the floor, in a corner somewhere.

Three men sat around the table eating ham pancakes and spilling beer
over the table, laughing and hollering. Håvard had talked with them at the
wedding but could barely recognize them; they looked much more tired and
hung over than Nordby himself, and all were roaring drunk. They greeted
him with loud yells but forgot about him immediately. One of them, called
Anders Flateby, he believed, kept repeating to one of the others, Sjønne
Strøm, or whatever his name was:

'You should be grateful, Sjønne! I would gladly sell half my soul for two
hundred dollars, sure would! Consider yourself lucky! I would gladly sell
half my soul . . .'

Sjønne, his head nearly touching the tabletop, didn't answer him. Once
he raised his face and gave a silly smile, but his face was grimy with tears, and
it was plain to see that he didn't understand a thing of what was said to him.
The third, the master at Nordset, was silent; his face had a black and angry
look even when he laughed.

Hans Nordby called the maid and ordered more ham pancakes.

'But first you shall have a drink!' he said to Håvard. 'And it has to be the
best. These other fellows can't see what they're drinking anymore.'

He went over to the cabinet and brought a bottle and a glass. Real French
brandy. His hand was shaking and he spilled some, so there wasn't much left
in the glass for Håvard.

'Skoal, and thanks for a very pleasant wedding!' Nordby said. 'It was a fine wedding, the biggest up in these parts in many years. But then, you know, Rønnau isn't exactly a pauper either!'

Again Håvard noticed his cold, suspicious glance. He thought, This is one of my next-door neighbors. I'd better watch my step here.

A fiddle lay on the table, in the midst of bottles, glasses, and splashes of beer. Håvard couldn't bear the sight of it lying there and picked it up. It was a fine fiddle.

'Where does this fiddle usually hang?' he asked.

Nordby said, 'The fiddle? Oh – I forgot for a moment. It was Sjønne who – . Well, the fiddle usually hangs over there.' He pointed, and Håvard went and hung it up. Strange to say, it hadn't been stained.

'Thank you,' Nordby said.

Shortly, the maid brought a new helping of ham pancakes. Nordby sat down to have a bite too, as he put it – well, he ate most of them.

Håvard, who had been hungry before he entered, had lost his appetite by now. He heard somebody moaning in the bedroom and turned his head.

'It's only Anne,' Nordby said. 'She has difficulty breathing, gets these choking fits every now and then . . . has been bedridden for more than ten years now. . . . Isn't worth the salt in her soup. But you've got to take the bad with the good, I guess.'

Hans Nordby began to talk to Håvard. He knew he was much more sober than the others, and therefore he thought he was completely clear and level-headed. But he, too, was somewhat muddled and said things now and then that he ought to have kept to himself.

Somehow or other the thought of Anne turned his mind to timberland.

'Timberland, there is wealth for you!' he said. 'The Baron and I . . . the Baron and I . . . To buy cheap, I mean. And hold on to it! And sell dear! But even better, don't ever sell!

'I understand, of course, that you plan to buy timberland up here. A smart fellow like you. It's all right with me, as long as you stay clear of my territory. Anders here, and Sjønne, they're my lambkins. But I wouldn't mind if you had a go at Nordset, should you feel like it.'

He talked about the three men without lowering his voice, as if they weren't there. They didn't hear him anyway.

'And who do you deal with?' he said, looking sharply at Håvard. 'With Anker, the proprietor?'[16]

---

16. This could be Peder Anker (1749–1824), a proprietor born in Christiania (now Oslo). Anker

Håvard answered every question evasively and managed to get away with it. You had to know a place better than he knew this parish before starting to buy timberland, he said. And competing with the master at Nordby at buying up timberland, that was certainly the last thing he would do.

Nordby was satisfied with that answer and began to talk about other things – how long he had known Bruflaten, the horse dealer who dropped by at the wedding, and things of that sort.

The other two were still having their bit of fun with Sjønne, repeating the same sentence over and over again.

Hans Nordby, noticing that Håvard was looking at the three of them, said, 'Don't mind them. None of them has got much to show for himself.'

Håvard looked around for the exit again, this time in earnest.

But something held him back. He had a feeling that was quite familiar to him, but he'd never noticed it as clearly as here and now. He could feel his distaste for it all penetrate his bones and had only one desire – to get away. But for that very reason he couldn't just get up and leave, because then the others would know why and feel put to shame.

He knew quite well that, considering the state the three were in, it wouldn't make any difference to them – they would forget him in five minutes – and the fourth, Hans Nordby, would probably think, He couldn't stand those guys.

Yeah, maybe. But the eyes of old Nordby never lost their suspicious look, and that made it hard to leave.

And so he stayed on, said 'yes' and 'I see' and 'perhaps,' while casting about for the moment when an occasion would offer so he could get up and say, 'I think I'll have to go now. Thanks very much.'

Suddenly Anders Flateby saw him for real. He straightened up in his chair.

'But look, there is our *missionary*, as the parson said!' he snuffled. And, quarrelsome all of a sudden, he went on, 'So you think we don't know how to use our land, eh? You want to show us some of the stuff they've taught you in *school*, do you?'

He replied, gently, that it certainly had never entered his mind to be a missionary here. He only thought he might improve Olstad a bit.

Anders couldn't understand and merely repeated his question, again and again. And every time he asked, he thought it funnier and funnier that a

---

was a member of the National Assembly at Eidsvoll and, after Norway's union with Sweden, a minister in Stockholm.

young whippersnapper like him, an outsider to boot, should come up here and teach them how to use their land. He burst out laughing, and once he'd started he laughed more and more.

'*Missionary*! the parson said. *Missionary*! he said. Ha-ha-ha . . .'

Håvard merely thought, Now it'll be even harder to leave.

Nordset sat at the far end of the table, dark and glowering. He too felt he ought to chip in with a word or two. 'We have no use for strangers up here!' he said.

Håvard didn't answer.

But Hans Nordby had noticed what he said about Olstad. 'So you think Olstad is poorly managed? You may have a point there; Ola, you know, had his mind on the forest, most of the time.'

Håvard hadn't meant to broach the subject, and certainly not on this occasion. But the silence seemed to turn into a living thing, something evil that rose up in the room and screamed soundlessly into his ear: Say something!

And so he answered Nordby's question, while the others went on with their sleazy talk. And before he knew it, he had said a word too many.

Anders Flateby was so drunk that most of what was said passed him by. But every now and then a door seemed to open before him and he *heard*. For some reason he heard what Håvard said about the cotters and found it terribly funny.

'Haw-haw! He wants to make big shots of the cotters!' he yelled. And then he burst out laughing again, lunged forward on the table and laughed; he howled with laughter and was unable to stop. He tried to imitate Håvard's voice:

'We'll just give the cotters better pay – and they'll be sure to give us more work!'

And then he laughed again till he cried.

'I haven't had so much fun as long as I can remember – haw-haw-haw! – not since last night anyway! Ha-ha-ha!'

His laughter was infectious. Sjønne laughed, without knowing what he was laughing at. Nordset laughed, even Nordby couldn't help laughing, mostly perhaps at the others, who sat there nudging one another and laughing, wiping their tears and laughing, trying to stop but constantly exploding in fresh laughter.

Then Nordby checked himself. He slapped Håvard's shoulder and said, 'You're very welcome to our parish! But as far as the cotters are concerned, you'd better forget what you just said, the sooner the better. It may be all right other places, but not here.'

Then he, too, exploded in another fit of laughter.

At that moment the maid rushed in, her face completely white: 'Hans, Hans! Come here this minute! Anne is having a choking fit, much worse than before! She . . .'

Hans Nordby got up and hastened to the kitchen. The others remained, laughing and wiping their tears, then laughing again. But little by little their laughter faded away.

Sjønne was the first to give up; he looked around in surprise, as if he'd just awakened – then he slumped forward on the table, his head on his hands, and immediately dropped off. Anders looked about him. 'Where did Hans go, eh?'

Nordset sat there with a scowl on his face, as before. 'Strangers!' he said.

Hans Nordby didn't come back for quite a while. Håvard got up and moved about a bit, mostly to get away from the three men.

He could hear a girl cry in the bedroom and a boy's voice: 'Mother!'

Then it was quiet for a moment. The three figures at the table were all asleep.

Suddenly Håvard heard a sort of joint lament from the boy and the girl in the bedroom: 'Mother! Mother!'

Then loud weeping.

A few moments went by. Then Hans Nordby came back, to all appearances completely sober.

'Anne has just died,' he said.

Håvard didn't know what to say. And as he stood there, somewhat stunned, he noticed that something was happening to Hans Nordby.

'It came a year too late!' he mumbled, more to himself than to the others.

His eyes stared straight ahead, with a look that Håvard couldn't make out; but it was quite evident that anger was slowly surging up in the man – his compact figure became more so, his face seemed thinner. It didn't last long. Håvard could see he pulled himself together.

'You'll give me a hand with these fellows, Håvard, won't you. To get them out. Time for them to stumble home now.'

They went over to the three sleeping men slumped over the table and gave them a shake.

'You've got to leave now!' said Hans Nordby. 'Anne is dead.'

It was almost impossible to revive them. They thought it was morning and mumbled that they would like to sleep a little longer.

'You've got to leave now. Anne is dead.'

Nordby said it over and over again.

Finally they managed to shake a bit of life into them. But they didn't know where they were; and they couldn't see at all why they had to leave.

Anne? Did Anne show them the door? That wasn't like Anne at all.

'Let me go to Anne!' Flateby snuffled. 'Anne would never begrudge a man a drink or two.'

And throughout they could hear children's tears from the bedroom.

They maneuvered them into the yard, at last. But the three were in the dark about everything and started fooling around. One of them, Sjønne apparently, was laughing without pause.

'Good-bye, Håvard!' said Nordby. 'I'd better lock the door.'

The three men were walking loops around each other, slapping their knees and getting trapped by their own legs, sending up sallies of silly laughter. That was the last thing Håvard saw.

Home to Olstad

*E*vening had fallen by the time Håvard rode out of the yard at Nordby. He could hear the shouting and laughter of the drunken men behind him. Before him lay the quiet hamlet with, on the left, the lake and the dark ridge behind it and, above that, the evening sky. The setting sun looked like a red sack, as so often after a blustery day. The wind had tapered off toward sunset, only a gust came now and then, chasing dust and dry leaves before it. Nobody was to be seen anywhere, either in the fields, the yards, or on the road. People had knocked off work for the day.

As he reined his horse through the gateposts at Nordby the sun went down, and the same moment there came a puff of wind; suddenly the entire hamlet turned wan, as though it breathed its last and died.

Something caught at his heartstrings, reminding him of the first time, last fall that was, when he rode this trail north, alone. Suddenly the hamlet stood before him like a wall, something he could only run his head against.

Oh – but there's Rønnau and I, he thought.

But suddenly Rønnau and he grew so small and the hamlet so big, so set and unshakable. Like a rock. And it was as though something inside him said, as it had said that time:

Now you're riding into the mountain, into the mountain . . .

He stopped his horse in the spruce grove directly below Nordby.

Suddenly it appeared to him as a misfortune that he hadn't managed to say a single word to Gjermund, his brother, when they parted. But he could still turn and ride after him; Dobbin was quick, perhaps he would catch up with him before he turned in – or if not tonight, then tomorrow. His brother had never liked to be on horseback and wasn't a fast rider; and besides he knew where Gjermund would be spending the night.

He would say . . .

Give my love to Mother! he would say. Give my love to Mother and tell her I'm thinking about her. Tell her that I didn't mean to betray Tonè – I can't say more about it now. She ought to meet Rønnau, don't forget to tell her that. To meet Rønnau, then she would understand everything. No, not everything, because – there is something here that no woman can understand.

I wasn't looking for wealth or a farm, tell her that. I wanted to keep my promise, but everything turned out differently. Don't forget to tell her that. She's in my thoughts every day – do you think you could remember to tell her that?

And remember me to Father. Tell him that if he has nothing but hard feelings, he doesn't need to give me another thought, I'll manage anyway. But if he cannot help thinking about me a little now and then, tell him to rest assured I'll conduct myself well where I am now. I won't dishonor myself twice, tell him that.

And you yourself, Gjermund. Don't hold it too much against me that I've gotten a bigger farm than you've got. I would much have preferred the home farm with its hills and stones to this rich farm in a strange parish. But the way things turned out, I didn't get Viland – nor you the cabinetmaker's shop you have always wanted.

Try to forget the times we have quarreled in recent years, and remember that we often had fun together in the old days, before I grew too strong for you and you got angry and cross and never wanted to talk to me.

Good-bye, Gjermund, we'll never see each other again.

He had made the horse do a half-turn, then reined it back again. It was too late, and besides it was no use. What was done was done, what had happened had happened. And he knew he would never be able to tell Gjermund any of the things he had just been thinking. Not a single word of it. And even if he managed to say something, it wouldn't help. Gjermund would look at him long and hard and clench his mouth shut – so, now the little brat wanted to make excuses, did he! With a nice big house and a smart wife and funds stashed away, did he want a halo around his head to boot, huh? To have his cake and eat it, now as always!

He had told Gjermund all that he could ever tell him.

Good-bye! he'd said. Good-bye, and remember me to Father and Mother.

There was nothing more to say.

He started the horse and rode on north.

Now he glimpsed the dark cluster of buildings at Olstad, slightly to the left. Straight north he could make out the church steeple, above the tall, naked crowns of the birches.

He stopped the horse when he got to the crossroads where the private road turned westward across the fields to Olstad, which sat far up the hill facing the lake, the outbuildings gray with age and the long main building dark, with a tinge of the evening sky in all the windowpanes. A fine farm . . . He could also see the buildings at Berg from here, the neighboring farm directly north and west – Kerstaffer's place, the farm with all those lunatics in the basement. There they were, just emerging from the door to the kitchen where they had eaten supper – the best of them, those who had been at work during the day. They were being driven out of the kitchen and down into the basement to the others. Kerstaffer himself stood at the corner with a whip in his hand, counting them as they went down to the basement, down into the stench to join the others, those who were hopelessly insane.

Håvard started Dobbin again, onto the old private road, where people had walked and ridden generation after generation until they had trampled the road deep into the ground. The lane went like a wide ditch between two rail fences. A black cat ran across the road like an evil streak. Ugh. He didn't believe in such things but . . .

A black bird was screeching in a treetop. What was it? A raven? Those were rare birds here, so far east. It was an omen of war, people said.

An owl hooted in the thicket on the right. It had turned up unusually early tonight. He rode step by step westward toward the farm. He had lapsed into a mood which made him take everything as an omen, like an old woman – he couldn't help it.

There came that well-known howl from one of Kerstaffer's lunatics, that ugly scream which portended a weather change.

He thought, It doesn't matter, as long as Rønnau will be on the porch when I round the corner of the house – as long as Rønnau will be on the porch.

There was no Rønnau on the porch.

The big yard lay there so empty and deserted. For three or four days it had been full of people, men and women passing back and forth with noise and laughter and merriment. Now everything was quiet. Down by the barn Martin Grina was taking down the stalls they had put up for all those strange horses. The other hired hands were through for the day; but Martin had been a sort of head servant here the last couple of years and knew his responsibilities; he probably wanted to finish this job before turning in. He carefully separated the logs and fussily put the nails in a box. He looked up sullenly as Håvard rode up, mumbled something to the effect that this big wedding in the middle of the worst spring shortage had made a big dent in the fodder.

Martin, a widower, was a cotter on the farm. He could hardly have looked very kindly on this new arrival, who perhaps intended to squeeze him out of his position, take away his power, and send him back to his miserable cotter's plot.

Martin was still a man in his prime, you could say – forty or so. But his back had the cotter's hunch, his legs the cotter's trudge; he was as slow as a funeral procession and had already acquired an old man's drip under his nose. It would hang there for hours on end, with him moving so slowly.

Now he began sweeping up the horse droppings behind the stalls, mumbling that you had to save what could be saved – the cows would be only too pleased to have the horse droppings. And so they too got a small taste of the wedding.

Martin's behavior gave Håvard something new to think about. Preoccupied, he stabled and fed Dobbin; preoccupied, he crossed the yard – there was still no Rønnau to be seen on the porch – and entered the house. There was nobody in the hall, which he regarded as another bad omen, though he immediately waved it aside, his thoughts being otherwise engaged. Absorbed by these other thoughts, he turned right, into the parlor, instead of left to the kitchen, where a meal no doubt was waiting for him.

There was nobody in the parlor. It had been tidied up and cleaned, but there still lingered an odor of tobacco, beer, and liquor and of many people sitting jammed together, sweaty from dancing for several days. Håvard went over to one of the windows and tried to open it, but it was nailed shut. Anyway, he knew that.

Lost in thought, he started wandering up and down alongside one of the rugs, from the window to the stove and back again. The fire hadn't been lighted and it was chilly in the room, but he didn't notice.

Finally he stopped by the window and stood there looking out into the yard with eyes which saw and still didn't see.

It was beginning to grow dark. The dairymaid came in from the cow barn with the last milk pails, one in each hand. There was a rattle of pots and pans in the kitchen, sort of far, far away. Down by the barn Martin had finished now, and nobody was to be seen in the yard anymore.

It had grown strangely quiet on the farm, as often happens immediately after a big party. Quiet in the house, quiet in the yard, which lay there so empty and abandoned, so big and desolate in the twilight.

The wind had freshened a bit for a little while. Sweeping across the yard and grabbing the corner of the house in jerky gusts, it picked up last year's dead leaves in the ditches and along the walls and sent them whirling, doing a shadow dance with them – it lifted the brown gossamer leaves into the air, dropped them again, whirled them up to a taper, dropped them halfway, swept them along the road, dropped them into the ditch again, then grabbed and lifted them into the air afresh. . . . Perhaps the leaves believed they were alive again while it lasted. There came a dry, dead rustle when the wind flung the dry leaves against the wall of the house.

Quiet.

But suddenly the quiet old house seemed to come alive. The wind grabbed it by the corners, shook the walls, made a thin whistling sound in the cold stove, and whispered in the door chink and the keyhole.

There were rustles and whispers.

The wedding and all that, now it was over, seemed suddenly so far away. But the memory of it lingered in the room like a specter of sounds, of talk and laughter, pale and remote – shadows of sounds, like the jingle of sleigh bells from a Christmas many years ago.

The floorboards creaked faintly, quietly bending in the big house, the walls softly resonated, echoing his footsteps or answering a flurry of wind from outside – there were sighs and whispers: has been, has been. What will be? Will be, will be – .

Shadows fluttered through the room, shadows of the past, shadows of the future. And of emptiness, uncertainty, desolation – of time past and of time to come.

Shadows crept out of the walls, old shadows from all the bygone years. There were low whispers, almost inaudible . . .

Someone is standing by the window. Håvard. Håvard, who is that? The new master. Haw. Haw. Håvard. The new master. We are the ancients on this farm. We sit in the walls, we creak around the hallways, we rustle and whisper in the door chinks, we are that which was and that which will be. The new master? Haw, haw, haw. Haw, haw, haw. You *are* – but we *were*, we were, we were; and we will be, will be, will be. Creak, creak. Were, will be. Håvard. Who is Håvard? Haw, haw, haw. Were, will be. Were, will be . . .

The shadows in the parlor thickened, grew larger. Other shadows joined them. Håvard, do you remember us? Yes, Mother, yes Father, I remember. Yes, yes, Tonè, I remember.

Are you still angry with me, Tonè?

Ha, ha, ha. Ha, ha, ha. Yes, it whispered. No, it whispered. A draft was coming from an unstopped window crack, and the chink in the door whistled so sadly. Oh yes. Oh no. Don't know, don't know.

A sigh, faint as the shadow of a sigh. Forgot you. Forgot you now. Forgot you now.

Håvard stood at the window with his back to the room, his back to the shadows, staring with eyes which saw and didn't see. Staring out at the dead leaves which danced their shadowy dance down along the road.

Forgot you now. Forgot you now.

Somebody was at the door. Rønnau came in.

'But darling, why are you standing here, in this cold room? I've been cleaning upstairs and didn't know you'd come home until Martin mentioned it. You should go and get something to eat.'

She came closer. She smiled. Her dark hair had a black sheen. Her white teeth gleamed.

'It's good to have you home again,' she said softly.

He could feel her warmth enveloping him as he put his arms around her – a living human being, not a shadow from the past or the future.

She laughed. 'What are you doing! You're getting my hair mussed up. What, are you mad?' She pushed him away as she whispered this, then drew him close again. Her high bosom, her warm skin, her quickening breath. Her mouth gave off a fragrance, tart and fresh, like cloudberry bogs in late summer.

She smiled again, but her smile faded and she grew serious; she threw her head back, and for an instant he felt her full weight in his arms – then she flung her arms around his neck. 'Håvard, Håvard!'

She whispered, 'No, no – are you mad! What if someone came in! No, no, we don't dare – not here – '

A moment later she whispered, as though they were doing something sneaky, 'We could go up to the guest room, you know – there nobody will disturb us.'

Rønnau was breathing calmly and evenly. She was asleep. Håvard lay beside her, awake. Outside, a blue evening sky.

Gone was the shadowy dance of last year's leaves and the whispering voices down in the parlor an hour ago. A calm strength, a calm confidence filled him like a song as he lay there watching Rønnau. A new voice spoke within him, a verse or an old jingle most likely.

What's done is done. What's happened has happened. Neither others nor you, alack, can stop passing time or make it turn back. If you've caused harm and grief and shame, shoulder it bravely and take the blame.

You've come to a strange parish, among people you don't know. Well, get

47

to know them then. You have married a house and grounds, and a woman you also don't know – not yet. But one thing is certain – she has more power over you than any woman ever had.

This is where you are now. Have you been bewitched, lured into the mountain? Perhaps. All right, you are inside the mountain. Turn it into a fine-looking mountain then – the best-looking mountain in the world.

The farm sat there, just waiting for him.

'It's a good farm, but it lacks a plow.'

It was Rønnau who had said this, the first time he was up this way; the first time he . . .

Did he sleep or was he awake? Somewhere in between, it seemed. He noticed, somewhat dimly, that he was mulling over something he'd been thinking earlier in the day.

The crops at Olstad are getting bigger. A new breed of cattle, milking more than the cows on the other farms, has arrived. The forest is being left alone, the timber is growing. Sledges loaded with grain drive into the city in the winter. Several people come to make inquiries, more and more – their heads cocked, making inquiries – .

The crops are slowly beginning to get bigger on the other farms too. There is a surplus of grain, potatoes, apples, cabbage, and carrots. What should be done with it? Haul it to the city. Next winter? No, in the fall, when the ground is bare, on wheels. But there is no road. Build a road. Who will build it? We ourselves will build a road. The freeholder, the cotter, everybody. Sneers and little sayings. More toil, certainly, until it's finished. But afterward everything gets more profitable. More work for the cotters, a shortage of workers – the daily wage rises. People shake and shake their heads. In my youth, they say. In my youth . . . in my youth . . . Plenty of work. Better pay. There are no beggars on the road anymore, the cotters are straightening their backs and won't accept whatever their master offers them any longer but demand a couple of shillings more a day, the same wages they are getting closer to town. Now the world won't last till Easter, things are really going too far, the cotters, God help us, come and *make demands*! In my youth . . . in my youth . . .

The master yells and curses and bangs the table. Everything is collapsing – here he had been so happy about everything, had seen the surplus from all these novelties he'd fought tooth and nail as long as he could, growing and growing and making such a nice pile in the coffer – *his* coffer – and then these slyboots, these miserable cotters, damn them, come and want to *share*! Share the benefits! Who the hell can enjoy a benefit if he doesn't have it all to himself?

48

Still, he has to part with his shillings. And if he is like some people, he will eat his heart out about it for the rest of his life. But if he is different, he'll remember quite soon it was *he* who went to his cotters and said: now we're making good money, fellows, so we'll share fairly – you've done a good job, and now you shall have a small raise, you bet.

And so one day the parish sits there, the same as before but no longer recognizable. New houses in many places. New cotter's cabins almost everywhere. Yellow grain fields and nicely kept yards. A real road which winds its way from one farm to another, up the hill and out of the parish. And horse-drawn vehicles – with wheels! – on every farm. People on the road, walking with straight backs and happy faces. Who are you walking so straight? asks a stranger on horseback. I? Well, I am a cotter going to work. He asks someone else, And who are you walking so straight and looking so happy? Oh, I'm a cotter on my way home from work, home to my wife and children. But who has managed to do all this? Oh, it's one and all, but mostly a stranger called Håvard, a man who had lost his honor in his native parish . . .

'Now you must wake up!' Rønnau said; she stood beside his bed with a candle in her hand. There was a tray on the table.

'I've brought you some food,' she said. 'Some of the party snacks. Why not? The workaday world, please God, will have to wait until tomorrow.'

The Dairymaid

*A*nd so the new workdays began.

Håvard had seen a new farm before him – a new parish, lush fields and meadows, well-tended forests, contented freeholders, straight-backed cotters . . .

Grand, simple visions.

But the first thing he had to tackle was small enough and neither nice nor grand. It was the way the dark, dirty cow barn was managed. And there he suffered a near defeat.

The outbuildings at Olstad were old and gray, many were sagging and going to ruin, and all were unpractical and inconvenient, built that way long ago because people had been building that way even longer ago. But the cow barn was the worst.

Old and lopsided, without a cellar or a foundation wall, it stood on the ground and had sunk halfway below the surface. Inside, it was dark and damp, with a single dirty little window. There was much too little room for

49

the big herd, but it had the advantage that the cattle kept warm, standing there underfed during the spring shortage. The dung hole was high up on the wall, as though contrived that way to make it as inconvenient as possible to clean the place. When, besides, you had a lazy dairymaid, as here, the result was that most of the manure remained inside. You waded through new and old muck to high up on your boots wherever you went. Here and there, haphazardly, roosts had been put up for the chickens – you bumped your head against them wherever you went. The chickens, some old, skinny wraiths, seldom or never laid an egg, but often, and quite willingly, dropped other things onto the heads of people who passed under them.

The maids slept in the cow-barn loft. Dark, damp, and unhealthy. Trying to change this, Håvard knew, was hopeless at the start. Up there it was nice and warm, and they were on their own, out from under the eyes of the master and mistress.

That they carried the cow-barn smells into the kitchen and the other rooms was an inconvenience you had to put up with. That's how it had been from the old days, that's how it was, that's how it should be.

Håvard realized he had to try and clean this barn.

The first thing he did was to set apart a corner for a hen house. Next, he moved the dung hole one beam lower down. Then the barn itself had to be mucked and washed. He asked the dairymaid to help him with this.

Berte, the dairymaid, was a big, stocky, sullen girl, stubborn and slow, unkempt and slovenly. She smelled of cow manure from morning till night. She liked neither the barn nor the cows, and Håvard was once more amazed at how often you found dairymaids who hated the cattle. Berte treated the cows like enemies, as though she had to get even with them for some secret offense. The cows were scared of her. She rarely walked past one of them without giving it a smack or a kick. She had nicknames for them. She never took the trouble to muck properly – that was a man's job, she said – but merely cleared away the worst mess directly behind the cows once a day. It was easy to see that she never had been inside their stalls with her scoop.

She didn't know how to milk. When getting ready to do so, she put the milking stool into the stall and herself on top of it, her boots steeped in muck. Then she would give the cow a hard smack with the flat of her hand. Come now! Move, will you!

Then she would milk, but much too hard, so that the teats hurt. The cows thanked her with a kick, or by flicking their tails in her face and into the milk every once in a while. Then with her clenched fist, she hit the cow straight in the belly, which was so mucky you couldn't see what it was made of.

50

It was the same with everything she did. She was lazy and ignorant, and even most of what she knew was wrong.

This was the woman Håvard was going to try and train.

In the front stall lay an old pauper.[17] She was called Mari and had somehow found her home on the farm. Rønnau reported that she had served a five-year stint as dairymaid there at one time. Later she became the wife of one of the farm's cotters; but when her husband went crazy and the parish sent him to Kerstaffer Berg's basement – he died a year later – she went back to being a dairymaid once more, until finally she got too old. And now she lived in the cow barn. She wasn't much good at standing or walking, so she stayed in bed most of the time, in the front stall.

Her bedstraw gave off an awful smell, as was to be expected – the wet from the cows trickled through from the next stall and was sucked up by the straw. Håvard got one of the housemaids to help him – the dairymaid said no, that sort of thing was no part of her barn chores – and the old woman was washed and groomed. Then he put a layer of boards on top of the stall flooring and got her fresh straw for her mattress. The old one didn't say anything, but let them tend her as they pleased. Only when Håvard asked if she wouldn't like to be moved up into the house, did she open her mouth. No, she liked it well enough where she was, with the cattle. Animals were good company. There was no deceit in animals.

After they had finished with her, Rønnau appeared. She laughed, 'Mari, oh my, you're real pretty – I suppose you'll start having Saturday gallants now!'

But she quickly went back to the house again.

It was easy to take care of Mari. It was harder to train Berte, the dairymaid.

He asked her to help him clean the cow barn, as mentioned, trying to explain to her the advantages of a clean barn. It didn't require very much work as long as you took care to keep it clean all the time. 'You should've seen Principal Sverdrup's cow barn at Kongsberg – it was as clean as a parlor, and the cows had such glossy coats you could see your own reflection in them. You have no idea how much fun it was to do chores in that barn.'

Berte stood there in silence, stubborn and surly. Explanations and jokes were wasted on her. She just stood there as Håvard cleaned out the stalls,

17. In Norwegian, *legdekjerring*; lit., *legd* woman. A *legd* was a certain number of persons or a set of farms organized to provide for paupers by receiving them in turn, or contributing to a store of provisions distributed by a poor-relief board. This system was continued until the year 1900.

doing little or nothing herself. You could tell by her face all along that now she was suffering a deep wrong.

She'd felt it as an insult from the very first that Håvard interfered with her work. She listened to his explanations with a sullen air and followed his work with hostile eyes, all the while muttering something under her breath.

The only thing one could read in those dull eyes, perhaps the only thing she understood, was that doing her chores the way Håvard said meant she would have more work on her hands.

She remained silent while Håvard cleared away the manure. But when he started heating water in the wash boiler and explained that now they were going to wash the barn, she couldn't take it anymore. Her feet grew leaden and she swelled with revolt.

Were they going to *wash* the cow barn? Perhaps they were going to wash the cows too?

Wash them, no, that wouldn't do. But curry them, sure, to rid them of the worst. So they could at least keep their coats fairly clean in this lean season, when they stood starving in their stalls and had scarcely the strength to moo.

At first she grew speechless from outrage. Then she just walked away and into the house, telling everybody who would listen that now this newcomer had gone mad – he wanted to wash the cows and put ribbons on their horns.

Håvard humored her. He washed the whole cow barn as well as he could. He made a carding comb for Berte so she could curry the cows. To be on the safe side, he curried them himself the first time. He thought she would eventually come around. Little by little, as he showed her what a clean and well-kept cow barn was, she was bound to like it, and to start liking her work.

But it didn't turn out that way.

When he went to the barn a couple of days later, things were nearly as bad as before. The cows hadn't been curried during those two days, and their flanks were once again covered with caked dung.

He didn't say anything but cleaned again and curried the cows once more. You had to be patient; sooner or later Berte was sure to learn.

But Berte didn't want to learn and wasn't at all patient. She tossed her head at the mere sight of him, if he as much as passed by. Her thick legs stuck in the ground like two logs, she stood there like an impregnable fortress in an armor of muck, refusing to be conquered.

Nobody was going to teach *her* how to take care of cows and cow barns; she had done nothing else all her life. Then along came this – this – she couldn't find a strong enough word, but with looks and frowns, with a mulish expression in her eyes, scornful shrugs of her shoulders and stamping of her feet, with contemptuous arm swinging and short furious gusts of laughter or groans of anger, she complained to heaven, calling on the whole world to witness the wrong that was befalling her. She was as bristly as a brush, as unyielding as a wall, not to be budged – you had to take a detour around her while pretending she wasn't there. Håvard went to the cow barn every day, cleared away the manure, curried the cows, and busied himself like an ordinary cowhand. The cows began to cast long glances after him, giving him a welcoming moo when he came and bawling when he left.

But nothing helped. Quite the reverse: when Berte understood that these new ways in the cow barn weren't simply a casual whim of her master but in dead earnest, she grew contrary, too, in earnest. She bridled at the mere sight of Håvard, turning up the whites of her eyes and trotting in the other direction. She didn't *want* to. She would do anything rather than learn something new – if things came to a head so she had no other choice, she would sooner jump into the lake, though there was nothing she disliked more in this world than water. As it was, she went to Rønnau and told her, if her work wasn't good enough, she could quit! She could quit this very day! She could go home, oh yes!

Home was a wretched small cotter's plot in the northernmost part of the parish, with two old parents who had scarcely a crust of bread but four small children to feed, left behind by their daughters on one of their flying visits. Berte had left one of them. If she went back home now, there would be even less gruel for everybody in the cramped, dark, drafty shack, and the children would get even thinner, their faces a shade more blue. She could go back home, all right! Her face puffy with hurt, she burst into tears with a loud scream, calling heaven and earth to witness what an unheard-of humiliation she had suffered; she stamped her feet, scattering muck all over, and screamed, 'It's blasphemy! He wants the animals to be kept cleaner than people! Never!' She would never put up with it – she for her part had nothing to learn from this newcomer, a stranger who spoke a language she didn't understand half of! But she could quit! Sure she could!

Rønnau laughed and talked calmly to her, stroked her, and got her to sit down. She threw herself forward on the table, her boots saying squish, squish, and cried until there was a wet spot on the kitchen table. But gradually she quieted down.

'Rønnau, you know, understood me *so well*!' she told the others, 'but she had to side with him a little too, seeing what it has come to between the two of them.' Anyway, what Rønnau had seen in that fellow was beyond her. There was more in this than met the eye – you had to understand what a man *said*, at least, before you let him into your bed!

Berte wasn't very well liked by the others on the farm, lazy, sullen, and stubborn as she was, and never willing to do anybody a favor. But now, when she kicked up such a row, they understood this much, the others too, that this newcomer must have treated her unfairly. They had better be on their guard with him, hold back a bit, stand stiff-legged as long as they dared, not let him bowl them over completely – but always with caution, so he wouldn't get any kind of hold on them. Better be wary. It looked like there wouldn't be much fun around here from now on for a while.

Rønnau heard a little of this and understood some more. She said to Håvard, 'You should treat Berte more gently. She's both lazy and stupid, and something of a pig. But good dairymaids are hard to find, the one I had before her was worse. Berte is good at one thing at any rate – she doesn't squander the feed.'

It was true. Berte underfed the animals with a will, you could almost say. The ceaseless bawling and bellowing of the hungry cows was enough to drive you mad. In the long run, Håvard couldn't bear listening to it. In the barn there was scarcely enough hay left for the horses. The hired hands were busy every day cutting young birch and osier so the animals could have something to munch on. But the cows were just skin and bones – the bones stuck out so sharply you could fairly cut yourself on them. A couple of the oldest weren't able to stand on their legs, and Berte barely managed to kick them to their feet when she was going to milk them.

When Håvard had waged this war of his in the cow barn for a week, he understood that something had to be done about it.

Rønnau and Håvard

'Y ou had better not play too much when others can hear you,' Rønnau said one evening in the bedroom.

Following the Telemark custom, he had taken out his fiddle and played some tunes. The servant, Lars, and the youngest maid had even danced a roundel. What's more, Kjersti, Rønnau's nearly twelve-year-old stepdaughter, usually so quiet, had ventured to take a turn.

Rønnau explained:

'I enjoy listening to you, of course – well, the others do too. But people up here are funny that way. A cotter can be a fiddler and so can a youth, even if he's heir to a farm. But a farmer, you know, is supposed to have outgrown such things. It's the custom around here. And customs have to be followed, if you want to avoid trouble with the neighbors.'

'I think we'd better go easy for a while, not make too many changes for our workers,' she said another time. 'They're used to the old way of doing things, you see. That's what they know, the new ways they don't know. Besides, they'll feel insulted if you push too many new things on them at once. They'll think you're telling them they don't know their work. If you forge ahead too fast, it may end up the same as with Berte, the dairymaid.'

What she said was well meant, he realized that. Maybe he'd been a bit impatient. He'd better remember he was new around here, an outsider at that.

Anyway, his efforts in the cow barn had ended in defeat. Or in something that had the looks of defeat. He couldn't get through to the dairymaid. Rønnau, stepping in, got Berte to put up with him at least, though just barely. When she saw him she gave choked snorts and groans like a sow in distress, but apart from that he was nothing to her – a mere smell, a bad one. She put up with his loitering in the cow barn and didn't protest when he mucked, curried the cows, or busied himself with other such nonsense. But she did her own chores the way she'd always done them. She stood by her words – if they were satisfied with her, that was fine; if not, she would be glad to quit any day!

In the long run it couldn't go on like that. Håvard had other things to do than fussing over the cows every day. They decided, he and Rønnau, to wait and see. Spring was around the corner and the cows would be driven to pasture; then came the summer and everything would change.

In the fall they would have to make different arrangements.

All this forced Håvard and Rønnau to talk a great deal about the management of the farm. And he discovered – to his great surprise – that Rønnau wasn't quite so eager to change the ways of doing things as he'd always thought. And not quite so willing to learn either.

'Do you really think that is necessary?' she would say. Or, 'Is it really so urgent?' Or, 'We've been doing pretty well here at Olstad before this, following the old ways.'

Once in a while she would use her late husband as a weapon. 'Ola wasn't very much interested in the land, if the truth were to be told – it was the woods that he cared about. Still, he was a man of experience, and he used to say that . . .'

She stuck to the old usages, everything that had been handed down from the old days.

Not always because she thought it was correct. On the contrary, often she knew quite well it was wrong, or that something else might be better. But, as she used to say, 'It's best to go by custom, if possible – as long as it doesn't lead to sheer folly, of course. That way you don't risk antagonizing people, and you're freer to follow your own bent in other things.'

She often laughed at the sort of things she would put up with, and at the things she did. But still she put up with them, did them too.

Leaving a bowl of porridge in the hayloft for the brownie Thursday night – this was just one of these things. Marking the door to the cow barn with a tarred cross on the eve of the first of May was another. She was fully aware that the porridge was eaten by cats, mice, and rats, and as for the witches who were said to fly over the roof of the cow barn on their way to Mount Brocken the night before the first of May, well, she didn't believe very much in them either.[18] But such were the age-old customs.

No, she didn't have much faith in all those old things. But he soon understood that there were exceptions. There were some old things – ancient customs and usages, often crass superstitions – that she accepted in dead earnest. And little by little he discovered that *these* were things she'd learned from her mother or father. Mostly the latter. *That* wasn't done, and so she could never do it with a smile. *This* was the proper way, it was *right*. To make her budge in these things was anything but easy, even if he was able to convince her – since she had a good mind – that what she did was totally wrong. Then she would correct it for a day or two, before going back to her old ways again. This is how Mother used to do it, she would say. Or, That's what Father thought.

All in all, she resisted a great many of his suggestions. It just wasn't done; this wasn't how her mother did it, her father . . .

He mentioned it to her one day, how she had changed. When he first knew her, she had been quite different. She had listened to the parson and wanted to make improvements.

'When I first knew you?' She repeated his words. 'That wasn't here, remember. That was at the wedding party at Millom, where you jumped clean over the circle of men who were after you. Remember?'

Quite true. But how about later, last fall when he came up here? She invited him, after all, because she wanted him to look over the farm and propose changes – because she realized things weren't going so well with those old-fashioned methods they were using.

18. Mount Brocken is a peak in the Harz Mountains in Saxony, Germany, where witches were believed to congregate for the Witches' Sabbath.

She stood still for a moment, looking at him with narrowed eyes. Then she said, to nobody in particular:

'That's men for you! What fools!'

This was during the day. At night it was different. In the bedroom at night, with nobody else around. Outside, the night was watching them; the wind had been rustling the leaves of the old apple trees in the garden, but now it had gone to rest. They were naked underneath the warm sheepskin. She always slept naked, her firm body against his, her skin sweet to the touch, her breasts firm like those of a young girl – who could believe she was a wife, with a child? Oh well, not quite, not yet anyway.

Her hands – how could she keep her hands so soft, with all the work she was doing? She played on him with those hands, tuned him, struck a note, one more, until a tremulous music arose inside him – she was the bow, he was the fiddle. Every once in a while he thought, vaguely, it ought to be the other way around. But whatever it was or wasn't, they did make music together – music that was new to him, strange tunes that kept rising and rising, making him dizzy and scared; they were wild and sad, and old as time, yet he'd never heard them before. They were . . . they all concerned the same thing, but each was different. They seemed to be about life, the whole of life, about love, and about death. Always about death. They were wild, as if coming from the black forest, from the dead of night. They were sad – or were they? Sometimes she would cry. Sometimes *he* would cry. Afterward, every now and then, he thought he could turn this tune into real music. He had even tried a few times, but then it was daylight and everything was different. He couldn't remember it, not well enough to play it anyway – it was almost like a dream. If he sat alone thinking about her some evening when she was away, he mused, then perhaps he would remember it and be able to play it. Sure. Because actually he knew it from before, had heard it as a child, or dreamed it – hadn't he? He couldn't say. But he could play it some night when he was alone – here or up in the woods.

Yes, at night it was different. Then nothing was difficult, everything was clear, and they understood each other perfectly. She understood him and he her, they would do everything to humor each other. He understood so well how she felt about the old things, and that people held on to them as something precious. He didn't want to trample on them either, not at all; quite the contrary. And *she* understood how his fingers must itch when he saw all that was wrong, the time and energy that were never used, all the waste. She shared his visions, saw a new farm before her, a new parish, with joyful people.

Then daylight came, and once more everything was different. Most of all, *she* was different.

He saw it and wondered, certain only of one thing: he didn't know her.

At times he reminded her of some remark she had made. Then, like as not, she would answer, 'That was last night!' Or, 'One says lots of things at night.'

His previous experience with women had all been in one vein. When he was with a girl she would melt, become wax in his hands or drown in tears. When he'd been with a girl a few times, he knew her inside out, like the pasture at home.

With Rønnau it was different. She was hot. She could be white-hot. But the next morning, when she had cooled off again, she was just as hard. Or perhaps even harder. Indeed, now and then she seemed to be spoiling for a fight precisely on such mornings, or to hate him for something.

If the girls he'd known previously reminded him of the family pasture, where he knew every stone and stump, Rønnau reminded him – he couldn't say why – of the big black forests encircling the farmsteads here. He had taken quite a few walks there by now and was getting to know his way around, as people say. Know his way? He could walk in these forests all his life and still not know them well enough to avoid getting lost in them – or ending up somewhere he'd never been so that he had to stop and wonder.

He didn't know her. But he felt faint when he got near her.

And she? He was quite certain she didn't know him. Not all of him any-way. (You don't either, he thought to himself.) It seemed to him she didn't even care about getting to know him. She was after something other than knowledge. Or – perhaps she already had it, the knowledge? Did she have it just like that? Did she sit on a peak, so to speak, surveying him from top to toe so that she simply needed to focus her eyes wherever she wished in order to see what there was to see?

He didn't know. But he did know one thing – he could tell from her eyes when they got near each other unawares that he wasn't the only one who felt faint.

He had better leave it at that – keep walking in this forest where he'd gone astray. It was too late to call for Mother now, as he did when he got lost in the pasture as a boy.

It had to take its course. Even if he knew, ten times over, that the devil himself sat in the corner biding his time.

No, the nights didn't present any problem. The days could be tough going.

But at other times things were different.

In the daytime everything went well. He threw himself into the work on the farm. He wouldn't tolerate quiet around him – neither breaks nor rest. There were hundreds of things to be done, one following hard upon another.

It didn't take long before the farm was buzzing with whispers that the new master was a scourge to his cotters; he was after them late and early and could be in several places at once; and nothing they did in their accustomed way was good enough. He meddled with their work routines, trying to teach them his new ways – far, far better than the old ones, of course. The old folks, it appeared, hadn't known a damn thing, really. In fact, the old folks had been born only yesterday. But this young puppy, well, he was old and wise as the hills, oh yeah. For as everyone knows, a new broom sweeps clean. That was obvious, wasn't it?

But he seemed so impatient, expecting them to master the new things at one smack. He didn't spare himself either, but went to work as if paid by the job, hoping to get rich from what little his own hands could accomplish. He who had discovered a much better way! For it wasn't with his hands he'd made his fortune overnight, that fellow! He kept speaking about an iron plow and about plowing deep. You bet! His plow, though, wasn't made of iron, oh no; still it had plowed well, and deep too!

The cotters would talk among themselves, chuckling and laughing, with admiration, anger, and contempt.

Håvard was vaguely aware of it and said to himself, 'You'll have to be more careful!'

Rønnau heard a bit more of what they were buzzing about, and understood still more – he could tell that much; it was one of the reasons she broached the subject with Håvard, asking him to tread more softly.

'Keep in mind, too,' she said, 'that Martin, the leader of the cotters – if leader is the right word – can't so easily forget that he isn't in charge here anymore.'

Kind of difficult, all right. Still, it was going pretty well – during the day.

The nights were worse.

Though it could be a bit up and down. Sometimes, after a bout of passionate lovemaking, he would fall asleep at once, sinking into an abyss that left him dead to the world until morning. Then he would awake cheerful and lively as he used to long ago, and suddenly he would catch himself singing while getting dressed.

Other nights were different. They might have had a glorious time to-gether and she had withdrawn from his arm and was asleep, with that calm, happy breathing he already knew so well. But he couldn't sleep and just lay there staring at the dark room. Creatures in all sorts of shapes appeared out there in the darkness. He dug his face into the pillow in order not to see – until he had to turn around to be able to breathe.

On such nights he was glad that summer was approaching, that the nights were getting shorter, daylight longer.

Other nights could be much worse. Though able to sleep, he didn't rest. He was dragging himself up an endless hill, trudging across a pathless heath, sinking in sand to his knees and into swamps that sucked at his feet and pulled him deeper and deeper down. But it wasn't sand, it wasn't a swamp – in his sleep he knew that he was slogging his way through shame and suffering, that his feet were wading through gray misery, sin and sorrow and misery; he knew it straight through his sleep and struggled to wake up but couldn't. Something was pressing him down, down into sleep, into the swamp. He had something on his back which weighed him down to earth, something he would have to drag along with him to his dying day.

Every once in a while he would dream that he walked like this through a crowd of people. The place, it appeared, was the church green at home, though there wasn't any sand or swamp there, none at all. People standing all around – they just stared at him as he walked around in circles, sink-ing deeper and deeper in sand and mud. Nobody said anything, they just stood there staring at him. And he – he couldn't utter a sound to anybody, didn't even dare look at them. Silence, his own and theirs. But sometimes he seemed to hear a word, a sort of song in the air as he walked on and on.

Astray . . . , went the song.

Every now and then Rønnau would rouse him at night. 'You're carrying on so in your sleep,' she said. 'You're probably lying on the wrong side.'

And in the semidarkness he could see her eyes upon him. Searching. A little scared? Perhaps a bit curious.

Did she know about it?

Was there anybody at all who knew about it?

He remembered how Rønnau had been closeted with his brother the second evening of their wedding party, and that she had refilled his glass several times.

Did she know about it? She hadn't said anything, but once in a while he felt that she knew. And he also felt that *this* was the only thing he found it hard to forgive her – that she knew.

Turn your back on it and don't think about it, then it won't be there. He had used that tack before, and things had gone all right.

When he had his hands full, when he worked or planned new work and one task followed another, then his thoughts would leave him alone – they weren't there, he was rid of them, he forgot.

Oh yes, in the daytime everything went well, as a rule.

Mari Tells a Story

O lstad sat on a headland fronting the lake. A small stream, or rather a big brook, ran into the lake on either side of the farm. North of the northern brook the ground rose steeply, and there sat Berg. South of the southern brook – it was somewhat bigger – lay the wide, flat fields of Nordby. East of Olstad, above the parish road and up toward the edge of the woods, sat Engen. There lived Hans the Haugian – Hans the Righteous, as they called him.

The road from Olstad to Berg, where Kerstaffer lived with his lunatics, was rather winding. First you had to go east to the parish road, which went north as far as the church; from there it turned westward, down to the brook separating the two farms, across the old wooden bridge and up the hills to Berg. The distance between the two clusters of houses was only three to four hundred yards as the crow flies. The road was more than twice that long. But there was a shortcut through the yard at Olstad and across the Olstad fields, down to a footbridge – constructed from three logs – which spanned the brook farther south, two to three hundred yards below the bridge. This was the path Kerstaffer used when he was in a hurry, as he usually was. Håvard had run into him in the yard several times. He knew him from the wedding, and custom required they should stop and exchange a few words. But Kerstaffer didn't stop, nor did he greet him; he merely gave Håvard a glowering look as he passed by – tall and thin, with iron-gray hair, a hawk-nose in his narrow face, cropped gray beard, and keen, too closely set eyes under bushy eyebrows. He had a slight limp – one of the lunatics had broken his leg, it was said – but moved along at a fast clip.

Anyway, Håvard was not the only one he didn't greet; he never greeted anybody. Håvard had seen him on the church green – he walked quickly through the throng without greeting anyone, and people fell back on both sides as though afraid to get burned. At such times he reminded you of a knife passing through butter.

After one of these encounters in the yard, Rønnau talked to Håvard.

'I think you should watch out for Kerstaffer,' she said. 'He bears a grudge against you. He proposed to me several times those years when I was a widow – well, I've told you about that. What he wanted was the farm, of course, more than me, as I knew quite well. Then you came, and now it looks as if you've stolen both me and Olstad from him. That's the way he is – when he's taken a fancy to something, little by little he comes to believe it is his. I could tell you many anecdotes about that. But you'd better watch out, for he'll never forget it!'

The following day, when Håvard had cleaned the cow barn and was currying one of the cows, the old pauper opened her mouth.

'I see you're fond of the animals,' she said to Håvard, 'and you don't forget old women either. The Lord in heaven will reward you for that.'

Oh, that fellow had so many things to remember, Håvard said. But she shook her fist at him:

'All that ye have done unto the least of my brethren, it says in Scripture. And by that he meant both children and animals and old people. That I've learned lying here in my stall for three years. And he doesn't forget what he's said, that fellow. Hm! He won't forget Kerstaffer Berg either – and the way he treats those lunatics of his. A day will come when he'll say to those luna- tics: "My poor lunatics, come over here to my right hand where there is bliss and rejoicing," he'll say. But then he'll say to Kerstaffer: "And you, Kerstaffer Berg, you step over to my left hand, where there's weeping and gnashing of teeth," he'll say. "For whatever you've done to those poor lunatics of mine, that, the Lord be praised, I'll do to you," he says.'

She certainly was well versed in the Bible, Håvard remarked. Oh, yes, she answered proudly. Her husband had been organ blower in the church for several years. He was so fond of all kinds of music, the poor dear. And in those days she used to sit in the organ loft every Sunday there was a service, seeing to it he didn't get plied with liquor – they got a kick out of that, to make him blow amiss so the organ would toot loud in the soft parts. They did have an organ in the church up here, as he'd probably noticed. There weren't very many churches that had an organ, as far as she knew. As it happened, it was Kerstaffer Berg's father, Old Erik, or Old Nick as they called him, who donated that organ – he'd somehow taken it into his head he might not have to go to hell if he did that; for everyone knew, and so did he, it was there he was going, and rightly so. What came to pass was quite a story, and though it had to do with Old Erik, who was dead, Håvard might as well know about it. For a farmer ought to be wise to his neighbors, and there were many who thought that Kerstaffer was a chip off the old block.

And so she started telling him.

It was wonderful to watch and listen to Mari when she told a story. The old wrinkled face, seasoned by wind and weather, though yellow rather than brown as occasionally happens with old people, composed itself.

She didn't look at Håvard as she told the story, and her voice acquired a slightly chanting tone – you knew right away that she'd told what she related now many times before, and to many people, and always with the same words.

Håvard knew the manner very well from his native village in Telemark.

The story she told was about Erik.

'For years, Erik was like a scourge to the parish. Mostly to the cotters and such naturally.

'He loaned out money, Erik did. Mostly to the poor. Gave them a loan of a dollar during the spring shortage, when many of them had to buy seed grain, and asked two dollars back for Christmas.

'Two days before Christmas he hitched his horse to a sledge and went from one cotter's plot to another collecting his Christmas toll, as people called it. If they couldn't pay up, Erik knew what to do, you bet. He unhinged the door to their cow barn, placed it on the sledge, and drove the door home to Berg, as a pledge.

'Then they would scrape together their shillings, most of the time anyway, and trudge to Berg to pay. But they had to carry the door home again on their backs.

'The old dean, he who served before the one who was here before Reverend Thurmann, was a man of authority. He knew how to *conjure*, oh yeah. He didn't stand in the pulpit talking about potatoes and winter rye, that fellow. Oh no, he spoke about the devil and all his works and about the eternal fire of hell until there was a smell of burning in the church.

'One winter two of Erik's cotters hanged themselves. A few weeks later he himself was taken ill and thought his days were numbered. Then the old dean dropped by. He had sworn he would provide organs for all the churches in his parish, and the worst sinners were going to pay for them.

'In the home parish the Mill had paid, and in the other parish of ease Baron Rosenkrantz had, it was told. But up here there was no organ.

'What the dean scared Erik with, you can imagine. And did he get scared! For he bought an organ. People said he paid several hundred dollars for it. And it was done quickly – he wanted to hear it at his own funeral.

'But, as it happened, that was long in coming. Erik recovered. Kerstaffer must have felt it took awfully long before he got the farm, because Erik didn't want to hear anything about retiring.

'One spring – actually the same spring he had donated the organ – Erik had been over to the west side of the lake and ground some barley. They had such a good flour mill over there, with nary a year without water.

'He drove home over the ice, the same way he'd come. But he'd been away for several days, and during that time the sun had been beating down on the ice every day.

'So he came driving toward the shore below Berg, in the afternoon it was. A brook runs into the lake just south of Berg.

'Well, you know that,' Mari said. 'People call it the border brook.

'The brook must have worn the ice thin. Anyway, as ill luck would have it, the ice gave way when the horse was a couple of hundred feet from the shore, and the next moment the horse, the load, and Erik lay there struggling.

'Kerstaffer was having his mid-afternoon meal in the kitchen with two of his cotters when they heard Erik's screams. The two cotters rushed to the rescue with long sticks and ropes. But Kerstaffer remained on the porch.

'"It's Father!" he said. "I recognize his voice. But I won't lift a finger. The devil helps his own!"

'And, indeed, he may have – or whatever. At any rate Erik made his way ashore. He lost the flour, but . . .

'He learned, of course, what Kerstaffer had said as he stood on the porch. But curiously enough he didn't get angry. He laughed and said: "Kerstaffer and I, you know, we are the same sort."

'But that summer Kerstaffer got permission to enlarge the basement and take in the lunatics.

'"I'd better permit him to make a little money," the old man said. "Then perhaps he won't begrudge me living to the end of my days."

'But somehow Erik died before his time anyway.

'When the so-called state bankruptcy came, Erik sat there with his coffer full of dollar bills.[19] Oh, yes, he had mostly bills, because they were a bit easier to get hold of than silver. And when he learned that every dollar bill was now worth only a few shillings, he became so angry that he took all his bills – people said he had several thousands of them – threw them in the fireplace and burned them, to the very last one.

'But the following day, when he sat down to figure out how much he'd lost – not only the dollars which the government had taken from him but all

19. This could be the state bankruptcy of Denmark-Norway on January 5, 1813.

64

the shillings he'd burned himself – he took it so to heart that he had a stroke, and two days later he was dead.

'But one thing he remembered at the very last moment. He'd gotten hold of the receipt for the organ and held it in his hand – held it so tight that nobody could pry it loose from his fingers after he'd died.

'His claws held it so tight, much like the way an owl holds a kitten. They had to let the receipt follow him into the ground. He had obviously meant to wave it before the throne of the Almighty. And the organ was used for the first time at his funeral – that, you know, was one of the conditions when he gave it away. And, believe it or not, people sat there weeping, however happy they were that he was dead. But whether he got to heaven on that receipt, well, you can't really tell – anyway, his ghost walks over at Berg. He stands down by the bridge on Thursday nights and stops the horses of people riding past.'

Mari looked at Håvard.

'Don't ever forget it!' she said. 'Berg strikes terror into people – the farm, the house, and the master. Nobody liked to meet Old Erik after dark, and the same is true for Kerstaffer. Nobody likes to cross the grounds even in daylight. Some of these lunatics, the best of them, work the tillage, often far afield, and walk back again to the house when they hear the gruel bell, and then you can meet them on the road. That's not to everyone's liking. And, you know, people say the place is haunted; the two dead wives, they say, bang the doors and whimper so pitifully: "Don't hit me, Erik! Don't hit me, Kerstaffer!" And so, day or night, people have come to prefer the path through cotter country when going north, though it winds along the edge of the wood and is almost twice as long.

'No servant girl will stay for long at Berg. Because of the lunatics, and other things too.

'Still, in some way, these lunatics are good for something too. A couple of them are simply wonderful at foretelling changes in the weather – then they hoot like owls and wolves. They have saved many a good load of hay and more than one shock of grain in this parish that way.'

Mari was thinking about a great many things as she lay there, it seemed.

'Kerstaffer complained awfully after his father died,' she went on. 'It was almost worse than while he lived, really. "He managed to make me a pauper anyway before the devil came to fetch him," he said. Kerstaffer was thinking of that expensive organ and all those dollar bills that had gone up in smoke in the fireplace.

'But it didn't take very long before Kerstaffer had money in his hands once more. He added a room in the basement and took in more lunatics. And then he made sure he became poor-relief officer. He kept the flour for the poor in the storehouse. But beside the flour sack there stood a sack of sawdust. And when the poor came to get flour, they received – in the opinion of some – equal parts of sawdust and flour in their bags. But Kerstaffer, of course, received *compensation* for pure flour.

'Whether it's true?' Mari said, looking up. 'Sure, I got some of that flour myself the year Lars was bedridden, before they drove him to Kerstaffer's basement.

'But he couldn't get away with it in the long run. One of the poor dropped in on Hans Nordby and showed him the flour. He got angry then, Nordby did. "I couldn't even have thought up anything so nasty as that," Nordby said. He went to the parson and told him about it. The parson – that was the former one – came for inspection, as he called it, and found the sack of sawdust beside the flour sack in Kerstaffer's storehouse. So next year Hans Nordby became poor-relief officer. But from that time on Nordby and Berg haven't been on the best of terms. . . .

'Hans Nordby? Well, he's your other neighbor, you know. And he's a hard man, no doubt about it, and a scoundrel according to some. But somehow he's all right too, in everything not having to do with timberland deals. Hans never cheats in little things, that he doesn't.

' "I'm no Kerstaffer, I refuse to turn thief to make a few shillings," he said once. That saying got back to Kerstaffer, of course. And since then Berg and Nordby have been on even poorer terms. . . . But if you can manage without having to sell timberland, then Hans might become a good neighbor – as things go in this parish anyway.'

'You've become friends with Mari, I see,' Rønnau said. 'You could've done worse than that. She knows a bit of everything, Mari does. She knows more than her pater noster, people say. Many people come to Mari for advice. She's a bit of a wise woman, they say – it's all right by me. Anyway, she saved two cows for me a couple of years ago – they had probably swallowed some poison. She was a fine dairymaid and in many ways a good wife. A pity her husband should go crazy. He sat in the basement at Berg over a year before he died. I'm afraid Kerstaffer isn't very kind to his lunatics. He seems to have so many things to take revenge for – upon all people – whatever it may be.'

To the Summer Dairy for Hay

*E*veryone had hoped for an early spring – the hungry animals were bleating and bellowing in every cow barn throughout the parish, so loud that it made your ears ache.

But there was no sign of such luck. On the last day of April there came a heavy snowfall, and the next few days it was cold as in February. Poor suffering cattle! people said, and everywhere in the neighborhood they chopped sprigs and evergreens, soaked them in a boiling juniper brew, added some horse manure, and fed the stuff to the animals. Down it went, though there was little enough nourishment in it – many cows around the parish couldn't stand on their legs anymore and lay in their stalls all day long. They were nothing but skin and bones, and so feeble that they could barely moo. Nor did they give any milk worth mentioning, and the dairymaid would just go through the motions of milking.

Up in the Olstad summer dairy there remained a couple of loads of hay, as far as Rønnau knew. It was decided that Håvard would take a hired hand along, drive up there with two horses and bring it home.

'I suggest you take Jon along,' Rønnau said. 'He may be something of a flap-jaw, but more of a man than these cotters anyway.'

There were five cotters at Olstad: Martin Grina, who had been head servant for the last three years, until Håvard came; Tjøstøl Inngjerdingen, Edvart Bakken, Amund Bråten – Amund Hungerstead as they called him – and Per Brenna. There were two additional cotter's plots; one of them stood empty, and on the other, called Huken, lived Jon – Jon the Hunter as he was called – and he wasn't considered a cotter. All the plots lay eastward, at the edge of the forest.

They didn't have much luck with their cotters at Olstad at the moment, Rønnau thought. Oh well, who did. Martin was probably the best of them, a bit slow, for sure, but otherwise all right, as long as he could do things his own way. Tjøstøl was old and worn-out – he was nothing but skin and bones and nosedrip; he had served his time and had one foot in the grave, as everyone could see.

Edvart was a braggart, and not much good for anything else. Amund was a man in his prime but terribly lazy, as Håvard must have noticed already. And Per was kind from morning till night, but clumsy with his hands and so stupid that if you told him that tomorrow the sun would rise in the west, he believed you.

'Really, you don't say!' Per said to everything and believed it.

No, it would have to be Jon.

Jon had come wandering north from the home parish one summer ten years ago and had stayed on because they were just adding a stable and a threshing floor, and he was a pretty good carpenter. Afterward they let him live in Huken, because all in all he was somewhat of an artisan. The rent was two dollars a year, and it was agreed he would do farm work at a cotter's wages to pay the rent, unless he paid it in goods instead. The rest of the time he was to do day labor when needed at twice a cotter's wages, or for three times as much when he worked as an artisan. But till now he'd never worked as a cotter, not for a single day. He paid the rent with grouse and fish, and every now and then with a shoulder of moose.

Jon was a skilled woodsman and certainly the best man for this trip. And he was lots of fun besides, Rønnau said.

Håvard had set his mind on Jon from the very beginning.

Jon was certainly no cotter. Nor did he look like one. He was tall and thin, with a straight back, bushy eyebrows, dark-brown hair, cold blue eyes, and a face reminiscent of a chicken hawk. You could tell at once that he was a hunter; and that was exactly what he was, life and soul.

Next to that, he enjoyed fishing in the woodland tarns and along the streams. He would turn up on the farm for regular day labor in the work seasons and any other time it suited him.

He lived alone up there in Huken, in a little shack which was black as a chimney. He liked it that way, he said. He picked at the tiny patch of ground as little as possible and kept no animals other than a skinny pig, a couple of still skinnier goats, and a shaggy, semi-wild cat.

When he was out hunting or fishing, the wife at Bråten nearby looked after his wretched animals for him. Amund Bråten put up with it – people said he didn't dare refuse. Jon had none of that timid, cautious cotter's manner; he looked you squarely in the eye and spoke his mind freely. When drunk, he could be dangerous in a fight. He was now well into his thirties. In his youth, people said, he'd had an affair with an heiress to a farm in the home parish – apparently she was pregnant with his child – but she was not for someone like him, a lowly cotter's son.

This much Håvard knew about the man he was taking with him on his trip to the summer dairy, plus the fact that he was full of yarns and awfully superstitious.

They took along provisions for two days and loaded the sledge with guns, both rifle and shotgun; wolves had been sighted down in the village the day after the snowfall. The pack had been as far as the lake, where they loped around howling, frightening people on the road to take refuge in the nearest house. They meant to look for this pack while they were up there. At the same time they figured they might be on the watch for grouse. Parson Thurmann was expected at Olstad the coming Sunday, unless he had to cancel the service due to bad weather and poor road conditions.

Håvard had a bottle of liquor in his bag. Rønnau had gotten it for him. 'Take this one along,' she said. 'Jon is a likable fellow and knows a little of everything. He can tell you all sorts of things about the way of the world up here which it will profit you to know, but you must help him get started.'

Most of the snow was gone down in the village, but in the forest there was much snow. Håvard had put his skis on the sledge, and when they had gotten above the fence and the horses started to show strain, he put them on. Jon had brought snowshoes, both for himself and the horses. He gaped at Håvard and the skis as he put the broad snowshoes on the horses' hoofs and then stepped into a pair himself.

'You use skis, do you. I spent some time at Finnskogen one winter – got way east by following a moose that fall.[20] There I met some Black-Finns, and they were great skiers, I can tell you. They would race down the mountainside, scattering snow all about them. It went so fast, almost like a bird in the sky. It occurred to me I ought to get myself a pair and try learning. But then, you know – the custom of the country and all that. I may be walking on thin ice as it is.'

Håvard knew from the parsonage that they seldom or never used skis in these parts. He asked Jon what the reason might be.

Hm. Jon couldn't say for sure. When he returned from Finnskogen, he dropped by at his grandfather's – he seemed to remember having seen a pair of skis in the attic there. And, sure enough, there they were. His grandfather could even remember a time when they were in use. They were different from Håvard's skis, though – one of them was long and narrow, the other short and wide and lined with skin; it was for holding back on the slopes, his grandfather had said.

Why they had gone out of use? Well, his grandfather thought it was because they had been so *misused*. It was mostly young people who used skis –

20. The Finnskogene district, about twenty-five miles northeast of Hoel's native township of Nord-Odal, constitutes a fifteen-to-twenty-mile-wide area along the border with central Sweden which was cleared and settled by Finns. Immigration was at its peak in the sixteen hundreds, especially the 1620s and 1640s. The culture the Finns brought with them remained fairly intact for 250 years, until the late nineteenth century.

grownups and older people stuck by their snowshoes. They were safer somehow and – yes, more dignified, his grandfather said. He had become sort of
devout toward the end. Sometimes he would even read his book of sermons
in the middle of the week.

Jon strode along in his wide snowshoes – it was like walking with a basket
on each foot. True, your gait did acquire a slow and dignified air that way.
Håvard went light-footed beside him.

The main reason why the skis had dropped out of use, Jon's grandfather
thought, was that they became so popular among the young. Instead of
making themselves useful in the winter, they were constantly out on the
slopes with their skis. And, naturally, that wouldn't do. For it was written
that in the sweat of thy brow shalt thou eat bread.

Jon snorted, full of disgust and contempt.

They had been going uphill for a quarter of an hour, and now it grew
lighter as they approached some open fields. After passing a gate, they were
at the lower end of a big, open tillage. The woodland trail went along the
fence, on the outside. Actually, the trail couldn't be seen, for nobody had
gone that way since the snowfall. The fields faced south, and there the snow
had melted. High up, almost at the horizon, they could glimpse a few gray
houses.

This was Lien, one of the best and biggest farms in the parish. According
to Jon, it wasn't the only farm up this way. There were five or six cotter's
holdings scattered around at the edge of the forest, and a couple of small
freehold farms behind the copse down below. All in all, you could say it was
an entire community.

In a way Lien was the best farm in the parish, Jon said. Good soil, large
fields – but that was not all. In the winter, when cold and winter fog lay
heavy upon the flatlands around the lake, Lien was often bathed in sunlight,
above the layer of fog. Therefore the winter was much milder up here than
in the main hamlet, the ground was less frozen, and spring came earlier; in
fact, they could start the spring planting as much as two weeks earlier here
than on the farms down in the hamlet. Large areas of timberland also came
with the farm. So the owner, Høgne, should be quite satisfied.

He was anything but, though.

Jon looked at Håvard with his sharp hawklike eyes. His glance expressed
a quiet mirth.

A story went around about Høgne. Maybe Håvard had heard it already?
No.

Jon chortled.

70

They were on a level with the buildings now. They sat neatly around a big yard.

Håvard noticed a strange thing. A path, or whatever it was, ran in a wide circle around the big, flat yard. Something or somebody had been walking there, slogging his way through the grassroots and right down to the black dirt.

'That is Høgne's circle,' Jon said.

They passed the yard. A face could be made out behind a windowpane but was gone immediately.

'He is sitting inside today too, just staring,' Jon said. 'I could see him out in the yard when we were down by the gate; but then he heard us and slipped in. He does that every time he sees someone coming this way. People say he sits there with the gun in his hand until they have passed.'

Otherwise he stayed in the yard most of the day, Jon continued. In the winter he would clear away the snow there, forming a sort of circle, quite big. And there, inside that circle, he would walk around like a tethered horse. He walked like that spring and fall, too. In the summer he mostly sat on the grassy bank in front of the porch. In recent years he'd rarely, if ever, ventured outside the yard.

By rights, Høgne should probably be sitting in Kerstaffer's basement. At any rate, many of those who sat there weren't much crazier than he. But – he was the owner of a farm, and he didn't harm anybody, so for that matter – . And Edvart Skuggen, his head servant throughout the years, ran the farm well enough, so for that matter – . And besides – even if they used four horses they wouldn't be able to drag him to Kerstaffer. For Kerstaffer was in a way the bane of his life.

Jon chuckled and laughed at the recollection. But suddenly he grew silent. They had gotten past the farm, and the road turned slightly to the right and cut across a big open meadow before disappearing into the woodland again farther north. The sun beat down here, and the snow had melted so that the meadow was bare. In the middle of the wide, open space lay a circle of huge stones, some fallen, some upright.

'Let's stop for a moment here,' Jon said. 'This, they say, was the place where the Thing met in ancient times – Lien was a kind of royal manor in those days, I've heard. And there were several farms up this way at that time. There may be something to it, because you can find good, deep soil from here on for quite a ways. Something must have happened. But Håvard, here you have to turn around: there, look!'

Håvard turned around. Below him lay Lien, and farther down, below the strip of forest they had driven through, he could see a large part of the parish – Nordby, Flateby, and Strøm to the left, Olstad and Berg directly below, with the church a little closer, more to the north, and Engen still a little closer to the edge of the forest. North of the church lay Moen. There lived Amund, a husky fellow with a beard the color of a wolf's pelt. Håvard had run into him at the wedding and had taken a great liking to him. It was rumored that he'd tossed his wife down from the barn bridge so she broke her neck, and now he lived with one of his maids. It was probably nothing but village gossip. They could see the smoke from the chimneys of several cotter's homes too, but the small houses were hidden behind the edge of the forest.

'It's a tough parish you've come to, Håvard,' Jon said. 'We can see seven farms from where we are standing, apart from Lien, and to my reckoning four murderers, or killers anyway, live on those farms. Well, I don't count Sjønne Strøm and Anders Flateby, they lack the gumption for that sort of thing. But Nordby – well, I know you were there when his wife died, and that, you know, was a slow murder, whatever the sheriff says. As for Kerstaffer, two of his father's cotters hanged themselves, and one of Kerstaffer's. And there is that lunatic he drove back to Sand because they had forgotten to pay for him – he chucked him onto the pile of snow in the yard so he froze to death – and finally the other loony whom he killed on the threshing floor.

'Then there is Hans Engen, one of Hauge's friends and all, who has flogged his son out of his wits so he walks around like an idiot – well, you probably haven't seen him yet. But, you know, I call that sort of thing murder. And Amund Moen – but that I can tell you more about tonight if you're interested.

'Hm. I really wonder if you're strong enough to manage with such neighbors on every side.'

'I can see you aren't particularly fond of Kerstaffer,' Håvard said.

'Kerstaffer? Well, he's all right. He's certainly rich enough. And he is getting richer every year.

'But Mari asked me to tell you a few things – much of what I know, in fact, I have from Mari herself. "We'd better let Håvard know about the sort of mischief he's surrounded by," Mari said.'

Jon glanced at Håvard with his sharp eyes.

'But now we'll have to go if we are to reach the summer dairy at a reasonable time.'

They entered the forest once more.

What had Kerstaffer done to Høgne? Håvard wanted to know.

But Jon said merely 'hush' and shook his fist. They had reached the deep woods now. The trail they followed was lined by a steep crag on the right and by the course of a stream down below to the left. Jon didn't utter a sound as long as they were driving alongside this crag. When they had passed it, he seemed to breathe a sigh of relief. He turned toward Håvard and said, 'Inside that crag lives a fellow I wouldn't care to meet. We call him the Old Man of Blue Crag.'

Håvard wanted to know a little more about that fellow. But Jon looked about him and shook his head. 'We'd better not say anything more here,' he said softly. 'There are many creatures around here who both see and hear, even if *we* can't see *them*.'

They drove on in silence for a couple of hours and reached the chalet meadow.

The terrain was open here. Four or five summer dairies were clustered around a little lake or a tarn. Everywhere was snow, fine tracking snow after the snowfall. Fox tracks crisscrossed the chalet meadow; but they hadn't seen any signs of wolves on their way up and didn't see any now either. Jon peered out across the white expanse of snow, disappointed.

'Oh, no. That fellow is so sly, he knew we were coming already before we started.'

The chalet cabin sat in he middle of the meadow, low, old, and gray. Down by the gate stood the cow barn and the little hay barn.

Most of the snow had melted or shrunk on the meadow itself. But directly outside the fence it reached to one's knees. Jon shook his head.

'Spring will be late this year, I can tell.'

It was cold and damp in the chalet cabin. It smelled of soot in there – some lumberjacks had used it this winter. Entering first, Jon did something, making passes with steel or whatever it was.

'You're casting spells against the troll people, I see,' Håvard said. Jon didn't answer him right away. But after a while he said, 'I just wanted to make sure we didn't disturb anybody in there.'

'You really believe in such things?'

Jon answered sharply, 'When you've spent as much time in the woods as I have, you will believe in all sorts of things too.'

They got the sheepskins down from the crossbeam, climbed onto the roof and removed the stone slab from the chimney, and went about lighting a fire – a good-sized heap of birch bark, birch logs, and pine wood lay stacked up in the corner behind the fireplace. Afterward they went to stable the horses and covered them with horse blankets – it was cold in the cow barn, with its cracked walls – went over to the dairy brook to fetch water for the horses and themselves, and gave the horses a good helping of the hay they had brought with them. Mountain meadow hay wasn't any good for horses.

Finally they loaded the sledges with the hay they found in the barn. It came to two good loads. Then they were ready to enter the chalet cabin, take a drink, and open the food pack.

Rønnau had even prepared a bag of coffee for them.

Soon it grew warm and cozy inside the little cabin. The flames fluttered in the fireplace, lighting up the table and the three beds as well as the myriad of initials people had cut into the timbered walls with their sheath knives; it was mostly young folk who did such things, Saturday gallants coming up to see one of the chalet girls, but many others too.

'You, too, should cut your initials into the wall,' Jon said. 'You're the owner of this place after all, and this is the first time you've been up here. I believe that those who stay here after we've gone home again would like it.'

Håvard obediently cut the letters H. G. V. into the timbered wall.

'You use your bachelor's name, do you?' Jon said. 'Anyway, up here they call you the new Olstad. "That new Olstad Rønnau's got, is he any good at all?" they ask. Well, what do you say yourself? Are you good enough?'

That evening Jon told him about the Old Man of Blue Crag, about Høgne Lien, and a little about Kerstaffer and Amund Moen – to give him a bellyful, as he said, and because Mari had asked him to.

The Old Man of Blue Crag was the biggest giant on this side of the lake. People said there was an even bigger one far away in the woods westward, but Jon didn't know very much about that fellow.

The oldsters had probably all seen the ogre of Blue Crag; but they didn't let the cat out of the bag, those fellows. Anyway, Old Anders Flateby became a bit strange after a trip to the woods one fall, and it lasted for several years; but he never said anything.

'A chalet girl once disappeared for a whole week, and they combed the country for her. Then she came back but couldn't say a word in explanation. She had a child before the end of the winter, and it looked like a troll. But this was a long time ago, before Mari was born.

'Then, not so many years ago, there was a cocky young fellow from Lang-set – the heir to the farm, as it happened. He wanted so badly to see the mug of this giant of Blue Crag, or so he said. And see him he did and talk to him too, you bet. In the late summer – it was a Thursday evening – he took a couple of friends with him and went up there. It wasn't dark, but it wasn't broad daylight either. This young puppy – his name was Søren – started calling the giant. "If you have any guts, why don't you show your mug!" But

74

no giant showed, naturally. Then Søren grew even bolder – they had taken a couple drinks on the way up – went right up to the rock wall and threw a stone at a hole in the mountain where people thought the giant had his entrance. "I'll rouse you, all right!" he said.

'And rouse him he did, and how. Some rocks jumped out from the wall where his stone had struck, rolled down and brought more along with them – in the end it sounded like a thunderclap, said those who were with him. And all of a sudden a stone leaped out from this rockslide, sailed through the air and hit Søren straight in the forehead so he fell plump to the ground.

'The others ran back to the village head over heels, too scared to look back. The following day some people went off to the woods to pick up Søren. He lay where he'd fallen. But the woman who washed the body said that Søren had blue and yellow spots all over, as if he'd been manhandled by someone with a really big fist. Since then nobody has shouted a word at the Old Man of Blue Crag.

'Hm. Well. Now you know about that escapade. Skoal! Good, strong liquor this, I should say.'

Then there was Høgne, Håvard reminded him, an hour or so and a couple of drinks later.

'Well. Actually, I thought Mari had told you all about *him*. I wasn't in the parish yet myself when that happened. But every word I'm telling you is God's truth, for I have it from Mari, and she knows everything that has happened in this parish in our time, well, further back too.

'Høgne is getting on in years now. Oh, he might be roughly Kerstaffer Berg's age, around fifty, or a bit more. But this thing happened when they were still youths, so to speak. At that time Kerstaffer's father, Old Erik, was master at Berg, carrying on worse than ever. People said Kerstaffer had such a sense of *humor* in those days. He wasn't quite so difficult, angry, and spiteful then as he became later, and not quite so raving mad about money and land and timber lots either. It was his father, Old Erik, who was called the Old Nick of Berg at that time, and nobody dreamed that Kerstaffer would take over that nickname from his father, together with the farm and the money and the timberland.

'He was constantly full of fun and frolic in those days and thought up all kinds of games and pranks – like that joke he played on Høgne, for example.

'They were friends of sorts, Høgne and Kerstaffer. At any rate, Høgne believed they were. He was always so trusting, Høgne was. So whenever he came up against a difficulty, he would tell Kerstaffer about it.

'Mostly it had to do with women, of course. Høgne had a soft spot for the girls, but he was so bashful, he couldn't bring himself to talk to them. And so he went to Kerstaffer and opened his heart to him, as they say. And from Kerstaffer it spread over the whole parish. Oh, yes, they had much fun with poor Høgne.

'Then it happened one summer that Høgne lost his head over one of the hired girls who took part in the haymaking on his farm. She came from a small place directly below Lien. Poor though she was, she was not a cotter's daughter, and she was certainly a pretty girl, and lighthearted to boot.

'Høgne went to Kerstaffer to ask his advice. He was so fond of that girl but couldn't get himself to speak to her, he said. "No need to speak," Kerstaffer said, "just push ahead." That saying of Kerstaffer has been repeated in the hamlet to this very day.

'But Høgne had even less of a knack for that sort of thing, as you can well imagine. Høgne was so timid, you see. And so he came to want the girl more and more. Finally he got the idea of marrying her, if only she would have him. He would never get a prettier or better wife, he said. Høgne's father and mother were both dead at that time, so he could just please himself. He went to ask Kerstaffer if he would be his go-between with the girl and her parents.

'Sure, he'd see what he could do, Kerstaffer said.

'And off he went to see the girl, had a good, long talk with her too. Not exactly about Høgne, though. And the girl was pretty, as I've said, and lighthearted, and the upshot was that Kerstaffer went to bed with her. And after a while the girl felt as keen on Kerstaffer as a mouse on a piece of cheese – every word he said was gospel truth to her.

'Then Kerstaffer hinted at this business about Høgne.

'"Come to think of it," he said as he lay in bed with her, "the truth is I was supposed to court you for somebody else," he said. The girl just snorted. She wanted Kerstaffer and none other than Kerstaffer, and more and more of Kerstaffer. She had lost the last remnant of her common sense and already saw herself as mistress at Berg.

'It was then that Kerstaffer had an inspiration, as they say. It was an old story he'd heard, supposed to have happened someplace in Ringerike,[21] which gave him the idea.

'He went to tell Høgne that the girl wasn't very willing, but she wasn't quite unwilling either. So if Høgne would just obey Kerstaffer in everything, *he* would see to it that the wedding took place, he said.

21. The area around the Tyrifjorden Lake northwest of Oslo.

'Høgne was so happy he didn't know which leg to stand on. "You are the best friend anyone ever had," he said.

'But what was he to do? he then asked.

' "All you have to do is to brew and bake for the wedding and get clothes for yourself and finery for the bride. Leave the rest to me!" Kerstaffer said. And Høgne began to bake and brew, and a shoemaker and a tailor turned up on the farm. And he himself took a trip to the city to buy liquor and silks and things. No expense was too great, it seemed. The evening before the wedding people arrived at the farm carrying presents. They carried and laughed, snickered and laughed as they handed them over, and stood doubled-up with laughter down the hill going home again. For Kerstaffer, of course, had made known everywhere what he meant to do. The only person who didn't understand anything was Høgne. Høgne was so trusting, you see.

'Then came the wedding day. A throng of people gathered at the farm. Everybody wanted to watch the show.

'The tables were set, and there was plenty both to eat and drink.

'Høgne was in the bedroom at the back.

' "You just stay there till I bring the bride," Kerstaffer said. "She's a bit stubborn, but it'll be all right, I think. We'll decorate her in the old house. We'll put the whole caboodle on your black mare and ride straight to church," he said.

'And he wasn't telling a lie either when he said that. For Høgne had a handsome black mare. And it was her Kerstaffer had intended to hang the bridal finery on.

'When the moment came, Kerstaffer and a couple others dragged the mare down into the old house and decorated her as nicely as – well, as a bride. And the girl helped with the decorations. Then Kerstaffer led the mare up on the porch, through the entrance hall and straight into the parlor.

'He called Høgne.

' "Now you must come, Høgne! Here's your bride," he called. And Høgne came.'

Jon stopped to nip at his glass.

'And then?' Håvard asked.

Jon looked at him a moment before he went on.

'Hm. All right. There were those who thought it wasn't as much fun as they had expected. For Høgne didn't say or do anything. He simply stood stock-still without saying a word. Not for quite a while. And besides, even if he had said something, they probably wouldn't have heard him. They were laughing so terribly, you see. But when it gradually quieted down, he looked about him – taking in all the people standing in the parlor – in such a way that some of them didn't feel very comfortable anymore.

'"Well, well. Well, well," he said. He turned around and returned to the bedroom, and nobody saw him anymore that day.

'Then it grew quiet again, for now they had nobody to laugh at anymore.

'And in the end there was nothing people could do except gather up their presents and go home again, each to his own. Thus ended the wedding of Høgne Lien.'

Jon sat for a moment, chuckling to himself.

'And then?'

'Hm. Well. From that moment on he was a little queer, Høgne was, as I've told you. The following day he shot his fine black mare – that shows you better than anything how crazy he was. And he never set foot in the village after that day.

'During the next few years he would sometimes walk about the woods and fields on his own property. But more and more he began to shun the woods. "People stand behind the pine trunks laughing at me," he told Edvart, his head servant. "You don't say!" Edvart said – he's such a simple soul, Edvart is. Anyway, Høgne didn't want to walk the woods anymore.

'He continued wandering about his own fields for another few years, mostly during the rest periods, when nobody was out working. But that didn't last either. He came to believe that the villagers lay behind the fence laughing and snickering at him. In the last few years he has walked almost nowhere except in his own yard – circling around and around, winter and spring and fall, like a tethered horse. In the summer he sits mostly on the grassy bank below the porch, as I've already told you.

'Well. There you are. His circle has grown smaller and smaller as the years have passed. Anyway, that happens to most everybody.'

'And the girl?' Håvard asked.

'The girl? Oh, she's still unmarried. Some people may have thought she'd disgraced herself by being part of such a prank. And as I've said, she wanted Kerstaffer; but *him* she'd never get, that much was clear. Kerstaffer, well, he married *money*, he did.

'And after some time had passed and he'd gotten his hands on the money, he started beating his wife, just as Old Erik was said to have beaten *his* wife.

'She died of pneumonia one winter, Kerstaffer's wife did. But people say she haunts the house, whimpering and begging for mercy.'

They sat in silence for a moment.

Håvard wanted to know if he thought that story about Høgne was funny.

Jon sent him a sidelong glance over his hawk-nose.

'When one big shot plays a joke on another, then I think it's funny!' he said sharply.

'But I can tell you,' he said a moment later, somewhat pensively, 'that I would be anything but pleased if something like that happened to me. I would use the knife then, I think.'

They put more wood on the fire, moved the sheepskins a bit so they would dry and get warm, and took a turn around the corner. It was a tranquil, starlit night, with a moon. They heard a hare coo just behind the fence. The next moment a fox yapped and howled at the moon, and the hare became quiet. From far away they heard another sound, a horned owl which hooted its nocturnal cry.

'It's doubtful if that hare will live to see tomorrow,' Jon said. 'Those two will know how to track it down, you bet.'

They heard the horses chomping their hay and shifting from one leg to another in the cow barn – it was such a peaceful sound.

They went back into the cozy chalet cabin again and took a drink.

'Something happened in this chalet cabin once,' Jon said suddenly.

'What?'

'It was a chalet girl. She hanged herself from that crossbeam over there.

'People said she was going to have a child with her master – Old Ola Olstad that was, grandfather to the Ola that married Rønnau.

'It's a long time ago, as you can see.'

They sat for a moment.

'So the place is haunted, is it?' Håvard asked.

Jon gave a short laugh.

'Oh no – a poor cotter's daughter won't haunt a place. She's resting quietly where she lies.

'But when you have a big wheel like Old Erik Berg, Kerstaffer's father, it's a different matter altogether. He's been dead and buried for almost ten years now, but Thursday evenings he still stands on the trail that leads up to Berg and stops the horses passing by on the parish road. Anyway, I suppose Mari has told you about it.

'At any rate, it's a fact that people prefer to go by way of cotter country Thursday evenings, even though it's twice as far. And about Andreas Engen, your neighbor Hans's grandfather – he had such a difficult wife, and people say he shot and killed himself in anger one day – about him people say that

79

he haunts the kitchen at Engen one evening every year. Then he smashes all the dishes he can lay his hands on, for that's what he did when he had a fight with his wife.

'And Karen, the old mistress at Nordby, cries and moans every once in a while in those dark hallways at Nordby, because she signed the paper which gave Hans the power to send Erik, the eldest son, to the basement at Berg. I haven't heard it myself, but still. She isn't loud, people say. "Erik! Erik!" she whispers, so you can barely hear it, and then she weeps, as though far away. It's when Nordby hears this, people say, that he goes on a binge; he'll have as many as ten drinks, keeping it up till he collapses. But that I take with a grain of salt. Hans Nordby is made of stronger stuff than that.'

He had promised to tell about Kerstaffer and the two lunatics too, Håvard reminded him.

'Yeah, sure. Not that those stories amount to much, but still.'

This happened after Jon had come to the parish, and he had witnessed it in a way, so it was *true* at any rate.

'The folks at Sand, on the western side of the lake, had sent a son to Kerstaffer's basement – they felt it was impossible to keep him at home. But then they forgot to pay for him. Kerstaffer sent word, but they forgot again. Then he tied the lunatic to a sledge, Kerstaffer did, and drove him over the ice to Sand, unloaded him in the yard and let him lie there in his rags.

'The weather was bitter cold – it was just before Christmas – and as it happened no one on the farm had noticed Kerstaffer. More than an hour passed before they found the bunch of rags which he'd left behind. Then the master at Sand drove his son back to Berg, and this time he took money with him. But the whole thing was more than anybody could take, even someone like that, and soon after, the lunatic died. From then on people knew they had to pay Kerstaffer punctually.

'The second time . . .

'Three of the cotter's cabins at Berg were vacant, however difficult it was to get a roof over your head in this parish. People would rather go begging than be a cotter at Berg. But Kerstaffer got the farm work done anyway – he let the best of the lunatics work on their own. He himself walked around with a whip in his hand, supervising. And he was a good, enterprising farmer, no doubt about it. "Run away? My lunatics run away?" he'd say. "Forget it. There isn't a dog in the parish that's better trained than my lunatics." But in one instance he'd made a mistake, nonetheless. He took one of the lunatics along to the threshing floor when he was going to thresh his barley. There were only the two of them. When they had worked awhile, the lunatic raised his flail and hit the small of Kerstaffer's leg so hard that the bone snapped. But Kerstaffer is no mouse – with a broken leg he stood his ground, giving blow for blow until he knocked down the lunatic with a punch to his head. And afterward he whacked away at him till he was sure he was dead! But since that day he's never put axes or other dangerous tools in the hands of his lunatics.

'He's had a slight limp in his left leg since then. And whether it was because of this or something else, he got stuck with the name Old Nick, just like his father.

'Whether Kerstaffer is evil through and through? No, it wouldn't do to say that. I have seen him stand with a lump of dirt in his hand, crumbling it between his fingers and sniffing it. Then, I could swear, he looks almost gentle. He's fond of the soil, Kerstaffer is.

'But look,' Jon said suddenly, 'now I have told you so much nastiness it will have to do for one sitting. I'll save Hans Engen for another time – and now I need a drink!'

Still, a little later he was telling him about Amund Moen.

'But with Amund it's different than with these other fellows,' Jon said. 'Some believe he killed his wife, others don't know what to believe. But Amund – Big Amund as people call him – is an honest and straightforward fellow, and if he did put an end to that sour, insufferable witch, he had good *reason* to, that's what I think!

'He was unlucky with that wife of his, Amund was. People said she had been awfully pretty in her youth; but with the passing years she only grew thin and stingy and sly and quarrelsome. She never had any children – she was *barren*, as they say. Little by little Amund may have fathered a brat or two on the side up in cotter country and, as we all know, women talk about such things, going from one house to another. This didn't make his wife feel any kindlier toward him, of course.

'At the time I'm talking about, Amund was probably sleeping with one of his maids – he's done so to this day, it seems – an uncommonly pretty girl, buxom and very likable. They have a son together now, and many wonder why they don't get married, once having gone that far. I think I know the reason why.

'But I was talking about his wife. One evening – it's more than six years ago now – Amund was busy on the threshing floor. Then this bitch of a wife came up the barn bridge to call him for supper.

'But she never did so without throwing in a couple of taunts. This time she may have hit the bull's eye. In any case, there are those who say that

Amund slapped her so she lost her balance, fell down from the barn bridge head first and broke her neck. Amund tells it differently – that she slipped on the ice at the edge of the barn bridge and fell over. It was in the middle of April, with clear ice at the edge of the bridge.

'Many had their own thoughts, perhaps, but nobody did anything about it. But then it turned out that a teenage boy from one of the cotter's plots had hidden in a corner of the barn. This boy knew about a nest with eggs in it in the hayloft down below, and he'd meant to sneak down there and steal a few eggs as soon as Amund went in for supper. He was stupid enough to tell what he'd seen – or rather what he claimed he'd seen – around the hamlet. Eventually it led to so much gossip that the sheriff came and began asking questions. But there he got nowhere, oh no.

' "Let me set eyes on that puppy!" Amund said. And when the poor boy came in, quite green around the gills – well, Amund just *looked* at him and that was the end of it. The boy had never hid in the barn and hadn't seen anything, and least of all had he meant to steal eggs!

'That was that.

'Since then Amund has lived in peace and harmony with his girl. She sleeps in the kitchen, not in the bedroom where that grouchy wife of his had stayed.

'And now the son has turned five. *He* sleeps in the bedroom with Amund!

'It's hard to imagine why anybody should feel offended by this. But there were some, to be sure, who thought it was going too far. They were mostly the friends of Hauge, of course. Hans Engen walked over to Moen one day to talk with Amund about his *scandalous living* – that's what he called it, I believe. Amund didn't answer, he just got up and *saw* Hans out of the parlor and the yard.

'But good old Mari thinks she knows something. Amund's wife belonged to a well-known breed with a knack for haunting a place and causing harm up to seven years after they're dead. It's six years now since his wife was buried. Amund isn't the sort who gets easily scared; but I guess he'd rather not expose the girl to any wickedness from the ghost.

'On account he's sleeping with her? Well, his wife had never cared much for *that* sport, not while she was alive anyway. No, it's the status and the position as mistress of Moen that she begrudges the pretty girl, Mari thinks.

'Just wait another year or so and you'll see there will be a wedding at Moen.'

Håvard had probably had a drink too many. He couldn't remember exactly what he'd talked about to Jon at the end – well, he did remember, in a way.

But now, waking up as he felt Jon's wondering eyes upon him, he asked himself if he hadn't made a slip of the tongue again.

'So you want to help the parish, do you?' Jon said. 'That you'd like to make improvements at Olstad I can well understand, but the parish? I've heard that the Bible speaks about such people. But I'll be damned if it isn't the first time I'm seeing one with my own eyes!'

He had let slip a word too many, all right. The reason, most likely, was that he was finding it too difficult to keep it to himself day after day.

'Eight shillings a day? For the cotters?'

'That would be sometime in the future,' Håvard defended himself. 'If all went well, I mean.'

'Hm. So you really want to help *others*!' Jon again eyed him with wonder. 'Even a poor miserable devil of a cotter!

'Let me tell you one thing. Watch out, and don't mention it to anybody!

'Have you ever seen a crows' parliament? A hundred crows sit in a circle, and in the middle sits the one who's *different*. And when those hundred have stared at it long enough, they hurl themselves upon it and hack it to pieces.

'Watch out, I tell you. In case you don't, they'll put you in Kerstaffer's basement. If they have the power to do so, mind you.

'But now I think we have to crawl under our sheepskins if we want to be in time to catch the birds tomorrow morning.'

The Mill Owner

*T*wo men came riding westward, down the cattle trail toward Olstad. It was the mill owner from the home parish and his scribe. At this time of year they usually took a trip through the countryside to come to an agreement about the burning and hauling of charcoal and the hauling of ore to the Mill the following winter.

Rønnau stood on the porch to receive them – erect and high-bosomed, with a sheen to her dark-brown hair, a silver brooch on her dark dress, and silver buckles on her shoes. The mill owner couldn't help wondering whether she dressed like that every day, or had seen them coming down the road.

Lars, the servant, took care of the horses.

A moment later Rønnau and the mill owner were sitting in the parlor; the scribe stayed in the kitchen. There was a roaring fire in the stove. When the maid had brought the coffee, Rønnau fetched French brandy from the cabinet – she remembered that the mill owner liked to take it with his coffee.

After a suitable interval he gave his errand. What he wanted to know was whether he could count on a little extra hauling of coal or ore – and a little extra burning of coal also of course – during the coming winter. They had planned to expand the Mill.

'I thought the Mill was doing poorly,' Rønnau said.

And so it had during the last few years. But now they had found out, he and the other partners, that they could turn it around if they extended their operations a little. Only, they had to be assured of getting enough raw material. A good deal of fine ore had been found up this way during the last few years, something Rønnau no doubt was aware of. Among other places, in the Olstad forest, if he remembered correctly.

That was so, no doubt. But this ore didn't seem to be quite as good as they had first believed. Jon, who knew about such things and had helped discover the ore, thought so anyway, and the poor pay they received could mean the same thing.

'Håvard, my husband, is away at the summer dairy to fetch some hay today,' she said. 'With Jon, by the way. They should be home fairly soon now. You'll have to talk to him, and maybe to Jon. But I'm inclined to believe that Håvard won't feel much like taking on more of that hauling than we're obliged to. We have talked it over, and he feels the work pays very poorly.'

'It's probably from you he's heard that,' the mill owner said. 'But it's customary to pay better for any hauling over and above the old agreement.'

The mill owner was a tall, quiet man with cold, pale-blue eyes. He was no longer young, maybe approaching fifty. He'd been running the Mill for ten years now.

Sure, they'd better wait until Håvard returned, the mill owner agreed.

'Come to think of it, it's strange I haven't met him yet – I have heard a great deal about him lately; he's obviously a very capable man; the parson misses him very much – '

It grew quiet in the room for a moment. They sat there sizing each other up.

It was the mill owner who broke the silence.

'It came up quite suddenly, this business between Håvard and you, didn't it?' he said. 'By the way, I had heard something to the effect that several individuals up here had set their sights on you.

'Which wouldn't be surprising,' he added, more to himself than to her.

'Suddenly, you say. Well, I don't know about that. Speaking for myself, I had realized where it would end up almost a year ago. From the very first time I met him, if you want to know.'

'And after that he had no more say in the matter?'

84

A tiny smile lurked in the corners of his mouth. His calm eyes gazed at her.

'Oh, yes. Håvard does have a say where women are concerned – in other things too. When you meet him you'll understand that he's not the kind of man who lets himself be pushed over by the first woman who comes along.'

'But you aren't, Rønnau.'

She didn't seem to have heard him; at any rate she didn't answer.

She sat for a moment, as though considering whether to say more or not. Her narrow gaze was fixed upon the mill owner all along.

After a while she said:

'He came north last fall to teach me a little about the new ways of farming. I had met him before, and asked him to come.'

'And then?'

'The upshot was that we made up our minds. A couple of things happened which were decisive – for me at any rate. And for him too, I think.'

Her eyes glittered.

Did she want to find out if she could hurt him?

Quiet. He sat watching her with his calm eyes.

'Then he must be the right one,' he said. 'You have always known what you were doing, Rønnau.'

She knew that she'd said too much now – far too much. It was because of those insufferable eyes of his. They would've tried the patience of a saint.

'Not at all,' she said. 'I certainly didn't know what I was doing when I took service with you. But it won't hurt you to know you're not the only man who can make love in such a way that a woman loses her head and thinks of only one thing. Håvard isn't any less of a man than you are.'

The mill owner sat without moving, fixing her with his calm eyes.

'And so it was decided?' he said.

'In one way, yes. But in another way, no.'

She had pulled herself together now and knew what she was saying.

She sat for a moment.

'In many ways Håvard is more of a man than you have ever been. But in one way . . . Well, you'll meet him shortly, so I might as well tell you. You notice such things anyway.

'He's strong, but he's weak too. He has one fault, or whatever it should be called – he has so many dreams and plans. It's mostly weak people who are like that, as you know. Or quite young ones.'

'I, too, was like that once,' the mill owner said.

'Yes. But you outgrew it. That's why you can see it in others. And I'm not sure whether you like such people. They've got something you have lost.'

'How old is Håvard?' said the mill owner.

'Twenty-eight.'

He thought, Rønnau is thirty-four. But it doesn't matter. Not for a good many years.

She seemed to know what he was thinking. She said sharply, 'Leave that worry to me!'

Once more she felt his calm gaze on herself; but this time it didn't reach her – she was absorbed by her own thoughts.

'He dreams of accomplishing great things here in this parish. In *this* parish! I've had to think it over time and again – I still have to.'

Her eyes weren't so narrow anymore. It almost looked as though she was asking this man for advice.

But he didn't say anything.

'There was something else too,' she said. 'He had a girl up there in Tele-mark. I didn't know anything about it then – when this thing came up with us. But little by little I understood there was *something*. It was hard for him, because he had given her a *promise*.'

'Did he tell you about it?'

'No. I was unaware of most of it until the wedding this spring, when I talked with his brother.

'When this girl learned that Håvard and I were to get married, she threw herself into the waterfall.'

She smiled.

He looked at her. 'You are a hard woman, Rønnau.'

She blazed at him. 'So what? Someone who has been in the clutches of a man like you can't help getting hard.'

It grew quiet in the room again, and it remained so for quite a while.

This time it was Rønnau who had to continue.

'Håvard is uncommonly proud – more so than you have ever been, I think. He feels he has lost his honor up there in his native parish.'

'Has he spoken to you about it?'

'No. I had some of it from his brother, and some I've understood – from one thing and another.'

Silence.

'So it will cheer your heart to know that everything isn't so easy here at Olstad either,' Rønnau said.

The mill owner sat for a moment. He wasn't looking at Rønnau now.

'But if he is as proud as you say he is,' he said, 'and if he had given her his *promise* – that, you know, can sometimes be almost dearer than life itself to a man . . .'

Rønnau didn't say anything.

He looked intently at her.

'*Did you tell him you were pregnant?*'

She didn't answer, and he seemed to interpret that as a good enough answer.

If Rønnau wanted at all costs to make this quiet man lose his composure, she had now managed to do so. He got up and took a few turns back and forth in the room, sighing several times. His face was no longer calm.

'Everything repeats itself!' he said at last.

She jumped up from her chair. 'No! Quite the opposite!'

She laughed. 'What you couldn't do, Håvard might bring off, don't you think?'

'What I couldn't do and Ola Olstad couldn't do,' he said.

'True; so what?'

Having calmed down, he could hear, or thought he did, that now she spoke in defiance.

He sat down again.

'Rønnau,' he said. 'We both know how you are. When you want something strongly enough, you believe that what you want really happens. But life isn't always so – obliging.'

'Sometimes life is good too!' she said.

'If Håvard is as you say he is,' he said, 'then it's dangerous to make a fool of him. I don't mean exactly that he may kill you; but you may kill something in him.'

Her eyes, which had grown narrow again, flashed at him. 'I have not made a fool of him! And I won't make a fool of him either!'

He didn't say anything, and she slowly regained her composure. But her eyes were still narrow.

'I told you that Håvard is no less of a man than you are,' she said. 'But he's more trusting. Once you look him in the eye, you can tell. And that does something to me. No, him I certainly won't make a fool of! And if he's weak, as you would call it, then I have strength enough for two.'

'You sure do!' said the mill owner.

There was another silence. And this time it looked as though they both had said all they had to say.

'You will stay the night, won't you?' Rønnau said after a while, in an entirely different voice, calm and courteous.

87

'Thank you, yes. If you want me to,' he said.

He laughed then, for the first time, and said in a jesting voice, 'I hope you don't intend to put an adder in my bed.'

She laughed at that, showing her white teeth.

'You can rest assured,' she said. 'It's too early in the season for that – the adders haven't crawled out yet, you know.'

They heard harness bells outside. And there the two sledges ground their way across the yard.

Rønnau asked to be excused for a moment, she had to go to the kitchen.

The mill owner went over to the window and looked out into the yard.

The sledges had stopped outside the cow barn. The two men stood side by side. They were the same height.

Jon was a tall fellow. So the other one must be Håvard.

Now Håvard grabbed a big handful of hay and carried it into the barn. He didn't return for a while.

The servant came running down to the two men from the kitchen. He explained something to them. Håvard let the boy take over one of the loads, said something to Jon, grabbed a couple of things from the load and walked up toward the house.

He carried two guns slung across his shoulder. A brace of wood grouse seemed to hang from the other.

His gait was unusually light, with soft springy steps, even now when he was carrying a goodly load which weighed him down.

The mill owner wondered a moment if he himself had ever walked that lightly.

Now he could hear Håvard's Telemark speech out in the hallway; Rønnau was receiving him.

'Two nice wood grouse!' Håvard said. 'They'll make a dinner for the parson. Jon shot one of them. Payment on the rent, he said. We got a bit delayed on the down trip, because we found some bear tracks; but with all that snow we didn't manage to get close to it.'

Rønnau said something in a subdued voice, and Håvard replied likewise.

After a little while Rønnau came in with a tablecloth and began to set the table. 'Håvard just went to fix himself up a little,' she said.

Some time passed before Håvard entered – freshly shaven, washed, in a clean shirt and his Sunday best. He still wore his Telemark clothes, the mill owner noticed. Was it in defiance? People up here took note of such things.

He could look a little more closely at Håvard now.

88

He saw a tall young man, remarkably well-proportioned. His hair was dark blond, his face thin with high cheekbones, quite common among people in the mountains. What made the face unique were the dark-blue, deeply set eyes, shaded by thick eyebrows which were darker than the hair and slanted up toward the temples. These eyebrows gave his face a passionate, even violent appearance; but his mouth said something else, being sensitive and friendly, and with a tiny smile lurking at the corners most of the time. A bit weak? Yes, perhaps, but even more very young, younger than his twenty-eight years.

His eyes? He couldn't make them out right off – it was only a man Håvard was facing. But Håvard had an open and honest expression, and he looked straight at the person he talked to.

How would he manage here in this parish? The mill owner blankly refused to make any predictions about that. It depended on so many things.

Rønnau had calmed down now that Håvard was present. The mill owner noted, with a little smile, how proud she was of his looks.

According to custom up this way, Rønnau waited on them but didn't sit at the table herself. They were served good beer – not brewed at home, but from the Mill – and good brandy. With another little smile, the mill owner noticed that she remembered what kind of food he liked best.

Afterward, when Rønnau had joined them, sitting somewhat apart from the men with her knitting, the mill owner broached his errand.

Håvard hedged, saying 'uh-huh' and 'yeah' but without giving a straight yes.

That hauling paid poorly, as Rønnau and he had agreed. If it hadn't been an obligation, he wasn't sure whether . . .

And besides, they had only four horses at Olstad this year, and that was somewhat short. Two of them were needed in the woods for lumbering a good part of the winter, the third was a fjord horse which he was reluctant to wear out with heavy loads.

The mill owner explained that the extra hauling would naturally be paid at a higher rate; but Håvard still didn't say yes. He would think it over, he said.

The mill owner didn't press him. They would come back to the matter, he said. If Håvard got to the home parish sometime in the spring or summer, he could drop by the Mill. They were trying out some new things in farming there, which Håvard might like to take a look at – he'd gotten the impression from Mr. Thurmann that Håvard was interested in such matters.

Rønnau stiffened slightly at that but didn't say anything.

89

Later they spoke about one thing and another until the evening.

The guest room was spacious, the bed was good, without so much as a trace of an adder.

The following day, after the mid-morning meal, the mill owner left. They hadn't come to any agreement.

At the Mill and in the Smithy

*T*he day after the mill owner had been at Olstad, Rønnau was taken ill and had to go to bed. Most likely, it was nothing but a slight cold, she thought, though it didn't quite feel that way. It was mainly that she felt so queasy. Would Håvard be so kind as to move into one of the guest rooms awhile? She preferred to be alone when she felt poorly. Håvard offered to help her in various ways, but she said no thanks, with a little smile. Men were mostly in the way during illness and such.

This was Wednesday. She remained in bed Thursday and Friday as well; but on Saturday she was up again, somewhat pale and quiet, but otherwise quite well, it appeared.

'It might have done me some good to stay in bed another day or two,' she said, 'but the parson is coming this afternoon, and I have to look over a few things.'

Sure enough, in the afternoon Reverend Thurmann, the rector, did come. It had become customary for him to be put up at Olstad. The parish clerk, who lived slightly north of the church, with a small plot of land and eight mouths to feed, was only too pleased.

Ola Viken, the new head servant at the parsonage, came along as a sort of bodyguard, with a gun suspended from the saddlebow – wolves had showed up several places along the road after the snowfall.

The parson got down from his horse, slowly and with difficulty. He'd grown rather stiff lately and seemed older than his years; for that matter, he was well over fifty. He beamed when he caught sight of Rønnau and Håvard on the porch.

The parson was his old self, kindly and talkative. And Rønnau was a good hostess. She had been well trained during those years when she was at the Mill, that was easy to see.

The parson talked mostly about how they neglected the soil in these parishes – that was his pet peeve in a way. And Nordbygda was even more backward than the home parish in everything.

'It's a boon that you've come up here as a missionary for the good cause, my dear Håvard!' he said.

Håvard winced.

At dusk he and Håvard took a slow walk around the fields. The parson had good eyes, and now it was his turn to wince.

'Neglected! Sadly neglected!' he said several times.

But when they came to the big water-logged meadow and Håvard explained to him what he had planned to do with it, he brightened up.

'Four acres!' he said. 'Unless the soil has turned sour, this could become the best field on the entire property, my dear Håvard!'

Last fall, when Håvard visited the farm to give Rønnau advice, he had hammered a couple of stakes deep into the ground down there. He had thought that, when he came up here again – the following summer, he'd figured – he would pull them up so he could take a look at the stakes and tell by the smell if the soil had turned sour.

He gave a pull at them now, but they were stuck in the frozen ground, as was to be expected.

The parson followed everything with interest.

'That reminds me of the almost mystical aversion for improvements which we meet everywhere, and many times most strongly in those who would reap the greatest benefit from such improvements,' he said. 'What can the reason be? It must be due to the general disposition of the people, who lack the ability to grasp the new ideas.

'Just look at these posts which stand there in the swamp, and which for some reason or other you want to pull up, because they offend you. Then you notice that they *refuse*. You can't pull them up. That sticky material in the swamp clings to them and won't let go, as though subterranean forces held them back with a thousand fingers. If you wish to liberate them, you have to undertake the laborious task of draining the entire swamp, dig ditches in all directions so as to allow the superfluous water to run off. And then some day – look! – you can go over there and pull up the post with a tiny little tug, because the swamp has let go its hold on it. But at the same time the entire swamp has been changed – it's no longer a swamp but fertile soil fit for cultivation.

'Yes. That's the way it is!' the parson said, animated. 'I plan to use this symbol in one of my future sermons. In other words, it's education that we need, more and more education. . . .'

The parson went to bed early, as always the day before a religious service.

But the following day he did not speak about the posts in the swamp. He had picked out as an independent text the parable *A sower went forth to sow. . . .* The spring planting was imminent, after all. He explained that what was right for the farmer was precisely to bury his talent in the earth, then he would get it back tenfold.

He also managed to touch on drainage, crop rotation, and growing potatoes – he had found out that the soil up here, with its sandy contents, was especially well suited for this plant, which so benefited people and pleased God.

The farmers sat there listening, or pretended to listen. Many of them had a hangover, one was snoring like thunder. But Pastor Thurmann was used to such occurrences. The important thing was to sow, and continue to sow, even if most of the seeds fell upon stony places.

At the very back of the church sat a group of Haugians. Most of the time they were looking at the floor. Only a couple of times, when the parson got more than usually engrossed in the blessings of crop rotation and the use of fertilizer, did they exchange glances and slowly shake their heads.

Spring was late in coming, but it came with a bang. Sunshine alternated with pelting rain, the meadows turned green and the frost in the ground thawed. It was May by now, and in two weeks, or at the latest in three, the spring planting could begin. Time was getting short for a good many things. Håvard pulled himself together – he knew he had postponed it for too long – and began checking the farm implements. He went to the storehouse to inspect the grain bins a little more closely at the same time.

It was pretty much as he had imagined, no better in any case. The implements were as he remembered them from last fall when he was here – scarcely a thing that was worth other than to be chopped up for firewood. Forks and spades were needed, as were hoes and picks, plow and harrow. But worse than that – seed grain was needed. The wretched mixed grain which filled the bins could at best be milled for summer fare, but it couldn't be used for seed grain.

Then he needed clover seed for his barley field, seed potatoes, and all kinds of seeds for the garden. Wherever he looked about him, he saw new expenses. Figuring and figuring, he realized that every scrap of whatever money he'd saved over the years would be used up already in the first round; it might even fall short.

Then there were the days after tomorrow to think about. Håvard knew well enough how costly it could be not to have a dollar or two stashed away, in case something unexpected should come up.

So he had to ask Rønnau. He felt fairly certain she had a bit of cash put aside someplace or other.

But he didn't like to ask her. That was the reason he had postponed this inspection far too long.

He went around being anxious, one day, two days. By that time he'd gotten sufficiently angry with himself to catch Rønnau alone and ask her.

The outcome was pretty much as he had anticipated – no, as he had feared.

She couldn't quite understand why these new things had to be rushed. The farm implements? Well, she didn't know very much about such matters, but as far as she could tell the implements they had on the farm were just as good as on the other farms, if not better. Were they that out of date? They had done service, such as it was, for people in olden times, they had been like that from time immemorial. . . . Forks and spades and plow and harrow of *iron*? Well, she didn't know very much about it, as she'd mentioned before, but – wasn't there an old saying that too much iron in the soil was poisonous?

Oh, yes, he said – he noticed he was getting impatient and forced himself to speak slowly and quietly – that was an old saying, for sure. About as old and as true as that the earth was flat.

No, she didn't know very much about it, as she'd told him, but . . . And the seed grain? The grain in the bins had been harvested here on this farm, from grain that had also been harvested here – as far back as anyone could remember, and even further. Even in 1809 and 1812,[22] when grain wasn't to be had for hard cash, Ola had provided grain for sowing, or so he had told her – this was before her time on the farm. . . . Otherwise Ola could be a bit careless in running the farm; he felt happiest in the woods, he did. Everything that had to do with lumber, he – well, it became the death of him too, when he felled a huge pine on top of him one day, as she'd told him – but he always saw to it that there was seed grain for two years in the storehouse, that was the custom on this farm from the old days. So . . .

That was precisely what was wrong with this grain, he tried to explain to her. It was old, and how. Poor grain. And impure. Barley and oats all

22. The long period of blockade during the Napoleonic Wars, followed by poor crops and the failure of fisheries from 1815 to 1818, caused a great deal of hardship in Norway. This is the period Rønnau is referring to.

mixed up in a big mess, and both parts a poor sort. Good enough for flat-bread, perhaps, but . . . It was pretty much the same as with the cows on the farm. They, too, were an old breed. Or several old breeds mixed together in a mishmash through the ages. They ate a lot – if there was anything to eat – and milked little. Nor did they yield much meat when slaughtered. But to acquire a new breed of cattle would take a long time, that much even he understood, although *she* might think he forged ahead much too fast in many things.

Anyway, she had agreed with him about all these things when he dropped by here last fall . . .

She gave a short laugh, sending him a sidelong glance.

Yes, that was so, she said. She gave a short laugh again – though she didn't really laugh but sat there smiling to herself. She glanced at him a couple of times, smiled a little and looked away. Against his will, he felt as though he was just childish and stupid, as though she sat there chuckling at some simple and obvious thing he didn't understand.

She grew serious.

Yes, that was so, she said again. And it was clear that what he thought had to be done, must be done. What she had wanted to say was only that they had to take it easy and not bite off more than they could chew. It was the cost she was concerned about. For if they were quite well off here at Olstad – and as far as she could tell, they were – they weren't exactly flush with cash. Still, she might have a hundred dollars or so put away. But she had learned that you should never be completely out of cash on a farm, because you never knew when something unexpected might come up. So she couldn't really say that she was eager to part with that money. But if it was that important, he could take half of it anyway.

No, he said. If that was how things were, she should forget about it. Then they had better wait with one thing or another until next year. With these words he left her, in a strange state of mind. If only he didn't feel in his bones that she *had* money – money she didn't want to part with . . .

He pushed it aside and sat down to figure things out once more. He could borrow a plow at the parsonage. Fortunately, under the circumstances, spring came a good week later up here in the woodland hamlet than out there in the home parish, with its large flat areas. They had two plows at the parsonage, and they had done most of the plowing last fall. As for seed grain, he would have to be content with sowing just enough to give him seed grain for next year.

But he had to get to Christiania to buy a harrow, and that would cost a lot of money.

94

All of a sudden he knew what he had to do. It tallied with what he had been thinking – that you had to pay dearly for being short of funds. But what he could achieve was more important.

The following day he saddled Dobbin and told Rønnau he would be away for a few days – he might take a short trip to the city. He took care of provisions for the road and rode off.

He said nothing about what errand he had in the city, and he couldn't help the impression that Rønnau was sending him some long glances as he left.

It was sunshine and clear spring weather. The hamlet lay there bright and friendly – even the forest was less black than it used to be. There was spring on the surrounding farms too, the manure had been carted out to the fields, and the lumber skidded down to the lake, later to be rolled into the water. Some of the birds had arrived, starlings sat on the rooftops singing their spring ditties, and at one place he saw a pair of wagtails tripping across a yard.

First he rode to the Mill.

He had realized that he was forced to take on that extra haulage next winter. He would ask for an advance, because he had to get that harrow.

He intended to talk about seed grain and clover seed while he was at it – perhaps he could bring up the matter of the breed of cattle, too. They operated a sort of model farm at the Mill. That much he knew.

He met the mill owner in a good humor. He was happy about the offer of haulage. And he could have the fifty dollars right away. Obviously it required a bit of extra expense at first to change the management of a farm.

Seed grain and clover seed? Sure, that would be taken care of.

When Håvard said a few words about the money – that for the time being one sack of barley and a small bag of clover seed would have to suffice – the mill owner showed obvious signs of surprise. 'Is that so?' he said. 'I thought there was no shortage of money at Olstad . . .' Then he checked himself, merely adding, 'But that is something which doesn't concern me.' Then he sat a moment without speaking, as his eyes sort of scrutinized Håvard, calmly, from the side. But he seemed to get into a better and better mood as he sat there.

No, as far as the money was concerned, he resumed, there was no need to worry. When you were from a farm like Olstad, with a wife like Rønnau – not to forget Håvard, whom he knew from the parsonage, where they had spoken favorably of him – you had something called *credit*. It could always be arranged. The Mill needed both charcoal and lumber – if Håvard had no objection, they could come to an agreement right away. Sign a contract too, for that matter; and in case he needed a bigger advance, that too was not impossible. As he'd told him before, the mill owner knew as well as anybody that it was expensive to start something new. . . .

When Håvard left he had fifty dollars more in his pocket than when he came, had made an agreement about delivery of lumber and charcoal, and had been promised a sack of barley, a sack of rye, and as much clover seed as he needed. Besides, it was agreed that next fall he would get two cow calves and maybe a bull calf on top of it, if it turned out that way at the calving.

He had made a good deal and ought to be satisfied. But he was not. No, he really was not. He didn't know what the reason was. The mill owner had asked so much about Rønnau. Several times. Well, she had been his house-keeper for a couple of years, so it wasn't that surprising perhaps. But he had – yes, he had seemed so strange. And why was he so surprised when he heard there was a shortage of cash? And why was he in such a good humor afterward? As if he sat there being amused by something?

At the parson's he was told yes at the very first word. He could borrow a plow, and a wagon for his trip to Christiania as well. A sack of potatoes, of course.

Mrs. Maren Sofie came out to send greetings to Rønnau. The next Sun-day there was a service up north and she meant to come along – she couldn't forget the coffee twist she had tasted at Olstad during the wedding.

Miss Lise didn't show herself.

Five days later Håvard returned to the parsonage with a harrow on his wagon. He came to an understanding with the parson and Ola about the freight. Ola was to go to the Mill and fetch the seed grain and clover seed, and then row up to Olstad with the harrow, the idle plow, the seed grain, the clover seed, the potatoes, and the other little things in Håvard's load. Håvard offered to send a man, but the parson thought that this was the least he could do for a missionary of farming like Håvard. Håvard only picked up a small package, which he tied to the front of Dobbin's saddle. This package contained dress material and a couple of other trifles for Rønnau.

He was home again at Olstad the same evening. Rønnau received him standing in the yard.

So now he'd gotten himself a plow and harrow, seed grain and clover, seeds for the garden, and a little of everything besides, both big and small.

But he still lacked spades and forks, picks and hoes. He dropped by the smithy – sure, there was plenty of iron lying around.

Starting the following morning, he stood there with Jon, himself a semi-skilled blacksmith, and worked from morning till night.

It was interesting work. While working, he realized he'd walked around being dejected for some reason or other, or perhaps for several reasons. Breathing the wonderfully pungent air of the smithy, he recovered. He sang as he swung the sledgehammer over the red, sparkling iron.

He sang a bit of everything, as it came to him:

My horse stands in the stable,
so handsome he is to view.
The shoes on his hoofs are gilded bright,
and his ears are colored blue.

Or this verse, which he liked a lot:

Once I traveled up in the north,
wanted to buy me some rye;
I bought a dozen gypsy wives
and forgot the rye to buy.

But mostly he sang the ballad about Vilemann and the Blue Mount.[23]

Sir Vilemann mounted his steed all gray.
The cuckoo did crow.
And so he rode to the Blue Mount away.
    The dew drifts along
    and the hoarfrost falls far and wide.

Sir Vilemann rode to the Blue Mount away.
Then his steed doth stumble and wanders astray.

Sir Vilemann he blew his gilded horn.
Then he stumbles, himself, and strays forlorn.

I do not see either dawn or sun.
And north and south to me are as one.

I do not see it throughout the long day.
And I do not know how to find my way.

---

23. It is ironic that this ballad, with its prefigurative function in the novel, is Håvard's favorite song. It was written by Hoel himself, though all the reviewers took it to be authentic. Hoel's love of folk poetry is confirmed by Olav Hestenes, who says that at intimate parties he would sing 'old ballads' (*Ordet* 9, no.8 [1958], p.334).

I do not see any stars in the night.
I do not know how to find my way out.

Jon was pumping the bellows, but every now and then he came over to watch – he wanted to learn, he said. He quickly got the knack of it, and thought it was interesting work.

He began humming and singing Håvard's ballads too. 'They've got some very strange songs up where you come from,' he said. 'I'm trying to learn them.'

And it didn't take long before he knew them either, though he couldn't quite manage the Telemark manner.

They worked in the smithy for several days.

One day the doorway darkened and a pious, tilted head appeared inside. It was the next-door neighbor eastward, Hans Engen, the Haugian – the righteous man in the parish, as they called him, and not only out of friendship. Håvard remembered him from the wedding, though he had been there only the first day. His face was marked by pious, sorrowful vertical lines, as though he had acquired stripes for mourning the world's evil. Half a step behind him was his eighteen-year-old son, his head slightly tilted like his father's, but with not quite as many lines in his face yet. The boy repeated everything his father did. If his father took a step forward, the son did too; similarly, when the father took a short step back.

Mari, the pauper, had told Håvard about Hans. He was a good farmer, especially after he'd turned Haugian – they would help and train each other, those fellows. But he certainly wasn't very cheerful company. And to have him for your father must be a real misfortune. Whenever the son, Little Hans, played a small prank as a child, Hans took his son aside, explained to him why what he'd done was wrong, and concluded by saying, 'Now you can think about this until Saturday.'

And come Saturday he took the boy down to the woodshed and beat him, often until he drew blood. They had heard the boy's screams on every farm in the neighborhood.

And so the boy had become what he was – a frightened shadow of his father.

'God speed your work!' Hans said. 'I can hear you're singing. That's a good custom. I often sing myself, as well as I can. One shouldn't forget HIM, whether working or resting. Hm. That hymn you were singing – I don't think I know that tune . . .'

'It is a hymn from Telemark,' Håvard said.

Jon stood laughing over in the corner as he pumped the bellows. The Haugian noticed but didn't let on. He didn't want to take offense and leave, being too curious about their work for that.

So, they were making spades and forks and hoes from *iron*, were they? That seemed odd. Wouldn't they be very heavy to use?

One had to use one's strength, Håvard said. It was written that in the sweat of thy brow shalt thou eat bread.

Yes, that was so, that was so. But he in all innocence had always been of the opinion that so much iron would poison the soil.

'We'll see,' Håvard said. Anyway, they hadn't noticed anything of the sort in those places where people had started using plows and harrows, spades and forks of iron.

That might be so. In the capital – and other big places like that – there they probably knew such things better than up here, where people in all innocence had merely been busy farming.

Håvard had nothing to say to that, and after another long look around the smithy the Haugian went away, piously and with tilted head.

'Perhaps you could teach me that hymn when you have a chance,' he said as he left. He wasn't stupid. If only he hadn't looked so pious all the time, as though he'd been blown straight out of Jesus' nose.

'Oh, go to hell! Phoo!'

Jon had to spit.

That such people should walk around with bowed heads and call themselves holy! With that half-crazed boy at his heels every minute of the day. Starting before the boy knew how to walk, he had flogged most of his wits out of him with leather straps, until the boy was running around like a frightened shadow of his father. Except for those times when he sneaked away and tried to hang himself. Jon had helped cut him down the last time. Oh, go to hell! Phooey! Even Kerstaffer was a relief after that.

It was as though he had called the devil. After less than a minute had passed, Kerstaffer poked his narrow, angry head and wiry gray hair through the doorway.

He didn't utter a word of greeting now either, but he wanted to see what they were doing. Really? Spades and forks of *iron*. But wouldn't the soil get poisoned?

If he thought real hard, Håvard was pretty sure he could remember that question now. The cotters would be the next to ask – those who weren't just content with gloating over him.

Kerstaffer got the answers he had asked for and left as he had come, without saying good-bye.

Rønnau was somewhat restless these days. She didn't ask what they were doing, that wasn't her habit anyway. But she did make herself an errand down to the smithy a couple of times, with a between-meal snack. And then she couldn't very well avoid seeing one thing and another.

Something was bothering her.

'So you are a master blacksmith, too?' she said. 'That's more than I knew. Looks as though I've made a better bargain than I had realized.'

'Oh, master . . . If need be I can make a paltry spade, I suppose – which will serve until I can afford buying a couple new ones.'

So. Did he intend to make himself a harrow and plow too? Because she had thought that those dollars . . .

But Håvard replied that he did not intend to make a harrow or plow, oh no. That was rather difficult, he thought. Besides, he had bought a harrow in the city, and he could have a plow on loan from the parsonage. In a couple of days Ola would bring everything in his rowboat. That was money saved. And money saved was money earned, he'd heard say.

He wanted to avoid at any price her offering him money – now. Why, he didn't know himself.

'I saw Kerstaffer drop by the smithy today,' Rønnau said in the evening. 'And I say, as I've said before, you'd better be careful with him, he's not exactly your friend. He feels you've stolen Olstad from him – well, I've mentioned it to you before.'

She laughed.

'I also had a visit from Hans Engen a couple of times when I was sitting here as a widow. He, too, was a widower at that time.

'Hans said he could prove that it was providence, a sort of divine dispensation, that Ola was killed by a tree up in the woods. The Lord had seen that the two farms belonged together.'

Today, by the way, she had noticed that Kerstaffer was hiding behind some trees beyond the smithy until he saw Hans leave.

For the man he hated most of all, perhaps, was Hans Engen. He had suffered an ignominious defeat there.

The fact was, as she had told him before, that when Kerstaffer had coveted a piece of land long enough, it seemed to him he owned it. Then he started moving boundary markers and suchlike. That's what he did with a part of the pasture which belonged to Engen and which directly adjoined Kerstaffer's pasture. Kerstaffer moved the whole fence, which was no small job, carried out at night to boot, so you almost felt sorry on account of all the toil and trouble.

He had frightened, and paid off, one of his cotters to bear false witness.

He probably figured that Hans was so devout he didn't pay much attention to what was happening around him in the world.

'But that devout Hans has never been.'

So there Kerstaffer had a really close shave. Too many people remembered where the fence had been, and besides they could see the marks in the ground. The poor cotter quite lost his nerve in court when he felt the eyes of Hans the Righteous fixed upon him – he began to stutter and stammer and ended by sniveling, saying he didn't remember anything. Kerstaffer was sentenced to move the fence back again.

People said that this gnawed at Kerstaffer like a sort of debt – he'd been over in Hans's field several times at night and trampled it down.

So people said anyway.

Therefore you could well imagine that, if he hated Håvard, he hated Hans even more.

And Nordby, who had taken away his position as poor-relief officer.

It was an advantage, one might say, that there were several who could partake of this hatred. Because it was so big, far too big for a single man.

Spring Planting

O ne evening Håvard said to Rønnau, 'You're working too hard, and doing far too many things. You've got two housemaids, after all. I don't know very much about such things, but I've heard that when a woman is in the condition you are in, she has to spare herself.'

Rønnau didn't answer right away. Then she said lightly – a bit too lightly?

'Oh, I don't need to spare myself any longer on account of that. And it's often good to have something to keep you busy. Then your thoughts will leave you alone while it lasts anyway.'

Håvard felt the ground give way under him. He waited a moment, but she didn't say any more. Then he asked, 'What did you say, Rønnau?'

She smiled at him. 'Don't you realize what the matter was when I stayed in bed during those days?

'There won't be any child this time, Håvard. Such things happen, you know. Not so seldom either.'

It came so fast, and so unexpectedly. Håvard felt numb, as after a blow so hard and sharp that it paralyzed him. Many thoughts sailed through his head, so many that he couldn't keep up with them. Gone astray . . . Nothing . . . Tonè in the waterfall . . . Without honor in Telemark . . . Wedding – and now funeral . . . Poor Rønnau . . . and me and . . .

'But . . . ,' he said, and couldn't go on. 'But . . .'

Rønnau had come up to him. She clutched onto him, burying her head in the hollow of his throat, and he could feel that she was shaken with tears.

It was the first time during the period he had known her that Rønnau cried – in the daytime.

At his wits' end, he awkwardly stroked her hair.

He had never been able to endure the sight of women crying.

'Easy, Rønnau . . . Easy, Rønnau . . .'

But he was still just as numb as before. His thoughts sailed on and on, he couldn't keep track of them.

Little by little she calmed down. She gently patted the nape of his neck, and he understood – though faintly surprised – that it was a shy, timid caress.

Finally she let go of him, dried her eyes, and went to sit down in a chair over in the darkest corner.

'You said when – when you didn't yet know what had happened – that I ought to spare myself at this time. I'm not sure my carelessness lay in *that*. I'm not sure whether I could have done anything at all to help it.

'Women are strange creatures – well, *you* should know that.

'The mill owner came here one day, remember. I hadn't seen him for several years. As you know, I was a maid at the Mill for two years, and afterward a housekeeper for two years. It was a good time in many ways, but a difficult time too; he wasn't always so easy to deal with, the mill owner, and the same goes for the people who used to come and go in the house – for a young girl like me, I mean.

'That visit upset me a little. Before you came – oh no, he wasn't familiar, far from it, he isn't that way, a married man and all, with a little boy of three. But it upset me nonetheless. And the following day it came.

'Well, I don't really know if that's how it happened. Maybe it wasn't meant to be.'

A little later she said, attempting what turned into a pitiful smile, 'I guess we'll just have to start all over again, Håvard.'

Poor Rønnau! he thought. . . . Poor Rønnau . . .

He still felt numb, as if he'd been paralyzed by something, by a blow or whatever it was.

This was the evening before they were to begin the spring planting.

He felt a bit under the weather in the morning – he hadn't slept much during the night – as he sat at the head of the table watching his cotters gathered around the breakfast table.

Next to Jon, Martin was probably the best of them. But he sat there with a sullen, impassive face – a fired head servant! That must be the way he looked at it. The others – well, perhaps he took a somewhat somber view of things this morning, but . . .

Ugh, what a sight they were. Thin and seedy-looking, tired from early morning on, and so filthy you felt like praying God to have mercy. And he knew all too well what their homes looked like. A wife, wallowing in dirt, walking around sloppy and down-at-the-heel all day long, dressed in the same rags she had slept in the night before in the stinking bed. When the husband came home in the evening, a little more tired than in the morning, he had to take care of the most pressing farm chores before finally knocking off, to enter a room which looked like a pigsty, with a sullen, grouchy, un-kempt wife and a flock of screaming, hungry kids – his own or the bastards of his daughters, which they had left behind on one of their brief visits be-fore being off again, back to the farms where they were in service. *There* they slept in the cow-barn loft, or in the servants' quarters with the hired men. Once the maidenhead was gone and the worst shame forgotten, producing a few more brats would be no problem. What did the girl say? We poor people need a bit of fun too in the winter time, when the nights are long and candles are expensive.

She could have added, And in the summer, when the body is wild and wanton, and you can bed down behind every bush.

How sad, oh how sad, was the cotter's life.

And never an end in sight. He who was born a cotter remained a cotter, and his children after him. They had to go into service almost as soon as they could walk. When they grew up the daughters had children, and so did the sons – with other cotters' daughters, and in the fullness of time they got themselves a cotter's plot where everything would be repeated.

Was it so strange that they were weary and unhappy and woefully slow in their movements?

Yet . . . it was with these men he was to introduce new methods of work and new ways of cultivation on the farm.

He did try to teach them a little, as best he could. Oh God!

Worst of all perhaps, in his new state of mind, which started while he was talking to Rønnau yesterday, he had second sight again, as had happened a couple of times before up here. He could see what they were thinking, he didn't even have to be anywhere near them to hear what they were saying.

He didn't need to have much second sight either.

He had mingled with them for a couple of months now and was begin-ning to know them. They had a special way about them, the cotters up here – they were like eels, constantly slipping out of your hands. They rarely looked you full in the face, their eyes always glanced sideways or down. They rarely said no, that's true, but never *yes* – not, that is, so you felt they meant it.

Well, know them? He'd noticed long ago that they probably knew him – or thought they did – better than he knew them. They had talked about him, held him up to the light so to speak, turned him this way and that and tested and weighed him – they had done this time and again when he himself was out of earshot.

All those new things he brought with him – new plow, new harrow, new spades and new forks, new seed grain, potatoes, new ways of plowing and harrowing – they accepted them all, calmly and quietly, without question as it were. Didn't say no, didn't say yes, looked sideways and said: Uh-huh! Sure, that's so. Certainly!

But there was something in *the tone*.

Still, every now and then they couldn't help themselves. It was Martin, the former head servant, who led the way. Martin's eyes always eluded him when Håvard *looked* at him. But once in a while when he turned quickly toward him he managed to see them, for a brief moment. And then they were not especially friendly, oh no. Poor devil anyway – a widower with two snotty teenage brats up on that measly plot of his. No doubt he had had high hopes for that position as head servant. Now there wasn't a shred left of that hope. If he had taken it well, a tolerable arrangement might still have been found for him. But he took it badly. He began stirring up the other cotters, managed to make them still a bit slower, made them pretend to be even more thick-headed than they were whenever they had to understand something new and unaccustomed.

Every now and then Martin felt he had to show off a little to the others.

So. They were to plow deeper. To be sure. In the old days people used to plow just as deep as the topsoil went. But obviously they were wrong. You had to go deeper. To be sure. Oh well, the old only did what they could back up by experience, they did. They had never been anyplace to learn things. In the city or over at the parson's, and far away in the West Country, there they understood these matters much better, that was clear. There was probably something in books too about such things. . . .

Plows and harrows of iron? Uh-huh.

And forks and spades of iron? To be sure. The implements became quite a bit heavier that way, but . . . And there was an old belief that too much iron poisoned the soil, but . . .

Not so? Indeed! Well, the people in the city no doubt knew about such things, that was clear. To learn farming you had to go to the city, that was clear.

He didn't say all this at one time, that was equally clear – it would never have worked. He dropped a sentence every once in a while during the two weeks the spring planting lasted. And mostly when there were several of them in a group, so that he had some listeners.

The flock stood silent behind Martin when he delivered these volleys. A silent chorus of mirth followed each of his sentences.

This silent, mirthful chorus – Håvard suddenly recognized it. He'd noticed it sometimes in the evening after supper, when they were all busy in the kitchen and Rønnau had asked him something and he'd become animated, whereupon she asked some more questions – in a friendly way, for sure, and in a spirit of curiosity, but still half-jokingly, with half a smile and a touch of slyness: of course, nothing that we knew from before was good enough nowadays.

You're just an eager little boy – that was roughly what Rønnau's smile said, without any malice on her part. But the others saw something more in it and thought they understood perfectly what she meant to say. And her they knew and trusted – she had been their mistress for several years and had made herself respected. *Him* they didn't know yet, nor were they clear about whether they had to respect him or not. He wasn't really master on the farm yet, and besides he was an outsider.

Martin had more than once sat among this flock gathered in the kitchen. Little by little they all knew how to look at him – as the stranger who had come to the parish uninvited and had gotten himself a home and grounds through sleeping with the owner. The cotters – well, they knew their place, they knew it was no use to say *no*, but they weren't slaves, so they didn't say *yes* either, and Martin even dared stick his neck out and say, oh so piously, almost like the missus herself, In the city, no doubt, they know all about farming. . . .

Quiet mirth. In the servants' quarters and in the cotters' shacks everywhere, as well as out in the fields when he wasn't present himself, the mirth wasn't so quiet, oh no.

What about their zest for work and their ability and willingness to grasp what he explained to them, when it had gradually been pretty much established that he was a footloose tramp and a crackpot?

It was hard enough to make them understand something they did their best to understand. It had been hard enough last year over at the parsonage, with Ola as an eager and steady go-between. But here? With Martin around?

Håvard would get so furious – he sometimes felt like barging straight into the flock thrusting them right and left, grabbing them by the collar and shaking them, scaring the wits out of them and then into them again, until they stood there like the sinners and poor devils they were before the Lord. Those lousy cotter souls . . .

Then he remembered who and what they were. Poor devils born in poverty and bred in rags, ill-used and put upon throughout the years, under-fed worse than the cows in their stalls, condemned to slave and toil for the freeholder late and early for meager wages or none at all. Rags in front and rags behind, drudgery and poverty from the cradle to the grave.

And then *he*, a footloose tramp, came wandering into the parish, and – hey, presto – there he sat on one of the best farms, giving orders and carry-ing on and requiring more and better work; for they were smart enough, however stupid they might seem to *him* and however wrong and worthless everything they had learned from childhood on, and their parents before them and their parents before *them* again – they were smart enough to understand one thing: the novelties that this stranger wanted to bring about so suddenly would require more toil and more thought than the work they were used to from before. And what did they get in return for it?

Not a shilling.

Uh-huh! they said. To be sure!

He plowed a few furrows with the iron plow to show them how it should be done. 'Look here – if the topsoil is shallow you let the plow run shallow. But if it's good and deep, then you let it grab as far down as it can.'

Poor devils, he thought once again when he finally had put them to work. But there remained a resentment in him against something or other.

If only he had somebody to talk to. He caught himself longing for Ola at the parsonage – slow, steady, and reliable. Ola, with whom he could talk when necessary, and be completely silent with when *that* was the thing to do. Still, to give the devil his due, every now and then Jon intervened, and with a bang. After all, he had lent a hand in forging these new implements.

'So this spade isn't good enough, eh?' he would say to Martin. 'Bring it here then, if you aren't man enough to lift an iron spade! Look here! Take this stick!'

And he threw him an old wooden spade.

Then there was silence for a while. They knew that if they started quar-reling with Jon, he could easily beat up two of them together.

And then there was the fact that he was one of them.

One of them? They knew, when they thought about it, that Jon was as far removed from them as the moon. He said what he felt like saying and did what suited him, Jon did. He was something that none of them could even dream of becoming – what was it they called it? *A free man.*

But Jon was only one of six. And he didn't show up every day. In the middle of the work season, when he figured the weather was right, he would go up into the hills and shoot grouse for a couple of days.

The spring planting took its course. To be sure!

Worst of all, the cotters were partly right. Or put themselves in the right. Due to mismanagement year after year, generation after generation, the top-soil had become shallow – in many places you didn't have to plow very deep to hit sand or clay. Anyway, here and there they did turn up. And Håvard, after all, wasn't familiar enough with the soil up here yet, so he couldn't tell them in advance, 'Careful here, go shallow there,' or, 'Let the plow dig in here.' But the cotters, who knew the plots inside out, let the plow cut especially deep where they knew that the topsoil was just a thin layer – let it cut down into the clay and thrust it up, an ugly sight which they afterward would point at with a silent sneer: look, there you have your field after the new fashion – just plow under the topsoil and turn up the clay, after the custom at the parsonage and in the West Country and *the city*!

Every once in a while, when there were too many things to think about – Rønnau and him, the baby, everything connected with it, and these cotters on top of it all – it happened that he drove himself too hard, as though try-ing to get even with the soil for everything. Then it happened, too, that Jon stopped him.

'Hey!' Jon said a couple of times. 'You're driving yourself too hard now. These cotters believe you expect them to keep up with you, and that they can't do – even if they *wanted* to. Something is bothering you, I understand that much. But you must try and control yourself!'

It went all right, after a fashion. The field turned out to be only so-so, plowed too deep where the soil was poor and too shallow where it was rich and deep. Poorly harrowed – you couldn't be everywhere – and the barley field manured only so-so.

But just wait till the fall, till the winter rye!

And the potato field was a great success.

He noticed, too, that the sarcastic remarks at the expense of the new im-plements gradually became more subdued. Those who had used the iron spade and the iron fork one day, quietly went to pick them up again the fol-lowing day as well. Not that they had been mistaken when they made fun of these implements beforehand – far from it. And if they had been mistaken, this stranger certainly wasn't right either, far, far from it. The new spade was beastly heavy, and it did poison the soil, that was for sure; there was a good old saying about that. But it wasn't *their* soil, after all, and you had to admit you could pick up more somehow with these new implements – you could take it easier and still accomplish the same as those who stood fiddling

107

with the old wooden gear. So when this fellow Håvard absolutely *insisted* on poisoning his soil, then . . .

'What has been going on?' Rønnau said one day – it was near the end of the spring planting. 'Some of the cotters walk around muttering that you have promised them eight shillings a day – and that's double wages, you know – but that you aren't at all serious about it, that you're just baiting the hook to get them to work harder than they're able to.'

'Eight shill . . .' At first Håvard didn't understand anything. Then something dawned on him.

'Oh. It must be Jon. We were sitting up in the summer dairy, you know, talking about all sorts of things while we had some drinks. In the end I may have said something to the effect that, if we could make farming pay, sometime in the future . . .'

They called in Jon and asked him about it. Oddly enough he expressed regret.

'I told Amund – it was sheer thoughtlessness on my part,' he said. 'Actually to make fun of you, Håvard – to show what a fool you are. But they have taken it differently, I can see that now.'

There was nothing to be done about it.

Sure, the spring planting went all right, after a fashion. But when it was all over Håvard felt worn out, as though after many nights of watching. Having thought things over for a moment, he packed some food for himself and took to the woods. He felt a deep craving to be alone, far away from people. Not to have to see or talk to anybody for a good many days. For a pretext he mentioned that a fox had showed up in the hen house at one of the cotter's plots and had slaughtered a couple of hoary, windblown hens.

The Waterlogged Meadow

*A*fter five days, when Håvard came down again from the summer dairy, he felt like a new person. He had walked around in the deep woods every day, mostly in what he knew or assumed to be the Olstad Forest, but farther on as well. He had been up on a couple of peaks, looked out across miles and miles of woodland on every side, and had felt as small as a gnat. When he returned to the summer dairy in the evening after a day like that and had sprinkled himself with cold water from the dairy brook, he felt deep in his soul as though he'd been bathing in a Telemark summer lake.

When he sat inside the chalet cabin in the evening, with a pine root burning with a yellow flame in the fireplace and a low, faraway soughing from the forest outside, he knew what it meant to feel safe – and yet a little fearful, because everything was so vast.

He walked down the dairy road with two fox skins tied to his scrip, knowing that now they were going to tackle the waterlogged meadow.

That meadow was, in a way, the big discovery he'd made when he was up here last fall. He had used a couple of days to examine it then, but now he knew more about it. He had driven stakes into it to a depth of four feet and knew that the soil was fine and not gone sour. At four feet he hit something hard, which he thought was blue clay. That was all right.

The meadow sat at the lower end of the property, not far from the lake, and sloped gently toward the west. It was quite big, at least several acres. The reason why it lay there so wet and waterlogged was – and this was his discovery – that a low rocky ridge ran immediately beneath the turf at the lower end of the meadow, between the meadow and the lake. It created a blockage, so that the water couldn't drain properly. It stuck up like a small hummock farther north, but then it went underground. It should be possible to make drainage ditches here, but a bit of blasting would be necessary, as well as a couple of covered ditches up through the meadow itself. Time would take care of the rest.

The same afternoon he'd returned from the summer dairy, he walked around the meadow one more time. But the matter was quite clear.

After a bit of blasting and ditch digging, this useless swamp would become the best plowland on the entire farm. He had bought blasting powder when he was in Christiania. Now he went over to the smithy and made a mining drill. Spades for the job, he had.

He sent for Jon and three of the cotters, Per and Edvart and Amund. With Lars, the servant, and himself, that made six hands, which should suffice. He didn't want to see Martin's sour face this time, and Tjøstøl was too old. He had two weeks ahead of him, with nothing else to think about than this job. Rønnau gave him a smile when she noticed how eager he was. Suddenly he realized he'd gone around harboring a resentment against her – for several reasons – but now it seemed to have blown away.

The next morning they got started.

First they dug a little here and a little there, to make sure where the rocky ridge was going. Soon they knew; they also knew that they had to blast their way through the ridge only at one point for the pond to spring a leak, so to speak.

But Håvard had further plans, and that was why he took such extraordinary pleasure in this work. He wanted to try something which even Principal Sverdrup had tried no more than once – he wanted to make covered ditches, with flat stones at the bottom, flat stones in the walls and on top, then a filling of round stones and earth on top of that again, so that no one could see there even *was* a ditch. That way you saved ground, too. In other countries, like France, he'd heard that such closed ditches had been in use for several centuries, it was only up here that they had never been used. But from now on they were going to be!

He saw it so clearly in his mind, now that he and the cotters were working together: in a couple of years there would be a rye field in this meadow, with stalks and spikes so tall that you could get lost among them. How they would stretch their necks then, those sour neighbors around here, shading their eyes and gawking. And the cotters would come over, perhaps not quite so skeptical anymore. It might even penetrate their thick skulls that, once he had developed the farm, part of the benefit would fall to them, the cotters.

In the middle of the work period they took a short rest.

He gave the three cotters a warm look as they sat there staring indifferently into vacancy. He remembered something that Principal Sverdrup had read to him, from a book of sagas or whatever it was, by a man named Snorre Sturlason, about a man called Erling Skjalgsson.[24] He took his thralls into the field and set them daily tasks, the book said. But if they managed to do more, they were credited with silver for it. And if they were able to work up so much silver that it amounted to the price of a thrall, they became free men.

He was somebody, that Erling Skjalgsson. If only one could do as well as he.

They would have time to spare, both he and the cotters, once he'd changed the way the farm was run. What should they use the free time for? Oh, in the river north of here there was a nice little waterfall. The farm grain mill stood there now. What if he mounted a saw there, for household use? The outbuildings needed fixing up, many of them more than that. And the cotters' shacks too.

Perhaps some of them would even understand that grain and potatoes could be grown on a cotter's plot.

'All right, fellows, we must get going again!'

His voice was so cheerful that they turned their heads and followed him with their eyes as they slowly got to their feet. That fellow seemed to feel

24. Also spelled Snorri Sturluson (1179–1241). Icelandic historian, skald, and statesman. Snorri is most famous for his history of the Norwegian kings (up to the year 1177). Erling Skjalgsson (ca.975–1028) was a powerful chieftain of southwest Norway.

work was just fun! Oh well, when you worked your own land and for your own riches . . .

The digging was coming along better than he'd dared hope. The second day the first blasting shot was fired. It was followed by a howl from the basement at Berg – they probably had a loony who was boom-shy over there.

It wasn't long before one of his neighbors came over – Hans Engen, the Haugian. He stood there so pious, his head tilted, and his son one step behind him. God speed your work! What were they doing to make such an awful racket? You don't say – so they wanted to drain this wild meadow? Hm. Well. A commendable task, to be sure. Hm. But – if it had been the Almighty's intention that this meadow was to be drained, perhaps he wouldn't have placed that rocky ridge in the way. Eh?

Håvard replied, mildly, that as far as he remembered, it was written that, if your eye offends thee, you should pluck it out. This rocky ridge offended *him*, and now he was plucking it out with a vengeance.

Certainly! Hm. That word about the eye wasn't meant to be taken quite in that sense perhaps, but . . . he was glad to hear that Håvard was so well versed in Scripture. If you read *that*, then you were never at a loss for an answer – that was certainly true.

Hans had gotten an answer to his question; but he didn't move on.

Hm! Since he'd come around anyway – . That new grain Håvard had purchased at the Mill, as he'd heard – that grain was supposed to be better, wasn't it, than the sort they'd used in this parish as long as anyone could remember?

When Håvard said that it might not be so much better exactly, but better sorted – barley by itself and oats by itself – Hans answered meekly that maybe he was right. Still, he had always heard that the grain turned out as the Lord wanted it – if he wanted it to be barley it came out barley, if he wanted oats, it came out oats. And if he wanted mixed grain, that's what you got. Mostly it turned out mixed, that was so.

He was even more doubtful about the potatoes. He'd heard the parson, of course, oh yes. But he had never seen that plant mentioned in the Bible. And the fact was, as Håvard would no doubt agree, that the word of God ought to be our guiding star both in spiritual and temporal matters, wasn't that so?

Håvard, who hadn't spent several years at a parsonage for nothing, re-plied that, sure enough, the Bible said nothing about the potato. Nor did it say anything about winter rye or, as far as he knew, about oats either. But it said that man should till the earth and subdue it. When the potato wasn't mentioned, it might have been because it didn't grow in Palestine. Nor did lingonberries or cloudberries, which weren't mentioned either, for the same reason. Still, they were good-tasting berries. Hans tilted his head and agreed. He quickly changed over to asking what the yield for the potato was, whether it was wholesome and nourishing food for man as well as beast, and what the current price per barrel was. He went away thoughtful, his son one step behind him. Two of the cotters, Amund and Per, nudged each other in the ribs: that Telemark fellow had the edge there, did you notice? Did you see Hans's head? It ended up even more askew – like this!

This was the first time Håvard felt that he had the cotters *on his side*. One of them pointed westward, in the direction of the alder woods, and laughed. Over there, half hidden among the bushes, stood Kerstaffer Berg, shading his eyes and gawking. He was consumed by curiosity but couldn't bring himself to come over now that Hans had been there.

They were working on the ditch behind the rocky ridge, getting close to the north end. Then, just below the turf, they bumped into a big boulder which they didn't quite know what to do with. It couldn't very well be left alone – then they would have to make a big bend in the ditch. They could drill a hole in it and blow it up with powder, but that would take several hours; or they could try to ease it up and out with pry and stake; but that too would require several hours of work, if they should succeed. That stone was a lift for three or four men.

Then someone said, 'Let's get Mons Myra.'

Håvard had seen Mons only two or three times; but he'd heard so much about him, from Rønnau, Mari, and Jon, that he felt he knew him inside out.

Mons was one of the cotters at Berg. He was a giant, good-natured as such people usually are, and so strong that he thought all fighting and quarreling among ordinary folk was just kid stuff. His own strength was something he could never get used to, people said – it was a source of constant wonder to him, something divine, or all but supernatural anyway. But he was happy with it. Every once in a while he took a walk through the hamlet. Then people were glad to give him an opportunity to show his strength, partly because they knew he really liked to, partly because they liked to watch and to have something to talk about for a while. Afterward he always got a meal. He ate enough for four.

Kerstaffer, whom he worked for, was in the habit of setting daily quotas for his cotters. He would always make them as big as possible, and if they couldn't finish their stint he threatened to evict them from their holdings. And this was by no means an idle threat – he made agreements only for a limited term with his cotters, and he *had* evicted a couple of them.

Mons was not particularly quick. Kerstaffer, who had to give him double wages and a double amount of food at every meal, gave him a double daily quota of work too. But when the work was heavy, often it couldn't be avoided that Mons finished his stint in less than the agreed-upon time. Then Kerstaffer would increase the work load, both for him and for the others. This was impossible in the long run, and the upshot was that Mons carried out the agreed-upon work in the agreed-upon time period and passed the remainder of the work period out in the field whittling ax handles or making brooms, beer bowls, and the like – he was quite handy with those huge paws of his. If Kerstaffer noticed this, he would come storming out into the field, shouting abuse at the top of his voice.

Mons would sit there watching the little man as he came nearer and nearer, trying to hear what he was saying; but he wasn't able to – people said his only physical defect was that he was somewhat hard of hearing. When Kerstaffer got to within a couple of hundred feet or so, Mons would rise and start lumbering toward his master – perhaps he felt it was a shame that this man, who owned the farm and all, should be forced to run the whole way.

Then Kerstaffer would stop, while continuing to sound off. Mons lumbered on, not fast but heavily, roughly the way you would imagine a rock moving, if it could get started. Kerstaffer began to back off – but he kept jawing away. Mons quietly followed. Finally Kerstaffer turned around and began to run, ranting and roaring all along. Mons plodded ahead, until he saw the master turn into the yard. Then he understood that his master didn't want anything with him after all, turned around, and went back to his beer bowl.

Kerstaffer stormed into the house; if at that moment he ran into his teenage son, he would hit him. Otherwise he never did, for he was proud of that boy: 'I believe Little Erik is possessed by the devil himself,' he used to say. 'That boy is worse than I am!'

The son grinned; he put up with it at those times.

But to fire Mons? It would never enter Kerstaffer's mind. He knew quite well he could never find his like for a cotter.

From where they stood in the meadow they could see that Mons was sitting out in the field making a broom. They sent Jon over to him. At the same time Håvard went into the kitchen and said, 'Prepare more food. Mons is coming!'

Mons came lumbering up. A wonder the footbridge held up under him – it was made of only three logs.

First they had to go through a short introduction – the three cotters reminded him of feats he had accomplished. 'Do you remember when you crawled under the belly of that stubborn horse over at Nordby and lifted him off the ground? How scared he got hanging there in mid-air – he's been as sweet as a lamb ever since.' . . . 'Do you remember . . . ?'

Mons patiently put up with these boasts. In fact, he was quite pleased.

Then he went over to tackle the boulder.

'I believe it's too heavy,' Håvard said. 'Jon and I have tried to budge it, but it feels like bedrock.'

Mons didn't answer. He grabbed the boulder with both hands and rocked it. Then he placed one leg on each side of the stone and got a better hold.

It went slowly. Now the boulder lifted slightly, and at the same time Mons sank into the ground a bit. The stone was pointed at the lower end and was somewhat bigger than they had thought. Now he'd got it level with his knees. He moved forward slightly – very slowly. His broad feet sank several inches into the ground at each step. He carried the boulder carefully, as though it was a rare kind of egg, laid there by some giant bird. Two steps – four – eight steps. Now he was at the edge of the meadow, where he dropped the stone with a crash. The pointed end sank well into the ground. He took a couple of breaths and stood there looking at the boulder awhile. The others didn't say anything. They really didn't believe what they had seen – that must have been a lift for four men.

Mons had gone red in the face. He looked down at the boulder again.

'I sure am strong, ain't I!' he said, glad and surprised.

Then they went up to eat. They were having gruel, pork, and flatbread – fine fare for Mons.

It was well into the month of June. The hamlet stood all green. The birds sang around the clock, built nests, and flew high and low after flies and gnats. They sang in the bushes and the underbrush surrounding the meadow. They darted around one's ears, so close one could feel the waft from their wing tips – for worms and other little crawling things turned up in delicious abundance as they were digging. Every time a blasting shot went off, the birds got frightened and were silent for a minute or so, about as long as they could remember something like that, or bothered to be frightened. Then they began singing again.

The sun was up when the men went to work at six in the morning, it was up when they went home, tired, at eight in the evening. Edvart looked up into the air, where the swallows were flying like dark arrows against the pale sky. He said:

'The swallows are flying high. The good weather will stay with us.'

Per could tell the same from his rheumatism – it wasn't there. They'd had almost too much of this good weather now – the grain fields and the potato patch needed some rain. For that matter, they were getting nice and green, everything was coming along fine; but there was an old saying that you could seldom have too much rain before Saint John's Eve.

As they walked up to the kitchen for supper, the song thrush chirped in the bushes along their path:

Look at them! Look at them! Digging ditches in the meadow!

Another answered, And digging worms for us!

And the first one answered back, That's why we let them dig, let them dig, let them dig!

Lars looked longingly in the direction of Berg – his girl was over there – and said, 'If it was summer all the year round, life would be easy!'

The work on the meadow went forward, day by day. After three days they were through with the blasting and the crosswise ditch farthest down and started on the three lengthwise ditches running up the meadow.

At one time this land had been part of the sea bed. At a depth of from three to four feet they hit blue clay. They worked themselves down to that point, lined the bottom and the walls with stones, filled in with round stones from the piles nearby, covered with slabs, and filled in with dirt at the very top. Now the water would have an outlet. Immediately a steady trickle began to flow into the open ditch lowest down. From there the water flowed through the opening they had blasted in the rocky ridge and along through the stone-lined trench they had made down below. It led out into the little stream which divided Olstad from Nordby.

When they had finished, the six men had been busy for exactly ten days. In two days it would be Saint John's Eve; on that day farm folk everywhere would take their cows to the summer dairy.

And then the summer would truly begin.

Summer

Rønnau, Håvard, and Kjersti went along to the summer dairy and remained there for a few days.[25] To find a place to sleep wasn't very difficult now in the summertime – Rønnau and Håvard slept on spruce twigs and sheepskins in the little barn.

Rønnau saw to it that everything got off to a good start. Afterward the dairymaid and one of the housemaids would manage by themselves. Håvard fixed a few things on the roofs of the cow barn and the cabin, dug up pine roots for the fireplace, and fetched and chopped dry wood for the first part of the summer – otherwise the chalet girls were used to doing these things by themselves. Even the dairymaid put up with the sight of him when she noticed what he was doing.

The evenings were long, and as light as an overcast day, the air so pure it did one good just to breathe. Everyone knew that people became well from staying at the summer dairy.

They sat on the broad door slab until near midnight, talking leisurely. You needed less sleep here than down in the village.

In the morning blue smoke rose from all the dairies around the tarn. You could hear conversations from far away in the still air. The cows gave one another friendly moos. Some bull calf or other scraped the ground with his forepaws, bellowed in a small way, and wanted to be a grown-up bull. In between the other sounds could be heard the barking of a dog – at the Nordby dairy they had a small watchdog which liked to be in on everything.

The cluster of houses could almost be called a small hamlet now during the summer-dairy season.

Little by little the cows' coats began to recover their glossy look. In the morning they walked one after the other through the gates and into the

---

25. Summer dairying (*seterdrift* or *seterstell*) was an important part of traditional Norwegian dairy farming; today it has been greatly reduced. Usually it took place in the mountains, where the cattle would graze during the summer months. The *seter* – variously translated as 'summer dairy,' 'mountain dairy,' and 'mountain pasture' – became the matrix of a veritable subculture, steeped in folklore and fantasy, as though the mountain setting released people's sense of the supernatural. Since the beginning of National Romanticism (ca. 1840), many echoes of this subculture have appeared in literature. The *seterjente* (*seter* girl) has been the subject of many a romantic song. One of several comic-satiric treatments of this figure is found in the second act of Ibsen's *Peer Gynt* (1867). Hoel's subsequent use of the *seter* motif (in the chapter 'The Bear' in Part Two) for launching a highly dramatic episode is more traditional. For a scholarly study of the *seter* tradition, see Svale Solheim, *Norsk sætertradisjon* (Oslo: H. Aschehoug, 1952).

woods, in the evening they came back again in the same order – the bell cow first both times. Oddly enough, she never walked exactly the same paths with her herd two days in a row – did she stand in her stall at night figuring out where to take the cows the following day?

Bears had sometimes been sighted up in these parts during the spring and fall, but the chalet girls weren't scared. Except when it was a killer bear – and nothing like that had been rumored for several years – it retreated farther into the forest as soon as it smelled the smoke of dry wood and heard the sound of human voices. There, far away in the deep woods, it seemed to live on ants, bumblebees' nests, field mice and roots, until the blueberries got ripe at the end of July.

After five days of a quiet existence, the three of them went back to the village again. Kjersti, Rønnau's stepdaughter, had turned twelve in early June. By next year, after she'd turned thirteen, she would be allowed to stay at the summer dairy for half the season. Then she would learn how to churn, make cheese, and prepare summer-dairy waffles – the best food there was.

Down home it was almost as peaceful as up in summer-dairy country – in some ways even more peaceful. At Olstad the sole housemaid was taking care of the pigs, the chickens, and the two cows they had kept at home. The sheep had been sent to the woods, the goats walked around in the pasture and came home by themselves in the evening. The cotters stayed on their own plots, so Håvard and Lars were the only men on the farm. The storehouse bell was silent, here as on most of the other farms at this time of year, between the work seasons. The yard was grass-green, and the paths between the houses were getting overgrown.

Håvard and Lars busied themselves with the necessary little chores – they checked over the fences, chopped wood for the kitchen, tidied up a bit in the barn so everything would be in order for the haying season. In a far corner of the lower hayloft they found a hen which had disappeared; it sat on some eggs, and they let it sit.

The hamlet was still all day long. Toward evening it grew so dead still that you could hear the voices of people carrying on a conversation on the other side of the lake.

'It promises to be a good summer,' one of them said.

'Yes, and the barley is coming along nicely.'

That was quite true.

There must have been a light breeze, though, because along with the quiet, faraway words there came a scent of wild clover and honey, of wet beach, of yarrow and dog roses and a hundred other kinds of flowers; it blended into a sort of fragrant flowery meadow in the sky and reminded you that it was summer.

It was early July. In ten days or so the haying season would begin. They could somehow feel it approaching – from over the crest of the hill. Then there would be a whirl of activity everywhere. You would hear, all over the hamlet, the shrill sound of the hired hands whetting their scythes, or the full, muted sound of grass falling before the scythe as the men walked their swaths, one after another, on all the farms. But as yet the entire hamlet was quiet from morning till night, so quiet that the barking of a faraway dog sounded like a yell at the wrong moment.

Everybody spoke more softly than usual during this period. The birds didn't sing as they had a month ago but darted high and low all day long, chasing flies and gnats for their greedy young. Some of them were probably baby cuckoos, but the cuckoo itself was no longer to be heard; it had gone south to a bachelor's life far away.

After supper Håvard rowed out on the lake and threw a net. Kjersti liked to go with him – she thought it was great fun to be in a boat and knew every fishing place around the lake.

Håvard was getting along fine with this girl by now. At first it had been different. He had acted friendly whenever he saw her, as was his wont. But days might pass without his setting eyes on her. She was shy and wary like an animal; thin and lanky, she would disappear like a shadow before he managed to turn around and look at her. Every once in a while he noticed that she was observing him when she thought he didn't notice – observing him eagerly, or curiously, he wasn't sure which, nor did he give much thought to it. Any time his glance happened to light on the dark corner where she sat curled up, those big eyes of hers were fixed upon him, and she quickly turned them aside, as though she had been caught doing something wrong. Now and then, when he was working on the threshing floor or in the stable, he would glimpse a shadow gliding past a crack in the wall. If he was chopping wood in the shed humming a ballad as he worked, a shadow might cross the streak of sunlight, and he would hear the crackle of a twig – it was Kjersti who had stolen behind the wall to listen to his song and had shifted from one foot to the other.

'Come in and I'll teach you that ballad,' he would say. But she was gone, without a sound.

That's how it was during the first couple of weeks. But from the day he had tended old Mari down in the cow barn, everything changed. They met at the old woman's stall, and suddenly it was as though her shyness and fear had been blown away. She chatted and asked questions, laughed and chatted again. And that's how it remained. Only when Rønnau was present did Kjersti fall silent as before.

Rønnau had her eyes about her and quickly noticed the change. It was nice that Håvard and Kjersti got along so well, she said. Kjersti was anything but easy to deal with, as she knew from her own experience.

'But perhaps it's easier for you who are a man,' she said, laughing.

Håvard threw his six nets in those places which Kjersti showed him. Then he took over the oars and rowed back home again. The lake was dead calm now in the evening; all colors were softened after sunset, and hills and meadows were mirrored in the lake with even more softened colors. Kjersti sat in the stern, quiet and pensive, gently rippling the surface of the water with a finger every now and then. In the wake behind her finger, the ruffled water shone like matte gray silk.

They walked back up from the boat landing, along the overgrown path. Dew was falling so their shoes got wet. The swallows were gone, but bats flew back and forth above their heads – now it was their turn to chase the flies. They flew noiselessly, like dark nocturnal shadows of a bird.

Kjersti lagged behind on the way up, picking flowers for a nosegay. Håvard knew she would put it in water, and in the morning she would bring it to Mari. They would probably be somewhat faded by then – such flowers faded quickly – but her gift was no less sincere for that.

Rønnau sat waiting on the porch. He could see that she was a bit startled when he turned the corner of the barn. She got up and walked a few steps down the yard to meet him, and he could feel his heartbeats, heavy and sweet, in his very throat.

They stood beside each other awhile, looking about them. Kjersti passed them and went in. Everything was so tranquil. Late evening, the month of July, summertime.

Rønnau drew a couple of deep breaths. Then she turned toward him.

'It's getting late. Time to go in.'

The Family Dagger

*T*he day he, Rønnau, and Kjersti came down from the summer dairy, Håvard almost begrudged himself the time to eat. He had to go down and look at the meadow. This meadow had become his child, in some way. Nothing had come of the other child, so . . .

But it didn't quite look the way he had imagined it would down there. As a matter of fact, he thought it was pretty much the same as before. It had gotten *a little* drier perhaps, but . . . And no water trickled down through the drainage ditch. It was quite dry.

He asked himself if it could be a mistake to make closed ditches. Had they collapsed so that the water couldn't find an outlet? But he chucked that idea right away – he himself had been present at all times, and he knew that the ditches were in order.

He surveyed the meadow one more time, checking if the grade was correct – sure, the water should be running.

But it wasn't running. And the meadow was just as wet. Nearly so, at any rate.

Did the water sit that damn tight in this swampy soil?

But he knew how impatient he could be. Take it easy now, he said to himself. Such a meadow, which has lain there waterlogged for a thousand years, won't dry out in a few days. Weeks or months may pass before everything will be all right.

Little by little he managed to persuade himself that everything was in order. He had to give the water a little time. Until around harvest time, then he would see. He forced himself to stay away from the meadow during the two weeks before the haying season. But he thought about it every day – had he made a mistake someplace? But he couldn't believe that either.

Then came the haying season, and he had more than enough to do for a couple of weeks.

Until around harvest time, he'd said to himself. But he couldn't wait that long. One day at the beginning of August they were through with the haying. They finished in good time before supper. In the kitchen they were cooking the traditional cream porridge, and he went down to the cellar and fetched beer and brandy; but then he couldn't help himself any longer – he went down to the meadow to take a look.

The meadow lay there just as wet. The only thing that was dry was the big drainage ditch. Everything was as it had been a month ago.

He couldn't understand it.

He noticed that two of his cotters gave him a queer glance as he came walking up the field again. They were Martin and Edvart.

He noticed that these same cotters were glancing over at him during supper, too. They quickly withdrew their eyes when he looked at them, and their faces at once grew serious and impenetrable. But he had perceived a gloating look in their eyes during the brief moment before they withdrew their glances.

Oh, well. They'd been to the meadow and knew that he had been down there, too. They were delighted that he'd worked to no purpose. It was as simple as that.

That was how the cotters regarded him, these two anyway. And what about the others?

He looked around him at the table. There sat Amund and Per. He knew all too well how far he could trust them. There sat Jon, the hunter. Him he could trust – that is, about him he knew that he didn't care a damn either about the master, his meadow, his many plans, or his crabby cotters. What Jon wanted to do right now was to go fishing in the woods.

The following morning he was down in the meadow once more. The cotters were at the farm that day, too – many things had to be fixed and put back in their places after the haying season.

In the meadow everything was as before. And he couldn't think of an explanation. The meadow ought to have been dry by now. Some water should be trickling through anyway.

There wasn't a trickle of water.

As he came back up he noticed that Martin and Edvart were putting their heads together. He liked it even less than before. He dropped by at Jon's and asked him to come with him to the meadow. 'Perhaps you'll understand more than I do,' he said.

Jon's face hardened immediately. He followed him in silence.

They surveyed the meadow together. But it was as he had seen it for himself – the meadow lay there as wet as ever, there wasn't a trickle of water, and no explanation could be found.

'Can you understand this, Jon?'

'Hm. No. . . .' Jon scratched his head. 'It looks like those underground ditches of yours have gotten clogged up.'

He said it a little too lightly, a tiny bit too lightly. Håvard remained standing – suddenly he *saw* it. He didn't say another word to Jon but went straight up to Martin and Edvart out in the field.

'We are going to take a look at those closed ditches down in the meadow. Would you get some hoes and spades and come along?'

Looking at them, he saw what he had expected to see – Martin's leatherbrown face grew a little paler.

They followed him. Their cotter's crawl had never been slower, to his recollection.

They set to work. The two of them took their time. Håvard pushed Edvart aside: 'You go and help Martin, I'll take this one alone.'

Jon steadily worked his way down where the third ditch was going.

Håvard dug down to the upper layer of slabs.

He saw it right away – the topmost flat slabs had been taken out and clumsily put back again.

He lifted them off.

The ditch was walled up at the bottom. Blue clay had been smeared in-between the round stones, to make a tight wall which not a drop of water could trickle through.

The ditch was walled up this way for about two feet. Immediately above, the dammed-up water was pressing. The whole ditch above this point was full of water.

A couple of strokes with the spade, and the water streamed like a spring freshet down into the drainage ditch.

It was becoming difficult to breathe. Håvard straightened up. Martin and Edvart hadn't yet gotten down to the upper layer of stones in their ditch. They pretended not to have seen what Håvard had discovered.

At last they got down to the upper layer of slabs and gave Håvard an innocent, questioning look.

'Lift off the stones.'

They did, slowly and deliberately.

'Well, did you ever see the like – looks like some blue clay has collected here.'

Martin looked up innocently – a bit too innocently. When you took a peek at the ditch, it was all too clear what had happened. The uppermost slabs had simply been slapped down again, but underneath them the blue clay had been carefully smeared in between every stone – in a couple of places you could see the mark after the trowel.

Martin had regained his calm now. It was obvious what he meant to say: Nobody can catch *us* in this. He looked up at Håvard but couldn't resist casting a backward glance at Edvart first. And then he said, still with a voice that was a little too innocent:

'It sure is strange – that the drain should clog *that* fast!' He sent a brief, almost invisible, sneer in Edvart's direction.

Then Håvard struck.

The blow was heavier than he had intended. Martin fell and didn't rise again, and the next moment Håvard sat on top of him.

'Hey there!'

It was Jon who cried out. He had sat down on the big boulder, the Mons stone, as they called it. Looking up, Håvard discovered that, without knowing it, he had pulled his knife and raised it, ready to strike.

He let go of Martin, got up, and replaced the knife in its sheath.

Then he turned toward the other one, Edvart. 'Did you have any part in this?'

Edvart squirmed now, and the sneer had vanished. His face looked ashen through the tanned skin as he stood there stammering.

'Only on one – the others Martin did alone.'

'Phoo!'

Jon, who had sat quietly on the boulder all along, relieved himself of a jet of tobacco juice.

When had they done it? Håvard wanted to know.

Oh, it was done a couple of nights while Håvard was staying at the summer dairy. Martin came and said to him one evening . . .

Jon blew his nose energetically. On edge, Edvart started, lost his thread, and stood there stammering. But he managed to say this much – it had happened a little over a month ago.

That is, just a few days after the work was finished.

'We did it just for fun!' Edvart said.

Martin slowly sat up. He rubbed his chin and spat red a couple of times – had bitten his tongue, most likely. He didn't seem too happy as he got to his feet and brushed off a bit of dirt and clay.

'Get into the field and go to work again!' Håvard said. And he added, in a furious rage which refused to simmer down, 'By rights I should hand you over to the sheriff!'

They shuffled off, the two of them. Håvard, who remained, felt like biting his tongue too. The sheriff! A self-respecting freeholder didn't call in the sheriff because he had a little row with a couple of cotters. He settled that sort of thing by himself.

Jon sat on the boulder as before, calmly watching Håvard. Håvard was still seething. Suddenly he turned to Jon.

'Did you know anything about this?'

Jon replied, slowly, 'I don't have to answer that.'

'Why didn't you let me know?'

Jon got up. He looked coldly at Håvard.

'I'll tell you. Because I don't give a damn either about you or your meadow. It's not my meadow, and not my ditches. By the way' – and his sudden anger vanished – 'by the way, I thought that what they did, Martin and Edvart, was a dirty trick. And I'd certainly meant to let you know. But then it occurred to me that, if you were worth your salt, you would find out for yourself.

'But remember – I don't give a damn!'

Håvard had to laugh. 'You don't mince your words, do you. But perhaps you could explain one thing. I realize that a cotter doesn't like to work any harder than he has to, for those miserable four shillings a day. But why would he get up at night and toil for hours to reduce his day's work to nothing?'

Jon looked away. 'Oh, they probably didn't hatch the idea by themselves,' he remarked. 'And you can't be sure they did it for nothing either.'

Håvard and Jon mended the three ditches and replaced the soil on top. Already before they had finished they could hear the purling of water in the drainage ditch.

Afterward Håvard was lost in thought. He seemed far away for a moment. Then he asked if Jon had decided to go fishing upcountry.

Yes, he had. Tomorrow, in fact. Had thought he would take along a couple of nets, a bit of salt, and a good-sized tub – he meant to salt and smoke some fish for the winter.

'If you pay well, I might let you have twenty-five pounds or so,' he said.

Perhaps. That wasn't what Håvard had had in mind, but . . .

He stood for another moment. Then he seemed to make up his mind about something.

'Could you come with me up to the smithy for a moment?' he said.

Then he went on to explain.

'This knife has almost made me kill a man twice. The first time was at my sister's wedding up in Telemark. Then they had to lift me off the poor wretch who was laid out. The second time you saw yourself, an hour ago. The third time it could be worse. I mean to forge it onto a scythe, so it won't cause any more misfortunes.'

He didn't mention Tonè, who had returned the knife before she jumped into the waterfall.

'It didn't end up in murder exactly today, but it sure was close!' Jon said. 'I could see your face when you swung the knife. So perhaps it's just as well to forge it onto a scythe – if the strength is in the knife, I mean.'

When they got to the smithy and had made a fire in the forge, Jon stood looking at the knife a moment.

'This is an awfully handsome knife!' he said. 'Longer than ordinary knives too. It's really too bad . . .

'I've heard that you can take the magic out of knives and such if you put them in a basin of water which somebody has recited a spell over, and place the basin on the church altar three Thursday evenings in a row. But you have to do it alone. And to risk that is a touchy business. But what a handsome knife!'

'You see, it's no ordinary knife,' Håvard said. 'Look at that knife handle. It's an old sword hilt. And the blade has a double edge, as you can see, so it looks more like what's called a dagger, but wider.

'They call this knife our family dagger.[26] It's blue, as you can see, and sharp – if I wanted to I could shave with it.'

He ended up by telling Jon the story of the knife – that it had once been a sword and had belonged to his ancestor, an outlawed knight who had sought refuge up there in Telemark.

He mentioned the threatening verse which the old witch had mumbled to him at his sister's wedding.

The family dagger is good as gold,
as good as the gold of Grane.[27]
But if you draw it in your own yard,
it will be to your own bane!

He concluded, 'Not that I believe in such things, but . . . Every now and then it almost feels as though there sits some power in this knife.'

'Hm.' Jon stood lost in thought for a moment. 'Sure, one has to pay close attention to such things. And that verse – it sounded old and *strong*. I think I would obey that verse.

'But you know, if the power to kill sits in that knife, it won't do much good to just forge it onto a scythe. In any case, you have to find someone who'll read a spell over it.'

Håvard remarked he didn't believe very much in such things, as he had told him. Then he heard a voice inside him asking: Why, then, are you forging it onto this scythe?

'I, too, had a family heirloom,' Jon said. 'That is, it wasn't a knife, but a ring . . .

'My mother was in service in Sweden for a year. That's where I was sired. My father was a Swedish captain; Mother even told me his name. It was something with *von*. But when she realized she was going to have me, this captain, you know, gave her a ring and a few dollars, and she went back home again. Then she married the fellow they used to call my father. Well, she had to give him those few dollars, of course.

---

26. This dagger plays an important role in both *The Family Dagger* (*Arvestålet*, 1941) and *The Troll Circle*. There was an old prophecy that once in every third generation a man of the Viland family would commit murder because of women; most recently it happened to Håvard's great-grandfather. When a witchlike relative scrutinizes Håvard at his sister's wedding (related in *The Family Dagger*), uttering a couple of sibylline quatrains (*stev*) with the warning, 'If you draw it in your own yard, / it will be your death,' he dismisses this as 'stuff and nonsense.' The following day, however, in a fight provoked by his drunken rival, Håvard comes within an inch of murder.
27. The horse of Sigurd the Volsung, Germanic legendary hero celebrated in several Edda poems and in the *Nibelungenlied*.

'That ring, though, she gave to me. Then, as ill luck would have it, I lost it when I was drunk.'

Really. So Jon, too, came of gentlefolk!

Oh well, everybody no doubt came of gentlefolk. If Adam was a gentleman, anyway.

Håvard chopped off the point of the scythe.

'I can make myself a knife blade out of this point, I suppose,' he said.

When they had finished, Jon made the sign of the cross over the scythe and said, 'I'll keep an eye on this scythe. I think it'll be an awfully good one.'

No sooner had Håvard forged the knife onto the scythe than he regretted it.

The family dagger – the finest heirloom he had – to have forged it onto a scythe as though he were a frightened cotter!

He probably didn't even have the *right* to do what he'd just done. This knife belonged to the family. He himself was only a kind of steward.

The power to kill – did he really believe that this knife possessed such an evil power? No doubt he did, since he'd come up with such a foolish idea.

His grandfather had the ill luck to kill a man with this knife, that was true enough. But no action was ever brought against him, because it was in self-defense – two men attacked him with a knife at a wedding, and one of them never got up again.

Håvard kept the handle, the old sword hilt. It was of iron or some similar material, but with rings of fine gold threads wound on top of the iron. If it entered his mind, he was man enough to forge the knife out of the scythe again.

But in that case he would do it by himself. Jon was just too superstitious.

Anton

ne rainy evening at the end of the first week of August, there came an unexpected visitor to Olstad. This was Anton Måsåmyra, a hired hand at the parsonage.

Since it was now between the work seasons, only the members of the household were in the kitchen – Rønnau, Håvard, and Kjersti; Lars, the young servant; and one of the housemaids. The other maid was at the summer dairy with the dairymaid.

It was cold and dark for early August, so they had made a big fire on the hearth, and the pine sticks in the chimney hold were lighted; they filled the large room with a fluttering yellow light.

Anton was drenched. His hair was sticking to his head, and his clothes were dripping wet as though he'd been lying in the lake – a puddle formed on the floor under his chair as he sat there with his cap on his knees. With his pointed nose, buck teeth and fidgety eyes, he resembled a half-drowned rat. But there was still plenty of life in him – his glance was so busy, darting hither and thither, from one person to another, it looked as though he was out to rob them with his naked eye.

Håvard was anything but pleased to see him – he knew him a little too well. Anton was a poor specimen, good at shooting off his mouth but no good as a worker. Nor was he particularly honest. You could easily tell he'd just been chased away from the parsonage. And so he came here to Olstad, hoping they might take him in.

The others looked him over – Lars with unconcealed wonder in his fair, freckled face, the housemaid rather indifferently – but then, Anton wasn't much to look at. Kjersti sat quietly in her corner. Rønnau had assumed her hard expression.

They were about to have supper, and Rønnau invited Anton to join them. She didn't have to ask him twice, and he helped himself generously to the offered fare, barley mush and curdled milk.

Afterward he just sat there, unable to say what he had on his mind. This was so unlike him that Håvard had to take a second look at him. But he merely saw what he had known at once – that Anton was in a fix again, and scared.

When Håvard and Rønnau were the only ones left in the kitchen, he finally managed to tell them that he had quit his job at the parsonage and would like to enter into service here at Olstad, if they could use him.

Why had he quit?

Oh, well – he hesitated – it was because of this new curate, he was such a stickler in everything. He had accused him of staying all night with the maid who slept in the kitchen, and it wasn't even true – he'd just sat on the edge of her bed for a little while, and only once. But the parson's wife sided with the curate – he'd become so grand after his engagement to Miss Lise, every word he uttered was like gospel truth.

This last bit of news, which Håvard hadn't heard, gave him something to think about. So poor Lise was getting herself a husband, after all. The new curate wasn't much to look at either, but . . . He was a pretty good preacher, though, and he even knew something about farming.

Håvard had lost the thread of Anton's story, and it was just as well. What he told them was probably a lie anyway.

He would have liked to tell Anton to go to hell but couldn't quite bring himself to do it; the poor fellow was so utterly down-and-out that it would almost be like stepping on someone who'd been knocked down.

The upshot was that they gave him a hay sack to sleep on in the barn overnight. They would talk about the rest in the morning.

On his way back from the barn Håvard thought it over. One thing was certain: to take on Anton as a hired man was out of the question. They were well served by Lars, with his youth, his red hair, and his freckles – he was smart, easy to teach, and reliable. But you couldn't simply kick him out either – the poor fellow clearly had nowhere to go.

Then something occurred to him. At the edge of the forest eastward they had a vacant cotter's plot, called Kleiva. It was the poorest of all the cotter holdings that belonged to the farm; the buildings were on the verge of collapse and nothing but sorrel grew on the small patches of tillage. But maybe they could let Anton move in there for the time being, as a cotter on trial, so to speak, for the rest of the summer.

Håvard didn't like that idea either, but . . . Later he discussed it with Rønnau in the bedroom.

Rønnau was somewhat doubtful. She thought this fellow had the look of a tramp. She knew a thing or two about his family, and it was anything but good. Their cotter's place was located near a bog, just barely inside the home parish. You could make out the little shack on your left hand when you rode to the parsonage from here, sitting at the edge of the forest – maybe Håvard had noticed it. Gypsies and such often hung out there. The fellow's mother was rumored to be a thief, and the same was true of several of the children. This one, Anton, she didn't know, but what she'd seen during those brief moments was enough to convince her that he was one of those who talked a lot and did very little.

She'd hit the bull's eye, and Håvard had to laugh.

There was still something else, Rønnau said. It was easy enough to take in a fellow like that, but not always quite so easy to get him out again once he occupied the plot. To be sure, you could come up with a pretext and throw him out with the law in your hand; but it would look bad and make the other cotters drag their feet even more – they were thick as thieves, he knew that. So once they took him in . . .

Still – perhaps there wouldn't be much of a risk if, as Håvard proposed, they let him stay up there at Kleiva on a sort of trial basis, until they knew a little more about what had happened at the parsonage.

'You shall have the last word on this,' Håvard said. 'But I would be glad if you could give him a place to stay, at least until we know some more.'

128

Håvard felt relieved. Or did he? A voice inside him whispered, Now you're doing something you'll regret.

So the following day Anton moved up to Kleiva. Håvard went with him and helped him put together a bed and a table. He got a straw mattress to sleep on, an old sheepskin, and a few pots and pans. Håvard realized that they would probably have to lend him some food and clothes, too – he evidently had nothing except what he stood up in.

Anton was given a bit of work to do at the farm and recovered surprisingly fast. His tongue started wagging again, he laughed and told stories, made fun of the other cotters, and always knew everything better than anybody else – after all, he came from the parsonage, where he'd been trained both by the parson and by Håvard himself. Slipping back and forth like a squirrel, he was everywhere except where he'd been set to do some chore.

He was thriving. Tales of all sorts streamed like a sickening vapor from his mouth. The other cotters were amused and occasionally sent Håvard a quick glance. So this was the fellow worker he had brought with him up here, that new master of theirs. . . .

A week went by. The following Sunday there was a service in Nordbygda, and Parson Thurmann himself came, accompanied by Ola Viken, as modest as ever – it had become established custom for the parson not to ride that lonesome road by himself.

This time the parson, reluctant to abandon the place altogether, stayed overnight at the parish clerk's, but after the sermon he came to Olstad for dinner. He felt happy at Olstad, the parson did.

As they were taking care of the horses, Håvard asked Ola what had happened to Anton.

'Oh, he probably stole something from the storehouse,' Ola said indifferently.

Ola couldn't stand Anton.

After dinner, while Rønnau was in the kitchen, Håvard questioned the parson about Anton. Had he been fired?

So, Anton had turned up here, had he? The parson grew silent and thoughtful. Hm! Hm!! Håvard finally had to ask him point-blank what had happened. 'Hm. Well. You see . . .' The parson looked helplessly at Håvard.

Mrs. Maren Sofie had noticed for some time that things were disappearing from the storehouse. Then one evening she caught Anton and one of the maids, the one who slept in the kitchen, red-handed. They were standing on the storehouse steps with a ham, a cured leg of mutton, and a batch of flatbread in their hands.

Anton denied everything, saying he'd just been passing by. But Mrs. Maren Sofie fired them both on the spot. As far as poor Anton was concerned, moreover, there seemed to be sufficient reason to suspect him of having been party to a theft that was perpetrated by a company of gypsies on a certain evening last fall. In any case, it was a proven fact that the gypsies had spent the evening in the house of Anton's mother, where Anton too was present, and witnesses had met the self-same company on their way south, with Anton sitting in the front cart. Anton for his part, however, stubbornly denied any connection with this theft, maintaining that he had only been given a short lift by the gypsies. When the company pitched camp about three miles from the parsonage, he parted from the gypsies and returned by foot to the parsonage.

Did the parson have any advice for Håvard?

Yes – . No . . . Mr. Thurmann showed obvious signs of embarrassment. If the truth were to be told, he, the parson, had been disposed to temper justice with mercy, in the hope that the fright which the good Anton had experienced on this occasion would serve as a sufficient lesson to him. But the plain truth was that Maren Sofie, Mrs. Thurmann, wouldn't even discuss it. And therefore, well – yes – no . . . 'But if you, my dear Håvard, are willing to take the risk that undoubtedly goes with having such an exceedingly unreliable person on the farm . . .'

On his way back home the parson was thoughtful and absentminded.

The following day Håvard went up to Kleiva and found Anton sunning himself by the wall. There was a smell of coffee from inside, wherever he'd gotten it from.

Anton immediately burst into tears when he heard that Håvard had spoken to the parson. And he told him an entirely new story at breakneck speed.

He hadn't told the *whole* truth the first time, when he'd related the episode with the maid, that was so – there had been a little something between them, sure enough. But only because he was much too kind and found it so hard to say no.

But then one evening, after everybody had – or should have – gone to sleep, he had dropped by the kitchen, but she wasn't there. So he took a stroll, as they say, to look for her. And there she stood on the storehouse steps, with a ham and a leg of mutton and flatbread.

Anton was so carried away that he forgot to cry.

'I got so scared. "Take it back again!" I said. But that same moment the parson's wife turned up. She must've been lying in wait.'

'Why didn't you tell this right away?' Håvard asked.

Anton burst into tears again.

'I didn't dare!' he stammered. 'I knew it must sound so without rhyme or reason. Who are you, Anton, I thought, that Håvard should believe you rather than such fine folk as the parson and the parson's wife?'

'But you couldn't help knowing that I would speak to the parson?'

'Sure. But I didn't dare think that far ahead.'

For that matter – and here Anton brightened perceptibly – *the parson* had not been quite sure. Actually, when he stopped to think, Anton was fairly certain the parson rather believed his story. But Mr. Thurmann, poor man, had nothing to say if the missus had set her mind on something, Håvard surely knew that. . . .

'By my soul's salvation, which is my hope, I swear I've spoken nothing but the truth!' Anton solemnly concluded.

And Håvard thought, Then this too is a lie!

But he didn't say anything.

Anton watched Håvard with a tear-stained face, scared and helpless but, as always, with something at the back of his shifty eyes. Scared, but cunning at the same time, and mildly expectant, as if experiencing a secret, uneasy pleasure: Will *this* play, I wonder?

'And what about that troop of gypsies which stole the salting tub from the parsonage storehouse last fall?' Håvard asked.

But Anton just waved his hands in protest.

That was sheer nonsense, nothing but slander. He rode in the cart a little while because it was so far to walk – he'd been home to see his mother, who was poorly. But when the gypsies pitched camp he left them and didn't stop until he got to the parsonage.

'So?' Håvard said. 'You told me – I had just come back from a trip to the city, remember – that you didn't get to the parsonage till the mid-morning meal or so, long after the theft had taken place . . .'

'Oh yes – no – .' Anton was confused, but only for a moment. 'I dropped in on a girl I knew!' he said.

Håvard thought, If you were involved in that episode, the devil should take you. It almost killed Ola.

'One thing is clear,' Håvard said. 'If I turn you away now, you'll have no choice but to hit the road and go begging. Do you understand that?'

'Yes,' Anton whispered.

Håvard said – with a sharper voice than he'd intended – that he refused to decide this matter. It concerned Rønnau as much as himself, and it would be up to her to say yes or no.

'You can wait here!' he said. 'I'm afraid this won't go well.'

When Rønnau had heard the story, she knew she had been right. If that bum was a thief as well, he had to go, the sooner the better.

She was so insistent that Håvard couldn't help remembering the parson's wife. The result was that he defended Anton more than he had intended.

'Mrs. Maren Sofie isn't always to be trusted that way,' he said. 'She's very hasty, and not a good judge of character.'

And he told her the story of the gypsies and the salting tub.

One night last September a troop of gypsies had stolen a big salting tub from the parsonage storehouse. The parson's wife suspected Ola, the farmhand, and had practically said in so many words that Ola was the thief. Ola – the proudest and most honest person Håvard had met up this way.

But everything was cleared up.

'I found Ola in the hayloft,' Håvard said. 'He sat with a piece of rope in his hand, staring up at a crossbeam. I had to call him three times before he heard me.

'What I wanted to say was only this,' Håvard continued, 'that, in reality, Mrs. Maren Sofie doesn't have much more proof against Anton than she had that time against Ola.'

He thought, Ola? Are you comparing Anton with Ola?

But he wouldn't give up, or couldn't.

He didn't tell Rønnau about the new things that had come to light, which might indicate that Anton had had quite a lot to do with those gypsies.

Rønnau was silent awhile.

'Do you believe, then, that Anton is as innocent as Ola was?' she asked.

'No!' Håvard said. 'But I believe he's had such a fright now that he will control himself. And if he doesn't, we'll just throw him out, without notice.'

In the end Rønnau gave in.

Anton could remain over the summer then, she said, but only on trial. They would see how he conducted himself. He could scarcely bring them to rack and ruin with his stealing during that time.

'In any case,' she said, 'from now on we must count on having a thief prowling between the buildings here!'

Håvard pushed it aside.

'One summer doesn't last for ever,' he said. 'In fact, it is late summer already.'

132

Håvard went up to Anton, who sat sunning himself by the wall, very small now.

'Rønnau will let you stay on trial,' he said. 'Only on trial. Rønnau will be keeping an eye on you. And remember, she understands a bit of everything and has sharper eyes in her head than the parson's wife. Now you know.'

'I'll behave myself this time,' Anton said – such a strange sentence coming from him that Håvard could only stare at him.

Once more the thought flashed through his head, Now you've done something you'll regret.

Nonsense! he thought the next moment. What kind of harm could a poor fellow like Anton do to anybody?

Still, it was a fact that for as long as he'd known Anton, he'd seen him become malicious if someone did him a favor. His mildest response in that case was slander. Strangely, he did seem to have a sort of pride, which made him think it shameful to accept help.

But he was constantly in need of help.

Fortunately he had the ability to forget – otherwise he would have had too much to worry about. After some time, the memory of favors bestowed gave way to an obscure dislike. A little more time, and it was all forgotten. He didn't bear grudges for long.

No, do harm to him? Håvard? That harm couldn't amount to very much.

But walking back home from Kleiva, Håvard still couldn't help wondering. Why had he gone so out of his way to help this poor fellow, whom he didn't even like, not one bit?

And as soon as he'd asked the question, he knew the answer.

He didn't like Anton, but he knew all his frailties. And therefore he seemed to give him a sense of security – became almost a sort of friend, at least compared to these cotters, about whom he knew only one thing: that they would gladly stab him in the back for any reason at all, if only they dared.

So Anton continued to live at Kleiva, on trial. And he did bring some trouble, as it turned out. After a few days a woman, no longer young, arrived at Kleiva. It was his sister, who was moving in to take over the housekeeping. He seemed unable to find himself a woman of his own, in spite of all his dirty talk and brag.

They got a goat on loan from Olstad, and Håvard helped him repair the little cow barn, so the goat wouldn't freeze to death at night come winter.

Håvard had to help with other things too, for they were as poor as church mice. Only trifles, but – one more sheepskin, a few more pots and pans, a bit of herring and flatbread, an old dress for this sister of his. . . .

But, surprisingly enough, Anton behaved better than before. He even curbed his tongue, at any rate when Rønnau was in the kitchen.

He was scared of Rønnau. But he worshiped her too, almost as if she were a queen and he her slave. He became virtually a mind reader as far as Rønnau was concerned, dropping whatever he was carrying and rushing up to give Rønnau a hand – he carried in firewood, fetched water, helped her bring in the wash, repaired the old mangle in the north attic.

Rønnau laughed, but she liked it.

Just before the winter nights, which fell in mid-October, she said to Håvard:

'I think we'll let him stay. He's no worse than the others.'

But in the meantime all sorts of things had happened.

An Evening in August

O ne day around breakfast time Lars, the servant, came rushing into the kitchen, his red hair on end – he was in the habit of running his hands through his hair whenever something special was up.

'Håvard, there have been thieves and scoundrels in your potato field!' he yelled.

Håvard went down there with him. And, sure enough, what he saw could only have been done by scoundrels.

This potato field was Håvard's luckiest undertaking. The sandy soil was just right, the field faced reasonably south, and he himself had been in charge of all the work. The plants were coming along fine and were now in full bloom. But someone or other hadn't been able to bear the sight of it: nearly one-fourth of the plants had been pulled up and lay scattered all over. The person involved had clearly wanted to do more damage, but he must've gotten frightened by something or other.

'I believe it was me who frightened him,' Lars said. 'Or them. Because there were two – I could make out talk. I came walking . . .'

Lars began to stammer, but this much was clear. He had been seeing Oline, his girlfriend, home in the evening – she was a maid at Berg. Returning by way of the footbridge, he heard two people talking in low voices after he got across. They must have heard him too, for they took to their heels in the direction of the bridge farther north.

'That's why I went down to the potato field early this morning,' he said.

'I wanted to see what they had been up to down there in the middle of the night.'

Håvard was so angry he felt sick.

He had a fairly good idea who it might be.

He went in and told Rønnau about the vandalism.

She didn't say anything, only gazed at him. And he knew they were both thinking of the same person.

They had a long day of it.

After the mid-morning meal Håvard went to the potato field with a bucket and a hoe. He filled his bucket with the small potatoes – it could have become a couple of barrels. But though the potatoes were small, the biggest were eatable – indeed, they would be party fare with herring and butter.

They would have them for supper, he agreed with Rønnau.

At first the cotters were suspicious – did this Håvard fellow mean to poison them too? But when they saw that Håvard helped himself, they cautiously followed suit. When they were through, there wasn't a single potato left in the big dish.

So they had learned, at least, that this new dangerous plant tasted quite good. But figured one way – two barrels of potatoes – it became an expensive meal; regular party fare would have been cheaper.

In the evening Håvard made himself ready for his night watch. He bundled up – it was chilly at night, and it might take time.

He had been to the pasture and cut himself a thick birch switch in the afternoon. It wasn't very likely that the same person would return again this evening. But if he was mad enough to try, he would get a rap he remembered.

Håvard didn't go down to the potato field until it had become fairly dark. Anyway, that occurred rather early, considering it was not yet the middle of August – it was a moonless night and the sky was overcast.

Only Rønnau knew what he was up to – the situation being what it was at the farm, they had better not say too much.

He sat there waiting for an hour, then another hour. People had gone to bed everywhere a long time ago. Nobody was likely to come tonight; still, Håvard had decided to stay down there till around midnight, perhaps a little longer.

If the scoundrel was the one he had in mind, he was anything but stupid. He might just figure that nobody would expect him to return the following night.

At that very moment, around eleven or a little later, he heard something – cautious, stealthy footsteps along the grassy slope.

Two shadows.

He waited until he heard them pulling up the first potato plants. Then he jumped up and ran toward the two shadows. He may have let out a yell too, but couldn't quite remember afterward.

He was able to make out both shadows now – they had taken to their heels, running away in different directions.

Håvard pursued one of them and was catching up with him, but not fast enough – he cursed his thoughtfulness in putting on such heavy clothes. He wasn't quite sure, but he had the impression that the dim shadow in front of him was dragging one of his feet. They were headed toward the footbridge across the brook.

When he'd nearly overtaken him, he swung the thick birch switch and struck with all his might. The blow hit the man, whoever he was, on his left shoulder. Håvard could hear the crunching of bones, followed by a grunt as he crashed to the ground. But the same moment Håvard himself was tripped up by a root or something and fell flat on his face. When he got on his feet again it was too late – the shadows were gone. He thought he heard a rustling sound among the twigs and leaves near the brook farther up, in the direction of the little bridge, but it was too late to do anything more about it now.

Håvard went in and told Rønnau, who sat up waiting for him, what had happened.

'There were two. I was able to give one of them a whack with the switch. I think he'll remember it for a few days – I thought I heard bones snapping. The blow hit him on the left shoulder.'

'Could you tell who it was?'

'No. But I think – I'm not quite sure – he dragged his left foot a bit.'

However it was, the following day they heard that Kerstaffer had fallen down from the barn bridge the evening before and damaged his left shoulder. Quite badly too, said the fellow who related it – they strongly suspected that bones had been broken.

After a couple of days had passed, they heard that Kerstaffer was poorly. A severe pain had settled in his shoulder – it hurt so badly he couldn't get a wink of sleep, either night or day.

It was agreed that Lars was to keep watch at the potato field. Håvard let him have his birch switch.

'But I don't think you'll have any use for it,' he said. 'I bet it'll be quiet for a few days now.'

And it turned out he was right. The potato field was left in peace.

A few more days passed. Then it became known in the hamlet that two of the cotters at Berg had had to take Kerstaffer to the little fortress town, where they had a barber-surgeon, or whatever they called it.[28] He was a German, it seemed, but had taken part in the war and knew a little of everything. The shoulder had gotten inflamed.

They had fetched a neighbor, a wise old woman. She was of the opinion the shoulder had gotten dislocated, but the arm hurt so much that nobody could touch it. In the end Kerstaffer lay there babbling incoherently. And so Mons Myra carried him down to the boat. They rowed him to the end of the lake, along the little stream and up the river to the fortress town. It was a trip of twenty-five miles each way, and it took them three days back and forth. Kerstaffer remained in town, and his seventeen-year-old boy stayed with him. The cotters related that the surgeon shook his head when he saw the shoulder. It was the first time in his experience that a fall off a barn bridge had had that kind of effect, he said.

People talked and talked about this when they met.

Another couple of days passed. Then, one afternoon, a rare visitor appeared at Olstad. It was Mons Myra who came lumbering by.

'I'm here on a strange errand, I must say,' he said. 'The fact is that one of our lunatics is dead set on seeing you, Håvard. In one way he's probably the craziest of them all, but in another way he's without doubt the wisest; at any rate he's got second sight, as one and all of us at Berg have noticed. By the way, he's one of those who howl when a weather change is coming. But enough of that – this lunatic sits there all day saying he wants to see you.

' "I want to see Håvard. I want to see that barn bridge which walks on two legs – and which fell down on Kerstaffer's shoulder!" he says.

'It makes the other lunatics so restless, and that's why I thought that if you'd be so good as to take a walk over to us . . .'

Håvard went with him.

'The basement looks worse than usual now that the old man is gone,' Mons said as they stood in the yard after getting there. As you know, Kerstaffer lets the best of these loonies work in the fields; he himself usually walks around supervising them, whip in hand. That way there is more room in the basement, and we can clean it every once in a while. But nobody else wants to take the responsibility for letting them out, because Kerstaffer himself is the only one who can keep them under control. So now they're sitting

28. The fortress town is Kongsvinger. Situated about twenty-five miles southeast of the novel's setting, the fortress was founded in 1681–82 as protection against the Swedes.

there behind locked doors, throwing porridge and filth all around them. I just wanted to warn you – it's an ugly sight you're going to see, and you'd better harden yourself to it.'

And an ugly sight it was.

They sat around the walls in the dark basement. The stench came at you through the door, thick enough to make you dizzy. It was dark down there, with a rattling of iron. What he'd heard was true – some of them were chained to the wall.

'We have tried to use ropes,' Mons said. 'But they chew them to bits.'

Facing the door sat a fellow dressed in sackcloth and rags. His food trough stood beside him. The pair of eyes he fixed upon the two who entered were the strongest and wisest eyes Håvard had ever seen. Sitting there silent amid the stench and the semidarkness, this man did nothing but *see*, as though he wanted to see holes through Håvard. The others were mumbling or laughing foolishly, beating the floor with their hands, or befouling themselves as crazy people do. He alone sat there quietly, looking.

'He's the most dangerous of them,' Mons said. 'Even Kerstaffer is scared of him.'

For days Håvard felt those eyes upon him, wherever he stood or went. And afterward, every time he heard the familiar howl at a weather change, he again could see them before him.

Quite a guy, Kerstaffer was. To have this fellow and the rest of them living under the floor every day of his life. What's more, to be able to thrive on it, as he seemed to.

'A couple of years ago, Kerstaffer felt it was really too bad that this big, strong fellow should never make himself useful on the farm,' Mons said. 'So one day he went down and released him from his chains – well, he did take me along. But no sooner was the man free than he had his hands around Kerstaffer's throat, and I had to use *force* to work him loose. Kerstaffer could only whisper for a whole week afterward.

'Since then he's been sitting like you see him now.'

The lunatic took a quick look at Mons.

'You be quiet!' he said, in a powerful, agreeable voice. Then he turned his strong, sort of shiny eyes on Håvard again.

'You, I see, have taken on the devil himself!' he said, still in his powerful, calm, agreeable voice. 'May the Lord help you – if he can.'

Then he made a little sign with his chained hands. It was as though he said that now they could go.

He didn't look at them again.

They left.

Word had spread all over the hamlet already that Kerstaffer had tried to destroy Håvard's potato field and had gotten a bone-crushing whack on his shoulder.

People didn't seem to be very sorry; that happened seldom here anyway, as long as the damage concerned someone else.

'So you are that barn bridge which fell down on Kerstaffer!' people would remark to Håvard.

Some tried to call him simply the barn bridge, Lars related. But the name didn't stick, it wasn't funny enough.

Greetings from Tonè

One morning a stranger rode into the yard at Olstad. He was a fairly young man, about Håvard's own age, and by his speech you could tell he was from somewhere in the west. He said he was a helper to Mons Bruflaten, the horse dealer. They had come by the woodland trail those twenty miles from the neighboring parish to the north, and were headed south toward the capital and from there east to Smålenene County.[29] Bruflaten sent greetings and wanted to ask if Håvard had a meadow or pasture where he could stay with his drove for two or three days. The drove consisted of twenty-two horses. Bruflaten himself would come, with the drove and the other helper, in a couple of hours, and intended to stop up the road.

Håvard asked the man to wait. He never made a decision in such matters without first talking to Rønnau. He asked her if she remembered Mons Bruflaten, the horse dealer who came uninvited to their wedding with six horses and sold every one of them before the wedding was over. He added, 'You know – that lame, one-eyed man with the smart nose. I knocked about with him a couple of summers, and we had meant to work together for one more year; but then this thing with you and me came in between. There is that open meadow up in the pasture, you know, and right now there aren't any horses or cattle there, so I thought . . .'

Rønnau remembered Bruflaten very well and had liked him quite all right. Sure, he was welcome to use that meadow in the pasture. A bit of horse manure would remain, if nothing else, so that next year the grazing would be somewhat better.

There was only one thing she would like to know – did Bruflaten intend to stay at the farm during that time?

29. Smålenene County was the name of what is now Østfold County, located south of Oslo, between 1662 and 1919.

Håvard didn't think so. Bruflaten always used to arrange such things ahead of time, and Håvard was glad to be excused – Bruflaten was in the habit of carousing till the wee hours of the morning when he traded horses.

'You know, with such a drove of horses around you, it's almost like being at a party,' Rønnau said. 'Everyone drops by and takes a drink or two, and everyone gets cheated – except for the horse dealer naturally – and most people are well satisfied afterward. That's how stupid farmers are.'

Håvard thought that Bruflaten wasn't one of the worst that way. He used to say that it was a poor horse dealer who cheated so big the first time that he couldn't go back and cheat once more. But one thing was for sure: Mons was always making money, regardless of whether he bought or sold.

Lucky that the meadow was so far from the farm, Rønnau said. They would probably still hear some of the racket.

A couple of hours later Bruflaten did indeed turn up. Håvard took him to the pasture, and he was quite satisfied – the meadow was free and open and lay in the middle of the hamlet, a convenient distance from the road. No thanks, he had made arrangements to stay with Amund Moen.

Håvard remembered that those two had hit it off very nicely at the wedding.

Rønnau and Håvard dropped by the first afternoon. Bruflaten had sold a couple of horses; usually there wasn't much trading the first evening; it was only the second and third day, after several people had picked out a horse they liked, that it started to move along briskly.

Bruflaten received Rønnau as though she were an old flame of his. She absolutely had to take a drink with him – he had French brandy in his nice silver pocket flask. 'A pity I met you too late, Rønnau!' he said. 'You know, I was once a handsome fellow, too!'

Bruflaten was also his old self in other ways – not sober, but not drunk either. He was in a good humor – the trading had been nice and steady all summer, from Telemark down to the low-lying areas west of the fjord. They'd been as far north as Hedemarken,[30] buying and selling. He'd planned to sell the remainder down in Smålenene County, where he could get rid of the heavy horses any time.

A handsome fellow? That must have been a long time ago, if ever. One

---

30. Now Hedmark. A large county north of Oslo which borders on Sweden in the east and South-Trøndelag County in the north. Nord-Odal, Hoel's native township in Hedmark County and the model for Nordbygda, is located sixty miles northeast of Oslo, between the district of Solør in the east and Upper Romerike in the west. The lake which is so frequently referred to is Storsjøen (The Big Lake). Sand, where Hoel was born and grew up, is on the west side of the lake.

eye missing, gouged out by the horn of a bull in his youth. The other one, though, had seen most things. But the most striking part of him was the nose, long and red and dented, with a network of veins – hundreds of purchase toasts had left a monument there. But this large nose was shrewd through and through, so it was a wonder that any farmer dared trade horses with it.

He had two helpers with him this time, and a woman besides, which went completely against local custom. Anyway, she'd just married one of his helpers, and they owned a farm where they would settle when the trip was over; but she wanted to see a bit of Norway first. 'Afterward there will be nothing except babies and diapers,' she used to say. A splendid woman, and as good at selling horses as any man.

'She's from Telemark,' Bruflaten said. 'Well, it's several parishes below where you're from, Håvard, so she doesn't know either you or your people. By the way, I stopped briefly in your home parish, let me see – it was around midsummer, as far as I remember. I even have a letter for you, from Jon the Schoolmaster.

'And there's something else I have to tell you. Gjermund, your father, was suddenly taken ill with pneumonia and died early this summer – he was a goner after three or four days. That's what Jon's letter is about, I expect.

'Oh, well. Gjermund, your father, was getting on in years, wasn't he. Over sixty, if I remember rightly.'

Bruflaten dug up the letter from one of his thick pocketbooks.

Even now, in an hour of sorrow so to speak, when Mons put up the most sympathetic face he owned, he couldn't suppress a sly, clever glint in the depth of his eyes. How would Håvard take this, eh? After all, it hadn't been all roses between Håvard and his father – long before this thing with Tonè came up. Gjermund was stubborn and felt that Håvard took everything much too lightly. And he had never made a secret of it either.

There was just enough daylight left so that Håvard could read the letter. It was quite short this time. Jon wasn't the kind of person who would forget Tonè.

To

The Esteemed Haavard Giermundsen.

I take pen in hand to inform you that your father, Giermund, was suddenly taken ill with pneumonia on June 13th and after 4 days of suffering with high fever and delirium died on June 17th, last. It was a big blow for your mother, and now she sits mostly by herself and doesn't speak. The funeral went very well, for you must know that your father was a highly regarded man in the parish and had no enemies.

Your brother, Giermund, intends to change his state, it is said. The maiden's name is Maria, and she is from Grave. But I suppose you know about that.

Your mother begs to be remembered and says she often thinks about you and prays for you.

Jon Tollefsen
Schoolmaster

Håvard read the letter twice, while Bruflaten looked on.

He had meant to take Rønnau and go home afterward – he didn't feel like staying any longer. But it wasn't quite that simple.

Suddenly it looked as though every farmer up here wanted to offer him a drink. Hans Nordby, Amund Moen, Anders Flateby, and a good many others he scarcely knew. And all of them wanted to talk about Kerstaffer.

'There you've gotten a friend for life,' one of them remarked.

Håvard said he found it hard to believe that Kerstaffer had wanted to ruin his potato field. Anyway, it was pitch-dark. And he merely struck at a shadow – though he did hit something, that was true.

This answer was correct, he noticed.

'But we know Kerstaffer!' said another. 'And it's more than strange he should fall off the barn bridge the same evening!'

There were too many drinks, and Håvard tossed them off quickly just to get rid of people. He didn't feel at ease among these good-natured, half-drunk people, not this evening anyway.

Lars, the servant, was at the center of a throng. He was a trifle tipsy – well, more than a trifle.

At last they got away. Dark fell quickly as they walked downward.

'Mons brought a letter from home,' Håvard said – he was holding Rønnau's hand, the path being a little difficult for her in the semidarkness.

'Yes?'

'Father is dead. It happened two months ago.'

'I'm so sorry,' Rønnau said. 'Were you fond of him?'

'You know – he was my father, after all. A different sort of person, but . . . Too strict, perhaps.

'He thought I was frivolous, as it's called. He felt that what I did was mostly wrong. Perhaps it was, in a way. But . . .'

'I understand,' Rønnau said, 'I had a strict father too. Still, it was quite strange when he died.'

Håvard stopped. 'Is someone following us?'

But Rønnau hadn't heard anything. 'Let's sit down in the kitchen awhile,'

142

she said. 'You need to talk a little about your father, I think. We'll light a candle or two.'

Håvard sat at the kitchen table, where two candles had been lighted. Rønnau sat on a chair somewhat on the side. He didn't look at her, but sat staring into vacancy, as though he were speaking more to himself than to her. Still, it was to her and nobody else that he spoke.

'You are quite right about that,' he said. 'It's quite strange to lose your father. I haven't really been able to talk to him since I was eighteen, but he was there anyway, like a sort of bulwark, or what you will, between me and the great Lord himself. Now that bulwark is gone.

'It was often a bit bumpy between Father and me before I turned eighteen, too. We were so different. You met Gjermund, my brother, at the wedding this spring. He's like Father, so you'll understand. Father was dark, squarely built, serious, and – well, like my brother. As for me, I took more after Mother. But old people used to say it was I who took most after the old Viland family. Perhaps it wasn't as strange as it may sound; for Mother too was of that family.

'I may have been rather wild as a teenager. More so than Gjermund, my brother, and than Father himself had been, I believe. Father felt I was erratic, and told me so. But things never came to a head. Mother intervened, you see.'

'I can well believe it!' Rønnau said, smiling.

'Then there was my grandfather. He belonged to the fair sort, and he and my father didn't have very much to say to each other.

'When Grandfather was near death – actually it was the day he died – he called me in. He gave me that knife which is called the family dagger in our family. In a way it was the finest thing we had, and by rights it should have gone to my father. But Grandfather gave it to me because I had the birthmark in the right place, he said.'

'Oh, the birthmark you have right below your heart?' Rønnau said.

'Yes. It is said that the outlawed knight we are supposed to be descended from had such a mark – put on him by magic, it seems. Nothing but an old wives' tale, sheer nonsense, of course. But that's how I got that knife. And Father, you know, wasn't exactly thrilled about it.

'For my part, I would have preferred to give it to Father. But Father felt so insulted that I knew he would never accept it.

'From then on it was rather difficult for us to talk. . . .'

'What is it, then, that makes that knife so fine?'

'That, too, is nothing but nonsense, or so I believe. But it was said that the knife had once been a sword and had belonged to that outlawed knight who sought refuge in our out-of-the-way valley. It's from him the family is supposed to be descended. The king's men found him, and he was executed at the Brunkeberg Church – beheaded with the sword and not with the ax, because he was of noble birth.[31]

'One hears so many things. Do you remember that old ballad I have sung for you – about Vilemann and Signe? They say it is about that knight. But I can't believe that is true, because it has some very different things in it.'

He started humming the first verse:

Sir Vilemann unto his mother did come.
The cuckoo did crow.
Why be you so quiet, your cheek so wan?
       The dew drifts along
       and the hoarfrost falls far and wide.

'You remember – he rides to the Blue Mount to find his sister, who has been lost there, bewitched. Then he himself gets bewitched, forgets everything, and doesn't even recognize his sister. But then, many years later, he hears the church bells, recognizes and saves her, but is himself killed by the troll woman.'

'I remember,' Rønnau said. 'It's a strange ballad. But I cannot see that it tells anything like what you just told me.'

'Nor can I.'

There was a moment's silence.

'It's all so stupid!' Håvard said, as though to himself. 'There was nothing I wanted more than to give Father that knife.'

His voice softened as he said this.

Rønnau sat still, watching him. She knew he was far away now, somewhere up in Telemark.

After a while she said, 'I think it's time to go to bed, Håvard. You have gotten the worst of it off your chest now.'

'Perhaps,' he mumbled. His head felt heavy and strange. The drinks, no doubt.

'You just go,' he said. 'I have to check on the horses. I saw Lars up there – he was quite tipsy, so by now he's probably lying in a ditch somewhere.'

The fall night stood dark around him as he crossed the yard toward the stable. He was still taken up with what he'd been talking about.

'You see, I didn't take everything quite as lightly as you thought I did,

31. Brunkeberg is a parish in Kviteseid, Telemark.

144

Father,' he said, facing the darkness.

But nobody answered him.

He opened the door to the stable. A friendly whinnying came toward him from in there.

He took a pair of buckets and went to fetch water, twice, at the water tub. Then he wanted to give the horses some hay for the night, but discovered that Lars had forgotten to bring any from the hay loft. The big wicker basket – the osier tub, as they called it up this way – was empty. It was large, made of osier twigs which had been twisted and woven together, and had two shoulder straps, also of osier. When it was packed tightly, it was all a man could lift. He slung it over his shoulder and went to the hay loft. It was pitch-dark in there, but he knew where everything was.

He thought he heard a shuffling sound on the threshing floor and stopped for a moment; but it was nothing – the cat perhaps. Still, the moment the basket was full-packed and he was about to sling it over his shoulder, he did hear something.

'Håvard . . . ,' it said.

It could have been from the threshing floor, or from farther away – it seemed so faint and distant.

Strangely, it was Tonè who had called him. There was no mistaking that voice.

He stood there listening.

'It's Tonè,' came quite faintly and from far away, like a breath of wind.

He froze to the roots of his hair. His forehead broke out in a cold sweat.

'Is it you, Tonè?' he said.

He was answered by a cold laughter, it too from far, far away, as though it had wandered over wide spaces and along desolate paths before reaching him. But it wasn't Tonè's laughter, not as he had known it at any rate.

'Do you want anything, Tonè?'

No answer. But all along a faint sound was reaching his ear – it reminded him of the thin, fragile tune of a faraway wind, which can be sensed rather than heard beneath a cold, star-studded wintry sky.

'How are you, Tonè?'

At first, nothing. Then that cold laughter once again, far, so far, away. And then came, but so faintly that he wasn't sure he'd heard it:

'You know where I am now, don't you?'

He didn't hear or say anything more.

As he continued to stand there – he didn't know for how long, but it was a good while – he felt he was getting cold. He grabbed the heavy basket, swung it over on his back, and walked out of the hay loft – very slowly, as he had walked when he was a boy and the grownups laughed at him because he was afraid of the dark, and he would go out into the pitchy darkness to force himself not to be afraid. There was always someone behind him then; he knew there was someone behind him but forced himself not to turn around.

In the stable it was cozy. The horses whinnied at him again. Slowly and carefully, he divided the hay between them, patted their necks, went out, closed the stable door, and paced slowly across the dark yard toward the house.

The kitchen was black as a pit, and there was a smell of tallow from the extinguished candles. He knew there were embers under the ashes in the fireplace. He found a couple of sturdy pine sticks, blew till they kindled, and put the sticks in the chimney hold.

His ears were buzzing, due no doubt to the fact that he'd taken a drink too many.

He put his ear to the bedroom door and could hear that Rønnau was asleep.

Afterward he sat down at the broad kitchen table. He sat there for quite a while, staring before him with unseeing eyes.

The following morning many things looked different.

Could it all have been a prank by Mons Bruflaten? He was crude enough to do it, and the girl they had with them was from Telemark.

It could have been her.

It could – it could . . .

Bruflaten had played such pranks before. Håvard had been part of a couple of them himself.

But how could they have known he would go to the barn?

Was the whole thing something he *imagined* he heard? He had taken those drinks, after all. Nothing but fantasy?

Some of it, perhaps, but not everything.

The more he thought about it, the more certain he became that it was Bruflaten. But he wasn't certain enough to want to talk to him about it.

Anyway, he didn't plan to see him again this time around.

He put a packsaddle on Brownie and made ready to go to the summer dairy. It was time to fetch some butter and cheese.

Dobbin had gotten harness gall in the hay harvest – it was that stupid Edvart who was responsible for it. He would let him rest up.

Rønnau was rather surprised. Hadn't he planned to go over to Bruflaten? She seemed to remember that Håvard meant to buy a horse.

146

He *had* meant to, that was so. But he'd given the horses Mons had brought the once-over, and he didn't like them.

'As I have told you,' he said, 'I traveled with Bruflaten a couple of summers. I learned a little about horses then, enough to make me think twice before buying a horse from Mons.

'Bruflaten claims that every once in a while he talks to God. And if he has sold a horse without cheating, the Lord becomes stern and says:

'"Mons! Did I make you a horse dealer, or did I not make you a horse dealer?"'

No, they were probably better off for not buying that horse this time.

When Kjersti heard that Håvard was going to the summer dairy, she begged to be allowed to come along. Rønnau, who happened to be in a good humor, said she could stay up there until the end of the summer-dairy season – it would be over in about a week now.

Just before Håvard left he told Rønnau that if Bruflaten came and wanted to pay rent for the loan of the meadow, she should say they didn't want any. It was a parting gift from Håvard, she was to say.

There were quite a few chores to do at the summer dairy. It was late afternoon before Håvard got started on his way back. But he was taking home a nice bunch of trout from the dairy tarn.

It was evening when he reached Olstad. He could hear noise and shouting from the pasture.

He baked trout in the embers for Rønnau that evening.

'You shouldn't sit here being love-sick for Mons Bruflaten, you know. We can make a party ourselves,' he said.

Mons had, indeed, dropped by to pay rent. When he got Håvard's greeting, he just said thank you and left.

The following day Håvard took off for the forest to gather birch wood for the winter. He took along a food pack and stayed away the whole day.

The next morning the drove moved on. Rønnau and Håvard stood in the bedroom watching it leave. Bruflaten didn't ride over to say good-bye – he understood things quickly, Bruflaten did, when he wanted to.

They counted eighteen horses. That meant he had sold four. But later they learned that he'd bought three as well, so in reality he had sold seven. And he said himself that he seldom made less than ten dollars on a horse.

This time, as they learned later, he had sold two crib-biters, one that was blind in one eye, and one which had windgall. But the rest were fairly good horses.

His next stop was in the eastern corner of the home parish where Rønnau came from. Rønnau had asked him to greet her sister if he met her. She was married on a nice farm out there.

As time passed, Håvard became more and more convinced that it was Bruflaten who had played a joke on him that evening in the hay barn. But there were a couple of things he couldn't understand – above all, the fact that he had recognized Tonè's voice at first.

A doubt remained, which he felt most strongly when he was about to go to the hayloft on those dark fall evenings.

It had been a custom in the old days that the dairymaid would hold a lighted pine stick in her mouth when she went to the cow barn in the evening during the fall and winter, carrying a pail in each hand. But Håvard had forbidden the use of open fire in the hay barn. On a trip to the city that fall he bought himself a stable lantern, the same kind they had at the parsonage. Instead of cod-liver oil, they used melted tallow for it. It didn't give much light, but there was company in it.

The Sister

Rønnau had been in the habit of going out to the home parish to visit her family for a few days in the quiet period before the grain harvest. This year she was eager to have Håvard come along. They could stay with her sister, who had a nice farm out there. This was an old understanding.

Håvard wasn't very eager to take this trip just now; he felt there were too many things to take care of at home. It didn't make it any easier that Lars, the servant, had a message from home that his father had been suddenly taken ill, so he had to ask for a few days off. Lars was the next eldest son on a small farm in the northernmost part of the parish.

But the same day – it was the day Bruflaten left – they also heard something which had to be called good news. A message had come from the small fortress town that Kerstaffer would be staying there for another couple of weeks.

And so, as it turned out, Håvard went along with Rønnau anyway. He sent for Anton and gave him two tasks – he was to take care of the horses and to keep watch at the potato field in the evenings.

To be sure, he didn't seriously believe that the potato field was in any danger now that Kerstaffer lay sick many miles away; still, he was a little uneasy as they left.

He would have preferred to take Dobbin; but he hadn't yet completely recovered from the harness gall and needed another few days' rest.

They arrived around noon and were welcomed both by the sister and her husband. The farm was called Moen – a good farm. Håvard had been there a couple of times before but didn't have any clear recollection of the sister – she was that sort of person. The husband was withdrawn and rather taciturn. He was seldom seen in the house. They had two children, a boy and a girl, both teenagers. They too were withdrawn, as though they had lived under a strain. They mostly resembled their father.

In the afternoon Rønnau, Håvard, and Hans Moen paid a call to Håkenstad, Rønnau's home farm, next door to Moen. Her eldest brother, Håken, owned it now. They were to have an early supper there, and afterward Håken and Hans had meant to go and look at Mons Bruflaten's horses – he was staying at a farm a little farther on. The sister, Randi, didn't go along. She hadn't been feeling well lately, she said, didn't quite know what it was, a pressure in her chest and a slight cough, so she preferred to stay home.

Håken was a tall, quiet man, somewhat fairer than Rønnau. His wife was blond and cheerful, and the three children, a boy and two girls, also teenagers, were not at all withdrawn; they were happy and trusting. These people were a good breed, no doubt about it. The farm, sitting down by the river, was good too, slightly bigger than Olstad perhaps. But neither the brother nor the sister had any of the luster that Rønnau gave off, like a bright shimmer.

After supper, when the two men went to look at the horses, Rønnau and Håvard returned to Moen. It had been a long day and they turned in early.

The second afternoon Rønnau was to call on a woman friend from her childhood. But she let Håvard off the hook. 'Mari isn't very interesting,' she said. 'Nor did she make a very good marriage. But she would be so unhappy if she found out that I'd been over here in the east nook without dropping by. You just take it easy, Håvard – take a look at the farm and such.'

So Håvard wandered about by himself all afternoon and most of the evening.

Hans had gone over to see Bruflaten again – a brown mare had caught his fancy the previous evening.

The farm was good and well cared for but run in a somewhat old-fashioned way. Håvard realized he didn't have much to learn here, and in the end he betook himself to the parlor of the sister, Randi.

One of the maids set the table for supper. Randi sat quietly in her chair. The two children stayed in the kitchen.

Afterward Randi had the maid bring beer from the cellar. She didn't drink any herself, but urged Håvard to.

There was something she wanted to say but couldn't. Her eyes scrutinized him, then slipped away, only to return once more. There was something she wanted to get off her chest, all right.

He looked at her a bit more closely. She resembled Rønnau, in a way. But in another way she didn't look like her in the least. She was a couple of years older, he knew. She was a little fairer, shorter, and somewhat stout. She had a sort of withered look, as though she had grown up in the shade. Håvard realized he didn't care for this woman. He also realized that she, Randi, didn't care overly much for her handsome sister.

It must have been strange, she said, for Håvard to have come from so far away, to a parish which was so wholly different from what he had been used to, going by what she'd been told anyway. And to be married in Nordbygda, a place which was no better than a backwater – well, she thought so anyway. Rønnau wouldn't agree with her about that, but . . .

Rønnau didn't admit any more than she cared to. Nor did she make any slips of the tongue. She bore whatever burdens were placed upon her shoulders and never complained. Not that she had any reason to complain, at least not now. Everybody said they had never seen Rønnau so happy and so, yes, so *sparkling* as she was now since she'd been a young girl.

At that time, in her teens and early youth, she may have gotten a bit spoiled.

'All of us worshiped the very ground she trod on – Mother and Father, not to mention Håken and me. She was sort of the golden child in our family. We loved her so, all of us! It was nothing but Rønnau and Rønnau all day long!'

Randi quickly wiped one eye with the corner of her Sunday apron.

But later she had had her share of trouble, Rønnau too. She never said more than she meant to, as she'd told him, but . . .

No, Rønnau's life had certainly not been *only* a bed of roses, oh no.

Randi was newly married when her father suddenly became ill and died. But Rønnau, poor dear, was unmarried. She could have continued to live at home; but then Håken got married and . . .

'Imagine, to be from a good farm and then have to go into service!'

She was at the Mill, with the mill owner, for four years. The first two years as a regular maid, the last two as housekeeper. Oh, well.

'She had her troubles, all right. And I for my part thought more than once, Why don't you ever come and open your heart to me, Rønnau! You must know that I love you more than my own self. But no!'

Once again she dabbed her eye with the corner of her apron.

She paused a moment, and Håvard thought, Here it comes, I expect.

She resumed.

'The mill owner was a widower at that time,' she related. 'A respectable man, but . . .' His wife had died of pneumonia, and they didn't have any children. Whether there was something wrong with the wife, or . . . No, it couldn't be *him*, because he was remarried now and had a son. . . .

Randi had lowered her eyes and sat looking modestly at the floor.

It was said that Rønnau and the mill owner were secretly betrothed. Rønnau never mentioned it, but it would have been neither unreasonable nor unbelievable. There wasn't a handsomer girl in the whole parish than Rønnau. And if you considered the family . . .

Randi looked up; against his will Håvard had to admire her. She had a knack for fixing you with her innocent blue eyes as though she didn't have the least ulterior motive.

'If you consider the family,' she said, 'the mill owner's grandfather was a common farmer who bought timberland; our family is *of noble birth* if we go back no more than four or five generations.'

Suddenly Håvard was annoyed because of all the things he'd told Rønnau about his own family – about the outlawed knight, the ballad about Vilemann and Signe, the family dagger, the whole lot. He himself, Jon, and now Randi, all of them were of noble birth. . . . Rønnau at least had never bragged about it. They probably had such legends in every good yeoman family, whether they were true or just lies. Mostly, to be sure, they were lies. Anyway, *he* hadn't seen any outlawed knight.

He was ashamed and felt like laughing.

Randi was looking down at the floor again.

However it was, the mill owner and Rønnau never did become a couple. Randi, for one, believed that the mill owner wanted to have proofs before he got married; but Rønnau, who was well – even strictly – brought up, probably said, no, marriage first!

But that her life was anything but easy during that time, you could tell by simply looking at her. It wasn't always so simple for a woman to know what was the *wisest* thing to do.

She looked up again, quickly, with those blue eyes of hers in which there wasn't a hint of ulterior motives. Håvard thought he would take it upon himself to remember her hereafter.

She lowered her eyes again.

Then, after four years, she married Ola Olstad, who was a widower in the prime of life and had that daughter whom Håvard had seen. But naturally he was eager to have a male heir.

'The mill owner didn't remarry until two years after *that* again. He was *mourning* – at least there were many who thought he was.'

But, as it turned out, Olstad didn't get its male heir. That was probably Rønnau's main regret. For Ola was otherwise a splendid fellow – Rønnau never had to content herself with less. . . . She went to several wise women and so on, but it didn't help. It wasn't meant to be, she wasn't going to get everything she wanted, Rønnau either. However many gifts the Lord had showered upon her – the prettiest girl in the parish during the years she was single, and the prettiest wife in Nordbygda today . . .

But that was why she, Randi, was so glad, so glad to see how Rønnau had gotten on top of things again. That Håvard was the right man for Rønnau, nobody could have the slightest doubt. So if only they gave themselves time . . .

Rønnau could probably also learn to love children – if only they were her own. . . .

And she glanced at Håvard again with that candid look in her blue eyes.

Håvard said in a dry, calm voice that everything would turn out all right, she should just wait and see.

He couldn't bring himself to say anything more.

She gave him a piercing look.

Yes, if only he was right. If only she dared to believe it! Because she, who was so fond of this sister of hers . . .

Håvard couldn't bring himself to get up and go either. He was somehow spellbound by the sight of this sister, who was so fond, so fond, of Rønnau. So fond, so fond . . . In the end she repeated it several times and had to wipe her eye with the corner of her apron again.

Oh no! he thought. To sow poison between Rønnau and me, that you'll never manage; that would take a far worse adder than you.

At that moment he could see the mill owner before him, first in the parlor at Olstad – that calm glance which passed from Rønnau to him and from him to Rønnau. Later in his office – how he had brightened up when he heard that there were no leftover dollars in Rønnau's coffer for a miserable harrow. . . .

After that he was prepared to grant him his every wish. Credit and clover seed and seed grain, and the promise of a heifer and a bull calf. . . .

Watch out now! he said to himself. Watch out – what you call having second sight doesn't have to be anything but suspicion, *isn't* anything else, in fact. Random suspicion at that.

Oh no, that damn jade was not going to bring it off.

He felt confident that his thoughts didn't show outwardly.

They talked about other things. This sister had meant well, she'd sown her seeds now; just give them time to sprout.

Oh, no!

'Really?' he said. 'You don't say.'

Rønnau came back quite late; she'd been rather bored, she said. Honestly, she preferred to talk to men. But Mari's husband had gone to take a look at the horses.

Håvard thought, Even if you have fooled me – which I neither will nor can believe – I have only to remember this sister of yours to fall in love with you as never before.

Soon after, the husband came home, along with Håken. Hans had bought a horse from Bruflaten. Håvard simply had to come out and take a look at it.

It wasn't one of the worst. Not one of the best ones either. Håvard knew it. So Amund Moen had sold his brown mare to Bruflaten. Or had traded it, more likely. If Hans had gone directly to Amund, he could probably have had it for ten dollars less. But there was no reason why he should blurt out that sort of thing. He merely said that, sure, the horse was all right.

Why Amund had gotten rid of it, he didn't quite know.

Hans got mighty proud and happy. He was a bit tipsy, but now he insisted that they should all take a couple of drinks. An extra purchase toast for a good deal.

It got late before they went to bed.

Håvard slept restlessly. In reality, he wasn't quite asleep; it seemed to him he was aware of things most of the time.

He was in a room with an adder. It turned and twisted and said, 'I am ssso-o-o fond of . . . ssso-o-o fond of . . .'

Then it struck.

He just laughed, flung it aside, crushed its head with his heel and said, 'Oh no! It will take a worse adder than you to . . . A worse adder than you to . . .'

Then he felt the poison starting to take effect – it became hard to breathe and he felt sick.

He woke up, noticed he felt woozy from the drinks, and turned on his other side with the thought, I'd better stay awake for a while so I can get out of that dream.

He and Rønnau had come home again. But something was wrong . . . something was the matter at Olstad. . . . He shouldn't . . . shouldn't have let Lars go. . . . There was something the matter at Olstad. . . .

He woke up several times, sat up in bed, and tried to get rid of those troublesome dream thoughts. But no sooner had he gone to sleep again than they turned up once more.

At daybreak he got up. This was getting to be intolerable. They had intended to stay another couple of days – he ought to drop by at the parsonage also; but he felt he couldn't feel sufficiently at ease for that – there was something the matter at Olstad.

He woke up Rønnau and told her he felt uneasy and had to get back home. He was afraid there was something the matter at Olstad.

'You and your visions!' Rønnau said, and laughed. But that was all she said. Since she met him, Håvard had seen things already a couple of times, and seen correctly.

'In any case, come with me to the kitchen and get a bite to eat,' she said. 'We won't wake my sister, and certainly not Hans – he's sleeping quite heavily this morning, I should think. I'll just say you had misgivings that something was the matter at Olstad.'

They had taken the two brown horses for this trip. Brownie, which he rode, was a good horse but rather heavy.

Something the matter at Olstad . . . This business of second sight was simply stuff and nonsense. Having second sight was nothing but suspicion.

If anything, it had to be the potato field – at any rate he couldn't think of anything else. But then it couldn't be Kerstaffer.

He put Brownie to a smart trot.

Once in a while he thought of the sister.

She was weaving the wind. Nothing but nonsense and old wives' tales. Old sister's poison. Weaving the wind.

He spurred Brownie to a smarter trot. There was something the matter at Olstad.

Why did he think so? Because this sister had filled him with her spiteful prattle? She was weaving the wind, weaving the wind. . . .

It was only that – such troubles never come singly, so therefore – something was the matter at Olstad.

It would be just like Anton not to keep watch at the potato field. But then he would have to go, this very day.

He couldn't see the trail he was riding. Brownie was in a lather when he turned into the yard at Olstad around the mid-morning meal.

Three or four cotters were gathered outside the stable. Cotters? They hadn't been ordered to do any work here for the time being.

They were so absorbed by something that they neither saw nor heard him. He dismounted. The same moment he heard the voice of Dobbin, but not as he was used to hearing it – this was a wild horse's scream. There was a roaring, rattling noise in there, he heard a man yelling, and then a thump against the wall. Then once more a roaring, rattling noise.

154

Alone

'*D*obbin! Dobbin!' Håvard called. Then he opened the door and entered the stable.

Dobbin was bleeding heavily. He had received two big gashes with a knife, one along the side and one down his left leg. He was trembling like an aspen leaf. He had smashed one of the partitions of his stall.

Directly behind Dobbin, flung up against the wall, lay Martin. His chest was completely crushed and he obviously had difficulty breathing. Still conscious, he gave Håvard a strange, deep look – it was without malice now, like a sort of good-bye. The same moment a stream of blood spurted from his mouth, and he stretched out and was dead. Dobbin scented the blood and kicked the wall smartly, with a bang.

'Dobbin! Dobbin!' Håvard made his way into the next stall so that Dobbin could see him, got hold of his forelock, and stood there patting him awhile.

'There. Dobbin, dear. Poor Dobbin.'

He quieted down a little.

Fortunately the stable was quite roomy, with stalls for six horses; at the moment they had only four, and two of them were away. The only one here besides Dobbin was Old Brownie. Frightened to death, he stood stomping the ground in the innermost stall, trembling and snorting.

'So. Dobbin dear.'

Håvard led Dobbin out of his stall and farther back, to the space beside Old Brownie. The horse had to step right beside Martin's body and kept as far away from it as possible, trembling all over again and snorting as though scenting a wolf or a bear.

Håvard tied him up in his new stall. Old Brownie stretched his neck over the partition and passed his muzzle along Dobbin's neck.

Håvard went out.

'Martin is dead. You'll have to help me move him.'

Two cotters entered the stable – the two horses snorted and puffed.

The three of them lifted Martin, put him in the front feeding passage, and straightened him. Håvard closed his eyes. The rest would have to wait.

When they came out again, Edvart took a step forward. His face was distorted, his eyes wild.

'It was you who killed Martin! I heard you strike him!'

The others stood there undecided. Håvard was so surprised he couldn't utter a word. They had been there after all and had heard how Dobbin lashed out, sending Martin flying against the wall with a thump.

But Edvart yelled once more, frothing at the mouth, 'I heard you strike him!'

It must have been Dobbin's last kick he'd heard.

But then the other three joined in, 'Sure. We heard you strike him!'

'Murderer!' Edvart yelled. The other three joined in – they, too, more and more beside themselves:

'Yes. Murderer! Murderer!'

Håvard stood still, looking from one to the other. He couldn't quite believe what he was seeing and hearing.

Brownie stood a short distance away. He was a quiet horse. He had laid his ears back at first, but was now nibbling at the grass.

The housemaid had come out on the porch, her face set in an open-mouthed stare. But the second time they called *murderer*, she let out a loud scream, without words, and ran back into the house.

Håvard prepared to put up a fight – anything could happen now. Four men – it might be a close call. But what he'd half expected didn't come. Suddenly Edvart shouted, 'We'll go get the sheriff!'

And the others joined in, 'Yes, yes! We'll go get the sheriff!'

The same moment the maid came rushing out, a big bundle in her hand.

'I won't stay in the house of a murderer!' she cried, wild-eyed, and joined the flock of cotters as they marched out of the yard in a tight pack.

Håvard remained alone.

He was lost in his own thoughts but didn't know what he was thinking about. He got back to the here and now when Brownie nudged his shoulder.

'Yes, Brownie. We'll take care of you first. But I don't think we'll stable you just yet.'

Having watered and unsaddled him, Håvard tethered him behind the house.

Then he went into the kitchen. He knew he had to try and wash Dobbin's wounds.

In the empty kitchen the remnants of the mid-morning meal stood on the table – porridge, flatbread, and curdled milk. A big kettle hanging on the hook in the fireplace was full of water. The water was clean and lukewarm. He swung it away from the piled-up embers, took a couple of towels and wrung them out. Then he went down to the stable.

Dobbin was quieter now and whinnied as Håvard entered. He had almost stopped bleeding.

Håvard spoke softly to him and carefully washed his wounds with the wet, lukewarm towel.

It almost seemed as though he liked it.

156

Then Håvard watered both horses and gave them hay. Dobbin got a couple of handfuls of oats as well.

The worst was over. Dobbin immediately attacked the oats. Håvard hesitated a moment – then he gave Old Brownie a couple of handfuls too.

He whinnied and chomped.

It was so peaceful here, as though nothing wrong or ugly had happened. Ten feet away lay Martin's body.

Håvard thought he'd better take care of the small things first. The two home cows still stood in their stalls, most likely; and had the pigs been fed?

He went down to the cow barn. There lay Mari in her stall.

Had the cows been milked?

Yes. And the maid had given them water and a wisp of hay. But the pigs hadn't been fed yet, she thought.

He could tell that much from the dissatisfied grunts coming from the pigsty.

'You heard what happened, Mari, didn't you?'

'I heard most of it,' Mari said. 'And understood most of it too, I think.'

'Martin tried to mutilate Dobbin – he gave him two big gashes, which were bleeding heavily when I came in. Then Dobbin must have gone wild, he broke down one of the partitions and kicked Martin up against the wall.'

'Yes, I heard that,' Mari said. 'It's real bad.'

Håvard didn't answer.

'Have *you* gotten anything to eat then, Mari?'

No, she hadn't.

'The porridge isn't rightly warm any longer, I'm afraid,' he said. 'Would you take it as it is?'

Mari would. Håvard went in and got food for her.

The two cows stood in the empty cow barn yearning for the summer dairy. He let them out into the pasture.

'I'll drop in again later,' he told Mari as he left.

Now the pigs had to be fed. He heated the water again, found the big tub of slops and made a couple of buckets of rich feed for the three pigs. It took him half an hour or so, and he was glad for every half-hour that passed. This day would be a long one.

Was there anything else?

Remembering that the chickens had to be watered and fed, he took care of it right away.

He ought to get a bite to eat himself too; but he didn't have any appetite.

He went in to see Mari again.

'You said you heard most of it,' he said. 'Something must have happened before I came. When I rode into the yard, four of my cotters were standing outside the stable. Martin, I learned later, was inside the stable. Two, Jon and Anton, weren't there.'

'So?' Mari said. 'I was fairly sure I heard Anton. But that was a moment before you came. Perhaps he saw you coming up the road and skipped out.'

'Did you hear what they were talking about?'

'Not all of it; but they certainly weren't in agreement. One of them said: "No, that would be a shame!" or something to that effect.'

'I think I can see it all now,' Håvard said. 'Martin had gone into the stable. Dobbin stood next to the outermost stall left of the door. But to be able to use the knife, Martin had to get over on his left side, so that Dobbin came to stand between him and the door – he must have been crazy not to understand that it was dangerous. When Dobbin broke down the partition, Martin tried to run past him and out; but that way he came to be directly behind Dobbin for a split second, and he lashed out. I heard the kick the very moment I entered the yard, and the thump as Martin hit the wall.'

'I heard the same thing,' Mari said.

'Dobbin had completely crushed his chest. He was still alive when I entered the stable, and conscious. He looked at me but couldn't speak. The same moment the blood gushed from his mouth, and he died without saying a word. It was a ghastly death, I must say. He suffocated and bled to death, both. If only I could understand . . .'

'I've been expecting something,' Mari said. 'Well, nothing like this, but . . . If Kerstaffer had been well and home on the farm, I would've thought he was the one behind this. But he's sick in bed miles from here, with his shoulder in splints. And he's supposed to be very poorly, people say.'

She thought for a moment, carefully choosing her words.

'There are a couple of things you don't seem to know, Håvard. He was smitten with Rønnau, Martin was, those two years he was head servant around here. God only knows what dreams he may have had – both of wife and farm, perhaps.

'He must have been a bit soft in the head already, or he would have under-stood he wasn't the right sort of man for Rønnau. Then you came and took both the wife and the farm, and he had to go back to his cotter's plot. It was more than he could take, I reckon. I could tell that something had been broken inside him. Still, I never imagined he would be *this* crazy. To cut up a horse . . .

'By the way, have you taken care of Dobbin?'

Håvard explained that he had washed the wounds with lukewarm water.

They had almost stopped bleeding.

'You should cook a mush of plantain leaves to put on. It may come out all right, as long as there wasn't poison on the knife. He will run a fever later today, but it may wear off.'

'What about the other cotters? They could hear, just as well as I, what was happening in the stable. And still . . .'

He sat for a moment at Mari's stall, pondering.

'That's one thing I can't understand. And the other is, how could they put up with Martin's mutilating a horse that had never done him any harm? Dobbin, you know, is as gentle as they come.'

'I can't understand it either,' Mari said. 'Come to think of it, that must have been what they disagreed about. What some of them felt would be a shame. It was Tjøstøl, poor fellow, who said that.'

She sent Håvard a look which said, more plainly than words, You must have made a stupid mess of it with your cotters.

There could be no doubt about that; but he didn't understand exactly how.

'I have never wanted to harm my cotters,' he said; 'but they seemed to think I was pushing them too hard. I never pushed them, really, but to them I probably seemed a bit faster than they were used to.

'There is one other thing. Jon and I were up at the summer dairy last spring . . .'

He told her what he had said – that if this farm was run the right way, it might be possible to give the cotters twice what they were getting now.

'I thought, in a few years,' he said. 'And besides I know a matter like that would have to be discussed with the other farmers, or they might chase me out of the parish with sticks.

'I would never have breathed a word about it. But Jon and I had had a few drinks and one word led to another. . . .

'The stupid thing was that Jon mentioned it – to Amund, I think it was. And *he* spoke to the others, and so they thought the whole thing was a bait I used, to get them to work harder.'

'Cotters aren't used to good deeds, you know,' Mari said, fixing him with her wise old eyes.

She lay for a moment staring vacantly. Then she turned her eyes toward him: 'Do you really mean to increase the cotters' wages?'

'I do. But today we'd better say I *did* mean to. I had meant to do it as soon as I could afford it and could find a way of doing it.'

She looked at him with tenderness, the way a mother looks at a small child: 'Håvard – you are, God help me, even more stupid than I had thought!' she said.

She again lay for a moment staring vacantly.

'What you have just told me explains some, but not all.

'You are an outsider, and it didn't take you long to come up in the world; that explains a bit more.'

'Then I knocked down Martin and scared Edvart when they had clogged up those ditches for me,' Håvard said. 'You must've heard about that.'

'Yes. That could explain still some more. But it's not enough.'

She lay again for a moment. Suddenly she said, 'Now it comes back to me, something Martin answered when Tjøstøl said he thought it would be a shame. "There will be only one fine!" he said, "and Kerstaffer has said he'll pay it."

'So, you see, Kerstaffer is behind it all the same. He must've told him this when – well, I suppose you know Martin was Kerstaffer's partner in the potato field?'

Håvard had imagined so but never known it for sure.

Mari nodded.

'Kerstaffer egged them on – he, the worst slave driver in the whole parish.

'You know how stupid cotters are.'

There was nothing left to talk to Mari about. He went out into the yard, took a turn to the stable and talked to the horses, dropped by the pigsty, went into the kitchen to heat more water, picked some plantain leaves and cooked a mush, then visited the stable and pasted it on the wounds. The flies had begun to gather where the clotted blood had spread down Martin's chin and neck.

Suddenly he remembered something and wondered why he had forgotten it till now.

He went down and looked at the potato field.

It lay there just the same as when he had gone away.

He dropped by the empty kitchen once more.

There was still a long wait. It would take the cotters four hours to get to the sheriff's. Then they would have to tell their story, and afterwards walk for another four hours to get back home again. They would hardly be back till around supper time.

He didn't know what to do with himself.

The farm lay perfectly still, as though it were dead.

He sat down on the porch.

He must have dozed off for a moment as he sat there – he awoke from the sound of footsteps not far away. Looking up, he didn't quite know if he was awake or dreaming, for the one who was coming toward him, and whom he couldn't remember ever having seen, looked like a cross between an elf and a gnome – well, he hadn't seen them either. He was a man getting on in years, small and withered, rather bald and with small, red-rimmed eyes.

Suddenly he understood – this could be none other than Høgne Lien. Now the world wouldn't last till Easter – with Høgne being seen outside his farm for the first time in twenty-five years.

The same moment it flashed upon him, hitting him like a blow: right now people were going from farm to farm all over the parish recounting what had happened – turning and twisting it, feeling amused or angry, or both, most likely.

Getting up, he walked toward the man.

'You are Høgne Lien, I understand?'

'We have never met,' Høgne said. 'But I have heard what has happened to you today and thought I would drop by.'

He stood for a moment. Then he said, more to himself than to Håvard, 'This parish breaks everyone.'

Then, after another moment, he added, 'You must either trample underfoot or be trampled underfoot.'

He stood for another few moments, staring into vacancy. 'It's all Kerstaffer's doing. I suppose you realize that.'

In a way Håvard agreed – if only he could understand *how*. Kerstaffer was sick in bed, and far away. . . .

Høgne said with conviction: 'Kerstaffer can do anything.'

Then he laughed, a thin old man's laugh. 'But you managed to give him a whopping blow, didn't you!'

Suddenly something occurred to him and he livened up. 'How is the horse doing?'

Håvard said he would survive. 'He's got two nasty gashes, but . . .'

'And the cotters have gone to the sheriff?'

'Yes. Though I don't have the faintest idea why. Martin was killed by the horse. His chest has been totally crushed, anyone can see that.'

Høgne stood for a moment.

'The world is wicked,' he remarked.

Then Høgne had nothing more to say. Håvard asked if he would like to come in for a drink – he had little else to offer him, since he was alone at the farm today. But, no, thanks, Høgne didn't want anything.

'Too early in the day too,' he mumbled.

There was nothing more to talk about. Høgne turned to walk homeward again and Håvard went with him. He accompanied him right up to the fence near Lien.

There Høgne said something strange. 'If you pass by some day, why don't you drop in,' he said.

When Håvard got back home he looked after the animals, talked for a while to Dobbin, fried some pork and prepared porridge for Mari and chatted with her a bit – but this time mostly about little things.

He went to sit on the porch again but hadn't been there for long when he heard footsteps a second time.

A big, husky, bearded fellow this time – Amund Moen himself.

'I've heard about this awful thing that has happened to you,' Amund said. 'Will the horse be all right?'

Yes, Håvard hoped he would.

'I have put on a poultice made from plantain leaves,' he said.

'Hm. You've been talking to Mari, I see. Sure, Mari knows her stuff.'

'And your cotters have gone to get the sheriff?'

It seemed they had.

'Hm. As far as I can see, you are on the good side of the law,' Amund said. 'Hm. You came into the yard the moment Martin was mutilating your horse in the stable. Was that it?'

'Yes.'

'Then you rushed into the stable, knocked down Martin so he fell under the horse's hoofs, and the frightened horse trampled him to death. Anyway, that's how I would explain it. The testimony of the four cotters doesn't have a leg to stand on, because they are under suspicion on account of this business with the horse, and nobody is going to be lenient about that sort of thing. No, in such a case all you need to do is stay calm, then they won't get anywhere.'

It took Håvard a while to realize that Amund actually believed he had killed Martin.

He told him as briefly as possible how it had happened.

'He died because he couldn't breathe, I think. Besides, at the end, he bled from the mouth – perhaps because a couple of broken ribs had entered his lungs.'

'Hm. Yes.' Amund looked a bit puzzled. 'Sure. That's no doubt a better explanation, sure.'

He obviously didn't believe him. How, then, about all the others?

'If Martin had been on his feet when I got to the stable, I don't know what I would have done,' Håvard said. 'But Dobbin had already settled accounts

162

with him. Come to think of it, Martin lies there in the outer feeding passage. Perhaps you could give me a hand to get him to the threshing floor?'

'Surely.'

They walked into the stable. The horses grew restless the moment a strange man entered, but Håvard quieted them with soothing words.

Amund examined Dobbin's wounds.

'The person who did this meant business, you bet. But he'll be all right, I think.'

They took the body and carried it between them onto the threshing floor.

When they had laid it out, Amund bent over what had been Martin and opened his shirt front.

'It might be interesting to see,' he muttered.

He straightened up again, amazed.

'I'll be damned – you've been telling me the *truth*, haven't you, my boy? This is a kick, no doubt about it. There are two marks in his chest, side by side, from the horseshoes, and it is the *front* calks of the shoes that have gone deepest. That means he was kicked and not trampled underfoot. The case is quite clear.'

'You think so, and I know so,' Håvard said. 'But what do you think the cotters are going to say? Having gone this far, they are bound to go further. What if they say – and swear to it if necessary – that they saw me knock down Martin in the stable and drag him under the horse's hoofs? Afterward, maybe, I slashed my own horse with the knife so it would look as though Martin had done it. . . .'

'No, it won't do!' Amund said. 'That a farmer mutilates his own best horse? They can't get anyone to believe that.'

'Oh, some will,' Håvard said. 'Remember, I am an outsider here.'

'Yes, that's true.'

Amund grew quite thoughtful.

'One more thing. People come to thank me because they think I broke Kerstaffer's left shoulder in the potato field. For my part, I don't know who it was I hit – it was pitch-dark that evening. But very little would be needed to turn this around, making me out to be a dangerous, violent person who recklessly attacks people. For now, you see, Kerstaffer is in a bad way, sitting there with his shoulder blade in splints, a semi-cripple.

'He who does one, can do the other.

'There's only one thing: Mari was lying in the cow barn with the door open and heard how it all happened.'

'You take a much too gloomy view of this,' Amund said. 'Anyway, speaking for myself, I'm willing to stand up in court and swear that the marks from the horseshoes are marks of a kick. If it should end up in court. But it won't.'

In the minds of the people you are a murderer yourself, Håvard thought.

Amund became absorbed in thought. It looked as though he'd become rather indifferent to the whole business now that he realized Håvard had not killed Martin.

'I understand you've got a litter of elkhound puppies,' Håvard said, mostly just to say something as he walked him out of the yard and up to the road. 'Could I order one? Preferably a male puppy, if there should be any.'

'That can be arranged,' Amund said. Then he laughed. 'Kerstaffer's next-door neighbor might well need a dog!'

He turned toward Håvard. 'I can see you don't believe it'll end up in court either.'

'We'll wait and see,' Håvard said.

But to himself he thought, It certainly will. And it won't be a joke either.

Not till he had heard himself say it to Amund did he really understand how hopeless his situation was.

He had put it the way it was – they had gone so far now, these cotters of his, that they might just as well go further still.

How far they would go or what they would say, nobody knew – it depended on how shrewd or how stupid they were. Perhaps it was lucky for him that they were rather stupid. Stupid people overdid it when they took to lying. So much so that nobody believed them. He would have to stake his hope on that.

And the fact that the horseshoe marks were from a kick and not from trampling? Oh, well, people saw what they *wanted* to see.

The only thing it would be difficult to get anyone to believe was that he, a farmer, had cut up his own best horse.

They would probably believe that Martin had done that, to revenge the attack last summer. Then Håvard appears, catches him red-handed, knocks him down, and throws him under the horse's hoofs.

It might end up not as murder, perhaps, but as manslaughter. That was bad enough. A big case could be made out of that, outsider that he was. With witnesses called in from all over.

The mere thought of it made his blood run cold.

Witnesses from home. About Tonè who threw herself into the waterfall. The whole story turned inside out in court.

Kerstaffer's shoulder – right now people were laughing and gloating over it, but public opinion about such things could change overnight, as he well knew.

This adventurer Håvard, this violent man with dead bodies and beaten-up people lying in his wake . . .

". . . As an aggravating circumstance due consideration has been given to the fact that the accused also previously . . .'

He noticed it didn't affect him, not much anyway, what people in this parish thought or said. But what if he were to lose his honor in his own parish once again! – no, better not think about it.

He went to the kitchen and heated some water. Then he fetched his razor set from his saddlebag. He washed himself carefully, shaved, and put on a clean shirt. If the sheriff came for him, he wanted to look decent.

It had turned four by now. He couldn't expect them in less than three to four hours.

He noticed he was holding the razor in his hand as he went out on the porch again.

The weather was overcast, but mild, almost like the middle of summer.

He realized he was extremely tired, which wasn't so strange, perhaps – he had slept very little last night and eaten nothing worth mentioning all day. He probably ought to get a bite to eat from the kitchen cupboard, but the very thought of food made him nauseous.

He sure was tired – or was it something else? His body felt as though it were soaring – as though his feet didn't touch the ground.

Now he would certainly never be able to go home to Telemark anymore.

He recognized that thought well enough from before. When it hit him full-strength, he felt numb and queer. He felt as though he were sitting in the parlor at night, there was a fire in the hearth, the pine stick was burning in the chimney hold, and he felt good and warm and secure – and then, all at once, something came and removed one wall, so that he sat there staring straight out into the darkness.

Actually, he hadn't thought about it very often. Or, if he did, he wasn't greatly affected by it, not always anyway. When there was plenty to do, when the work went briskly, when things were going well – sometimes even when they weren't going so well – you felt happy and warm inside, as though you were filled with a summer's day. But there were other days – and he didn't always know where they came from – when he would suddenly perceive a cold blast and an ominous darkness coming at him through the open wall.

Now, as he stood on the porch, this thought hit him harder than ever before.

At the lower end of the yard, slightly left of the cow barn and with a view of the lake, there was a biggish round knoll. People said a ship had been buried there. A tall old birch tree grew on top of the knoll. They said it was an ancient burial mound.

Every once in a while he had gone to sit on that mound in the evening. When he sat there looking out over the lake, it almost seemed to him he was sitting on the knoll below the buildings at home, in Telemark. The knoll was almost the same, the birch tree nearly identical. And the view too – well, it was much flatter here of course, but he could see the fields sloping down toward the lake – even the hills on both sides faintly reminded him of it. Sometimes he took his fiddle along. When he sat there by himself late in the evening, after people had gone to bed and he didn't see a living soul or hear a human voice, he would plunk a bit at his fiddle – cautiously, so it wouldn't be heard on the other farms round about.

At the moment he was walking down to this mound, where he sat down to look out across the lake for a while.

He opened his razor and looked at it – and then he didn't rightly know what happened.

It seemed to him he cut his throat with the razor, making a huge slash all the way across. The odd thing was that it didn't hurt; but he died immediately. He soared out of himself and saw his own body lying there on the ground with a big, gaping wound in the neck.

It didn't greatly upset him to see himself dead.

The wound didn't bleed much either.

He hovered quietly in the air, feeling wonderfully free. Suddenly he knew he wanted to go home again, to Telemark. A trip home again, for the last time, he thought.

He rose aloft and headed southwest.

He flew high up, the way the cranes do, increasing his speed. It was a long journey, and he had to get there before dark.

He flew over wide flat country, seeing yellow fields and green meadows far below him. But it wasn't his country, so he flew higher up and picked up speed. He saw a couple of cities far down to the left but didn't stop, they weren't his places. He was passing over Vegardshei Heath with its vast dark forests[32] – he'd been through there with Bruflaten one summer, with a sizable drove of horses. He recalled how nice and cool it had been in the forest, with its fragrance of resin and heather; but he didn't need to stop there this

32. A hilly, wooded area ten to fifteen miles north of the coastal town of Tvedestrand in Aust-Agder County.

time. Now he was over Telemark. Here he knew most of the parishes, and in many places he'd visited almost every farm. He started going down and flew more slowly. He looked at each field, at each green meadow, as if he was seeing them for the last time. He thought it was beautiful. And then he remembered that this *was* the last time. He felt sorry about that, but reflected there was nothing he could do about it.

Now he was over his own hamlet. He thought it was the most beautiful of all.

Here he knew every farm, every farm yard, every field and fence. He dropped still lower down, until he could nearly touch the treetops. Few people were out and about, it was evening already. Dew was starting to fall, and he perceived the fragrance from the yellow grain fields. Soon the grain harvest would begin here too.

Then he stood on the porch at home.

But the door was locked, and he understood it had gotten very late.

At first he was bewildered; but then he remembered he was dead, after all. He walked straight through the door.

In the parlor stood his mother. When she saw him, she became so glad.

He felt awful about saying what he had to say, but he knew he couldn't help it.

'Mother, I am dead!' he said. 'You see, Mother, I have killed myself.'

She began to cry, and he understood she cried because she loved him.

Then he realized he had been frozen stiff but hadn't noticed. Now he was thawing, and it felt both good and painful, but mostly good.

He was glad because his mother cried but felt bad that he should be glad because she was grieved; yet he was glad, so glad that he also began to cry.

Waking up from the sound of tears, he straightened up where he sat on the grassy knoll, still holding the open razor in his right hand. And the same moment he knew that now he wanted to live.

Strange – he hadn't had the faintest idea he meant to take his own life.

The same moment he heard men's voices from the trail between the parish road and the house. Maybe that was what he had heard while asleep, and now it had awakened him.

Five men were headed toward the yard. Four of them were those cotters of his. The fifth he didn't recognize right away; but he saw that it wasn't the sheriff.

He stood up, shut his razor, and put it in the pocket of his jacket.

The fifth man walked one step ahead of the four. He knew him now, having seen him at church a few times. His name was Hans Olsen Tomter,

167

and he was a Haugian living on a roadside farm in the far south of the parish. Håvard had noticed him because he was so quiet and looked as though he was at peace with the whole world.

'Here I come with your cotters, Håvard,' Hans said. 'Satan had tempted them, and they were wandering down evil paths. But the Lord helped me to make them listen to reason. We should have been here earlier, but we stopped to hold a brief prayer meeting together. They are repenting their sins and beg your forgiveness from the bottom of their hearts.'

He looked up into the sky and said – and the strange thing was that when *he* said it, it sounded neither false nor foolish:

'God be praised, who turns evil unto good.'

Edvart, who always had difficulty keeping silent, looked up into the sky too, took a step forward and said:

'We have seen the truth and found God!'

Aftermath

*T*oward evening the next day Rønnau rode into the yard with her brother-in-law, Hans Moen. The rumor had reached Moen around dinner time that day. But they hadn't heard it had all ended well – for how else to describe it?

Håvard discovered that he'd never seen Rønnau angry before.

For the maid, who had stood on the porch shouting *murderer*! and now was pacing back and forth in the kitchen weeping, she had only one sentence: 'Out of the house!'

And she wanted to evict the cotters. They had broken every agreement and contract – let them go begging, each and every one, even if it meant that every cotter's plot would remain vacant for years.

Hans and Håvard tried to make her listen to reason, but they could have saved their breath. When Håvard said that the poor devils had been converted, as far as they ever could be – Anton reported that they sat at home in their shacks singing hymns – Rønnau merely answered that she didn't give a penny for that kind of conversion. What else could they have done? But now they could apply to the Lord for a cotter's plot.

Hans said – rather mildly – that they had to think about the grain harvest; but she just snorted. Out they should go, even if the crops were to rot standing.

This was as far as they got with her at first. Anton, who for once hadn't done anything wrong but was so unused to it that he was slinking about frightened to death, was sent up into cotter country to summon the four cotters down to the farm – at once.

They came, their backs and knees more bent than usual.

It was Rønnau who spoke. She explained to them as they sat around the kitchen table – without food this time – that after what they had done, Håvard and she had the right to evict them without notice, and not a single farmer in the entire parish would lift a finger to help them.

When Edvart made a modest attempt to quote Scripture at her, she silenced him, 'Shut your mouth! I get sick just listening to you.'

It turned out to be poor Tjøstøl who saved them all.

Unlike the others, he hadn't converted, strangely enough. Håvard noticed that the others looked at him rather coldly – whether for that reason or for some other, he couldn't say. He sat somewhat apart from the others at the table.

Suddenly he blurted out, 'I knew it was wrong all along. And now I'll go under ground with shame, on top of everything!'

Rønnau stood and gazed at him for several moments. They noticed she was simmering down.

'You can stay, Tjøstøl,' she said. 'You haven't been one of the worst.

'As for the rest of you' – as she looked at them, one by one, they shrank from her eyes – 'by rights you should be sent packing tomorrow morning. But you do have wives and children, so I'll let you stay on. But don't you forget, you Edvart and you Amund and you Per, that the *next* time – if there should be a next time – you will be out of here on the spot. You can go now.'

They padded quietly out of the kitchen.

It probably was the best solution. But Håvard felt strangely out of it all. When he watched these cotters, he felt neither anger nor hatred, as though he were completely devoid of such feelings. He just felt it would be nice to be spared the sight of them awhile.

But he wasn't; for in a couple of days the grain harvest began.

He noticed that the bad experiences he'd had lately had changed him in some way.

What had happened out there at Tomter, on Hans Olsen's farm, was like a miracle: it had saved him. But he had gotten to the point now where he asked, In what way will I have to pay for it?

Some new outrage, he feared, would come from somewhere else when he least expected it.

In the next few days rumors and reports reached Olstad from several parts of the parish. Little by little they could follow the cotters' trail from one farm to another, all the way to Hans Olsen.

They had stopped at every farm, had told their story and been offered a drink. At first they needed the drinks because they were scared, later they accepted them because they felt brave.

When they got to Tomter, they were riding very high. They had worked on their story going from place to place, and now they felt it was ready.

Well. What it amounted to was that Håvard had attacked Martin the moment he entered the yard, knocked him down, as he had done once before, dragged him into the stable, chucked him under the horse's hoofs, and then cut up the horse himself to have a sort of excuse.

It was Edvart who spoke. He was the one who had spoken for them all along.

'Now you're lying, Edvart,' Hans said in his calm voice, fixing him with his calm eyes. 'No farmer will use a knife on his own horse.'

And so the whole thing fell apart for them. It hadn't been thought out any better.

Rønnau said, 'Good, at least, that our cotters are so stupid. Had they been smart to boot, it might have gotten quite awkward.'

Quite awkward? She had no more idea than anyone else what a close brush with disaster it had been.

Otherwise it didn't look like Håvard would have to pay for anything, not at once in any case. It was as though the evil had purged itself. Nothing untoward happened for a while. They brought the cattle down from the summer dairy without mishap. The grain harvest went well – they were lucky with the weather and got a good-sized crop. They dug the potatoes and were luckier than expected – eight barrels!

Only, the strange thing was that Håvard took so little pleasure in it all.

The cotters were meek as lambs, and little by little they tried, cautiously, to get on speaking terms with Rønnau and Håvard again. The conversion seemed to hold up – they were carefully watched by the Haugians, of course, and had to go to a good many prayer meetings. But they may have been quite sincere, perhaps they were sorry.

Jon thought so anyway. 'When such poor devils don't get away with their pranks,' he said, 'then they are really sorry. Being sorry, for such people, just means to be scared.'

Kerstaffer had come back home again but scarcely had much to say for himself, not at first anyway. His shoulder was in splints, he could barely move his arm, his back had turned crooked, and he was awfully skinny. He rarely showed his face in public and put Mons Myra in charge as head servant.

He never again crossed the yard at Olstad.

Hans Nordby put it this way. 'Kerstaffer is in a pitiful state, that's clear. But to *feel* pity for him, no, I can't – he would have to be dead first.'

Dobbin recovered. The only reminder of the slashes were two long scars.

But he had changed. He grew uneasy whenever one of the four cotters, or Anton, entered the stable. And only Håvard and Jon could handle him; with the others he refused to budge.

So perhaps it was true what Mari had said, that she'd heard Anton's voice outside the stable.

One evening Amund Moen dropped by. He had brought one of his elk-hound puppies.

He didn't want anything for it. 'You can take it as a small gift from this parish,' he said. 'It has certainly done all it can to thwart you so far. The parish, I mean.'

The puppy thrived. It was most devoted to Rønnau, Håvard, and Jon – it seemed to know from his smell that Jon was the hunter. Limber-jointed, it walked about with a rolling gait, tried its teeth on everything it came across, and rolled on the floor like a baby.

But if no disasters swooped down upon Rønnau and Håvard from the out-side, there occurred a couple of things which stemmed from within them-selves. It wasn't very much to talk about perhaps, but . . .

Håvard and Rønnau

*E*arly in October a man came from the Mill, with a heifer and a bull calf on a leash. Both were of the right kind, the red, hornless Smålenene cattle.

And now Håvard knew he could no longer delay the conversation he must have with Rønnau about the cows in the barn.

When it came, it was worse than he had imagined.

He proposed that they sell or slaughter three or four cows, in order to have sufficient fodder for the remaining ones. It was a real torture to listen to the starved animals as they stood bawling in their stalls all spring.

He had known it would be a battle, of course. From the old days every farm took pride in having a big herd – even if the cows were nothing but skin and bones and gave little or no milk when spring came around.

But Rønnau took it more to heart than he had expected.

'Run the farm your way and let me take care of my things my way. You have acquired this farm through sleeping with the owner, but you have not acquired any authority in the house or in the cow barn by your exploits – not yet anyway.'

He turned cold as ice. He looked at her for a moment before answering.

'Since you were so cozy drinking with my brother at our wedding, you must know that it wasn't my intention to catch either you or your farm by going to bed with you. But a man does many a thing without stopping to think. It happens sometimes that others think for him – I won't say whether it is to his advantage or not. But I can tell you one thing – if you like, I am willing to go right now, taking nothing except what I had when I came to this farm. And I believe I'll be just as happy then as I am here and now. You can choose.'

She stood still for a moment, taking a couple of deep breaths. The color came and went in her face. Then she said, in a voice that was quite calm, 'I think it would be best for both of us if we forget what we just said.'

He replied, 'If you can forget it, fine. I'm pretty sure I can. If you can't, if you add it to all the other things you have in your coffer, I can do likewise.'

Then he turned on his heel and left.

Several days passed before they exchanged a word about anything except the most essential things. But then one night she came snuggling up to him, as warm and tender as before, asking his forgiveness and whispering words he hadn't heard from anybody else. . . . And he gave in.

The following day she was as before, calm and confident. He couldn't help recalling a saying she had uttered a couple of times:

A decent person should know how to remember, and how to forget.

She knew how to. Now she had forgotten their little squabble. That is – she had put it in her coffer. He knew he himself couldn't do that. *He* was the kind who would walk around brooding. And he understood what it meant – that she was the stronger of the two.

They didn't talk any more about the cattle. He knew Rønnau would never give in on that point.

Shortly before Christmas he bought five loads of hay on a couple of farms in the northernmost part of the parish and carted them home. That cost him a few of the measly dollars he had, but it couldn't be helped – he simply refused to listen to the bawling of the cows anymore, not from the Olstad barn anyway.

Otherwise there was little change – on the surface. They were just a bit more cautious than before about what they discussed.

But something had happened.

He could tell by several things – by many small and a couple of bigger things – that he was no longer the same.

After that clash with the cotters, Rønnau never made fun of his work again. She seemed to have understood at last that there had to be something to this work, since so many tried to hinder it.

She even began asking his advice and guidance again, almost the way she had done when he came here the first time, a year ago.

But, perversely enough, her zeal had awakened at a time when he himself had become rather indifferent.

Double the crop? Of course they could, and more. But who was he working for? For Rønnau and himself? But they could manage well enough as it was on this good farm.

After that quarrel she was, if possible, even more ardent and affectionate than before when they were by themselves in the evening. The days had become shorter now, and it grew dark long before they went to bed. They had as good a time together as before – or did they? Now as before they would lie stark naked under the warm sheepskin. With her firm body pressed against his, her skin felt good to the touch, her breasts firm like on a young girl. Who would take her for a wife with child – but of course she wasn't, she wasn't, she wasn't . . .

It was nothing but a tiny little thought, like a gnat there in the bedroom. He pushed it aside – that sister of hers would never be able to poison . . .

But, after all, he'd thought the same thing himself.

Occasionally it took a long time before he fell asleep. Rønnau lay beside him, breathing quietly.

They never again spoke about the child they were going to have but didn't get. It would have been no use. What's gone is gone, for good and all.

In the daytime another little gnat would buzz its fine tune at the back of his head. But was it really another gnat? Something told him that in one way or another it was the same.

It was buzzing constantly, but so subtly that it was almost impossible to hear it.

It buzzed:

He had a new faith which made him happy. Then he set out to teach people the new faith, and the new knowledge that went along with it, in order to make them a little happier than before. But nobody wanted to listen to him, and nobody wanted to learn anything from him, and some people sought to take his life and he didn't get anywhere. In the end he grew heavy-hearted, and he who is heavyhearted cannot make other people happy. He forgot where he'd come from and what he'd come for, and he abjured his faith and became like the others. And then everything went well, oh, so well, and he came to have dollars in his coffer and silver candelabra on his table. Not till long after did he understand, at the very back of his head, that he had been bewitched, lured into the mountain, the mountain, the mountain, that the silver was mere tinsel, the bread cow cakes, and the wine bull's piss. . . .

The tune was so fine, so fine, you could barely make it out.

Anyway, most of the time he didn't hear it. Only once in a while when he lay at night unable to sleep, or now and then in the daytime when he wandered around by himself and fell into a reverie, without thinking about anything in particular. Otherwise it wasn't there.

Something else had happened, and he noticed it now and then both day and evening. He just couldn't cross the yard or walk around the tillage and think, This is *my* farm. It was a strange farm, a strange yard. Sometimes on his walks, he felt as though unfamiliar eyes were staring at the back of his head: Who are you?

Occasionally it had been like that before too, for as long as he'd been around on this farm. But this fall it had gradually grown worse.

It would slowly wear off, he knew. It would wear off as soon as he got to know the place better. You had to get to know a farm – every patch of ground, every animal in its stall, every person who worked here.

But that would take time, it appeared.

It was all a circle, and he didn't quite know where it began or where it ended – he would come back to the same places time and again, like a man who has gone astray in the woods.

He never spoke with Rønnau about it.

Gradually there came to be many things he couldn't speak about with Rønnau.

And as the weeks went by and became months, Håvard began to notice that a wall of unspoken things had built up between Rønnau and himself.

First, there were all those things he didn't say, and that was quite a lot – all, or very much, of that which concerned the past: Tonè, himself and

Telemark, and his dishonor in his native parish. He had to keep to himself all his thoughts about these things.

Then there were all the things he couldn't ask her about. The mill owner? It was forbidden. Whether she had *known* she couldn't have children? Forbidden, forbidden – and perhaps it wasn't even true. But no new child was expected, that much was true, or certain, anyway.

Finally there were all the things *she* didn't say. How much that was, he couldn't know. But probably quite a lot – some of the things he couldn't ask her about perhaps. But Rønnau was strong, she could cope with such things.

Every once in a while he could see before him the stones in this wall of silence – how they came and arranged themselves, one by one. Soon, perhaps, the wall would get so high that they couldn't see each other, and so thick that they couldn't hear each other, but would just stand there, lonely, on opposite sides – Rønnau, Håvard – where are you?

Whether Rønnau felt the same way, he didn't know – it was one of the many things he couldn't talk to her about.

The Passing Years

*T*ime passed.

As the weeks became months and eventually years, the relationship with his cotters sank to the level of everyday life again. They had become more peaceful, the four of them, and tended their work a little better than before. It could be because they were afraid; but it could also be because Martin was no longer around to egg them on. Throughout the winter, when there was little to do on the farm after the threshing was over, the cotters carted coal and ore for the Mill at regular daily wages. Then it turned out there was an advantage to that conversion of theirs – they didn't get drunk anymore, fearing the other Haugians.

By the time spring came, Håvard had repaid the advance received from the mill owner and had a hundred dollars coming to him.

That winter Håvard spent part of his time in the woods with Jon. Jon knew the Olstad forest inside out and helped Håvard find good timber for beams at a short distance from the nearest log-running river, thereby reducing the transportation costs and increasing profits. The Mill, which operated a large sawmill now, accepted all the timber that could be found.

Just before the beginning of the summer half-year, around mid-April,

Mons Myra came lumbering to Olstad one day. It was a well-known fact that Kerstaffer hired his cotters only for one year at a time, so he could have them more at his mercy. But now it backfired on him. Mons, who was the best man he had, wanted to quit and came to inquire if he could be a cotter at Olstad and move into Grina, Martin's place, which had stood empty throughout the winter.

Grina was so convenient too, next-door to where Mons was now, just straight across on the other side of the borderline brook.

'I like it less at Berg than before,' Mons said. He remarked later that Kerstaffer couldn't be in his right mind anymore – he sat in his bedroom talking aloud to himself, cursing and swearing, almost all day.

To be on the safe side, Håvard and Rønnau went to consult Hans Nordby, in order to ascertain whether Mons had the right to move. He did. Nordby reminded them that Kerstaffer had lost two cotters before the same way. 'But Kerstaffer never learns, we know that.'

So they accepted the offer. They figured that Kerstaffer could hardly get much angrier with them than he was already.

With Mons – and Jon, who came more often to the farm than before, not least to watch Mons show his strength – they had received more than double compensation for Martin.

At the end of April, shortly before the first anniversary of Rønnau and Håvard's wedding, Amund Moen married his pretty, cheerful maid. People thought they had waited rather long – their boy was six years old by now. Only a few were familiar with what Jon had told Håvard – that the old lady belonged to a type which had the power to haunt and make mischief for seven years, but no longer.

It was a nice, gay wedding, but it lasted only a day.

When Rønnau and Håvard rode homeward at night, Rønnau stopped her horse as soon as they were by themselves some distance down the road. She leaned against Håvard and said, 'We have been married for a year now, and we have known each other for almost two. And it is as good as ever.'

Håvard didn't quite feel that way. But he was glad that Rønnau did.

Again, weeks and months passed by. Everything was as before, or about the same as before. He himself was as before. Or nearly so. And so was Rønnau.

They never discussed having a child again.

The only change he could perceive in himself was that he'd lost something. He'd lost his faith in, or his dream of, something – he seemed unable to find the right word for it even if he tried.

As *the long day* receded into the past – the day he sat alone waiting for the sheriff – he seemed to be able to see it all as part of a certain pattern. It had made him wiser, perhaps, but not more lighthearted.

He no longer believed it was any use, it seemed. Or no longer dreamed of getting something accomplished up here.

It didn't concern the farm – he knew exactly what he had to do there. If something or other went wrong, with crop failures, a lack of money and such, his work might have to be delayed, but that was all.

It was all the other things. He'd had a childish dream of transforming this parish into a happier and better place – goodness, hadn't he even dreamed of making the cotters into free men? He had probably figured like this: Though the parson, who is a stranger, isn't getting anywhere, it might work when one of their own people . . .

He knew, of course, that he wasn't one of them either, never would be in fact. First, he was an outsider. But more than that, he understood – it was incredible how much you could understand in a short time if the circumstances were right – he understood that if by some miracle one of them were to come up with something new, something that went contrary to what they were thinking and doing every day in the year, many times a day, from that very moment he was no longer one of them.

Next to a rock, there was nothing as inert as a peasant.

And that idea of turning the cotters into free men . . .

It had been the most childish dream of all – he didn't even have to think to figure that out now. They had been pushed around for too long. Give them livable conditions from today on, and a hundred years from now their great-grandsons might have relatively straight backs.

He didn't get anywhere with the freeholders, he didn't get anywhere with the cotters. If he behaved wisely and cautiously, he might be in a position to improve his own farm, that was all.

The dream was gone. Otherwise everything was as before – or about the same.

A dream – it was such a small thing, thinner than a veil, a fancy, nothing. If it got shattered, everything else was still the same – the soil and the forest, fields and meadows. The sun rose as before and set as before, the work took its course as before, meals and rest periods came at the same time as before.

He told himself all this, many times over, but it didn't help. He felt that everything had changed, and it made him wonder.

Weeks, months, and years . . .

After three years he had doubled the crops at Olstad. He was satisfied with that but didn't think too much about it – he knew that the crops could be trebled with time.

The same summer the rye stood shoulder-high in the field which had once been the waterlogged meadow. He took a walk down there every once in a while and – yes, he was fond of that field. But Parson Thurmann who went with him, old and stiff and limping, was more proud of it than he was.

Among other happenings in Nordbygda during these years, the favorite topic of conversation was no doubt the sad fact that Hans Engen's son stabbed his father to death with a knife. No action was brought, because the son was stark raving mad and had to be chained to the wall in Kerstaffer Berg's basement.

'It had to end that way, of course,' people said. But nobody had dreamed, beforehand, that it had to end that way.

Hans Nordby bought the farm – some timberland came with it. The widow received a good pension and continued to live there. Hans found himself a capable head servant – it happened to be Lars, who had been trained at Olstad. He married, moved up there and ran the farm.

Anders Flateby had to sell half of his farm and timberland to Hans Nordby on account of overdue debts, a hundred dollars which had increased to two hundred.

Flateby was somewhat peculiar after that day.

Otherwise everything was as before.

Håvard dropped by at Høgne Lien's a few times, and Høgne received him well. Høgne was obviously cheered by having someone to talk to. Not that he said very much; if you listened to him as you would to a songbird, he had only two very simple tunes. One was, *This parish is hard*, and the other, *Kerstaffer is evil*.

Høgne might not be quite in his right mind, but he wasn't quite mad either. He believed that everyone in the parish was laughing at him, and it was virtually true, after all. He believed that Kerstaffer was behind all the bad things that happened, in this part of the world at any rate. In that he was somewhat mistaken, of course. Kerstaffer no doubt felt he was able to accomplish far too little.

Høgne liked Håvard and trusted him, first because he was an outsider, and then because he'd broken Kerstaffer's shoulder.

Once he even invited Rønnau. 'She, too, is an outsider,' he said.

But even more strangely, once he invited himself to Olstad on Christmas Eve itself. Feeling good, he thawed and laughed his old man's laugh.

There was moonlight that Christmas Eve; still, Håvard walked him back home, all the way to the Lien gate.

'Poor man!' Rønnau said. 'How good he would have been to that stupid wench – just think of it!'

The puppy, which they called Truls, grew up to become a fine hunting dog. Håvard and Jon went hunting with it every fall and mostly brought down a moose or two. They shared equally – Håvard kept the dog, but Jon was a better hunter.

Walking the woods with dog and rifle was a fine life, no doubt about it. There weren't such open vistas here as in the Telemark mountains; but the forest was vast, it was itself, and the treetops sang, I am free.

'You've grown more reticent in the last few years,' Rønnau said one day.

He replied that perhaps he'd learned something from this parish – people up this way didn't exactly let their tongues run away with them.

'You never sing anymore when you're working,' Kjersti said another day.

'I don't?' he said, wondering a moment. Then he knew it had been a long time since he sang when working.

Part *II*

The Troll Circle

The Bear

O ne year, during the second week of August, Håvard was at the summer dairy to finish the haying. They were through at the farm, and he was glad to give himself this week up in the woods afterward; it was so peaceful there, and so different.

Kjersti, Rønnau's stepdaughter, had turned twenty-one this spring and was at the dairy as a milkmaid.

Håvard, too, had a special reason to be at the summer dairy this year. For the first time in many years, killer bears had turned up in the area around the dairies. Mauled carcasses of sheep had been found in the woods, and a couple of weeks ago the cattle had come stampeding home in the middle of the afternoon, bellowing and scared to death. As it turned out, the bear had killed a heifer from the Nordby herd only a quarter of an hour's walk from the dairies. They had sent up a man with a gun from Nordby – he was up here with a dog but hadn't gotten a crack at the bear yet, had only seen a glimpse of it three miles east of the dairies.

Håvard had taken a gun along in the faint hope of catching this bear, but so far he hadn't come across any fresh tracks. It had most likely moved farther east, deeper into the forest.

This evening he was mowing above the chalet cabin. The sun was setting, the dew had started falling, and his scythe was cutting very nicely. For that matter, this particular scythe cut any kind of grass nicely – he was using the dagger-scythe this evening.

Håvard had often thought of forging the dagger out of the scythe and fixing it onto the handle where it belonged. But he'd never gotten around to it. For one thing, this scythe was so out of the ordinary, and it made itself useful both during the haying season and the harvesting. So instead he had forged a new blade for himself, as nearly identical to the original one as he could make it, and hafted it onto the old sword hilt. But he had a feeling it was fake, and as soon as he had a chance he would . . .

But right now he was mowing with the scythe, and it was cutting the soft mountain meadow grass very nicely. Everything was so quiet up in these woods – he could hear the voices of a pair of chalet girls at the other end of the tarn. He didn't see the cow barn from behind the cabin where he was mowing, but he heard the faint brass tinkling of the bell cow in there and

Kjersti singing a ballad while milking – in fact, it was one of the ballads he'd taught her many years ago.

Kjersti sang:

Sir Vilemann rode to the Blue Mount away.
  The cuckoo did crow.
Then his steed doth stumble and wanders astray.
  The dew drifts along
  and the hoarfrost falls far and wide.

Kjersti was a grown girl now, and well behaved. On the quiet side, which probably wasn't all that bad. And she had become a pretty girl, too, really. Light brown hair, big dark blue eyes that looked almost black – perhaps because of her eyebrows, which were darker than her hair. Those eyes reminded him faintly of Rønnau's eyes, curiously enough – they weren't kin after all – but Kjersti's eyes were bigger and seemed to shine with a light of their own now and then. She was still on the skinny side, but you could easily see she was a grown-up girl.

She hadn't found herself a boy yet, and that was all to the good, considering, for when she got married she was entitled to take the farm by allodial right.

She sat and sang:

Sir Vilemann he blew his gilded horn.
  The cuckoo did crow.
Then he stumbles, himself, and strays forlorn.
  The dew drifts along
  and the hoarfrost falls far and wide.

It was so peaceful everywhere, as on a Sunday evening. But suddenly, in a twinkling, it all changed. The bull started roaring, the cows were bawling and bellowing and carrying on, there were cries and shrieks and clatter – and now Håvard had a distinct impression that he heard the growl of a bear.

He rushed off, around the corner of the chalet cabin and down toward the cow barn. There he saw the bear standing in front of the open door to the barn, but in the doorway stood Kjersti, keeping it at bay with her broom and crying, 'Shoo! Get away from here, will you!'

Now everything happened very quickly. Håvard saw and heard a good many things at once: the bellowing cows, the bull and a couple of cows which had broken loose in the barn and were crashing about in there with no place to go, because the open door led straight into the jaws of the bear – then the shriek of the dairymaid, who had managed to escape from the barn and into the cabin, where she lay screaming with the door open; the furious baying of the Nordby dog as it came bounding toward them, eager to get at the legs of the bear; another roar from the bear as it swung its right paw, which Kjersti met with the broom: 'Shoo! Get away. . . .' It wasn't Kjersti the bear wanted to get at – it had obviously caught the whiff of a cow or a heifer inside the barn but Kjersti stood in its way, and now it would probably strike . . .

'Hey!' Håvard yelled, very near now.

The bear turned and took an instant dislike to Håvard. It roared again, more viciously than before, got up on its hind legs – a huge hulk of a bear – and raised its forepaws.

Håvard saw its gaping jaws and caught the pungent wild-animal smell; he was holding the scythe in his hand, holding it exactly as he had done when mowing the grass behind the cabin – he couldn't stop and think, so he just swung the scythe, aiming his stroke at the bear's flank with the thought, This is the end. But he didn't have time to get scared.

The sharp point of the scythe entered the bear's flank; it was checked briefly by something soft, like a sack, but sank in, penetrating deeper. The bear had raised its right paw to strike Håvard, but the blow never came – it flailed the air with its paws as though it had gone blind, and went down headfirst. Falling, it tore the scythe handle out of Håvard's hand, then lay there kicking at a tussock, scattering dirt and heather all around. After a choked final growl, it was still. Håvard didn't dare believe his eyes, but there lay the bear – blood gushed from it in a stream down the slope. He must have hit it straight in the heart. He could hear shouts and screams from the two neighboring dairies, and quite a way down he saw a man with a gun in his hand running full tilt; his dog, which was there by now, rushed up to the bear and started pulling and tearing at one of its hind paws, but the bear remained still. It was dead.

Håvard didn't quite know how the whole thing had happened, it was like a dream. Now he felt Kjersti, her arms around his neck, trembling like an aspen leaf against him, and he stroked and stroked her until she calmed down. Then came the tears. He let her have a good cry, after which she smiled, looked at him with shining eyes and said, 'I got so scared!'

They stood like this for another few moments, until her cheeks suddenly turned red – she let go of him and turned away. But she couldn't stand on her feet and let herself sink to the ground. 'My legs won't carry me,' she said without looking at him, making an effort to laugh.

He felt numb and strangely far away as he stood there. Far away. Gradually he came back to where he was: there lay the bear, there sat Kjersti, the

Nordby dog was pulling and tugging at the bear's leg, and he heard mooing and clatter and commotion – the animals in the barn were as wild as ever. They probably had been all along, he just hadn't heard it. Still very far away, he could hear something – what was it? Church bells. He definitely thought he heard church bells. He wondered – just stuff and nonsense, of course; no church bells would be ringing now, Friday evening, and he couldn't have heard them even if they had been ringing, not here, a good six miles up in the woods. . . . He passed his hand over his forehead and, feeling his knees were wobbly, went into the barn to the cows, which quieted down somewhat when they saw him.

When he stepped outside again, people started coming from the other summer dairies. The first person was Ole Bråten, a cotter from Nordby, with a gun in his hand. Hard on his heels came a teenage boy from the Flateby dairy. And then several from the other dairies, altogether quite a crowd. The Nordby dog let go of the bear and kept jumping up at his master, wanting to show him the big bear it had killed.

They were all talking at the same time.

The Olstad dairymaid, who had finally managed to come out of the cabin, was talking and pointing – 'I'd milked a pailful and was going up to the cabin with it, and there he stood right in front of me – the first thing I knew I was lying in my bed – he stood there with gaping jaws. . . . The first thing I knew I . . .'

Håvard got Ole to help him pull the huge bear down the slope, since they were upwind from the cow barn and the cattle wouldn't quiet down as long as they had the pungent smell of bear in their nostrils. But first Håvard pulled the scythe out of the bear's carcass. The blade had been twisted when the bear fell headlong with the scythe stuck inside it – hammering it straight again would take some time. To begin with, Håvard contented himself with wiping the steel clean of blood, every drop of it – bloodstains tended to cause pitting.

The others followed and formed a circle around them as they started skinning the bear. They were all jabbering away, as though each and every one of them had killed this bear – with his bare fists. The dairymaid kept telling her story: 'I'd gotten my second pailful of milk and was going up to the cabin. I thought I'd heard a thud, all right, and I'd noticed that the last cow was getting so restless. That must've been when the bear jumped the fence. Anyhow, the moment I came out, pail in hand, there he stood the size of a house, with gaping jaws. I dropped the pail, spattering milk all over, and I believe it was this saved me. Then the first thing I knew I was lying in my bed inside the cabin. . . .'

It takes time to skin a huge bear. Little by little the crowd thinned out and Håvard barely managed to catch the teenager before he left – he wanted him to run to the village first thing in the morning and send Anders, the new servant, up to the dairy with a horse and a summer sledge. 'And ask him to bring a scythe, handle and all!'

Håvard had remembered that the following day he would have to drive home to the village with the bear.

As they were skinning it, they could see the track of the scythe a little better. Through the thick fur, midway between two ribs, smack in the heart and clean through it.

'I can't believe it, Håvard,' Ole said repeatedly. 'Looks like the Lord is keeping a watchful eye on you. Because this is nothing less than a miracle, you know. The odds against it were over a thousand to one.'

Håvard too marveled at the incredible luck he'd had – that the point of the scythe went in just at the right spot. Slightly more to one side or the other, and it would have been stuck in the rib – and then, where would he be now?

'It's a huge hulk of a bear, all right!' Ole said. 'I could swear it's just as big as that killer bear I shot down on the Flateby property east of here twelve years ago.'

It was true, Håvard had heard it from Jon – Ole had actually slain a bear once, a killer bear at that. It was from that moment he was called the Hunter, and that name – well, the feat too – was the only thing on earth he was proud of. Anyway, Ole seemed to be an all-right fellow.

They carefully skinned the bear, hung the skin on a pole to dry, cut up the carcass, dropped by the dairy to fetch some containers for the innards, and chucked all the refuse into the woods down below the fence.

'The fox and the marten will get at it tonight,' Ole said. 'But if we leave the rest by the cabin wall covered with spruce twigs, it will be safe there till tomorrow morning. Animals don't like to get that close to houses.'

They went over to the dairy brook to wash. Afterward Håvard entered the cow barn once more.

The cattle had quieted down; a couple were munching some new-mown hay, but most had settled down for the night. Cows couldn't remember something that awful for more than a short while.

The dairymaid came to say that she and Kjersti were preparing some cream porridge in the fireplace. Ole was welcome to join them, too.

Ole had sort of acquired a small share in the bear by now.

Håvard took him inside the cabin but didn't stay; he went to hammer the scythe into shape, then walked up behind the cabin and started mowing again. He was trembling all over, and he felt he couldn't sit quietly on a bench quite yet.

He noticed he was singing as he mowed, and wondered. It had been a long time since he sang while mowing. Several years, he believed.

He was singing the last part of the ballad about Vilemann and Signe. But every now and then he would stop and listen – what was it? Once again he had a distinct feeling he could hear church bells.

They called him in for cream porridge and summer-dairy waffles. They talked all at once and laughed. This couldn't be called haying porridge, to be sure, but . . . well, they could call it scythe porridge.

Håvard had taken a bottle along, and now it was brought to the table. On his way up he'd had a secret hope of drinking a hunter's toast. And now it had come to pass. . . .

Håvard, Ole, and the dairymaid had their drinks. Only Kjersti didn't want anything. 'My head is swimming as it is!' she said. Anyway, she was rather quiet at the table and seemed to be far away several times; she glanced at Håvard every so often, blushed, and looked away.

No wonder she was preoccupied – a couple of hours ago she had been smacking the muzzle of a huge bear with a broom, slip of a girl that she was. . . .

Ole told them more than once about the time he'd shot down the killer bear on the Flateby property to the east. That bear tended to grow bigger and bigger as the evening wore on. Perhaps it was due to the two or three drinks. . . .

But one thing Ole knew for a fact: aside from *that* bear, this one was the biggest bear he'd ever seen.

They had to call it a day at last. When Håvard saw Ole off, the August sky showed dark above the treetops. In the distance they could hear a fox. 'He can smell it already,' Ole said. 'He'll turn up in an hour to take his part. But the marten will get there first.'

When Håvard came back, both girls had gone to bed. He himself crawled under the sheepskin in the third bunk. He felt terribly tired. What a day! he thought – nothing more. Once again he felt, vaguely, that he could hear the church bells; then he fell asleep.

Afterward, not so very long afterward either, he would think, And you who almost believed what people said, that the Lord was keeping a watchful eye on you! Sure. And went around thinking you had second sight every now and then. Still, you couldn't read the signs when you thought you heard the church bells. You had forgotten everything!

Had forgotten that, when Tonè and you really *saw* each other for the first time as teenagers, it was a Sunday and service time, and the church bells were ringing that very moment.

But he also understood, afterward, that it wouldn't have been any use even if he could have read the signs. It was meant to be, as the old folks used to say, and he couldn't have changed it one bit.

Around noon the following day Anders came up to the dairy with a horse and a summer sledge. He had been smart and taken the quietest and strongest of the horses, Young Brownie. He wasn't so young anymore, twelve years and some, and Old Brownie had been dead for some time; but Young Brownie was his name and would continue to be as long as he lived.

It took an hour to prepare the load and lock it in place with ropes so that everything was steady and secure. Young Brownie snorted a bit at the bearskin – perhaps he had had a great-great-grandfather who had run across a bear in the woods. But then he calmed down; he seemed to understand that this particular bear was dead.

They were all gathered in the chalet meadow as Håvard drove off. Kjersti stood by herself. She waved after him once, then quickly entered the cabin.

Håvard was singing as he drove along. Wasn't it against village custom to sing like that? Then it was high time, damn it, that it *became* the custom. The folks up here were people too, weren't they, not just bodies with a belly?

In the late afternoon he drove past Lien and dropped in to say hello. Høgne came out, all eyes. 'This is really something!' he said. He wasn't a man of many words, old Høgne, or choice ones either, but he managed to call after Håvard that he should come up some evening and tell him about the 'adventure.'

When he got out of the woods, he saw there were lots of people abroad this evening. It dawned on him after a while that they had come out to greet the man who had slain a killer bear with a scythe – to make sure it was true and that the bear was really there, of course.

Hans Nordby came to meet him way up the road. He stood looking at the huge bearskin for quite a while.

Finally he repeated what Ole had said the previous evening, 'I could swear the Lord is keeping a watchful eye on you, Håvard.'

Then he turned and went with him.

They greeted one person after another, now and then flocks of people, as they walked slowly down the road beside the horse. Half the neighborhood was taking a walk this evening to see the strange sight – a killer bear slain with a scythe. But there wasn't any conversation to speak of with these people, nor did they detain them for long; they stood too much in awe of Nordby for that.

But Håvard had to tell the story to Hans Nordby, of course. And when Nordby had heard it, he said once again what he'd said to begin with – anybody could see that the Lord was keeping a watchful eye on Håvard.

He walked with him as far as the Olstad road, which turned west from the parish road. In the end he was mostly silent, and he seemed in no special hurry to get home.

Nordby had remarried six years ago. He'd found out about a widow over in the home parish, with no children, but with a farm and timberland. That's how it happened. But people said this was the first time ever that Nordby had been cheated on a timber deal. The woman was a troll, and sharp as a razor, as childless women sometimes are. 'We don't mean Rønnau, of course, you know that,' people said when they mentioned this to Håvard. She was stingy and cross in the house and mean to Hans's two children – as far as she dared. That wasn't terribly far, really, and not for very long. Nordby remained master in his own house. But there was no cheer at home anymore. And so he would often come down to Olstad in the evening, even if it was just to sit there.

Rønnau was standing in the yard.

She had decked herself out in her party finery, with silver brooches and silver shoe buckles.

She shook hands with him as though he were returning from a long journey. Then she stood looking at the bearskin awhile.

'This, you know, could become a nice sleigh apron!' she said.

Her eyes shone when she looked at Håvard. They said, without words: 'Håvard! Oh, Håvard!'

Trouble Brewing

R ønnau and Håvard roasted the bear's heart in the embers of the fireplace the same evening and ate it together. There was an old saying that it would make you strong and brave and wise. The taste, though, was anything but good – it was almost like chewing shoe leather.

'Now you are my honey bear!' Rønnau said, laughing. But the next moment she grew serious, paled, and held him tight.

'My honey bear, my own – more than ever before!' she mumbled against the hollow of his throat.

Hans Olsen Tomter, the Haugian farmer who had once sent Håvard's cotters home again to Olstad, ran a small tannery on the side. He made a sleigh apron of the bearskin for them.

'May it be a blessing unto you!' he said when he delivered the skin to Håvard.

He was one of those who could say such things without making them sound either sickening or absurd.

In a more prosaic vein he said, 'I reckon it is the biggest bearskin I've ever seen. It must have been a touchy business to go at a brute like that with a scythe.'

Håvard merely said, 'I didn't have time to get scared!'

Then Hans said that sentence which Håvard had heard twice before and now heard for the third time.

'It was a miracle that you escaped alive,' Hans said. 'It almost looks like the Lord is keeping a watchful eye on you.'

Håvard liked this sentence less and less with each repetition. He knew too well that the person the Lord kept a watchful eye on didn't have much of a chance of pulling through.

Riding homeward on Young Brownie with the big, heavy bearskin draped over the horse's back in front of him – Brownie didn't snort now, because the skin no longer reeked of live bear – Håvard looked right and left as he headed north at a walking pace.

Did the farms around here show any traces of the work he had put in at Olstad during these years?

Yes and no. It hadn't gone as well as he had once dreamed. Not by a long shot. But it hadn't gone quite so badly as he'd feared while waiting, alone, for the sheriff during *the long day* either.

People had noticed the clover fields at Olstad – they did stand out – and quite a few had dropped by to purchase grass seed from Håvard, or get it for free. Some had also gotten hold of pure barley for seed grain; they had gathered this much from what they saw: the pure barley was better than that wretched mixture of barley and oats they had used before.

But that was about all they had grasped. They thought nothing of rye, no matter that the rye fields at Olstad stood shoulder-high. And as for crop rotation, the very basis of everything, they didn't understand it at all.

It was the last week of August, and Håvard couldn't help noticing how green and thriving the potato plants looked in one potato field after another alongside the road.

Oh, yes, people up here had gotten around to growing potatoes. And that was fine. But it was due neither to Parson Thurmann's sermons nor to the good crops Håvard had been able to muster. If the truth were to be told, it was due to the new law which again allowed people to distill liquor from their own produce by paying a liquor tax on the assessed value of their land – which all had to pay anyway, whether they distilled liquor or not. This was the reason the farmers up here had come to appreciate the potato.

Håvard felt as though he was enjoying a second honeymoon. What Rønnau had whispered against the hollow of his throat came true – he did become her honey bear – *her man* – even more than before.

She was all ardor – flaming hot. Suddenly there was no time to lose, as though their hours together were numbered and she could never have enough of him during the short time remaining.

Sometimes she swept him along, so that he grew wanton and wild himself, but he wasn't quite sure he liked it altogether. Now and then passion seemed to turn her into a stranger, a stranger who frightened him a little.

Every once in a while – this happened in the daytime – he would ask himself whether Rønnau had been quite well lately. She would be extremely impatient with the hired girls, and she had never been like that in the past.

She could be impatient about other things too.

Unavoidably, he had to tell the story of the bear more than once – whenever there were visitors, in fact, at least for a while. Then, of course, he had to tell about Kjersti too, how she stood in the doorway to the cow barn smacking away at the bear's muzzle with a broom, as though it were a dog. But the third time he related that part, Rønnau interrupted him.

'She couldn't have stood there for more than a moment!' she said. 'You were mowing above the chalet cabin and rushed down there right away.'

Afterward Håvard didn't feel like telling this story. Just as well too; you soon get tired of stories like that.

Shortly after the middle of August, Håvard went up to the summer dairy to fetch some butter and cheese. He used good old Dobbin, who still bore two long scars on his left side.

The heather was in bloom on the moors now, and there was a smell of honey throughout the forest, laced with the scent of sun-burned resin and ripe blueberries and cloudberries.

192

Everything was so free and pure up here – the air seemed freshly washed and everything was so peaceful and so remote from the world – that Håvard felt like staying a few days. But he had no excuse for something like that. A farmer had to watch the calendar, and in eight to ten days it was harvesting time.

Kjersti – hadn't Kjersti changed, become more grown-up, during these last couple of weeks?

Perhaps he just imagined it. But it certainly looked like it. He stayed overnight up there, and in the evening Kjersti helped him throw a couple of fishing nets he'd taken along; an old flat-bottomed punt lay moored where the dairy brook flowed into the tarn. The following morning Kjersti and he drew the nets, and they caught eight or ten fine trout.

Kjersti was very quiet throughout.

Rønnau felt it had been unnecessary to stay the night – you could easily make it back and forth in a day – but she sweetened up when she saw the fine trout.

There were no more trips to the summer dairy.

Instead he proposed to Jon that the two of them should go on a two-day excursion to the cloudberry bogs way off east in the woods. People said the cloudberry crop was unusually good this year. And they were now just ripe for picking.

It was always fun to walk the woods with Jon. Hunter and angler both, he knew so much, and not only about the giant of Blue Crag.

They came back with as many cloudberries as they could carry, and Rønnau – who hadn't been very keen on letting them go – was extremely pleased. Jon handed over his berries at the farm. This spring he had delivered four wood grouse, so now his rent was paid up for this year. And he had a quarter twist of tobacco to his credit.

Then came the day when they brought the cattle home from the summer dairy.

There was no doubt about it – Kjersti had changed. She would blush and she had opened up, the way a flower opens up; her hair had more luster, her cheek more color, and somehow she was more grown-up. She had changed in other ways too. Curiously, she seemed happier, but she was also more serious. When she gazed at you with her big eyes, she could be strikingly attractive. Those last few weeks at the summer dairy had certainly done her a lot of good.

But she and Rønnau didn't seem to be getting along very well. Rønnau didn't welcome her back home, nor did Kjersti say a word to Rønnau.

The following day the grain harvest began.

The last couple of years Kjersti had come along to the fields. As a rule she gathered up after Håvard. He had trained her, and she had become both fast and good at binding the sheaves, lithe and nimble as she was. But this year Rønnau kept her in the kitchen and sent the youngest maid to work in the field.

Evenings Rønnau would be very short with Kjersti. As time wore on, Håvard found himself hoping that the cotters and the other workers would remain in the kitchen as long as possible, because Rønnau would try and check her temper when others were present. He caught himself bringing up topics of conversation that could just as well have been put off.

Kjersti paid more attention to her clothes this fall – probably for the simple reason that she was growing up. In the evening she helped in the cow barn – she was to be a fully trained dairymaid, after all. When she was through in the barn, she would go to her room and wash and change, to get rid of the cow-barn smells, as she said. Rønnau, who was always nicely dressed herself and insisted on cleanliness from everybody around her, resented it where Kjersti was concerned. 'So, you've gone and decked yourself out again!' she would say. 'We aren't having a party tonight!'

Kjersti grew defiant. You could see she was thinking: Someone who has fought off a bear with a broom doesn't have to back down for an angry middle-aged woman.

Or maybe she didn't think that. Maybe it was Håvard who did. So much the worse, if true. Anyway, he couldn't repress the feeling that, in these clashes between Rønnau and Kjersti, Rønnau was the unreasonable one.

There was often little enough cheer in the kitchen when they sat there by themselves, the three of them.

And it was getting worse rather than better. When Rønnau picked at Kjersti and Kjersti talked back – sometimes she did, contrary to the accepted ways – Rønnau would go white in the face with anger, and then she didn't always mince her words.

As a rule Kjersti withdrew and went to bed early – there was really nothing else she could do – and, left alone, the two of them were rather quiet; it wasn't easy to find something to talk about. The upshot usually was that Håvard dropped by the stable – they had built an addition and had more horses now – though he knew he could trust Anders that way. Anders was extremely fond of horses.

One evening Rønnau mentioned that she had had a visit from a suitor for Kjersti not long ago, with matchmaker and all.

Kjersti asked who that might be.

It turned out to be a middle-aged widower from the home parish; his name was Julius Haugom.

Kjersti burst out laughing. 'That old fool!' she cried.

Rønnau asked her, more sharply than one would have expected, who she thought she was anyway. Suitors couldn't be had for the picking, like cones on a spruce.

But Kjersti just laughed, and Rønnau grew angrier and angrier. This was how that evening ended.

Håvard felt strange. He didn't know very much about this fellow Julius, but he'd heard he was a fool. Why be in such a terrible hurry to get Kjersti married, almost before she was an adult? And what would Rønnau gain from it? When Kjersti married, she would have allodial rights to the farm.

The following day, when Håvard dropped by the shed to chop some wood, Kjersti suddenly appeared. It had been a long time since she'd been there.

'I want to tell you, Håvard,' Kjersti said, 'that you have to put a stop to this business with Julius. Or I'll run away!'

Then she was gone.

Håvard could scarcely believe that Rønnau was in earnest. But that evening, just in case, he took a walk up to see Hans Nordby, who was both godparent and guardian to Kjersti.

Nordby just laughed.

'Julius?' He snorted. 'A middle-aged fool who doesn't even have a regular farm – you know, he's running Haugom with his brother, and it is the brother who's the *man* in that house, though he's single, and though Julius has been married and has a son. . . .

'And Kjersti of all people, a good-looking girl and one of the best matches in the parish, heir to Olstad and all. Rønnau must have gone completely out of her mind!'

The last words hit Håvard like a blow. Gone out of her mind? During these last few weeks the same thought had occurred to him a couple of times, and in dead earnest. A couple of times Rønnau had really behaved toward Kjersti as though she was out of her mind.

He waved it aside.

Another thought occurred to him. Had Nordby set his mind on a match between Kjersti and Pål, his son? They were about the same age.

Then there would be hard bargaining. Hans would be sure to try and get hold of Olstad by hook or by crook, and Rønnau would never part with that farm without a fight.

He waved that aside too. No girl in this parish was good enough for Pål, not even Kjersti.

The result was that Nordby promised to talk to Rønnau. And he must have done so, for Julius was never mentioned again however many insults Rønnau took it into her head to hurl at Kjersti.

One evening Rønnau slapped Kjersti. It happened so quickly – Håvard hadn't noticed anything special and Kjersti hadn't said a word, as far as Håvard had heard anyway; but suddenly there was a smack. He jumped up. The two women stood facing each other, Rønnau pale, Kjersti with her left cheek flaming red. Neither said anything, but their flashing glances as they crossed back and forth made you think of lightning. Then Kjersti went up to her room, without a word.

Håvard waited a moment.

Then he asked, 'Has Kjersti done you some harm?'

'You ask about that?'

'Yes, I do. I, for one, haven't seen anything.'

'You? You never see anything!'

That night he dreamed a dream which roused him from sleep. Though he didn't like it, he thought little of it – the first time anyway.

He dreamed that a she-bear was standing on its hind legs before Kjersti, paws raised and ready to strike. Then he swung the scythe and stabbed the bear so it collapsed – no, it wasn't the scythe, it was the knife, the family dagger, and it wasn't a bear, it was Rønnau – but was it Kjersti? Wasn't it . . . ?

When he woke up he felt uneasy, but didn't quite know why. For that matter, he probably wasn't fully awake. Why did he dream about a she-bear? It was a he-bear, real as they come, he had cut down with the scythe; and it didn't stand before Kjersti on its hind legs either. Nothing but stuff and nonsense! he thought, half asleep.

Sometimes it was Rønnau who slept poorly during this period – when she finally managed to fall asleep. At times she would moan so loud that he awoke. It wouldn't stop and he woke her up.

'Did you have a bad dream, Rønnau? You were moaning so in your sleep.'

'Yes,' she said. 'Yes, I had such a bad dream. I dreamed . . .'

'She'll kill me some day!' she said once when this happened. But that was all she said. She held Håvard tight, burying her head in the hollow of his neck. She gradually calmed down and, her head cradled in the crook of his elbow, she finally fell asleep.

A little later he freed his arm, which was getting numb. But he remained

196

awake. He couldn't stop thinking, and he didn't like what he was thinking about.

A couple of times she told him – in the evening after a good time together – told him before he got around to asking her:

'I have been unreasonable with Kjersti, I know. The girl can't help it, after all. . . . I'll watch out. . . . We've got brains in order to use them.'

That sounded like the old Rønnau, and he thought, Thank God!

But the following evening it was just as bad, or even worse than before.

Then it would come back, that dream of his. It was a little different each time. But nearly always a huge she-bear would stand on its hind legs before Kjersti – or Tonè. He knew now – those two got mixed up with each other when he dreamed. The bear raised its paws to strike, and he swung his scythe, or his knife.

The result was that he became scared of that dream and tried to stay awake to avoid it.

Another dream which returned every once in a while during this period also troubled him. It became interwoven with the dream about the she-bear, and the first couple of times he didn't understand why. But whenever he awoke from this second dream he also felt uneasy.

He dreamed about an episode from the war of 1814.[33] Strange that such an old thing should pop up again so many years afterward. And strange, too, that it was this very episode which caused him to be summoned in front of the lines and be promoted to corporal.

One day that summer, on a scouting mission in the forest, he bumped into three Swedish soldiers who were out there on the same errand. It looked as though his goose was cooked, but chance made it turn out differently. He had a loaded rifle, and so did the three Swedes. But it took a bit of time to position such a rifle properly. Håvard did something requiring less time – he stabbed the foremost Swede with his bayonet. It went right through his heart, and he fell. The hindmost Swede took to his heels, and the third, who must have thought he was a victim of sorcery, dropped his rifle and put up his hands.

The one with the bayonet through his heart remained prone in the heather, giving a few kicks with his legs before he died. Håvard felt sick at the

33. The War of 1814 was a short war (July–August) with Sweden, in protest against the Treaty of Kiel whereby the Great Powers had handed over Norway to Sweden after the Napoleonic Wars, in which Denmark-Norway had been allied with France and Napoleon.

sight of it, and when he had brought the other Swede up to the Norwegian lines he had to withdraw and vomit.

As the bear lay kicking on the ground, setting the heather and dirt flying, Håvard felt sick for an instant, without understanding why at the time. He understood now.

Due to that experience with the soldier, he had never since been able to take part in butchering, whether the animal was big or small. He had done it once, and when the cow started twitching he had to put his head between his knees and throw up like a little boy.

At the parsonage they had laughed at him when they saw how he felt. Here at Olstad he had more control over such things; here he got a butcher to come to the farm and he himself took to the woods or disappeared until it was over.

Strange that he was able to go hunting. But it didn't bother him, at any rate when he went after big game. Perhaps because he knew the quarry had a chance of getting away.

But this episode with the three soldiers, together with the reference from Captain Rosenvinge in which he was cited for it, was in a way the reason why he was taken on by Parson Thurmann in Telemark. And that, in turn, was the reason he came up here – why he parted from Tonè, got acquainted with Rønnau, deserted Tonè, and turned murderer, or felt like one. . . . It was all connected within a single strange web with some pattern or other, which he glimpsed a little of but not all. He felt if he could see the whole pattern, he might be able to turn his fate around. For there was no mistaking it: right now he was skidding pretty badly.

He disliked these dreams, coming back time and again as though they wanted to warn him. And he disliked these thoughts, which came to him at night and wanted him to understand them, whispering, But don't you see . . .

He saw part of it but not all by any means, and it troubled him.

Meanwhile the month of September was moving along. They gathered in the grain and the potatoes; that part of their lives went on as before. It was a bumper year, and when he went over the figures the crops turned out to be three times as big as the first summer he was here. But he found only small satisfaction in it.

Between Rønnau and Kjersti the situation became worse, if anything. And in the evening, when he and Rønnau were alone in the bedroom, she was so impatient and insatiable that he sometimes wilted in her arms. Then she was beside herself and fretted, 'You're tired of me! I knew it!'

They debased themselves. She begged him to come, come, and some-

198

times he had to think about another woman to be able to come – the very woman he knew he should never, never think about in that way.

He understood that this wouldn't do in the long run.

He thought and thought to find a way out but couldn't see any for a long time. By the end of September life in the house had become extremely unpleasant, and when he couldn't think of anything to do out in the fields, he stayed mostly in the stable or the barn.

Then one Saturday afternoon, in the woodshed, he suddenly thought he could glimpse a solution.

What if he talked to Mr. and Mrs. Thurmann and asked them if they would take Kjersti into their home so she could learn housekeeping and the like? Others up here had done similar things; Hans Nordby's daughter had spent a winter in the house of Baron Rosenkrantz himself. She had even gotten engaged in the city, it was told, but Nordby nipped it in the bud; he didn't want to have an office drudge in the family, he said. And now the girl was going around crying, her eyes red and swollen.

But it didn't have to go that way with Kjersti. For that matter, there wasn't any eligible man at the parsonage, as far as he knew. Though young men eager to turn the heads of young girls could be found everywhere, that was so.

Unluckily, Parson Thurmann was in such poor health this fall, being confined to his bed with asthma and other trouble, that the curate, Mr. Paus, had to take care of the services. The latter had married Miss Lise, the parson's daughter, several years ago but felt he couldn't look for a parish as long as the parson felt so poorly.

There were services in Nordbygda the Sunday after Håvard had come up with this remedy, and he made a hint to Mr. Paus. But he was told that Mr. Thurmann was very sick, spent all day in bed, and spoke only to his wife.

Håvard thought perhaps he'd better go out to the Mill and have a talk with the mill owner.

But the idea no sooner occurred to him than he dismissed it out of hand. *That*, anyhow, was impossible. Instead, he would ride out to the parsonage and talk to Maren Sofie, the parson's wife, one of these days.

But first he must discuss things with Rønnau; he felt fairly certain she would accept his proposal.

And before everything else he had to speak to Kjersti. He couldn't very well send her away against her wishes.

The trouble was that Kjersti had begun avoiding him again, as she used to do just after he had arrived at the farm. He never managed to be alone with her.

If only good old Mari had been here! he thought. But Mari had died several years ago.

And, as ill luck would have it, one day it was too late.

It Strikes

One evening after supper Håvard sat in the kitchen whittling an ax handle. Rønnau had just lighted some pine sticks over by the fireplace. Kjersti was down in the cow barn with the dairymaid, one of the red cows being due to calve.

Håvard was just thinking that tonight he must have a talk with Rønnau and Kjersti; it couldn't wait much longer. And if they could agree on this one point, he would ride out to the parsonage first thing in the morning and speak to Mrs. Thurmann and the parson, to see if it could be arranged. Both had seen quite a lot of Kjersti since childhood and knew she had always conducted herself nicely.

Then Kjersti came in. She said that Dagros had calved and that everything had gone well.

Håvard was glad and got up – he wanted to go down and take a look at the calf before talking with the two of them. Just then Rønnau said something mean to Kjersti, and this time she talked back. He didn't hear what she answered, but noticed that Rønnau was losing control. Now everything happened so fast that it was like a dream. Rønnau, who had been cutting up the pine sticks before lighting them, turned sharply toward Kjersti and brandished her big carving knife. Håvard sprang forward, noticing from the corner of his eye that Kjersti, quick as an animal, had jumped out of her way and now stood over by the kitchen counter. She had picked up a chopping board with her left hand, and in her right she held the other carving knife which had been lying there. Her eyes were ablaze and he thought, Now they have both gone out of their minds! and quickly raised the ax handle to ward off the blow, wherever it might come from. Rønnau, who may have thought he meant to attack her, made a leap backward, driving the sharp iron rod in the fireplace – the kitchen crane as it was called – straight into her back. She let out a scream, fell backward with the weight of her whole body and banged her head against the edge of the chimney ledge. She remained motionless on the floor. Bending over her, Håvard noticed that she lay with her eyes closed. She must have fainted. He called her name again and again, but she didn't hear him.

Finally he could think of only one thing to do; he asked Kjersti, who stood there spellbound, to light a couple of candles, carry them into the bedroom, remove the bedspread, and push aside the sheepskin on the bed. Then he lifted Rønnau from the floor – she was heavy – brought her to the bed and undressed her. Rønnau was breathing, but her body seemed dead, quite different from the quick Rønnau he knew. Her eyes were closed, her breath heavy and coming in fits and starts.

Between her shoulder blades, where her back had crashed into the iron rod, she had a big blue spot, but it didn't bleed. The back of her head, where she had hit her head so hard against the chimney ledge, was bleeding a little. Håvard washed the wound – it wasn't much of a wound really – and wound a wet towel around her head. He put another towel on the pillow, so it wouldn't get blood-stained. She was bound to have an awful headache when she came to again.

It seemed to hurt when he touched the back of her head; she moaned a couple of times but remained unconscious.

'What is it?' Kjersti whispered. She was pale and trembling – knowing, most likely, that she had been only a hairsbreadth away from being stabbed with the knife.

'I'm not quite sure,' Håvard said. 'I think, when she backed away so abruptly and rammed her back up against the iron spike, she may have gotten a kind of crick. She screamed with pain, fell backward and hit her head against the chimney ledge, as you could see. It was quite a bang, and since then she has been unconscious. . . . But there's something else – it feels as though her body is paralyzed. Not her arms, but her body and her legs. Her body feels as though – well, as though it were dead.'

He sat down by the bed. Kjersti remained standing. She couldn't do anything, just stood there. In the end Håvard had to speak almost angrily to her to make her go to bed.

'You can't do anything here anymore, Kjersti. I can't either, I was about to say. I only sit here so I can help her when she comes around again – it can't take that long. If I need you, I'll call.'

That being said, she had to leave, and Håvard began his watch.

It was a long night. Rønnau was breathing, unevenly and a couple of times with a slight rattle. But otherwise she lay stock-still in bed, as though she were dead. Toward morning Håvard dozed off in his chair but awoke again, got up, and made coffee for himself. Otherwise nothing happened during those long hours.

When the hired girls entered the kitchen in the morning, he told them what had happened – without mentioning the quarrel and the knife – that Rønnau had tripped and hit her back against the iron spike, had lost her balance and hit the back of her head against the chimney ledge. He sent the youngest girl up to Teppen, for Maren, the corpse watcher, as she was called; but now Håvard thought it was such an ugly name that he called her the night watcher. The girl was to ask her to come as quickly as possible – she was home at present as far as he knew, since nobody was seriously ill in the neighborhood right now.

She came, and Håvard gave the same explanation to her as he had given the girls.

He hoped that Maren, who had seen so many sick people, would be able to help with something or other. But when she had looked Rønnau over, felt the blue spot in her back and passed her fingers over the back of her head, she just shook her head.

'She's got a whopping blow right there!' she said, pointing at the blue spot, where there was a big swelling. 'I think she's paralyzed from the waist down, that's how it feels. But she can move her arms, so they're okay. She gave a loud scream when she hit the iron spike, did you say? I suppose she got a crick, as they call it, or something worse. I've seen people get paralyzed for life from that. And then she fell backward and hit her head, and that's the worst of it, I'm afraid. She's been lying like this for twelve hours, you say? I'll be blessed if I know. She's able to swallow, I see. I don't know what to say; we'll have to wait and see and trust in the Lord. I'll need a bit of water in a cup, and a dish of water with a rag in case she should begin perspiring. Has she vomited? No? That's sort of odd.'

She passed her fingers over the back of her head once more, very gently. Rønnau moaned but didn't open her eyes.

'It feels as if the back of her head has been damaged, there might be some broken bones. And I'm afraid there may have been bleeding, in the head. That, you know, can be very serious. I find it worrisome that she doesn't come around. Twelve hours is a long time, you know! But as I've said, there's nothing we can do but wait and see.'

It was a long day. There wasn't much work at the farm these days, so Anders could manage it by himself. But the rumor of the accident had spread, and all the cotters dropped by, one after another, asking for news.

Jon was in the woods; he had borrowed Truls, the dog, and was going after moose.

Nobody uttered a word as they sat eating in the kitchen. Kjersti, pale and red-eyed, didn't say anything either.

In the afternoon Håvard took a nap for a couple of hours in one of the guest rooms. In the evening he sat with Kjersti in the kitchen awhile, but they didn't speak. Later the same evening Kjersti made coffee for Maren and buttered a few pieces of *lefse* for her. Then she went to bed. As long as Maren got her coffee, watching two or three nights in a row didn't bother her.

Håvard stayed up for a while, though he realized he was helpless. He went to the guest room and lay down but asked Maren to call him at once if anything happened.

But Maren didn't wake him, and in the morning there was no change.

Håvard stayed in the kitchen the next morning, or sat in the bedroom with Rønnau while Maren rested for a couple of hours. But nothing happened. Rønnau's lips were dry and cracked, and now and then he brushed them with a wet towel; that was all he could do.

In the evening – Kjersti had gone to bed – Maren came to Håvard in the kitchen.

'She seems to be a little better,' she said. 'Anyway, she's mumbling a few words once in a while. But there's no sense in what she's saying.'

Håvard followed her in.

Rønnau was mumbling, a jumble of meaningless sounds. Only at rare intervals were they able to catch a word or two. 'My honey bear!' she said once. Then she started mumbling again.

'*Damn Kjersti!*' she said suddenly, clearly and distinctly. Then she mumbled again for a while, just words without coherence or sense.

Then, abruptly, there came a sentence. 'Håvard, where are you?' she said in a clear voice.

'I'm here, Rønnau. Your Håvard is here. I'm sitting by your bed.'

But she obviously didn't hear him.

After a while Maren said, 'Quite frankly, I think she's sleeping. And if that's the case, I believe she'll pull through. You go to bed, I'll make a drop of coffee myself. Kjersti has prepared some food, I see. If something happens, I'll let you know.'

Nothing more happened that night. But Rønnau did not get better. In the late morning the following day – Håvard was sitting in the kitchen – Maren came in.

'She's conscious now!' she whispered. 'But I think the end is near.'

Rønnau was conscious, but she was obviously tired, very tired.

Maren came along in case she should be needed, but she wasn't.

Rønnau was lying with her hands on top of the sheepskin. She tried reaching Håvard with her right hand but wasn't able to. Håvard had to take her hand himself. She smiled at him, and it was as though the hard features in her face, the lines which had appeared during the last few weeks, vanished one by one while Håvard sat there looking at her. It was as though a big invisible hand brushed her face and smoothed out all her wrinkles and lines. She grew many years younger in a few minutes. It was like time travel; he recognized her face as it used to be ten years ago, when he had first met her. He felt as if he were taking this journey with her and became younger and more carefree; all the painful things that had happened recently were erased, and now everything would be well. . . .

He passed his hand over her hair.

'Rønnau!'

She looked at him and smiled again.

'Håvard . . . ,' she said, feebly.

Then a film settled over her eyes.

Olstad Without Rønnau

*I*t was as though Rønnau's sudden death paralyzed everybody on the farm. The kitchen was quiet, and the maids walked about with red-rimmed eyes. Nobody spoke, except when someone or other came to inquire about things that Rønnau had used to decide.

Still, during the first few days there was inevitably a lot of hustle and bustle, as always before a funeral. To the funeral there came people from the entire neighborhood, in addition to members of the family, who sat there in utter silence. It wasn't a cheerful funeral. The fact that Håvard walked around looking as grave as an undertaker didn't help. But besides, people felt this death to be a sad one. Rønnau had never gone out of her way to make friends. It appeared she had some anyway.

The day after the funeral the house sat there empty and desolate, as though it had been abandoned. Rønnau had been the center of everything that took place indoors. Now she was gone, and the place she had occupied was so empty that everybody fell silent.

Two days after the funeral Håvard went for a walk to a small cottage up in the nearby cotter country. The place was called Kroken; Goro, a widow, lived there. Her husband had been a carpenter and a turner, but he died early. Since then Goro had eked out a meager living by weaving homespun and linsey-woolsey for the farms all around. Most of the food she needed she grew herself on the couple of patches of ground she owned.

It was always so spotlessly clean and shiny in Goro's house. She herself was freshly scrubbed and her hair combed each day of the week, every vessel on wall and counter was clean and polished, and the floor was always strewn with fresh, chopped-up juniper greens.

'It's always Sunday at Goro's,' people used to say. 'Still, her loom never rests, from morning till night.'

Håvard had been up there a few times before. Now he came to ask her if she could see herself moving down to Olstad.

It was a fact, he said, that gossip was apt to spring up if a single man, not too old at that, lived by himself with a grown-up girl, which Kjersti by now had become. So he had looked around and had set his mind on Goro, if she could see herself moving down to Olstad, keeping an eye on Kjersti – she might leave home to learn something when occasion offered – and in general, as far as possible, standing in for Rønnau. She would have a nice room on the second floor – it had been empty but was easy to furnish – and could otherwise arrange things as she pleased.

Goro didn't reply right away. But it was an honorable offer, as she said. It was a difficult task, though. To take over after Rønnau was certainly no joke.

Håvard mentioned her wages – he had in mind to offer her three times what the eldest maid received.

Goro pretended, as custom required, that she hadn't even given a thought to the question of wages. No, it was the responsibility. . . . It was a long time since she'd been on a big farm on a daily basis.

Goro was the daughter of a freeholder and didn't ever let anyone forget it.

'We'll keep an eye on your house and tend the grounds for you,' Håvard said. 'And you can take your loom with you, that's clear. You're fond of it, aren't you, and there may well be an idle moment now and then, like in between the work seasons and at other quiet times.'

'You think of everything, don't you, Håvard,' she said. 'What you just said almost tempts me to say yes.'

And so Goro moved down to Olstad. She brought her loom along with her and set it up at once for linsey-woolsey.

She took to Kjersti right away and Kjersti to her.

'But you'll have to give notice to one of the maids, Håvard!' she said. 'There won't be as much housekeeping now as in Rønnau's time, and I suppose I should be of some use too.'

It was the eldest maid who had to go – she was in the family way anyhow, three to four months gone already, and her sweetheart had a cotter's place.

Goro was able and easy to deal with. Gradually it became more pleasant at Olstad again. The cotters said among themselves: There is an old saying that life must go on, though people pass away.

One day Jon came and said, 'It's no use your moping around here from morning till night. Tomorrow we take to the woods to hunt moose.'

Håvard felt the proposal as a relief and agreed.

They took along Truls, the elkhound.

The second night they slept at the Olstad summer dairy. The previous day they had been on the track of a moose, but it swam across a tarn in difficult terrain and got away.

Håvard had brought a bottle of liquor with him, knowing that Jon liked it. And besides there might be a chance to drink a hunter's toast.

'A bit of liquor is essential on the hunt,' Jon said. 'It loosens one's tongue, and none too soon, by God. People in this parish have a padlock on their jaws – except when they stick their heads together behind other people's backs, of course.'

From this sentence Håvard understood that Jon had something he was eager to talk about.

As the years passed, Jon had become the person whom Håvard trusted most among those he knew in this parish. Jon had grown older, his hair had a touch of gray. But he was the same tough woodsman as before, and just as good a hunter. He had a big mouth, as Rønnau had said already ten years ago. But one thing Håvard knew from experience – he said nicer things about you behind your back than straight to your face.

This evening he first talked a bit about Kerstaffer.

'You have had your share of worry this fall,' he said, 'so you probably don't know about everything that has happened in the parish. It isn't that much, of course, but . . . Kerstaffer has bought timberland, have you heard?'

No, Håvard hadn't.

Sure, Kerstaffer had bought timberland. Two hundred hectares. For six hundred dollars, neither more nor less, cash on the table. A good price too, you'd have to admit. The timber prices had gone up a little recently, but . . .

The one who sold was Sjønne Strøm. So now Sjønne had only three hundred hectares left. Some day he would probably sit there without even a farm.

It was doubtful whether Sjønne would be very much upset about that. He had his fiddle, after all. As for his wife and children, that was another matter – once you had been foolish enough to provide yourself with them . . .

'Yes, there you've been shrewd, Jon,' Håvard said, somewhat thoughtlessly.

'Yes, I've been lucky that way,' Jon said, suddenly speaking in such a bitter voice that Håvard started.

206

Several moments passed before Jon returned to the story of the timber sale.

'That timber deal, you know, bypassed Nordby.' People were saying Sjønne's wife had sworn that Hans Nordby would never get to buy any more wood lots at Strøm, even if they all had to go begging. He was supposed to have cheated Sjønne scandalously in a timber deal ten or twelve years ago, Nordby was.

Who would have thought that this old devil at Berg was interested in buying timberland, as long as it was possible to steal? But that was Kerstaffer for you, not easy to figure out, even capable of making an honest deal.

Anyway, people said it was to give his son, Little Erik, something to keep himself busy with that he bought that timberland. Just as Old Erik in his day let Kerstaffer enlarge the basement and take in lunatics for pay. To be reasonably insured against an accidental death, *he* had said. And Kerstaffer could probably say the same.

Jon was silent awhile.

'Everything repeats itself,' he said, more to himself than to Håvard, it seemed.

People said when Little Erik was born that nobody understood how such a stingy man as Kerstaffer had been able to part with so much of what was his that a child could come of it. But now they had turned it around and were saying that Kerstaffer hadn't really had any expenses there – he had merely put out a little of his own malice at interest.

'Can you understand, by the way,' Jon said suddenly, 'why Kerstaffer has never set fire to your place?' The barn and the stable, or something. He's certainly more than spiteful enough to do it.'

Håvard replied that he'd thought about that more than once, which was true. But Kerstaffer wasn't stupid – he knew well enough he would immediately fall under suspicion.

'And then you know, don't you,' Håvard said, 'that with the way you have trained Truls, it isn't easy to set anything on fire undisturbed at our place.'

They let Truls stay out at night, except in freezing winter weather. Jon had trained him so well that he never went outside the area of the farm, but, still, people found it safest to make a detour around the Olstad fields at night.

Truls lay on the floor a little way from the fireplace. He opened his eyes a crack on hearing his name; but when he found that nobody wanted anything he went to sleep again.

He was getting on in years now, Truls was. But when he understood they were going to the woods to hunt moose, he became happy as a puppy.

These things were not what Jon was getting at tonight. Håvard had figured out that much.

They had another drink – and now it seemed to come.

'It was smart of you to hire Goro only two days after the funeral,' he said. 'There's a lot of gossip, you know, about how Rønnau died so suddenly – died an accidental death, as you might call it.'

Håvard felt himself stiffen.

'In this parish everything becomes gossip,' he said, 'so naturally Rønnau's death had to be turned into gossip too.'

Jon didn't answer right away. And when he did answer, you could tell that he was choosing his words carefully.

'Just before she died,' he said, 'Mari invited me to the cow barn, into her stall, one day. Then she said to me: "You are a fool and not worth much. But we have a bigger fool among us here who is worth more, and he may need a piece of advice every now and then. Give him some advice then – if you have the brains to do it."

'Well, that was Mari.

'And let me tell you one thing. It is not so very strange if there's some gossip now. The whole parish knows it was rather bumpy between Rønnau and Kjersti during the last few weeks. They were never friends – you know that, and all the rest of us know it.' (No, Håvard hadn't really known.) 'But those last few weeks – if you want to know, from the day Kjersti came back from the summer dairy where she slapped the bear with a broom – it got much worse. Tell me, Håvard, are you really as stupid as I am afraid you are? Can't you understand how Rønnau was eating her heart out at the thought that it wasn't *her*, but Kjersti, who stood in the cow-barn doorway slapping the bear on the muzzle with a broom?

'This is what I think. Other people think what's worse. They think about what they have seen or heard – that Rønnau was completely changed during those last weeks. And then they figure: Rønnau was between forty and fifty by now. Håvard is between thirty and forty. . . .'

'I'll soon turn forty,' Håvard said. 'And Rønnau was only forty-two or so.'

'All right. And Kjersti is just over twenty, and a very pretty girl. She hasn't had any suitors . . .'

'She's had one, but she turned him down. And I agree with Kjersti. She'll find a better husband than Julius Haugom. She shall have the man she wants.'

Jon waved it aside.

'The one she wants? She will never get him. But don't let us talk about that. I'm simply asking you if you understand it might lead to gossip.'

208

'Yes, I understand it might lead to gossip,' he said, 'just as everything decent people do in such a parish can lead to gossip – because most people can never understand that anyone behaves decently. Tell me, Jon – do you remember when my cotters mutilated my horse and went to the sheriff to denounce me for murder? If they hadn't stumbled across Hans Tomter, I would have been *condemned* for murder. And why? Because I was drunk and told you that I was dreaming about giving my cotters eight shillings a day instead of four. They thought it was a cheat – because they couldn't imagine that any human being wished them well.'

'Yes, I remember,' Jon said curtly; he didn't like to be reminded of that episode.

'And do you remember what has happened since? I give my cotters four shillings, now as then – the other freeholders won't agree to more. But I have fixed up every single cotter's shack and rebuilt two from scratch. I would have rebuilt your house too, if only you'd let me. And when the cotters help me with this work, they get full daily wages, not a cotter's wages.

'This has caused anger and annoyance among the farmers up here. But do you think the cotters have become any friendlier?'

'Perhaps, and perhaps not,' Jon said. 'Those who have brains remember it a short while, perhaps. But listen, why don't you laugh at such things? I have heard that you were so merry and lighthearted when you were at the parsonage – before you came up this way. Why don't you laugh as you used to? Most people don't deserve anything else than to be laughed at!'

'Now you are the one who's right, Jon. Let's not talk any more about it. What you say is true – this parish has drained me of some of my lightheartedness.

'I might as well tell you one more thing while we are at it – do you know what enabled me to fix up the cotters' shacks? It was you, because you showed me the way about the woods, so that I cut the right timber. Olstad Farm made several hundred dollars from that. So, if you wish, you can say it was you who rebuilt the cotters' homes at Olstad.'

Jon grumbled; but it was obvious that he liked to hear it.

They sat silent for a while.

'What do you plan to do now?' Jon said, abruptly. 'I know what I would do if I were your age and had money put aside and all. But you? Do you plan to stay here in this parish for the rest of your life?'

'No!'

Håvard himself hadn't known he was so confident on this score until he heard himself say the word. But from then on he knew.

'The only bond I had here was Rønnau. Can you understand that? Now that she's gone, I'll bow out. I have improved the farm, though I suppose you can always find someone capable of running it down again. I have a few dollars stashed away – how many of them are mine after everything has been settled, that I don't know, but some of them are.

'Do you think I plan to sit here on a farm which people can say I've gotten by sleeping with the owner? Then you'll have to think again. The farm belongs to Kjersti, and she's the one who shall have it. But I'm not a fool either, I want to be bought out in proper fashion, because I have put ten years of work into this farm. With what I get, big and small, I should be able to buy myself a farm, but preferably far from here. I'm not hoary with age yet – no, I'm not thinking about another wife; for someone who's known Rønnau it isn't easy to imagine another wife. But a *farm* . . .'

And then he said something he hadn't meant to say.

'Høgne Lien now – you know something? Perhaps you think he isn't in his right mind? Believe me, there's nothing wrong with Høgne's mind – only he doesn't have much trust in people. He does trust me, though, and he did trust Rønnau – we were outsiders both of us, as he said. A week after the funeral he came to see me and asked what I intended to do. I could scarcely think of settling at Olstad, he said, because Olstad was Kjersti's farm – this was how far *he* thought; but do you think anybody else up this way has thought that far? Oh no; they believe I want to latch on to this nice farm, every one of them, they can't think otherwise. But can you guess what Høgne offered me? *To buy Lien.* The best farm in the parish – for a thousand dollars, plus a generous pension, that's true. If I accepted his offer, Høgne would live very well, indeed.

'I do have those thousand dollars. And I bet I could improve Lien so it would give me several hundred dollars a year.

'I didn't say no, because I didn't want to hurt him. But I didn't say yes either. And I'm not going to accept his offer – I plan to go away, far away. To some place or other where there's nothing that will remind me of Rønnau.'

Jon was crying, clasping his head in his hands.

'I haven't been so glad for many years,' he said, 'as I am because of what you just told me. That you're leaving, I mean. Well, you must understand me correctly – may I burn in hell if you're not the only person in this damn parish I'd give three shillings for, now that Rønnau is dead, I mean. And there's nothing that'll make me more unhappy than your going away. And yet, if I've ever been so happy about something I've heard over the last few years as the fact you'll be leaving, then the devil break my ass – even if I won't have a damn soul to go hunting with or spend time with!'

They woke up the next morning with a roaring headache.

That day they shot moose.

As they were on their way down with the moose the following day, taking a breather while the horse rested, Jon asked casually – a bit too casually:

'Have you seen Anders Flateby lately?'

Håvard was surprised.

'Anders Flateby? I haven't talked to him in many years. Anyway, isn't he half-crazy these days?'

He'd heard a rumor that Anders had become a bit odd from the day when Nordby squeezed two hundred hectares of timberland and the third of his tillage out of him. He would walk the road talking aloud to himself, it was said, and had gotten into the habit of seeing visions. The latest Håvard had heard – and that was last spring – was that Anders had seen Old Nick in the shape of Hans Nordby straddling the roof of the barn at Nordby one Thursday evening. That it was the devil himself and not Nordby he had realized from the fact that he sent out green and yellow tongues of flame from where he sat.

'Yeah, sure,' Jon said. 'More than half-crazy, I'm afraid.

'By the way, I've heard he's really got it in for you.'

'Me?' Håvard was flabbergasted. 'I barely know the man.'

'Well, you see, there is a sort of explanation for it. When Anders lost a third of his farm, his wife was furious. They quarrel so you can hear them way down the road. And Berte holds you up as a model to him day in and day out, they say. "Why can't you ever make the farm pay?" she says. "Look at Håvard down at Olstad! He gets the farm to pay off, he does!"

'You know, Anders has always been a poor farmer. Still, I can understand that he might get tired of hearing your name mentioned every minute of the day.

'And then he's probably noticed that you and Nordby are friends – that you can stand to have anything to do with that cold fish is more than I understand, but . . . And so he mixes you up with Nordby in a way and gets as furious with you as he is with him. Actually, there are some who think he's even more furious with you. Because, you see, you are an outsider to boot!

'That's why I thought it was a bit odd when I heard he goes around boasting, or whatever, that he has talked with you several times this fall. You and he are having *consultations*, he says.'

'Stuff and nonsense!' Håvard said. 'I haven't exchanged a word with Anders in – well, it must be at least three years. And what would I have to talk with him about?'

'If you ask me, then I ask you!' Jon said.

But he seemed relieved.

'Gossip is what it is!' he said.

When Håvard came back again from the woods, there lay a letter for him on the bedroom table. It had been brought by a messenger from the parsonage, Goro said.

It was from Telemark, from Gjermund, his brother. It was written by Peder Trondsen, schoolmaster. Gjermund had never bothered to learn how to write, and good old Jon was probably dead, as was to be expected.

The letter related, in brief, that his mother had died, after being confined to bed for a period of time, on August 27th last, in her seventieth year.

That was nearly two months ago. He remembered that day very well – it was the day he went out to Hans Olsen Tomter to fetch the bearskin. He who once in a while believed he had second sight hadn't thought about her in particular on that day. So she must have died peacefully, as was to be expected of her. She had died of the infirmities of age, the letter said.

But he felt certain that she had thought about him that last day – as he rode north thinking about the bearskin.

He *had* thought about her, though. He recalled thinking, arrogant and proud, My mother should see this bearskin!

But she had had other things to worry about that day.

At the end of the letter were a few lines which evidently expressed a deep concern of Gjermund's.

'Your brother Giermund sends greetings and wishes to let you know that your mother left a couple of things she would like you to have in remembrance of her. There will be a new settlement of the estate most likely, and your brother bids me to let you know that you shall have your part, if you so wish. But there will probably only be some small articles for you, he bids me tell you, with his regards.'

So. Gjermund had thought about himself a little on that day too. And Håvard, after all, had become so rich.

Håvard sat there awhile, staring vacantly ahead of him.

He had searched for some means of seeing his mother again, if only once, as long as possible. But now it was too late.

He felt he'd become more alone in the world than he'd ever wanted to be.

Kjersti came in. 'Was it something important, Håvard?'

'Yes and no. It was only from my brother – he writes that my mother has died.'

Preliminary to Settlement of the Estate

*T*he day before the funeral Håvard had gone up to Hans Nordby. He asked him if he would be willing to come an hour or so ahead of the other guests the following day.

When Hans came, Håvard took out Rønnau's bunch of keys.

'I know what most of these keys are for,' he said, 'and almost all of them are for drawers and cabinets which have to do with the management of the farm. There are only two keys here which I'm not quite sure about, but I think I know what they are for, too. This big one here, I think, is the key to the traveling chest Rønnau always kept in the bedroom, and this small one must be for the till which is inside the chest. There, I know, she kept the change she needed for everyday use. I haven't opened the chest – I hope you believe me when I say that.

'As you can see, she had two more chests, and they are much bigger. But where she kept the keys for those, I cannot say I know. I would like to hand these two keys over to you right now. We can put them in a wrapper and seal it, if you wish. Some day we'll have to open those three chests – if we can find the keys; I have an idea they are in the traveling chest. But there's no urgency about that, and the keys will be safe with you.'

They agreed on that.

Some time passed before the traveling chest was opened. Nordby and Håvard were both busy, and as far as he was concerned Håvard knew he almost dreaded opening those chests. Then it would be over for good.

But one afternoon early in November, Nordby dropped by. He happened to be free that evening, so they might as well take a look at the things.

He took out the sealed wrapper with the keys. They called in Kjersti.

'You have to be in on this so it's all done properly,' Nordby said. 'It's you who have the allodial right, you know, and as soon as you get married you will take over the farm.'

The key, nearly the size of the storehouse key, fit the lock of the traveling chest. Håvard had seen Rønnau open it several times and knew roughly what he would find there.

In the chest itself lay three or four shawls for use at regular church services; two silver brooches, also for ordinary Sunday wear; two pairs of silver shoe buckles; and a broad, black leather belt worked with silver. Kjersti and Håvard had seen all of this numerous times, Hans Nordby too for that matter. But now they made a list and signed it, all three of them.

In the till to the left – it was dovetailed into the wall of the chest like a sort of shallow drawer and had a wooden cover with a padlock – they found something which Håvard also knew was there, Rønnau's money for every-day use. There were some dollar bills and a few silver dollars, besides smaller coins in silver and copper. All in all about thirty dollars. This was money that Rønnau used for minor expenses – when she hired women outside the household for a big wash, when she paid for the sewing of an everyday dress for herself or for Kjersti, and the like.

They wrote it down and signed their names.

In the innermost part of the till lay a key ring with two keys, and they made a guess that they were for the two chests.

The bigger key, sure enough, was for the smaller chest. They opened it and found that here was all the silver. On the bottom lay a carefully kept list, where it was noted what was Rønnau's own and what belonged to the farm – all they had to do was add up and tick off on the big document.

'Paper from the Mill!' Nordby said.

Rønnau's own things, which occupied one-half of the chest, included twelve silver spoons, evidently from Håkenstad; two large precious silver brooches; three gold rings; three pairs of silver shoe buckles, bigger and more ornamented and no doubt much more precious than those she put on for a regular church service; a couple of bracelets, also of gold; and two belts, one of pure silver, the other worked with silver.

'This is worth quite a bit of money!' Nordby said.

In the other partition of this chest they found all the silver that belonged to Olstad Farm – a silver mug, with the year and initials pricked in, and two dozen spoons were the chief articles.

'A good old farm, this is!' Nordby mumbled. 'That silver mug is awfully old; but twelve of those spoons Ola Olstad bought in the city after he'd made a good timber deal. He was fond of silver, Ola was. I was with him when he bought them. He bought a bracelet for Rønnau at the same time.

'There is silver here worth hundreds of dollars!' Nordby said. 'They didn't deliver any more silver than they had to here at Olstad either, I see, when the silver tax was levied.'

The list was now complete. As it happened, the part which concerned Rønnau had been signed – most of it anyway – by the sheriff 'as witness' fifteen years ago. That must have been just before she married Ola Olstad.

They signed here too, all three of them.

'And then there is the big chest.' It was Nordby who spoke all along. 'This is the key, I suppose.'

There were two keys in the silver mug, one big and one small.

It was the big key which unlocked the chest. What the small one was for, they didn't yet know.

214

There was a smell of camphor when they opened the lid. The chest had two partitions. The larger partition was packed with holiday attire – at the very top a set of silk shawls, heavier and finer than those Rønnau used Sundays and in church.

In the lesser partition there was a big box – the little key unlocked it – and, in the same manner as in the other chest, an exact list of all her dress clothes. It began as follows:

At the bottom, my confirmation dress.

Then followed, one after another:

Dress presented to me by my father when I turned 21.

Dress bought at the Mill for my first year's wages.

Then, a little further down:

My wedding dress when I was married to Ola Hansen Olstad on the 11th of April, 1814.

And quite a bit lower down on the list:

My wedding dress when I married Haavard Giermundsen Viland on the 22nd of April, 1818.

There was a good deal more – Rønnau had been fond of clothes, and it was all written down, most of the articles with the year and date when she had received or bought them. But there were a few exceptions. Three or four dresses which were entered on the list and lay in the chest, so they had to go back to the time before she married Ola Olstad, were without a year and date, and without further information. Most likely, they were from the years she was in service at the Mill – and Håvard felt as though he was prying into things which didn't concern him.

Nordby, who had touched each silver article as though it were a beloved little child, didn't greatly appreciate women's clothes and was visibly relieved when they were through with the list.

'Kjersti, you will have to put everything back again, so we can be sure it will be done right,' he said. 'When did she air these clothes, by the way? They didn't lie like this year after year, did they?'

Kjersti could relate that she had helped air them twice a year, mostly when the menfolk were in the woods.

Now only the big box was left. It had a complicated lock, the key had to be turned back and forth several times in a certain way before the box opened. When the lid sprang open, Nordby explained: 'First twice to the right, then once to the left, and then once more to the right. We have the same kind of box at Nordby.'

In the box lay, on top, three canvas bags marked with Roman numerals II, III, and IV, and under them again a large sealskin bag.

'The sealskin bag is the oldest, it seems,' Nordby said. And it proved to be so.

In the sealskin bag, at the bottom, lay a big canvas bag marked with a Roman numeral, I. In it lay, wrapped in thick paper, ten rolls of silver dollars, altogether two hundred dollars. In a wrapper beside it lay a fat bundle of dollar bills, two hundred all in all. In another wrapper were two hundred more. Altogether there was six hundred dollars in silver and bills in the canvas bag.

Besides these packets and wrappers, there lay – somewhat apart – a document inside the big sealskin bag. They could see at once that it was written in the hand of the mill owner. But it was signed by Rønnau, with the mill owner himself and the farm steward at the Mill as witnesses. The document was written six years ago, in the fall.

It was a kind of will.

In case I should die before my husband, Haavard Giermundsen, I wish to declare the following:

The money in Canvas Bag I (two hundred dollars in silver and four hundred in bills) was in my possession before I married Ola Hansen Olstad. The two hundred dollars in Canvas Bag marked II was the amount I received at the settlement that was undertaken when I was going to be married for the second time. I consider this to be my money, and I wish that this sum of altogether 800 dollars – to wit, eight hundred dollars – shall in full go to my surviving husband, Haavard Giermundsen, provided the law permits it. If not, as much as the law permits shall go to my husband, Haavard Giermundsen. But prior to any settlement he shall be paid 200 – two hundred – dollars, which was a personal loan from him to Olstad Farm during the first two years of our marriage, when he purchased new implements for the farm, together with seed grain, cattle, etc.

Furthermore, I wish that my surviving husband, Haavard Giermundsen, shall inherit all the silver (noted on a separate list) which is my personal property.

If my surviving husband, Haavard Giermundsen, should marry after my death, all these testamentary gifts are null and void, and the money as well as the silver shall be divided equally between my brother Haagen, my sister Randi, and my stepdaughter Kjersti.

Below was written in Rønnau's own hand:

Written at the Chief Residence, the Mill, after my dictation on the 3rd of September, 1821, and hereby signed by me.

Here followed her name and the names of the mill owner and the steward as witnesses.

Below, Rønnau had written an addition in her own hand, dated April 22, 1827, that is, last spring:

216

Of the 800 – eight hundred – dollars in the Canvas Bag marked III, which is money brought in by Olstad Farm during the time since 22nd of April, 1818, part – how much I cannot say, but the law will know – belongs to my husband, Haavard Giermundsen. The remainder must, as far as I understand, be divided equally between me and my stepdaughter Kjersti. However, if the law permits it, I wish that at my death my entire part shall go to my surviving husband, Haavard Giermundsen, or, if this is not permitted, as much of this amount as is ruled allowable under the law.

Håvard understood one thing: this will was a sort of apology because Rønnau had sat on her money the first year, when Håvard needed plow and harrow.

'That is some document!' Nordby said. 'Whether it is valid according to the law is more than I can answer. She must have had a guardian, and he should have signed, I think.

'Otherwise, I have to see to it, of course, that Kjersti won't lose anything she has a claim to.

'But I have to say that Rønnau must have had good advisers, since she managed to save her money throughout all those difficult years.'

He was probably thinking of the mill owner, Håvard thought.

Then Nordby brought up something else.

'Håvard, do you happen to know what caused Rønnau to make a will at that time?'

Håvard couldn't give a definite answer to that. 'But,' he said, 'Rønnau was seriously ill that summer – most likely it was what is called pneumonia. She was in bed for a whole month and felt poorly for several weeks afterward. During that time she rested up at her brother's and sister's for a while. It must have been then that she went to the mill owner and got that paper written.'

'Yes . . . To be sure . . . That must be it. So, the only thing that's not clear has to do with those three hundred and twenty dollars found in the fourth canvas bag without any explanation.'

Håvard knew the explanation but didn't say anything.

When Olstad began to yield a sizable annual surplus, Rønnau came to him one day – this was six years ago – and said that, things being as they were and Kjersti being entitled to take the farm by allodial right when she was married, in eight to ten years most likely, it seemed to her that Håvard and she had the right to think a little about themselves and about getting compensation for their work, because they both knew enough about allodial appraisals to be able to guess that from *there* they couldn't expect very much to come their way.

It was after this proposal that they started figuring wages for themselves – forty dollars a year for Rønnau, eighty dollars a year for Håvard. The wages to be figured from the day they were married.

These were the three hundred and twenty dollars. She hadn't yet added the wages for the last year – they used to settle up between themselves when Håvard had received payment from the Mill.

Håvard himself had fifteen hundred dollars stashed away in his own chest. They were the two hundred he had when he came here, the six hundred and forty he had taken as wages, and in addition the sums he had made over the years as a middleman in all the buying and selling which took place between the Mill and the farmers in Nordbygda.

That money he kept with a good conscience. He had worked hard for it. Olstad had become the best farm in all of Nordbygda, worth at least twice as much as when he came here. Kjersti was rich, but it wouldn't show up in the allodial appraisal – that would be about the same as it was ten years ago, when an appraisal was made before the previous settlement. At that time the entire farm was appraised at a thousand dollars. Håvard knew that if he could buy it today for three thousand, he would make it pay.

They had been busy with this inspection for several hours, and it was now evening. Goro came in and said the table had been laid in the parlor.

'I suggest you set a place for Kjersti, too,' Nordby said. 'We have to pretend we are gentry this evening and allow women to sit at the table. She'll have to be in on it anyway when we start talking about the settlement of the estate and all that.'

Kjersti sat at the table without speaking and barely touched the food. But Nordby ate and drank his fill and talked enough for three.

'That was a lot of money,' he said. 'Kjersti will be rich, the best match in the whole parish, regardless whether that will of Rønnau's is declared valid or not. And you too, Håvard, will be rich. But we don't need to undertake any settlement yet. Kjersti doesn't have the right to demand it till she gets married, and I, as guardian, won't insist on it. According to the law – and this I know – you, Håvard, have the right to use Olstad till that day comes. And as we all know, the farm couldn't be in better hands.'

Afterward they discussed what to do with the keys and the three documents. They agreed that the chests should be locked as they had been. The documents would stay where they were, but Håvard was to write a summary of them and get Nordby's signature on the paper, which would be kept at Nordby together with the key to the traveling chest.

The only remaining question, Nordby thought, was whether Håvard needed some money for the daily operation of the farm.

'I have the money for that,' Håvard said. 'Besides, I have some money coming to me from the Mill, too. According to the agreement, I can pick it up in December.'

But he had a feeling that the mill owner might ask for another deferral. Håvard had several hundred dollars on account there now. During the last three to four years the Mill had had an uphill struggle.

Goro cleared the table and brought beer and French brandy. Nordby spoke about one thing and another.

When he left, quite late in the evening, Håvard opened the doors to the hall and the porch. Goro had been keeping the stove going, and the air was thick with the smell of the tobacco Nordby had been smoking in his long-stemmed pipe.

The two candles on the table fluttered in the draft.

Kjersti sat a little ways from the table, watching Håvard.

This evening her eyes seemed to shine more brightly than usual. Håvard couldn't help remembering how she would sit in the chimney corner in the evenings during his first year up here – would sit there motionless, without saying a word, but with her eyes fixed on him every time he happened to look in her direction.

When he thought he had aired the room sufficiently and had closed the front door – he was faintly surprised that Kjersti hadn't gone up to her room to prepare for bed – she said his name:

'Håvard . . .'

She said it in a faint voice, as though from far away, or as though it was hard for her to utter this one word. In a flash it occurred to Håvard that this had happened to him once before.

'Yes?'

'That evening – when Rønnau swung the knife at me . . . and afterward hit her head against the chimney ledge . . .'

She didn't get any further.

'Yes, Kjersti . . .'

The next thing Kjersti said came so softly that Håvard could barely hear it.

'When she fell . . . had you hit her then?'

It came so surprisingly that Håvard was speechless for a little while.

'No, Kjersti, I hadn't. I was standing with the ax handle in my hand, don't you remember? If I had hit her with that, there would have been marks after it. But – you were there. Don't you remember what happened?'

'No!' she whispered. 'I saw her swing the knife. Afterward I remember nothing until I saw her lying with her head against the chimney ledge.'

Håvard wondered, and wondered again. Had she really forgotten? People surely were strange, there wasn't much more to say about that.

He could see it – unforgettable as it was, even the recollection seemed to come to him through the corner of his eye – could see how Kjersti quick as lightning backed away from the knife, grabbed the other carving knife which lay on the kitchen table and held it in her hand, ready to defend herself with a knife if necessary. But at the same moment he, Håvard, had jumped in between them and, with the ax handle poised, stood ready to ward off the blows wherever they came from.

'Rønnau must have thought I had meant to hit her,' he said. 'Otherwise I can't explain . . .

'I have thought back and forth about what happened in this house the last weeks Rønnau lived. She was so utterly different that I didn't recognize her anymore. I don't believe Rønnau was quite in her right mind toward the end. Jon, who isn't stupid, says the same. She was like another person, he says – and he saw only a small part of it.

'If she'd been in her right mind, it would never have occurred to her that I could take it into my head to hit her.'

At the very back of his head was the little gnat. So? But when you were dreaming, toward the end . . .

'It must have been for this reason she made that backward jump,' he said, 'ramming her back up against that iron spike. . . . You remember, don't you, how the iron rod stuck out from the fireplace, with a pot on the hook?'

Kjersti was still whispering, as though there were hidden shadows in the room, shadows that mustn't hear anything.

'Oh, yes, that I remember.'

'There was hot water in the pot, and Rønnau had swung the rod forward just before she lighted the pine sticks – and that, in turn, was just before you came in. I believe she had meant to wash something or other. She often did in the evening, you remember. That was why the iron spike, the outermost part of the kitchen crane, projected straight into the room, and so she drove it into her back the moment she jumped away. That was the great misfortune. The odds against it were over a thousand to one. . . .'

Thoughts came and went: the scythe which sank in between the killer bear's ribs – the odds against it were over a thousand to one. . . .

He continued:

'When she drove the iron spike into the small of her back, it must have been terribly painful, and I think she must have damaged her back so that her body got paralyzed or something. She let out a loud scream, lost her balance – or so it seemed – and fell flat on the floor, and without softening her fall with her hands or anything, banging the back of her head against the chimney ledge.

'Was that when you came to again, or whatever we should call it?'

'No,' Kjersti whispered. 'Not right away, I think. The first thing I remember is that Rønnau was on the floor and that you stood bent over her, saying, "Rønnau . . ."'

'But I think I vaguely remember that you had said her name several times.'

He had. He had said her name at least four or five times before he realized she was unconscious.

'Then you asked me to light two candles, lifted her up, and carried her into the bedroom; I pushed the sheepskin aside and you undressed her – I felt I shouldn't watch that – and you said her name again and again, but she didn't answer and was unconscious.

'I remember all that. And still it's like a dream. . . .'

Håvard sat for a moment.

'So all this time,' he said at last, 'you've been thinking that perhaps I had killed Rønnau. What was going through your mind as you went around thinking you lived in the same house with a murderer – or, well, killer?'

She didn't answer right away. But when the answer came, it made him speechless for a while.

'I was thinking,' she said, and for the first time she didn't whisper, 'I was thinking I could go through fire and water for you.'

When he was able to speak again, he first tried to laugh it off.

'No, I didn't kill Rønnau,' he said. 'The misfortune is bad enough as it is, but *that* bad it isn't, and you won't need to go through fire and water for me on that account.

'Rønnau killed herself, in a way, without meaning to. Or it was sheer bad luck. Or fate – I don't know . . .

'But what did you think when you came to and saw Rønnau lying there – do you remember that?'

Now she whispered again, 'Oh, I got so scared.'

Once again the shadow of a memory darted through his head, but he couldn't catch it.

He didn't say any more.

But she hadn't finished yet.

She said, now speaking quite softly again, 'Sometimes I dream – about that evening . . . And then I'm the one holding the knife. And I get so scared!'

Håvard didn't say anything.

Kjersti continued, but now in her ordinary voice, 'Why do you think

Rønnau was – that Rønnau wasn't in her right mind toward the end?'

'Oh . . .' – he would rather not go into that. 'For several reasons. Among other things because suddenly, without any warning, she became so spiteful toward you. It was no use talking to her either.'

Kjersti's eyes were intent on one of the candles. She sat as though lost in thought, far away.

'Oh . . . ,' she then said. 'It didn't come that suddenly, not really. And – I understood quite well why she hated me. She didn't have to be crazy on that account. I hated her too!'

She looked at Håvard, with a sort of defiance and triumph in her eyes.

'Kjersti!' Håvard said. 'You mustn't even think such things, much less say them. I could see quite clearly that Rønnau was awful to you toward the end. But she's dead now. Remember that, Kjersti.'

'Yes, Håvard,' Kjersti said obediently.

The stairs creaked. It was Goro coming down, wrapped in a shawl. She stopped as soon as she could see the inside of the parlor through the open hall door.

'I thought I heard you walk Nordby part of the way, and so I wanted to check on the fire,' she said.

'No,' Håvard said, 'I only let him out. But then I aired the room after him. That may have been what you heard. You could give it a more thorough airing tomorrow.'

Kjersti rose and walked upstairs.

'You will put out the lights then, Håvard, won't you!' Goro said.

Håvard smiled at her, and she, who knew why he smiled, turned around and shyly returned his smile.

Omens

*H*åvard couldn't recall that the dark weeks before Christmas had ever been quite so dark before. The frost set in right after the funeral – several weeks earlier than usual – but no snow came. After a couple of weeks the weather changed and turned mild, and then came rain, but no snow. It was during this time that Håvard went moose hunting with Jon.

The weather continued mild, with overcast skies and rain. It was already dark at midday, like evening. The pine sticks were burning in the chimney hold from morning till night.

At Olstad people would barely exchange a word as they walked past one another. It was silent around the kitchen table – everyone sat with lowered eyes or looked sideways. That was certainly so when Håvard threw a glance at someone or other at the table. After supper the cotters were in such a hurry to leave it almost seemed they were dying to get home.

After that conversation with Jon at the Olstad summer dairy, Håvard knew – or thought he knew – what the reason was for all of this. *Gossip* was scouring the parish, spawning and growing like mice and rats in an underground hole. The women went with their knitting from house to house more often than before, forgetting about the cattle and their husbands and the evening chores a little longer than usual, because they had such dark, terrible things to talk about.

'Have you heard the latest I've heard . . . ?'

Kjersti wandered about looking pale; she had obviously heard something. Goro was quiet and despondent – she had no doubt heard more.

Jon showed up more often for work this fall than he used to, though he had no obligations that way. Håvard knew what the reason was: he wanted to keep the cotters in some kind of check and shut the mouths of the worst ones.

Every once in a while Jon would remain after the others had left. Then Håvard saw to it that Goro, too, was present – he did this as a rule anyway, thinking it wise to sit alone with Kjersti as little as possible. And both Goro and Kjersti seemed to understand that.

Jon was the same as ever – he joked and laughed and told wild stories of the hunt. Sometimes he made both Goro and Kjersti laugh. Then Håvard might get up and go tap a pot of beer in the cellar. Anyone who happened to be outside the windows peeping in at such times – and they all knew there was often somebody there – must have wondered how they could be so lighthearted in this house, where death had been a guest only a few weeks ago.

Then they'll have that, too, to talk about! Håvard thought. Let them!

The first Sunday of Advent there was a religious service in Nordbygda. Håvard took Kjersti and Goro along and went to church. Seeing that an open space formed around them on the church green, he wondered whether the two women noticed it. They probably did – women were often as sensitive as animals about such things.

It was the curate, Mr. Paus, who officiated. This time he had brought Lise along – they had been married for several years now.

When the service was over, Håvard went up to Mr. Paus to find out how Mr. Thurmann was doing. He was poorly, confined to his bed every day.

'I'm very sorry,' Håvard said, adding, 'There's something I'd like to speak to him about. But I guess it'll have to wait.'

Mr. Paus said it would be better.

Lise kept in the background. She greeted him, but mostly kept her eyes on the ground.

Nearly ten years had passed since Håvard had talked with her and her sister, Anne Margrethe, on a daily basis.

It was like thinking back to a different existence.

On Monday Håvard went down to the woodshed, where Jon was struggling with the firewood for Christmas. Jon never went to church and hadn't seen the open space on the church green, with the people standing in a circle on the outside.

He asked Jon about the gossip – whether it was getting worse or wearing off.

'Well, you know, it tends to get worse,' Jon said. And here, alone with Håvard, he was neither merry nor lighthearted.

He added a couple of words on his own: 'I'd never thought this parish would prove to be worse than I had expected. But it has happened this fall. If people had something to go on, it could get dangerous.'

After a pause he said, 'The worst thing is I can't for the life of me find out who is blowing on the embers. There is someone, and my guess would be Kerstaffer. But he's in bed, and very sick, they say.'

He paused again.

'Nobody has anything to go on, as far as I have heard anyway. Well, there is Maren Teppen. She has somehow taken a strong dislike to Kjersti, keeps complaining that Kjersti was so cold and hard – she didn't utter a word of grief when Rønnau died, she says.'

'That may be true,' Håvard said. 'That's how Kjersti is. She shuts herself up when others spill over. She has certainly shut herself up this fall. It is easy to see that she's been unhappy since Rønnau died. But, you know, if somebody wants to do you harm, everything can be misinterpreted.'

Jon didn't answer.

The snow came in December at last – scantily, but enough for sleighing, and the farmers could start the hauling of coal and ore to the Mill. Håvard himself drove out there one day to pick up the settlement of his account; but it turned out as he had expected, and he returned home with a piece of paper instead of money – the mill owner asked for a year's deferral this time too. 'It is no secret anymore, the Mill has been in difficulty again these last few years. If it doesn't get better in a year's time, we may have to accept Baron Rosenkrantz's offer of another subsidy, which means that he will take over the whole works sooner or later, and then you won't find me in this chair anymore.'

224

Håvard knew quite well that at one time there had been something more than friendship between Rønnau and the mill owner. But that had been long before he appeared on the scene – and anyway, the mill owner could hardly have behaved shabbily toward her, for in that case Rønnau would never have gone to him when she wanted to write her will. Whatever the truth of that old story, Håvard had taken a liking to this big, quiet man.

'Let's hope it will turn around,' Håvard said. 'It can't be denied that Baron Rosenkrantz has a greedy streak, judging by what little I have seen of him.'

He had taken over two more farms in Nordbygda in the last two years – with Nordby as go-between, of course – and two farmers who had previously been free men now sat on these farms like cotters of sorts, at the mercy of the Baron.

'We'll see!' the mill owner said. 'Things have turned around a couple of times before.'

Two weeks before Christmas, Håvard, Jon, and Anders, the servant, drove to the capital with three loads. It was a change, anyway. On their return Håvard asked Jon if he was expected somewhere on Christmas Eve – if not, he was welcome at Olstad.

'It probably won't be a very cheerful place this year,' he added, 'but . . .'

Jon accepted the invitation and said that, once they had tapped the keg they were carrying in their load, it would get cheerful, all right.

And it did. Even Kjersti laughed.

Christmas was quiet at Olstad. They didn't have any visitors and weren't invited anywhere, except to Amund Moen, who celebrated the baptism of his third child, a girl. Håvard was a godparent. The baptism took place in the home parish church between Christmas and New Year's – it was considered grander to have your child baptized out there. They were a large troop as they drove out to the home parish together. Håvard put the bearskin on the big sleigh and took Kjersti along.

Afterward they drove straight back to Moen.

Amund was unchanged. He was unusually jovial, and very gallant toward Kjersti. 'If there was going to be a dance here this evening, I would certainly have opened the dance with you, Kjersti,' he said. 'The prettiest girl first, that's my custom. And had it been twenty years ago, when I was a merry young bachelor, I would have gone courting to Olstad, as sure as sin. And I wouldn't have courted you for your money either.'

Kjersti thawed for a moment.

The other guests kept their distance, and Håvard took Kjersti and drove home early.

That they weren't invited any other place didn't have to mean anything, of course. It was only three months since Rønnau had died.

Didn't mean anything? Håvard knew better.

On January 2 there was another service in Nordbygda, and the curate came. Mr. Thurmann was still confined to his bed – it had been over three months now. As usual Mr. Paus stayed with the parish clerk. Håvard went to church alone this time, not wanting to expose Kjersti once more to being at the center of a circle of staring eyes.

Nobody talked to him – Amund Moen wasn't there – but he'd gotten used to it by now.

After the service, as the people were slowly dispersing, Ola Viken, who was Mr. Paus's coachman, followed Håvard down the road.

'I don't know . . . ,' he said, and stopped. Håvard also stopped.

'I really ought to speak to you about something, Håvard. . . . But I don't know . . .'

He didn't make a move, nor did Håvard, until all the churchgoers heading their way had passed them.

Ola still waited awhile, until he was certain they were alone in the road. Then he said – but first he looked carefully around him once more:

'There is an awful lot of gossip about Rønnau, who died so suddenly.'

They were walking slowly down the road.

'I've gathered that much,' Håvard said, with a touch of coldness in his voice perhaps. So now the gossip must have spread to the home parish.

'Hm. It isn't just ordinary gossip anymore. The sheriff has been up here twice and talked to people. They say there might be a *trial*.'

'*Trial?*' Håvard said. '*Trial?* Of what?'

Ola lowered his eyes.

'They say there will be an investigation to determine if Rønnau died a natural death or if she died in – in a – well, if she was murdered. I just wanted to let you know.'

'But this is pure nonsense, Ola. Rønnau fell backward and hit her head against the chimney ledge.'

Ola still stood with lowered eyes.

'That may be,' he said. 'But anyway, the sheriff has been up here, as I've told you.'

'But what can he find out here? Kjersti and I were the only ones who were in the kitchen with her. . . .

'The only other person who might know *a little* is Maren Teppen, the night watcher. And she must've seen . . .'

226

Håvard stopped. What could Maren have seen, really?

They had stopped where the private road turned west toward Olstad.

'Maren Teppen is one of those the sheriff has called on,' Ola said. 'Well, I just wanted you to know.'

Håvard still didn't move. He needed a little time to collect himself.

Up to now Ola hadn't looked at Håvard even once. Now he suddenly fixed him with his eyes.

'Listen, Håvard, why don't you just clear out!' he said, in an intense, urgent voice – Ola was scared. 'If you come over to the parsonage I'll help you, so that nobody will know where you're going.'

'I won't run away because of gossip!' Håvard said, angrily. Then he added, a bit more gently, 'And besides, if what you say is true, it is too late to run away. But thanks anyway, Ola, for your good intentions.'

Ola didn't say any more. He turned and went back to the parish clerk's.

Standing there alone, Håvard felt numb.

Ola! Even Ola believed he had killed Rønnau.

At Olstad they were awaiting him with dinner. Kjersti had seen them up the road and, curious in women's fashion, asked what Ola had wanted this time.

Håvard replied that it wasn't of any importance. Anyway, they could talk about it later.

But he barely managed to swallow his food.

Håvard didn't talk to Kjersti till after supper. He had to think it over first.

But in order to think he had to have peace, instead of seeing Goro's frightened eyes fixed upon him all the time. He went down to the stable and sat there with the horses for a couple of hours.

It was so still in the stable. The crunchy sound of horses' teeth against hay and the tiny stamp when one of the horses shifted from one foot to the other made the stillness even more peaceful.

He could trust these horses. They weren't like people anyway.

He calmed down a little, sufficiently to be able to reflect at least. But he couldn't see any way out worth considering. If it had been summer, then perhaps . . .

He might be able to help Kjersti, though. If people hadn't gone completely out of their minds, that is . . .

After supper he saw that Goro had intended to join them in the kitchen. He went over and talked to her in a low voice.

'Goro, I think I must have a little talk with Kjersti. I have to try and get her away from here. It isn't healthy for her to be here, in the midst of all this gossip.'

'Yes, if only you could, Håvard!' Goro had tears in her eyes. Then she went quickly up to her room. Kjersti and Håvard were left alone.

They sat a moment without speaking. Håvard felt uneasy.

'You know Kjersti, don't you, that there is quite a bit of gossip in the parish,' he said.

'Yes, I know.'

Kjersti looked away.

'It isn't just ordinary gossip either. It's quite a bit worse than that. People – I don't exactly know who, and that's almost the worst part of it – people have the idea that Rønnau didn't die a natural death but was killed, by us – by me, I guess they mean,' he quickly corrected himself.

Now Kjersti looked at him.

'I have felt something like that,' she said. 'People have become so strange. . . .'

'Those who wish me well up here – but that's not many – don't dare to come to me with all they've heard. But I think people are saying there was *something* between you and me, and that this was the reason why Rønnau changed the way she did. And in the end, this is supposed to be the reason why we – why I took her life.'

Kjersti looked at him again.

'But Håvard – you've said yourself that you didn't touch her – that she hit her back against the iron spike and fell, slamming her head into the chimney ledge.'

'Yes, I have said that, and it's true. But that's not bad enough for people. They have to make it worse. And so they invent this thing about you and me.'

Kjersti sat a moment.

'That there was *something* between you and me. . . . Do they mean that . . .'

'Yes. And if that had been true, we would have been guilty of a crime. A serious crime too. It's called incest.'

Kjersti hesitated a moment.

'Incest? I know what that is. That's when near kin go to bed with each other. But we aren't kin, are we, Håvard?'

'According to the law we are, Kjersti.'

'Then it must be a stupid law. I wasn't kin to Rønnau either. And I am certainly not kin to you.

'I never called you Father. Even Rønnau had to give in on that point.

'You were never a *father* to me. You were *Håvard*. You noticed that, didn't you?'

Håvard had to smile in spite of himself. 'Oh, yes, I noticed.'

He grew serious again. 'But you did call Rønnau Mother?'

228

'Yes, because she forced me to. But inwardly I said only Rønnau. And when I grew bigger and she treated me worse than usual, I said to myself, *Damn Rønnau!*'

Quiet. Håvard thought Kjersti was more honest than it was healthy for a human being to be.

Suddenly Kjersti said, 'Håvard – why can't we go away together? Far away?'

And then she added, as sincerely as a child, 'That stupid law surely can't be valid in other countries!'

'Oh, yes, Kjersti, I'm afraid it is.'

Kjersti sat a moment again.

'But if we went someplace where nobody knew us – then it wouldn't do any harm, I mean.'

It occurred to Håvard that Kjersti didn't quite realize what she was saying.

'I'm afraid we could never go so far that they wouldn't find us,' he said. 'If they wanted to find us, that is.'

He had to change the subject to something else.

'For the time being we'll have to be content with *your* going away,' he said. 'The fact that you and I are living in the same house is the reason for much of this gossip. I'm inclined to think so anyway.

'Therefore I thought I would go out to the mill owner tomorrow and ask if you couldn't get a situation in the house there for a while. In the kitchen, or as a parlormaid. I know you could learn a great deal there. And then people would have less to talk about. But I won't do it, of course, if you don't want to go.'

He had gotten up. This conversation had lasted long enough. A little too long, perhaps.

Kjersti also had gotten up.

'That will be far away from you, Håvard.'

'Oh – you know, once in a while I go there too.'

'And how long should I stay there?'

'I don't know – a year perhaps.'

What she said next reminded him of something.

'A year – that's a long time, you know. I'm not sure I can think that far ahead. . . .'

She looked at him with those strange eyes which were innocent of ulterior motives and went straight through him. And he knew: she could be amazingly open, but she was no longer a child.

'Håvard . . . ,' she said, softly, and as though she found it difficult to breathe, 'Håvard – do you love me?'

'Of course, you know I do,' he said, evasively, without looking at her.

'You know very well what I mean. Do you *love* me?'

'Yes, Kjersti, I guess I do.'

'Oh!'

He felt her arms around his neck and her body up against his, tight, as though she wanted to press herself into him. 'Then nothing else matters. I'll gladly stay at the Mill for three years, if you want me to!'

He thought, This is getting dangerous! and gently freed himself.

She didn't say anything when he let her go. She stood there looking at him with starry eyes, scarcely knowing that her feet touched the ground.

A bit wobbly, he tried to dismiss it with a smile.

'Goro is in bed waiting to hear your footsteps on the stairs,' he said. 'We'll talk more tomorrow before I leave.'

She seemed to wake up.

'Yes,' she said. 'Yes, I'll go up now. Good night, then, Håvard.'

He took a turn down to the stable. The quiet horses made you feel so peaceful.

Conversation with the Mill Owner

*T*he following day Håvard drove out to the Mill. The sun shone with a pallid winter light and it was cold, so he took the big sleigh with the bearskin. He didn't know then that this was the last time he would use it.

The snow-covered road was fine and smooth, so he used Dobbin – the horse had been stabled awhile and liked to get a little exercise.

He thought as he drove along that he'd traveled this road many times now, at all seasons and in all kinds of weather and road conditions. Today the weather was nice and the hamlet all white on every side, but he doubted if he'd ever been on a darker errand.

Running away – that and nothing else was what it boiled down to. Running away because of gossip.

He wouldn't have hesitated if he'd known who his enemies were. But that was what he didn't know.

There were many sleighs in the yard at the Mill. The mill owner had visitors. But Håvard had become a well-known person around there. He was shown into the office wing, and a moment afterward the mill owner came.

The years and good living had left their marks on him. He'd grown stouter, and some of his light-colored hair was gone, so that his forehead had become higher. He'd developed bags under his eyes, and his face was too red, his cheeks too fat.

When they had wished each other merry Christmas and happy New Year, Håvard said, seeing that the mill owner was somewhat rushed for time, 'I've come to ask you a couple of favors this time.'

'Oh, well,' the mill owner said amiably, 'you've done me several favors over the years, so it would only be pleasant for me to do something in return.'

He looked more closely at Håvard.

'You don't look very happy, Håvard. Well, I guess there's no reason why you should . . .'

They had talked about Rønnau's death once before Christmas. Otherwise Håvard had noticed long ago that the mill owner didn't speak about Rønnau more often than he had to.

'No, there's no reason why I should be particularly happy,' Håvard said. 'We're unhappy because of all this gossip, both Kjersti and I.'

'I understand. I, too, have noticed there's some gossip. But in such a parish nobody can escape that, as long as he's visible.'

'It's not ordinary gossip this time,' Håvard said. 'I'm used to that – I don't come from this parish, as you know. But this time it's worse. There are people – who it is I don't quite know – who are spreading rumors that Rønnau didn't – didn't die a natural death, or something to that effect. That Kjersti and I killed her, one way or another. People look the other way when we happen to meet. We weren't invited anyplace at Christmas – well, that might have been because Rønnau had died so recently. Anyway, we didn't miss those parties, so as far as that goes . . .

'On the church green Kjersti and I find ourselves alone, with an empty space around us. It doesn't bother me. But Kjersti, who's young, little more than a child, doesn't like it. She feels lonely, and she's not happy. Therefore – and this is the first thing I wanted to ask you – I've come to ask you if you could find a situation for her here at the Mill for a year or so while all of this is simmering down. In the kitchen or – as a maid, or . . . Kjersti is clever, but she could learn quite a number of things in this house.'

The mill owner walked up and down the room a couple of times.

'Well . . . ,' he said. 'Surely . . . I have seen Kjersti a couple of times, and she strikes me as a straightforward and likable girl. Surely, it could be arranged, I think. That, too, will give rise to gossip, of course. But, you know, everything gives rise to gossip. . . . I'll have to discuss it with my wife, but I am confident that it will be all right. If you don't hear otherwise, you may bring her here in a week. The wages will be only the usual ones, but I assume you'll agree to that.'

Håvard agreed.

'That was one favor,' the mill owner said, visibly relieved and in a better humor. 'And now the other one.'

'The other one may be bigger,' Håvard said. 'But I don't know . . .

'Kjersti has now turned twenty-one. Sooner or later she'll find herself a man, I suppose, and get married. She's a good match, judging by a farmer's standards. She's pretty, too – most people seem to think she is anyway. And the day she marries she's entitled to take Olstad by allodial right. That means I don't have a permanent place here in Nordbygda. I might as well prepare for that now rather than later. Actually it suits me fine. I have done the bulk of what I can do at Olstad. Someone else can take over now, it won't be difficult – at any rate if I could train him for a year or so. If he knows something about farming, that won't even be necessary. I have trained Jon, almost without his knowing it.

'To be brief – I am unhappy in Nordbygda, almost more so than Kjersti, now that Rønnau is dead. I would like to go away, preferably far away.'

The mill owner nodded.

'I understand.'

'I've heard,' Håvard said, 'that the Mill owns a couple of farms on the other side of the border. I don't know whether there might be a post for me there, but . . . It occurred to me that if you have a manager there who would like to move, then I, for my part, would very much like to do the same. So that he managed Olstad awhile, I mean, and I took over his work. I don't know . . . I've thought about other things too – several other things. With the dollars I've put aside I could start as a horse dealer, if I cared to – only, I don't know if I care to. I could also perhaps manage to buy a farm someplace or other.'

'I have heard a rumor,' the mill owner said, 'that this recluse, Høgne Lien, has taken a fancy to you and has offered you Lien for a thousand dollars and a generous pension. Is that true?'

'Yes, it's true.'

'But it's dirt-cheap, Håvard.'

'I know it is. But I'm not happy in this parish anymore, as I've told you.'

'Hm. I understand. Between us, I also think it is a dark and dismal parish.'

The mill owner took another couple of turns back and forth. Then he stopped in front of Håvard.

'We might as well speak frankly, even brutally so, about this matter,

Håvard. For you are right about one thing – the gossip which goes around is not just ordinary gossip, it's far more malicious. There are those who claim that you – or Kjersti, or Kjersti and you together – attacked Rønnau, so that she fell and hit her head against the chimney ledge, with death as a consequence.'

'I know,' Håvard said, quite calmly.

'Then answer me one thing, Håvard. Is there any kernel of truth in this rumor?'

'No. Rønnau's death was pure accident. She stepped sharply backward and drove the iron spike of the kitchen crane over the hearth into the small of her back, lost her balance, fell down, and hit the back of her head against the chimney ledge. Neither of us as much as touched her. Anyway, if we had, there would've been marks on her body. We hired a night watcher the following forenoon – she washed and tended her the few days she lived – and she can no doubt testify that no such mark, or marks, existed.'

The mill owner scrutinized Håvard.

'This night watcher has made a statement!' he said. 'And I have the impression that she harbors a suspicion toward Kjersti.'

'Kjersti is as innocent in this matter as a babe unborn!' Håvard said, showing strong emotion for the first time during this conversation. 'If we are to talk about the cause of the misfortune, then, I'm sorry to say, it lay with Rønnau herself.

'Rønnau was – how shall I put it – she wasn't herself this fall. She made Kjersti a target for her hatred. Why, she never explained to me; but it grew worse and worse. That last evening she swung the carving knife at Kjersti. I stood there with an ax handle I'd been whittling. I jumped forward, raising the handle to ward off the blow. I moved quickly, of course. Rønnau got scared and jumped a step back. She must have thought I meant to hit her. – Me hit Rønnau! But that was how she came to drive the iron spike into the small of her back.'

The mill owner stood for a moment, reflecting. 'Yes, Rønnau knew how to swing a knife, all right!' he said.

Then he turned around and looked straight at Håvard. 'Did she have any reason to hate Kjersti?'

'None that I can see. But all in all, she had changed so sharply this last fall that once in a while I asked myself if she – if her mind hadn't become clouded for a while.

'She lay unconscious for three days. But toward the end she came to and was lucid. I sat beside her bed. Then I could see how this darkening of her mind, or whatever it should be called, slipped away from her, like layer after layer of clouds; her face became smooth, she looked at me and smiled, and was like I'd known her at the beginning of our acquaintance. She spoke to me – well, she said only my name – and then she died. The night watcher was witness to all of this.'

'So I have heard,' the mill owner said. 'She has related that, too, around the parish. But she said something else first – Rønnau, I mean – before she said your name.'

'What?'

'*Damn Kjersti*! From what I have heard, anyway.'

'True,' Håvard said. 'But that was before she was clearheaded. She said a lot of things while she lay there talking irrationally. Mostly things we couldn't make anything of.'

'Hm.' The mill owner took a couple of turns around the room again.

'To continue being brutally frank – Håvard, people in the parish say that Rønnau's mind was anything but clouded, as you call it, but that she was simply jealous of Kjersti. Have you heard that?'

Håvard sat a moment.

'No, I haven't,' he said. 'But it doesn't surprise me – no piece of gossip surprises me anymore. But if people are correct in that – if Rønnau was jealous, as you say – then it shows precisely that her mind was clouded.'

'Hm. Let me be brutally frank once again,' the mill owner said. 'People also say – some say, I should perhaps add – that there existed a more than friendly relationship between you and Kjersti, and that this was the cause of – of everything.'

Håvard hesitated a moment.

'That I haven't heard,' he said, 'at any rate not in so many words. But I have understood that such things were being said. Let me tell you one thing, Sir, I'll swear to it, if you wish. There was *no* such relationship between Kjersti and me. What's more, I feel absolutely certain that no man has touched Kjersti – in that way.'

The mill owner was silent a moment.

'I believe you,' he said. 'I believe you completely and unconditionally, and I'm happy because I believe you.

'But Rønnau's mind didn't have to be particularly clouded, as you call it, for her to get jealous and spiteful toward Kjersti. Remember, she was five or six years older than you. You are a man that women will turn around to look at more than once. Kjersti is an adult now. And – one more thing. Rønnau was here at the Mill for four years. I got to know her and – well, I'll put it this way: she took what she wanted. So if for some reason or other she imagined that Kjersti wanted you, it wouldn't be surprising if she imagined that Kjersti too might – oh, well – use every possible means to catch you.'

'According to the law, you know, I am her father,' Håvard said.

'I know, I know. But the law is one thing, life is another, my dear Håvard. Of course, all this is only conjecture on my part. But Rønnau may have been a victim of what some people call nemesis and others call a vicious circle. Up in these hamlets, by the way, it's called a *troll circle*. The past which avenges itself, fate which bites its own tail, like a serpent . . .'

The mill owner appeared animated.

'Odd, isn't it?' he said. 'Didn't you ever hate Rønnau?'

'Why do you ask about that, Sir?'

'Oh, I've heard a few things, I've seen a little more, and I've figured out a thing or two by myself. Some things even Rønnau – well – not exactly confessed but indirectly admitted, I might say. You see, she did have, despite her dislike of my person, a kind of confidence in me.'

'I know,' Håvard said. 'We have seen her will, Kjersti and I. Hans Nordby was with us. He's Kjersti's guardian, as you probably know.'

'No I didn't. But listen:

'I believe I know, to continue with my brutal candor, that Rønnau told you she was with child and this way got you to marry her, but that she wasn't.

'And you were betrothed to another girl but betrayed her – and so she took her own life. Is that true?'

'Yes, it is.'

'And still you didn't hate her?'

'At first I may have hated her, now and then,' Håvard said, 'after I got wise to what had happened. But in the long run it wasn't so easy to hate her for what she'd done. She did it, after all, because she wanted me.'

'Many things have become clear,' the mill owner said. 'To me it's all quite clear. Unfortunate circumstances . . .

'As far as our properties east of the border are concerned, by a stroke of luck, I might say, the manager of one of these farms – he's a Norwegian by the way, and a very good farmer – is no longer on friendly terms with the proprietor, who, I might mention, will be here this very day. In my judgment it is essentially the proprietor's fault, but the manager is also a headstrong man. I have no doubt that you could get along with them both. This man might certainly consider taking over the management of Olstad Farm for a year or two while you managed that farm in Värmland.[34] I'll see what I can

34. Region in western Sweden east of Oslo, Norway.

do. If it works out, the agreement will take effect from the beginning of the summer half-year. . . .

'Don't mention it, my dear Håvard; it has been a pleasure.'

The mill owner tried to make Håvard partake of a mug of beer and a bit of Christmas fare with him in the servants' hall. When Håvard declined, he ordered brandy to be brought in and drank a glass with him.

'Good luck in your new position,' he said. 'I am fairly certain I can arrange it in the course of a few days.'

But no such arrangement came about. Three days later the sheriff came and arrested Kjersti and Håvard on suspicion of having caused Rønnau's death.

Trial

*W*hen Håvard sat facing the bench in the courtroom one Monday morning in February, it occurred to him that, in reality, he had known it would come to this some day. But at the same time he knew that it wasn't so. It was just that what he was facing now reminded him of the court session he had imagined during *the long day*, as he was waiting for the sheriff.

He tried to imagine something else too – that all he was seeing here and now was only a dream he would awake from, so it wasn't really there, never had been. But he knew it was real enough – it was life itself suddenly forcing its way through the door and showing its teeth, with jaws that filled the entire doorway. That long day as he sat waiting to be charged with murdering Martin he'd seen one such glimpse of life, real life; and this was another glimpse of it. The ten years in between, years which had seemed to be so peaceful in every way, *those* years were a dream, a deceptive dream. This was no deception. What had happened ten years ago was merely a friendly warning. This time it was for real – that he had discovered these last few weeks while the preliminary hearings were going on. This time, the powers were out to get him.

They were in the southernmost, largest room of the Court House, or Community House as they called it up this way. Håvard was seated approximately in the middle of the room. To his left, but a little farther back so that he couldn't see her except by turning his head, sat Kjersti.

In front of them stood a heavy long table, and behind that sat the members of the bench: the judge and the two co-judges. The judge was an aging man with gray hair, muttonchop whiskers, and long tufts of hair protruding from his nose. Håvard had heard people say that he was strict.

'Strict but just!' the young defense attorney had said.

He knew the two co-judges: Ola Nordset, big, heavy and dark and rather slow-witted, and Hans Olsen Tomter, the Haugian who had saved him from his cotters almost ten years ago and who afterward had prepared the bearskin for him. His hair had turned gray lately, but otherwise he looked as always, his face enveloped by this mysterious thing called *peace*. But today he looked stern.

Behind the members of the bench, closer to the two windows facing south, sat the old tax collector in a big log chair at a smaller table. At the same table sat the curate, Mr. Paus. He had brought writing materials and was taking notes. So did a pale, long-haired and sharp-nosed fellow at the end of the long table.

Between Håvard and the bench sat the two lawyers, the prosecutor and the defense attorney, each at a separate smaller table.

Behind Kjersti and Håvard there were a couple of rows of chairs for those among the farmers who wanted to listen. At the moment most of them stood outside in the cold. Among those who were present was Kerstaffer Berg. Crooked and rheumatic, he had mostly stayed in bed lately. But today he'd dragged himself out of bed and had himself driven here by his son.

Behind these rows of seats, beside the entrance door, was the big square stove the old dean of the parish had persuaded the Mill to donate to the Community House long ago. There was a big fire of birch logs, and the hindmost would be sure to get their backs toasted.

There was a hawking and a spitting behind him — he could hear it during every brief pause in the proceedings, and he also heard, from the sound of the hawking, that Hans Nordby occupied one of the seats behind him. He knew that Hans Nordby had been summoned as a witness but had been disqualified because he was Kjersti's guardian. He could have been a good witness to have. He didn't know who else sat in those seats behind him. He only knew that those who were going to testify weren't there – they weren't allowed to listen until after they had given their testimony.

Håvard saw and heard everything which happened in the little courtroom so sharply that his eyes and ears ached. He saw the old tax collector as he sat nodding in the log chair, the sharp face of Mr. Paus, and the tufts of hair in the judge's nostrils – they quivered when he breathed – and he saw the faces of the two co-judges, feature by feature, the sharp, hooked nose of the prosecutor, and the friendly, somehow unfinished face of the young defense attorney. Outside, the February sun stood low in the sky, and a sunbeam entered the room through the left window, to come to rest at the small pile of paper on the table before the prosecutor.

He saw all this with such excruciating sharpness that it claimed too much of his attention. But the area behind and beyond the *here* and *now* seemed to be covered by a fog. What was going to happen was outside his ken. No, he didn't have second sight. The authorities evidently felt they had some sort of evidence against him – and against Kjersti. But what it amounted to, he didn't know. There was nothing either within him or around him that whispered anything about that.

The first day – morning session and afternoon session – passed slowly, as slowly as a louse on a tar brush. Håvard knew it all from before, as if he'd been through it a hundred times. Actually, he *had* been through it a hundred times, during the hearings as well as alone in the jail.

First the court summarized the case itself. Rønnau Larsdaughter Olstad had died on the thirtieth of September under suspicious circumstances and so on. The suspicion focused increasingly on the two accused, Håvard Gjermundsen and Kjersti Olsdaughter.

As far as the appearance of the deceased, Rønnau, was concerned, all statements agreed: the explanations of the two accused as well as the testimonies of the night watcher, Maren Teppen, and of the woman who had washed the body, Marte Svingen. The deceased, Rønnau, had a distinct mark in the small of her back after a mighty jolt; according to Håvard Gjermundsen's statement, she had incurred this mark when she slipped on the floor and with great force slammed her back against the iron spike of the kitchen crane, a rod extending from the fireplace – up this way called the chimney – which was used to hang pots on for cooking.

In addition the deceased had a wound in the back of her head, which she inflicted upon herself, according to the accused Håvard Gjermundsen, when, after damaging her back, she fell backward and hit the back of her head against the edge of the fireplace, also called the chimney ledge. This wound had bled, though not much. The testimonies of Maren Teppen and Marte Svingen confirmed the statement of the accused, as far as the wound itself was concerned. How it may have been caused, the court would go into later.

Other external injuries couldn't be detected on the body of the deceased. Since all the statements were in complete agreement as far as these external facts were concerned, the court had found it superfluous to have the body exhumed.

Then Håvard and Kjersti were called.

Håvard presented his statement, which he'd known by heart for some time. He told the truth – though not the whole truth. He didn't mention that Rønnau had swung the knife nor, consequently, did he mention that he himself had raised the ax handle. Instead, he said that Rønnau had slipped – the floor was slippery because some water had spilled on it from the pot.

In the continuation he carefully stuck to what had actually happened.

Kjersti's statement, which Håvard now heard for the first time, was quite brief. She had come in from the cow barn, where Dagros had just calved. Håvard sat whittling an ax handle; Rønnau – she quickly corrected it to *Mother* – stood over by the hearth. She herself went up to the kitchen counter and stood there with her back turned. The next she knew, there came a scream from – from Mother, then a fall, and when she turned around Mother lay on her back with her head against the chimney ledge, and Håvard stood over her calling her name, but she didn't hear.

'You don't call Håvard Gjermundsen Father?'

It was the judge who asked.

'No, I didn't use to. I was almost twelve years old when he married Mother, so . . . And I thought Håvard was such a pretty name.'

Even the judge smiled then.

Kjersti's statement could be true, or it could be a barefaced lie. It couldn't be decided one way or the other on the basis of the statement itself.

Neither the prosecutor nor the judge seriously went into any of the statements this time around.

It could only mean they had something up their sleeves. Otherwise there was nothing to build a case on.

First a number of witnesses were called – farmers from Nordbygda – who were asked to state their impressions of Håvard.

As their declarations came one after another, it seemed to Håvard there was something oddly familiar about every one of them. They were precisely the sort of declarations he had expected in that trial ten years ago, which never materialized.

Still, he was a bit surprised.

At that time he had been up here for half a year, and nobody could know much about him. Now he'd been here for ten years, and they ought to know what sort of reputation he had. More than once they had demonstrated that they knew it too.

He had loaned clover seed, seed grain, and seed potatoes to this one and that one and more, and he had provided them with a new and better breed of cattle, though most, to be sure, didn't have the sense to keep them clean. Every one of the farmers who now stood there testifying had come to him at some time or other, asking his advice and guidance, and had been given it. Most of them didn't have the brains to take advantage of the advice he gave them, that was so. . . .

Nor, as time went on, did they come to him at night, like Nicodemus, either. It had become an accepted thing that this Håvard fellow knew a little of everything. And now they stood in this court making statements that were as cold as ice.

They admitted – several of them – that Håvard was a good farmer. But otherwise they couldn't say they knew him. He was an outsider, after all.

Several of them managed to say the word *outsider* in a tone that could be interpreted, roughly, as follows: an outsider might be capable of all sorts of mischief.

There were two exceptions among the witnesses. But it wasn't easy to tell what effect they had on the court.

The first was Amund Moen, calm and self-assured.

He declared that Håvard was a capable and peaceful man. To kill, not to speak of murdering – no, Håvard just didn't have it in him.

'There may be some murderer or other in this parish,' he said. 'But Håvard isn't one of them.'

The prosecutor said, 'Isn't it a fact that some years ago you yourself were on the point of being charged, on suspicion of having killed your wife?'

Amund straightened up and gazed at him for a moment.

'This case of yours must be in really poor shape if you have to fall back on common village gossip, not only about Håvard but about the witnesses in the case too,' he said. 'If you'll come outside with me, I'll explain to you what we think about fellows like you.'

The judge used his gavel. The prosecutor had turned very red in the face.

'How close I got to being charged that time fourteen or fifteen years ago, I don't know,' Amund said. 'There was some gossip, that's true. But there's always gossip. In this parish, as you ought to know, each and everyone gets suspected of everything by everybody. The sheriff came to my house, that's also true. And when it turned out that the fellow who had spread the gossip ate his own words, no action was brought against me. And now I would like to hear if you have any more gossip to peddle while you're at it. What kind of gossip have you managed to sniff out about Håvard?'

Again the judge used his gavel, and Amund was dismissed from the court-room as quickly as possible.

The other person who had requested to be called was Høgne Lien.

A hum passed through the hall when, old and withered, he took his place in the witness box. Most people didn't know about the friendship between Høgne and Håvard, and thought this was the first time Høgne had been outside his own yard in almost forty years.

What Høgne had on his mind was quickly said.

'Kerstaffer Berg is the one behind everything!' he said.

He didn't really have anything more to say; but to him it was clear as day-light. This trial was a shame and a misfortune, and the one who was behind all shame and misfortune in this world was Kerstaffer Berg – it had been that way since he, Høgne, was a young man.

But every listener knew that Kerstaffer had been staying in bed for the most part during the last few years, and that he'd never been quite himself since that evening nearly ten years ago when Håvard hit him with the birch switch in the potato field. He'd hit a little too hard that time also, Håvard had – and the Lord only knew what had happened in the stable at Olstad the day Martin was found dead, though Håvard was let off the hook that time, sure enough.

And whatever you might say about Kerstaffer, he certainly hadn't killed Rønnau, because at that time he was confined to his bed. . . .

When the court and the public perceived – and they perceived it simul-taneously – that Høgne didn't have anything more to say, a rare thing hap-pened: the court and the public burst out in a chorus of laughter. Even Kerstaffer Berg joined in the laughter; and while this volley of laughter was reechoing from the walls, Høgne quietly slipped out of the courtroom. He sort of melted away and was gone, nobody knew exactly how.

For the second time in his life Høgne Lien had become a laughingstock to the whole parish on account of Kerstaffer Berg.

At the end of the first day's session the servants at Olstad were interro-gated, though not Goro, who had been hired only after Rønnau's death. All were asked if they had noticed any change in Rønnau toward the end, and everybody answered that they had. What kind of change? They answered cautiously, as might be expected, but agreed that Rønnau had appeared rest-less, something which was entirely new for her, and that she would often be impatient.

Håvard and Kjersti had been the same as ever; at any rate, nobody had noticed anything. Well, perhaps a little more quiet than usual.

Sure, little love had been lost between Rønnau and Kjersti.

Håvard couldn't quite understand what the prosecutor was driving at with all these questions. But he did accomplish one thing – it gradually became clear that it hadn't been very pleasant at Olstad during the last few weeks before Rønnau died.

The second day it became quite clear what the prosecution was driving at. Maren Teppen was the first to be examined. Håvard had been prepared by his conversation with the mill owner. But Maren was more dangerous than he had imagined. Not for him, Håvard – he had been miserable and had sat by the bed much of the time. The last thing Rønnau said when she regained consciousness just before she died was also addressed to Håvard. She said only his name, but she said it so sweetly.

Maren, however, was hostile toward Kjersti. Kjersti hardly ever showed herself in the bedroom and never sat by the bed. She scarcely said a word and never wept, not even when Rønnau died. . . .

Maren didn't lie, quite the contrary – she recalled everything very precisely; but she interpreted everything in her own way. Rønnau's exclamation 'Damn Kjersti,' which she let out while she was still delirious, became, to her, the first thing Rønnau said when she was coming to. The fact that Kjersti was numb and mute during those days was, in Maren's opinion, due to her being completely indifferent and cold.

To a question by the prosecutor whether she suspected Kjersti of having killed Rønnau, she answered quickly, obviously well prepared: 'Who killed Rønnau I cannot know, for I wasn't there. But I do know who didn't grieve when Rønnau died.'

Here the defense attorney interrupted to protest against the prosecutor having used the expression 'killed Rønnau.' It hadn't been proven that any act of killing had occurred; on the contrary, it was up to the prosecution to prove or make it appear probable that such a killing had occurred – if it could.

But Håvard had the impression that nobody in court attached any importance to what the defense attorney said. For the first time he thought there appeared a break in the fog, and he thought, This will end badly.

But the day's principal witness was Anton Olsen Måsåmyra, or Anton Olsen Myren, as it was dictated into the record of the proceedings.

Håvard thought, What does this mean?

242

He soon found out.

Anton Olsen, a cotter at Olstad for nine years past, had taken an evening walk on the second of January – it was such nice, clear winter weather that evening. It so happened that his path took him past Olstad, and he chanced to look in through the kitchen window. Then he saw Håvard and Kjersti standing on the kitchen floor and holding each other in a tight embrace, as though they were sweethearts. . . .

Of course. Håvard ought to have known it must have been Anton when he saw the imprints of a pair of boots outside the kitchen window – when was that? After he returned from the Mill.

Anton was called Peeping Tom throughout the hamlet. He had been caught several times staring at people through the windowpanes, especially on fall evenings. Once or twice he'd been slapped thoroughly for his trouble right there and then. It had gotten to the point where two of the farmers in the hamlet came to Håvard to complain, and Håvard had promised to talk to Anton – which both he and Rønnau had done. But Anton lied himself out of it, as was his custom. 'I get blamed for everything,' he said, 'simply because I am an outsider!'

This was an explanation which both Rønnau and Håvard could understand.

And, true enough, he was not the only Peeping Tom in the hamlet, though he may have been the most ardent one.

This practice of peeping had become somewhat of a nuisance, and quite widespread too.

A couple of farmers – among others, Hans Nordby – had hinted to Håvard that one ought to start hanging curtains before the windows in the evening. Then perhaps they would stop this peeping, after making their rounds in vain a few times.

But nothing had come of it. It hadn't been a custom to cover one's windows in the old days – that would be like admitting you had something to hide. Nobody wanted to be the first to do that, and so nobody did it.

Of course it had to be Anton. Håvard ought to have known the very moment he saw the imprint of those boots.

And of course it had to happen exactly that evening, at precisely those moments.

Håvard felt the cold shivers running down his spine. And for the second time he thought, This will end badly.

And there it came.

Anton went into detail. The two of them stood in the middle of the kitchen floor, as he had said.

'Kjersti had her arms around Håvard's neck, and Håvard had his arms around Kjersti's neck. They stood like this for a long time.' Anton wouldn't say that they did anything more than just *that* – then and there. But they did it thoroughly.

Anton paused and looked around him. He had been well coached by someone, whoever it might be.

It was deathly still in the courtroom.

'Afterward it looked like they said a few words to each other. And then, clinging to each other, they went into Håvard's bedroom.'

'That's a lie!' Håvard cried.

The judge used his gavel. But after a little back and forth, Håvard was allowed to speak, and the upshot was that Goro would be called as a witness. As Håvard said, he had hired Goro, and given her a room on the second floor beside Kjersti's room, just so she should be there and make sure that things of the sort Anton had right now falsely alleged, *didn't* occur at Olstad.

Håvard caught Anton's glance for an instant and gazed into a burning hatred.

He went numb. That Anton didn't like him he had known – he had done the poor fellow too many favors for that. But such hatred . . .

He knew that Anton had had a soft spot for Rønnau – more of one than Håvard thought that fellow could have for any human being. But now, in a flash, he saw something which made his blood run cold:

Anton believed that Håvard had killed Rønnau.

While they were waiting for Goro, Håvard was given the floor for a supplemental statement.

He remembered well, he said, that he had talked to Kjersti that evening. Various kinds of village gossip had reached his ears, and he decided it would be good for Kjersti to get away for a while, until the slanderers had been obliged to pipe down. He suggested that he go to the Mill the following day and ask the mill owner if he could find a situation for Kjersti, either in the kitchen, where she would learn cooking, or as a parlormaid, so she could learn a bit more about how to take care of a house.

It appeared that Kjersti herself had heard some of this gossip and was so unhappy about it – though she hadn't dared speak to Håvard about the matter – that when she understood he wanted to help her get away for a while, she flung her arms around his neck in sheer gratitude. But it was anything but a long embrace, contrary to what Anton had said. And that Kjersti afterward should have gone to his bedroom with him was an even more harebrained allegation. He was confident that Goro could confirm that. It wasn't that long ago, after all, and Goro had told him several times that she was always the last person in the house to go to bed, precisely because she felt her responsibility.

The prosecutor asked, amiably, if it was news to him that Kjersti was unhappy. Håvard answered that he'd been aware of it. But he hadn't known until that evening how unhappy she was.

'Both Kjersti and I were unhappy at Olstad after Rønnau died, and we both knew it. We felt the house was empty after her. Kjersti wanted to get away. As for me, I was looking around for a farm; for I knew that when Kjersti got married she was entitled to take the farm by allodial right.'

He stood maundering like this for some time, knowing full well that he wasn't doing either Kjersti or himself any good.

When he said that Kjersti and he were unhappy at Olstad, he felt the others' thoughts like a cold wind blowing in his direction. So, they were unhappy, were they? Well, it would be asking a bit much, wouldn't it, to expect that they should be *happy* in that kitchen, where they had killed Rønnau. . . .

A well-bred young girl of good family, brought up strictly, as Kjersti in fact was, wouldn't go and embrace a man, and certainly not her stepfather, just because he had promised to do her a favor. Farmers and farmers' customs weren't like that, and they all knew it, those who were in the room. That statement of his had as many holes in it as a sieve. Everyone on the bench knew that here Håvard was, at best, holding back something.

They went on for hours, back and forth, with Anton's testimony. Goro, who personally made a good impression, swore she had never closed an eye before she knew that the whole household at Olstad had each gone to their rooms. She remembered the evening in question very well – she'd heard them talking for quite a while after supper. Then Kjersti came upstairs. Afterward Håvard took a walk to the stable, as he always did before turning in, and only then did he go to his room. Sound carried easily at Olstad, as in all such old houses, and her hearing was very good.

She slept lightly too, as it happened. She used to wake up in the middle of the night if Kjersti as much as turned around in her bed.

Well and good. But Kjersti had embraced Håvard.

Then appeared Anders Olsen Flateby, called as a witness at his own request.

Håvard thought, What in the world can he have to say?

But Anders could relate some strange things.

In the course of September Anders Flateby had had several meetings with the accused, Håvard Gjermundsen. Or rather *consultations*. Twice during these consultations Håvard had said, Something has to happen. In the long run Rønnau and I cannot live under the same roof.

Anders had found this statement to be so strange that he remembered it word for word.

As far as the rest of this testimony was concerned, the judge dictated the following into the record:

'The accused, Håvard Gjermundsen, requested to speak and declared Anders Flateby's testimony to be a lie, pure and simple. He, Håvard Gjermundsen, hadn't exchanged a word with Anders Flateby during the last three years and had never expressed himself, as alleged by him, either to him or to others. It also seemed to him obvious that if he had had any plans to take Rønnau's life, which was a lie, he would have been insane to communicate such plans beforehand to his fellow parishioners. Finally, the accused would like to know when and where the said meetings were supposed to have occurred.

'The witness replied that the accused had strongly urged that these meetings be held secret. One meeting occurred in the woods, another after dark in the servants' quarters at Flateby, which stood empty for the time being. Concerning the purpose of these meetings he could only say that the accused, Håvard Gjermundsen, on both occasions had attempted to procure all sorts of information about Hans Nordby. The accused, who was an outsider, was a man of great ambition. He was already a go-between in buying and selling between the Mill and the farmers in Nordbygda and had planned to squeeze out Hans Nordby as a buyer for Baron Rosenkrantz. If he were to accomplish this, however, he would have to get hold of more damaging information about Hans Nordby than he, who was a stranger, possessed. But he, Anders Flateby, had refused to let himself be used for such a purpose, having even less confidence in the accused, Håvard Gjermundsen, than in Hans Nordby.

'To the contention of the accused that he must have been insane to disclose his plans beforehand, the witness wished to say that the man who planned to kill Rønnau was already insane.

'The accused declared once again that every word of this testimony was a lie.'

Håvard didn't attach much importance to Anders Flateby's statement – it was quite obvious that here was a half-crazed man telling a cock-and-bull story he had concocted. And someone or other who was not a party in the case was bound to come forward and explain what was going on with Anders.

But no such witness came forward.

The day ended with a strange occurrence. The prosecutor had examined Kjersti once more without getting anywhere with her – she had heard Håvard's statement, repeated it in every detail, and didn't let herself be budged or confused.

As far as Anton's allegation was concerned, she merely snorted.

'There isn't a soul up this way who believes a word of what Anton says!' she said. 'We all know he's lying.'

She took the embrace very lightly. 'When Håvard told me that he was going to the Mill the next day to try and find a job for me there, it made me so glad that I put my arms around his neck. It was the first time I had done something like that, and it lasted only a wink. But, of course, Anton had to be standing ouside the window exactly at that moment. And the next day Håvard *did* drive out to the Mill and was promised that I could go there.'

Kjersti had never been so calm and self-assured before.

Then the judge intervened.

He spoke to her in a friendly way, and slowly she melted at his friendly voice.

He asked her first about a number of harmless things – whether she had ever been out of the parish before, whether she knew the mill owner and his wife, when she had planned to go, whether she didn't feel sad at the thought of leaving Olstad, all the same. And Kjersti melted.

Finally, he gave her a friendly look over his glasses and said, even more gently than before, 'Tell me, Kjersti Olsdaughter – do you love Håvard Gjermundsen, who is sitting in this room?'

She looked at him with her big luminous eyes.

'Yes!' she said.

She realized at once what she had said. Bursting into tears, she rested her face on her hands, and afterward nobody could get another word out of her.

It caused such a commotion in the courtroom that the tax collector woke up.

In the evening the defense attorney came to see Håvard, who lay there in his chains, without sleeping – he slept little or not at all during this time.

He had a great deal to relate, and Håvard noticed that he was somewhat jittery as he related it.

The mill owner – he was staying at Olstad with Goro at this time, together with the district doctor – had been busy. He had visited the tax collector – who was staying at Nordby, along with most of the members of the court – and received permission to do what he afterward undertook. The mill owner was a friend of the tax collector (who was no friend of the judge) and knew that the tax collector was a kindly old man who felt sorry for Kjersti, this attractive young girl who'd gotten herself mixed up in this ugly business.

To be brief, the defense attorney said, the district doctor went to Kjersti and explained to her that, if she had a good conscience and wanted what was best for Håvard, she would let him, the district doctor, examine her in order to establish, in a medical sense, whether she was a virgin. At the moment Håvard's situation looked very bad (that her own situation was just as bad, he didn't say). But if she was willing to accept the discomfort which such an examination naturally entailed for a modest young girl, and if it should turn out that she was a virgin, then the entire foundation of the accusation both against her and against Håvard would collapse. For she must have realized that the whole case was built on nothing but village gossip. All the gossipy women had been buzzing and whispering from one end of the parish to the other that a relationship had existed between her and Håvard, that they had decided to get rid of Rønnau, but that one or both had gotten cold feet at the very last moment. Still, they had managed to harm Rønnau sufficiently to cause her to die from her injuries – which in the eye of the law was tantamount to manslaughter, or murder, if it could be regarded as premeditated.

If it could be demonstrated that Kjersti was what was called a virgin, the whole incest charge no longer applied, and at the same time the motive for the killing, or the murder, whatever you might call it, mostly disappeared. And so the very foundation of the case went up in smoke. And now it all rested on Kjersti, for he, the district doctor, thought it only fair to tell her that he couldn't compel her.

But when Kjersti understood that she could save Håvard, she was willing at once. And with Goro as a witness, the examination was performed. It resulted in the finding that Kjersti was a virgin, *virgo intacta*, and that therefore no sexual contact in the legal sense could have taken place between her and Håvard. The statement had already been written by the district doctor and would be presented to the court tomorrow.

The defense attorney, who actually had had very little to do with these things, was proud as a rooster.

'With this finding, in my opinion, the case is settled,' the defense attorney said. 'The prosecution might just as well withdraw the entire charge, and I wouldn't be surprised if it did.'

Håvard didn't say anything. The fact that strange men had laid hands on Kjersti was such an intolerable thought to him that he couldn't have said a word even if he'd wanted to – despite the fact that he fully understood that the mill owner and the district doctor had acted with the best intentions.

Yet, this night was the first in a week that Håvard had a few hours of deep, dreamless sleep.

The following morning the defense attorney requested leave to speak. He gave the background – all the gossip which had circulated in the parish – revealed the mill owner's initiative, and ended by reading the district doctor's deposition.

There was a moment of stunned silence. Then the prosecutor stood up and requested that the court withdraw for half an hour to consider the new situation.

The bench agreed to this – they stayed away for an hour, though – and when they returned the judge rapped the table with his gavel, cast a stern look around the room and said, 'The case will proceed.'

It seemed to Håvard that, if the court had undergone any change during that hour, it was this: it had come back more hostile than it had been when it withdrew.

The judge spoke and said that since the deposition of the district doctor had been put forward without being requested by the court, and in the absence of judicial and legal-technical models, it must be deemed as of no importance to the case and would not be placed in the record.

'As it must be assumed that the district doctor has said all he has to say in the statement which has already been presented, the court finds no reason to accept his kind offer to be a witness as well and must consequently decline said offer with thanks.'

The defense attorney's face was flaming red.

The prosecutor then resumed his examination of Kjersti.

It was plain that Kjersti now looked at all the members of the court with suspicion. Yesterday she had allowed herself to be fooled by the judge because he spoke to her in a honeyed voice. She wasn't going to let herself be fooled a second time. She gave curt answers to all of the prosecutor's questions, and in nine out of ten instances the answer was that she didn't remember.

It was clear – as evidenced by the faces of the members of the court – that with every minute that passed in this way Kjersti was hurting her own case. The prosecutor grew more and more triumphant, his tone of voice more and more amiably patronizing – he had obviously learned from the judge's demeanor yesterday.

'We have heard from various witnesses,' the prosecutor said, 'that you, Kjersti Olsdaughter, and your stepmother, Rønnau Larsdaughter Olstad, were on noticeably poor terms with each other during the last few weeks Rønnau was alive, that is, before she – hm – met her death in such a grievous manner. Do you have anything to say to this?'

But Kjersti didn't answer.

It began to be obvious that the defense attorney, young and inexperienced as he was, had given Kjersti a very poor piece of advice. He must have said, 'Nobody can punish you for saying you don't remember.'

But another thing began to be plain. Today they were after Kjersti.

'But, my dear Kjersti,' the prosecutor said, amiably – a little too amiably: 'That you should have forgotten, not only most of what happened that unfortunate evening, but also the many things that happened repeatedly during the preceding weeks – things which, according to several witnesses, clearly showed that you and Rønnau were *not* on good terms with each other – this the members of the court will find it extremely difficult to believe. Can't you remember anything at all of all this?'

Kjersti was silent.

'And can't you remember *anything at all* of what happened that last evening, the consequences of which led to the tragic death of Rønnau Larsdaughter? Wasn't there, then, any disagreement or quarrel at all between you and her?'

Kjersti's eyes darted hither and thither, like the eyes of an animal when it knows it has been caught in a trap. Then, time and again, her eyes would come back to Håvard.

Håvard had turned toward Kjersti now. But he knew that everybody in the hall was watching him very closely, with hostility, and would misinterpret the slightest play of his features, every expression in his face. He looked at Kjersti with an impassive face, unable to help her.

Kjersti had realized by now that she couldn't go on pretending as though she didn't remember anything at all. Still, she didn't know what to say. Her eyes darted hither and thither.

The prosecutor repeated, amiably – a bit too amiably, 'Can't you remember anything at all from this last evening?'

'She swung the knife at me!' Kjersti blurted out.

There was some movement among the members of the court. Sounds of chairs scraping against the floor were heard among the public, where there was also some movement. A murmur arose, on the bench as well as among the public. What Kjersti had said was a completely new piece of information in the case.

250

The prosecutor's voice cut through the noise; and now it was no longer friendly or ingratiating:

'So Rønnau swung the knife at you. You remember that, at last. Was it in consequence of a quarrel, or so to speak the final argument in a quarrel?'

But Kjersti was silent.

'Do you recall what happened afterward?'

Kjersti found her voice again.

'No.'

'Nothing whatsoever?'

Kjersti stammered, 'No – that is – not until I saw her lying with her head against the chimney ledge.'

Another murmur.

'Are we to understand, then, that you cannot give an account of anything that happened after Rønnau swung the knife – whether or not, to take an example, you attacked her and, younger and quicker as you are, nudged or pushed her against the iron spike extending from the hearth – are we to understand that you cannot confirm or deny any of this, any of these possibilities, insofar as you cannot remember what occurred until you saw her lying against the chimney ledge, her head crushed? *Answer*, Kjersti Olsdaughter!'

But Kjersti was silent. Only her eyes, bewildered and helpless, darted from one to the other, coming to rest on Håvard.

Håvard gave a hint to the defense attorney that he would like to speak.

He knew that if he didn't help Kjersti now, she was lost. The prosecutor could drive her up any corner he wanted.

Håvard stood up. He had to stand a moment before the tremor in his body receded, a tremor which appeared every time he stood up, making his chains rattle so that he felt their weight in a new way. He knew from experience by now that he couldn't utter a word until that tremor was gone.

He would like to offer a brief supplemental statement, he said. What Kjersti had said was true – Rønnau swung the knife at her. Not to stab Kjersti with the knife – that he, at any rate, would rather not believe. But naturally, he couldn't know anything for certain about this. He preferred to believe that she swung the knife because she happened to have it in her hand – she'd been trimming a pine stick, had just lighted it and put it in the chimney hold, when Kjersti came in from the barn where one of the cows had calved. He himself was whittling an ax handle, but had just got up to go to the barn and look at the calf. At that moment everything started happening so quickly that there was no time to think. Rønnau swung the knife, and he jumped forward and raised the ax handle to ward off the blow.

Rønnau, who may have been startled when he sprang forward so abruptly, made a jump backward, ramming her back against the iron spike, lost her balance and fell against the chimney ledge, as he had stated previously.

And, also as he had stated previously, neither Kjersti nor he had touched Rønnau when she fell.

The reason why he hadn't mentioned this matter of the knife earlier was that he would have preferred to spare Rønnau's reputation. The truth was, as far as he could see, that Rønnau's mind was clouded now and then toward the end – for about a month or so. It expressed itself through fits of temper without any warning. A couple of times her temper had vented itself upon the maids – which they themselves had reported here in court. At times, mostly in the evening, it would vent itself upon Kjersti. He himself had never been the object of any of these outbursts; but it had happened that Rønnau felt sorry afterward and poured out her troubles to him. He also had to admit that these fits had grown more severe, if anything, as the fall wore on. But when she came to on that last day, just before she died as it turned out later – he was sitting by her bed, as he had previously related – he could see at once that this whole sickness had slipped away from her and she was herself again, as she'd been in her happier days. But soon after she died.

There was silence in the hall as Håvard sat down. All the members of the court were looking intently at him. And suddenly he saw that, in their eyes, he had now made a confession, or something which was worse than a confession. Hardened till the very end, he had confessed to as much as was necessary because Kjersti had made a slip of the tongue, but no more.

To think that he had sometimes imagined he had second sight! He realized now that he never had second sight beforehand, when it might have helped him, but only afterward, when it was too late.

He could see, or thought he could see, what the men on the bench were thinking. The judge and Ola Nordset thought, Now we've got him! Hans Olsen Tomter's innermost thoughts he couldn't read. But that the trial as a whole, and most of all his supplemental statement, had gone against him, that he could see most clearly from the face of Hans Olsen. This Haugian face, which otherwise was so gentle and peaceful and had always been so friendly whenever Håvard met him, had become impassive and hard as iron in the course of these days. There he had already been condemned, there no mercy was to be found.

The prosecutor now had roses in his cheeks, from joy and triumph. The defense attorney was pale – he, too, couldn't believe what Håvard had just related.

252

Mr. Paus, the curate, sat looking at him. He wasn't hostile, but he seemed troubled.

Beside Mr. Paus, in the big log chair, sat the tax collector. He was asleep.

Håvard felt that all was lost. *The truth*, all agreed, they would never get out of him. Nor was it necessary to do so. They knew now that Håvard had forcibly pushed Rønnau against the iron spike and – in all probability – had banged her against the chimney ledge.

Håvard felt cold, despite the heat in the room, and had a sinking sensation. He felt as though he were sinking down into another room, identical to this one; but it was cold there, and he was alone. He knew he would remain down there in the cold, until he sank down into yet another room, colder still, where he would be even more alone.

Only one thing still gave him a warm feeling. He had accomplished what he had sworn to himself the day they were arrested, Kjersti and he.

He had sworn – he didn't know whether in the name of God or the devil – that whatever happened or didn't happen, Kjersti should not lose her life for his sake. *One* Tonè in the waterfall had to suffice. He was guilty of Tonè's death, in the eyes of God he was a murderer, and so, in a way, he deserved to die. And if it was true, as they had said, that God kept a watchful eye on him, then he was *doomed* to die. But Kjersti, who was innocent, was not going to share his death. She should go on and grow up, forget him as best she could, meet some other man, come to love him and have children with him, and only now and then become lost in thoughts she didn't let her husband know anything about.

He had managed to save Kjersti, he saw that much. They were satisfied with having one murderer. And whatever they were thinking or not thinking, the word incest – he could see that also – would never again be mentioned at this trial.

The judge shouted at him, in as loud a voice as he could muster, 'Håvard Gjermundsen – do you admit that, in your first testimony, you knowingly and deliberately gave false information to this court about what occurred that evening in the kitchen at Olstad?'

Håvard replied that he denied having given any false information. Everything he had said the first time was true. But he admitted having reserved a couple of pieces of information. He did not mention the fact that Rønnau had swung the knife at Kjersti and that he had had to intervene. He had kept quiet about that in order to spare Rønnau's reputation – to protect her against the truth of the matter, which was that toward the end her mind was clouded as far as Kjersti was concerned.

He realized himself that it sounded like a feeble explanation, and he could hear one of the members of the bench snort in contempt. In their view, Rønnau's mind hadn't been clouded in the least. On the contrary, she had, earlier and clearer than others, seen that Håvard had cast his eyes upon Kjersti and had wanted her, Rønnau, out of the way. They realized they might never know precisely how he'd brought it about and whether everything had been done coldly and deliberately, nor whether his courage had failed him at the last moment, hindering him from giving her the deathblow while he was at it. But they knew enough now – and Rønnau, well, she had died.

The judge dictated for the record:

'The accused, Håvard Gjermundsen, now endeavors to excuse his previous suppression of facts in the case by alleging that it was due to his regard for Rønnau Larsdaughter's reputation after her death. . . .'

What happened later that day might seem amusing both to the court and to the public; but Håvard knew that it was of no importance to the case.

Anton appeared, requesting permission to make a supplemental statement. Permission was granted.

He stammered a bit as he explained that he had stood outside the window at Olstad one more evening – and, as it happened, it was the very evening when Håvard pushed Rønnau against that iron spike.

On being questioned why he hadn't related this before, he replied that he hadn't dared to – nobody would have believed him if he'd told that sort of thing about a rich man, a big shot like Håvard.

He went on with his testimony, and what he said tallied with what Håvard had stated, apart from the fact that he claimed having seen Håvard push Rønnau.

But this time it was quite plain that the court didn't believe him. The fact of the matter was all too clear – Anton had been standing outside the Community House, had heard about Håvard's statement and thought he ought to improve on it a bit.

Håvard was permitted to put a question to him.

He asked, 'If you stood outside the window as you say, you must have noticed where Kjersti was at the time?'

Anton got confused and walked into the trap. He stammered, 'She . . . she had thrown herself on the floor . . .'

'It's a lie. Kjersti managed to skip aside and stood over by the kitchen counter holding up a chopping board to protect herself in case Rønnau should come after her with the knife.'

Håvard saw no reason to relate that Kjersti had gotten hold of another carving knife and was holding it in her right hand.

That everybody realized Anton was lying may have been well and good. Still, he had said exactly what most members of the court believed, or wanted to believe.

The next witness was the mill owner, who had requested to be heard. He related that Håvard had been to see him on the third of January to ask whether Kjersti could have a situation in his house – she was unhappy at Olstad after Rønnau's death and felt uncomfortable because of the gossip, about which she knew a little. Håvard knew somewhat more, but he, too, lacked a clear understanding of how widespread, and how malicious, the slander was.

He was promised the situation he wanted for Kjersti.

But the principal reason why the mill owner had asked to be heard as a witness was that, in the course of the long conversation he'd had with Håvard that day, the latter had told him, about Rønnau, word for word what he had said here in court in his supplemental statement. He had also used the word *clouded*, but added that he intended to keep this a secret out of respect for Rønnau's reputation after her death. This was at a time when he still didn't have the slightest idea that an action would be brought against him. And the reason why he mentioned it to the mill owner was that he would like to know if the latter had noticed anything similar in the course of the four years Rønnau was employed in his house.

As it happened, the mill owner *had* for a brief period, shortly before Rønnau quit his service, noticed something similar. This might conceivably be of a certain interest.

But the faces of the bench were all impassive, even worse – they were hostile. The mill owner wasn't particularly popular among the farmers – they didn't know the Mill had fallen on hard times and felt the wages he paid them were too low. Among the Haugians his reputation was even worse. He threw blasphemous parties, once even on a holy day, Good Friday, and it was said that one of his lady friends had danced on the table.

The last witness, who had requested to be heard after Anton had testified the second time, was Jon.

Jon wasn't in the least bothered by the court.

He said, first, that when he had asked to be heard, it was first and foremost because he wanted to say a couple of words about Anton.

None of the others who had worked at Olstad, neither cotters, servants or others, had imagined even for a moment that Håvard and Kjersti could have attacked Rønnau with the intent to kill her. And, after all, it was the hired people on the farm who knew them best. About Rønnau and Håvard he wanted to say that they had been so fond of each other throughout the years that they were practically like sweethearts.

'I couldn't help laughing at them sometimes. But it was pretty watching them, too. And what I saw was their everyday lives – it has been almost ten years now.'

It had been almost ten years, too, since Håvard in his kindness took in Anton, when that creep came tramping to the farm like a gypsy after the parson and his wife had kicked him out for theft. Håvard gave him a roof over his head and was like a father to him in every way. Anton was of the sort who couldn't take care of himself; but he hated anyone who helped him out when he was up the creek, and that happened quite frequently. That Håvard sooner or later would reap ingratitude for his goodness, he, Jon, had realized many years ago. And now the poor devil had seen his chance.

About Anton's truthfulness he would say this much: he had known him for ten years now, but he had never heard him utter a true word except when he made a slip of the tongue.

It was a good piece of testimony, and it might have had an effect on some other court. But Håvard knew, as sure as death, that *this* court had made up its mind. Hans Olsen sat there with a hard face, like iron. You could read the verdict there.

Afterward the prosecutor and the defense attorney had the floor. Håvard knew beforehand what they would say, and they said it.

But he noticed that the prosecutor neither mentioned nor hinted at incest. So the deposition by the district doctor had had its effect, all the same.

About Kjersti the prosecutor merely said that, because of the state of the evidence, he would not insist that she be punished. It appeared that the court had quietly dropped the charge against her.

The defense attorney underscored once again that, in this case, there was nothing which, with any semblance of justification, could be called evidence.

While the defense attorney had the floor, Kjersti leaped up, looked around in confusion and said, 'I was the one who swung the knife!'

But everyone realized that she was raving. After uttering that sentence, she sort of woke up, looked around in surprise and sat down again. The defense attorney continued.

The following day, in the afternoon, sentence was passed.

At the Parsonage

*W*hile the trial was taking its course in Nordbygda, Anne Margrethe came to the parsonage for an unexpected visit. She came, she said, to see her father, who had been ill for so long, but also to say hello to her mother, Maren Sofie, and her sister, Lise.

Anne Margrethe, the younger and more attractive of the two sisters, was married to Mr. Daae, a very prosperous department secretary in Christiania. She had taken along her son, Andreas, who was now almost nine years old. He was her only child.

Lise had, after four years of marriage, been blessed with a daughter, Sofie. She was now asleep on the second floor of the curate's apartment, while the two sisters were drinking coffee in the parlor.

As the years passed, Anne Margrethe and Lise had come to look more alike in a way.

Anne Margrethe had put on a little weight, but was otherwise well preserved. But then she was only about thirty, or a little more. With the passing years, she looked more and more like her mother.

So did Lise, who had also put on weight; but in her case it was only to her advantage – her nose didn't look quite as long as it had in her first youth; and when she was sitting her slight limp wasn't apparent.

When Anne Margrethe arrived, one of the first things she heard about was this trial of Håvard and Kjersti.

'Everybody is talking about it up here,' Lise said. She was not looking well these days, pale, with swollen eyelids, as if she had cried a lot or slept poorly.

'I heard something to this effect just before I left,' Anne Margrethe said. 'It's simply incredible! Imagine, Håvard! He who couldn't even bear to be present at a butchering! It's just comical – isn't it, Lise?'

'People up this way don't find it comical at all,' Lise said. 'Papa takes it so much to heart – he's gotten worse. And Mama – well, I don't actually know what Mama thinks.'

Mrs. Maren Sofie was upstairs with the parson.

'Comical! Simply comical!' Anne Margrethe said, passionately. 'Just imagine, Håvard!'

'The trial is now in its fifth day,' Lise said. 'Henrik sits up there too, in case he should be needed for some reason or other.'

Outside the weather had turned mild, with sticky snow. It was rather late in the afternoon, but still full daylight. Anne Margrethe turned toward her son.

'Håvard, run out into the garden and make a snowman, will you!'

The boy went.

'Håvard? Did you say Håvard?' Lise had raised her head. 'But the boy's name is . . .'

'Of course. Sheer thoughtlessness on my part. We were talking about Håvard, you see, that's why.'

A deep blush had mantled Anne Margrethe's cheeks.

The two sisters gazed at each other in silence for a few moments.

It was Anne Margrethe who broke the silence.

'Håvard, indeed!' she said. 'But do they have any *evidence* against him?'

She didn't get any answer to that, not from Lise at any rate. For that very moment they heard the sound of sleigh bells in the yard, and shortly the curate, Henrik Paus, entered the parlor.

'How did it go, Henrik?'

Lise's face had turned ashen.

The curate didn't answer immediately. He too was pale, and his under-shot jaw was more strongly marked than usual. He gazed at Lise awhile, as though trying to instill some strength into her by simply staring.

'It ended with the death sentence,' he said, in a faint, colorless voice.

'For both?' It was Anne Margrethe who asked. Lise's hands were clutching the arms of her chair.

'For Håvard. Kjersti was acquitted because of the state of the evidence. I can add as my personal opinion that, given the evidence at hand, which actually does not exist, the verdict could just as well have been conviction for Kjersti and acquittal for Håvard, or condemnation for both, or acquittal for both.

'But listen, Lise' – Mr. Paus was slightly embarrassed – 'I'll have to ask you for a cup of coffee before I recount this grievous story. I haven't eaten anything all day – I couldn't swallow a morsel at Hans Nordby's after the sentence.'

At the coffee table he gradually became more like his old self, clear but a bit dry, as he went through what seemed to him to be the main points of the case. Only once or twice did he have to consult his papers.

'I had been assigned a seat at the tax collector's table behind the bench. My pretext, which had been accepted, was that I should function as a sort of extra reporter, if it should turn out that the church had an interest in the case. From where I sat, I directly confronted both of the accused every moment.

'They sat a short distance apart, with their faces turned toward the bench and thus also toward me. She sat a little behind him, in such a way that she could see Håvard, but he had to turn his head in order to see her. Whether this was done on purpose by the judge, I don't presume to have an opinion of. But this placement, I believe, proved fateful.'

Mr. Paus leafed through his papers for a moment. He would first, he said, go through the entire course of events, postponing his comments till afterward.

It had grown dark outside. Andreas, who had returned from the garden, had been sent to the kitchen. The coffee was still on the table in the parlor, but nobody had touched it for some time. Two candles had been brought in, one on each side of Mr. Paus. There was a draft from somewhere or other and the candles fluttered, alternately casting light and shadow upon the three faces – the curate's sharp and thin; Lise's tired, with dark circles under her eyes; and Anne Margrethe's suspenseful and strangely greedy, as though she had an unquenchable desire to hear more and more of the somber tale.

Mrs. Maren Sofie had come down for a little while, but on hearing the outcome she said she would wait for the rest until the evening, when she could have it all without interruption.

Later she had come down once again, but very briefly.

'It's a pity he's so emotionally attached to Håvard,' she said; everybody understood it was Mr. Thurmann she was speaking about. 'For when all is said and done, our good Håvard is only a peasant!'

Both sisters responded to that sentence with icy silence. After a while Mrs. Maren Sofie felt frozen out and left, deeply offended.

A moment after she had left, Anne Margrethe said:

'Oh, I must tell you, Lise – out of curiosity I asked a friend of my husband to investigate in Copenhagen whether there is reason to believe that the legend about Håvard's noble lineage had any basis in fact – that he was descended from an outlawed Danish knight who got caught and executed at Brunkeberg Church – well, you remember the story, don't you. And, strangely enough, it appears likely that the legend does have a historical basis. In that case, Håvard is of considerably better family than we are!'

Lise didn't answer – she didn't seem to have heard a word of what Anne Margrethe had said.

The curate had at long last finished the report itself and was trying to sum it up.

He said: 'There wasn't a single witness to the crime, if there was a crime, that is; one was dependent upon the confessions of the accused. But no confession ever came. How, then, could the court, and evidently with complete conviction, sentence Håvard to death?

'I shall now try to explain this.

'The prosecution's charge was entirely based on the hypothesis that there had existed a sexual relationship between Håvard and Kjersti, that Rønnau had found out about it, that the two guilty parties had decided to get rid of her in order to indulge their criminal passions to the full, but that their courage had failed them at the very last moment so they didn't complete their crime. This did not, however, preclude their deed from being called murder, for Rønnau died from her injuries.

'One could say that the different parts of this hypothesis supported one another like the cards in a house of cards.

'To start with, there was very little ground for the accusation; and I had to declare my agreement with the leading man up there, Hans Nordby, when he said that if Håvard hadn't been a stranger but a native of good family, no action would have been brought against him.

'However – fooled by the judge, Kjersti admitted that she was in love with Håvard.

'It was then that the mill owner intervened. With the tax collector's permission – the mill owner can make the tax collector do anything – he let the district doctor undertake the examination of Kjersti that I mentioned, and the following morning the deposition lay on the judge's table: Kjersti was a *virgo intacta*.

'This ostensibly removed an essential part of the motivation for a premeditated murder – which also seemed downright improbable in view of the entire sequence of events. I, for one, thought, The entire case will collapse.

'That the court became confused goes without saying. It took a recess to appraise the new situation. I was requested to participate in these deliberations – a request I can find no other explanation for than that the court, to use a somewhat blasphemous expression, considered me to be a kind of expert on virgin birth.

'The following hour was to me fearfully instructive, as far as earthly justice is concerned.

'That the judge was deeply insulted by the mill owner's high-handed behavior is a thing apart. I guess it could be called simply human.

'It appeared immediately that the whole court, led by the judge, felt hostile toward Håvard, hostile toward Kjersti, hostile toward the mill owner, and now also hostile toward the district doctor, who, the judge alleged, had insulted the dignity of the court by his intervention.

'But behind this resentment there lay a belief that came close to being what in a secular context is called a sacred conviction. The members of the court had entertained a sacred conviction that Håvard and Kjersti had been involved in an incestuous relationship – a relationship of a criminal nature and, for that reason no doubt, all the more passionate. This hypothesis or, should we rather say, this considerably inflamed sexual fantasy, had become so dear to them that they neither could nor would abandon it.

'Their attempts to get around the clear declaration of the district doctor could have been called touching if they hadn't at the same time been so outrageous.

'One of the co-judges, a very foolish man named Ola Nordset, said, "*Oh – such outsiders, you know, can always find a way!*"

'Just a laughing matter? Not up there.

'But the most dangerous of the co-judges was the Haugian Hans Olsen Tomter, a well-known and highly respected man.

'He banged the table and said, "*They are guilty! Just look at her. Her face radiates sin!*"

'Hans Olsen's words carried extra weight, because everybody knew that many years ago he had saved Håvard when the latter was accused – unjustly – of having killed one of his own cotters.

'But I understood very well the reason for Hans Olsen's complete change in attitude. I shall come back to that later.

'After this deliberation I knew one thing:

'In their hearts the members of the court had – partly for widely different reasons – already sentenced Håvard and Kjersti and only searched around for something which could be called a kind of proof.

'It was the judge who resolved the touchy problem concerning the district doctor's declaration. As the court had not requested this declaration, it could be considered to be nonexistent in the legal sense and would not be entered in the record.

'This was of course sheer rubbish. From then on the court in reality skirted the entire incest charge. They were searching for another pretext to condemn the two of them.

'This pretext they were offered by Håvard. When Kjersti had been driven into a corner by the prosecutor, he presented his so-called supplemental statement, perceived by the court as a disguised confession. He did it in order to save Kjersti, *and he did save her*, but was himself condemned.

'The mill owner's testimony, which was offered at the last moment in an attempt to save Håvard, only made matters worse. A very wise man up there, Hans Nordby – I have already mentioned him a couple of times – said to me after the sentence had been read:

'"People say that the mill owner is such a wise man. But then we can also say, using an old adage from up here, that no man is wise from morning till night. The farmers up this way think of him as their natural enemy – they supply the Mill with coal and ore for what seems to them insufficient wages. What's more, in the eyes of the two Haugians in court he's the devil's hench-man. The air is thick with rumors about the parties at the Mill. If the mill owner says no, the court says yes, if it can."

'Thus far Hans Nordby.

'But what I knew sitting there was far worse. We all know, don't we, that the judge, with all his excellent qualities, suffers from one human frailty – that he filches silver, snuff boxes, and the like when he is at a big party. Two years ago – this I am telling for your benefit, Anne Margrethe, we up here know about it – he was caught in such a theft for the second time at the mill owner's. Whereupon his sleigh was driven up to the entrance and he himself was informed by the mill owner that his conveyance was waiting for him. Since then he hasn't been invited to the Mill.

'This is where I have to ask myself, Could the mill owner, who is such a wise man, have had a moment's doubt that a statement from him in favor of Håvard was bound to have a contrary effect on the judge?

'Naturally, the verdict rests on next to nothing and will go to the Supreme Court. But the court reporter who was keeping the record of the proceedings had previously been employed at the Mill – he was dismissed a year and a half ago on account of a small embezzlement. Subsequently he was hired by the judge's office as a demonstration against the mill owner.

'What this down-and-out, besotted, profoundly cynical person can do with the record, together with the judge, to aggravate Håvard's situation, I don't presume to know. I only know that they will do all they can – on the part of the judge, no doubt, with the best of intentions.

'I cannot help thinking that, in this court, Håvard was all in all a victim of such an unlucky interplay of circumstances that the odds against it happening to anybody were a thousand to one.

'And yet, I can't say I feel certain about anything in this case. I'm not even certain that Håvard was innocent.

'"*She radiates sin!*" Hans Olsen said.

'Translated into a less Haugian language, I can say this:

'The expression in Kjersti's eyes and face could be read like an open book. She *worshiped* Håvard. She worshiped the very ground he walked on. He was her God, her one and all in this world. Her eyes, which appeared to be strangely luminous, were intent upon Håvard all along, in a supreme ecstasy of self-forgetful love. We all saw it.

'One could say that the sight of such love – she is also a very attractive young girl – is moving. But to the court, whose imagination had become obsessed by the idea of incest, this sight was a shocking fact which the declarations of all the world's district doctors would not have been able to erase.

'And so it could be said that, if a single person is the cause of the death sentence on Håvard, it is Kjersti; first by her *yes* to the judge, then her sentence *She swung the knife at me!* which forced Håvard to change his statement, and last but not least by that look in her eyes. It is profoundly tragic that she – yes, she – would undoubtedly have been quite willing to die in his stead.

'We could see Kjersti's feelings for Håvard, because she was so young and couldn't hide them.

'Håvard's feelings for Kjersti – if there were any – we couldn't see in any comparable way. But he intervened when Kjersti's situation looked most dismal and in reality sacrificed himself in order to save her – though he could scarcely have known at the time that he sacrificed his own life in doing so.

'What if his supplemental statement wasn't complete either? What if, in order to save Kjersti, who was so precious to him, he attacked Rønnau and, during his attempts to wrest the knife away from her, was unlucky enough to give her that fateful push which, in the last analysis, led to her death?

'In that case he must have felt guilty, at any rate as a killer.

'Or what if, in fact, Kjersti was the guilty one?

'Her statement that she couldn't remember anything that happened during the crucial moments may very well have been true. In any case, it is quite conceivable that she didn't remember anything *clearly*.

'But what if she succeeded in wresting the knife from Rønnau, and Rønnau, when Kjersti in turn swung the knife, jumped backward, up against the iron spike?

'In that case Håvard was quite aware of it when he rose to hear the reading of his own death sentence.

'I can't forget that terrible moment this morning when the sentence was read.

'Everybody stood during the reading. I paid particular attention to Håvard. I was standing only eight feet away and could look him full in the face the whole time. He didn't look at me, and I don't believe he saw any of those present. His face was impassive – not the slightest twitch was caused either by the section where Kjersti was acquitted or by the immediately following section where he himself was sentenced to death as a murderer.

'It was as though he had foreseen everything, both the acquittal and the sentence, as though the whole thing seemed to him to be part of an inexorable fate.

'At the last word of the sentence, where he was condemned to death, Kjersti fainted and fell to the floor; she had to be carried out. But he stood as before, impassive, as though his face and figure had been carved from wood.

'It might appear as though he was hard to the point of being beyond the reach of all feeling. But I admit it can also be interpreted quite differently. He may have felt a despair verging on petrifaction – here combined with a freeholder's sense of honor, which requires that he remain *calm* in every situation.

'Or it could have been something quite different from all of this. During the whole trial Håvard was – I may have forgotten to mention this – chained hand and foot. When he stood up his chains clattered in a disturbing way, and a couple of times I noticed that an expression of profound disgust passed across his impassive face. Håvard was, according to all accounts, a very proud man, but here he stood chained like a slave, which symbolically stamped him as guilty in advance. Was it the shame and disgust at this which ended by petrifying him?

'I don't know.'

'Oh! These men and their incredible stupidity!'

It was Lise – she found it difficult to control her voice.

'If the court could see Kjersti, Håvard could also see the court, couldn't he? And he knew what he could expect from that quarter, from people who hated him because he was what they were not – a man loved by women and admired by his equals. Should he now give them a cheap triumph by seeming crushed as he stood before them?

'And how about this – should the fact that Kjersti loved Håvard be a reason for handing down a death sentence? That she was unable to keep her love a secret merely shows, after all, that she was innocent. *All* women who met Håvard were captivated by him, and this was one of the things which made other men hate him. I could tell you . . .'

'Lise!' Anne Margrethe said sharply.

In the Prison

*T*he people in the courtroom quickly dispersed when the sentence had been read and the meeting adjourned. The sheriff sidled up to Håvard and patted his shoulder, 'Well, here we are, the two of us.'

When Håvard walked out with the sheriff upon his heels, he noticed a man still sitting there – he hadn't gotten around to seeing his way out yet. This was Kerstaffer Berg. Kerstaffer looked old, shriveled, and crooked. But he managed to sneer at Håvard anyway.

Outside, where the sheriff's horse was waiting, people drew aside from him, over into the piled-up snow, as though he were a leper.

First the sheriff took him to Olstad. Håvard would have to count on a relatively long stay in prison in one of the cells at the fortress, and he received permission to pack a traveling bag and a bentwood box with some clothes. The sheriff, who knew how cold these cells were in the wintertime, advised him to take along plenty of clothes. Also, the sheriff – Aarsæter was his name – knowing better than anybody that Håvard was chained hand and foot, left him alone in the room on the second floor where he kept his chests.

Håvard did his packing thoroughly and thoughtfully, and didn't forget to take his razor along. The only thing that disturbed him in his work was the clanking of his chains. He just couldn't get used to that sound. Outside the door he could hear the sheriff carrying on a conversation with Goro in an undertone, and he understood that Kjersti had been taken home and put to bed. He hesitated for a moment when he got to the small leather purse with the fifteen hundred dollars. Then he stuck the purse in the traveling bag.

Goro and the sheriff stood outside. Goro was pale and red-eyed, but quiet. He had forgotten that she was so small.

'You will be good to Kjersti, won't you, Goro,' he said. 'She'll need it.'

Goro wept and couldn't utter a word, but nodded her head.

She walked downstairs with the sheriff and Håvard.

In the kitchen he found, as he had thought he would, Jon and Mons Myra.

They weren't particularly cheerful company – they sat on the bench as though gathered for a funeral.

'Good-bye then, Jon, and you too, Mons,' Håvard said. 'And now, with witnesses present, I would like to say that I appoint you, Jon, to look after the farming while I am away. For that you shall be paid twenty-five dollars a year, besides your daily wages, which you shall collect as before. Hans Nordby will arrange the payment. Do you agree to that?'

Jon's face kept twitching, but he nodded to indicate he agreed. Then the usual Jon got the upper hand for a moment, and he said, 'I agree on one condition: If Anton should turn up here, I want to have the right to chase him away with a stick.'

Then it was time to go. Håvard and the sheriff took their seats in the big sleigh and drove off.

The sheriff had removed the harness bells.

'We're not exactly going to a wedding,' he said, 'so it seems to me there's little cause for bell ringing.'

The first night they were to stay at the sheriff's house out in the home parish. The following day they were to drive on to the fortress prison.

The sheriff was a reticent man. He said only one sentence during the three-hour trip.

'I have driven all kinds of people in my time,' he said. 'But I've never before driven a man who's condemned for murder. And I certainly hadn't thought that you would be the first one.'

They hadn't really spoken with each other during the trial. But Håvard had noticed, and had also been told, that once he had completed the preliminary hearings, the sheriff had concluded that Håvard was innocent.

It didn't matter what Aarsæter's opinion was, Håvard knew that. But the fact that the sheriff considered him innocent made it a little easier to sit in the same sleigh with him.

They arrived at the fortress before noon the following day, and the sheriff handed Håvard over to the governor, a deserving old noncommissioned officer.

Håvard hadn't slept much the night before – he couldn't get used to sleeping in chains. Now he stood there half-asleep, hearing the governor call somebody or other. An aging man with a limp, clearly another retired noncom – he was wearing a sort of uniform – came in with a big, jingling bunch of keys.

'Take him to the empty cell directly below the stairs, Gunder, will you.'

Gunder came limping up. Håvard, rousing, looked at him and recognized him. In 1814 Gunder Pilterud was a corporal, no longer young, small, and rather withered in the eyes of the young recruits. He must now be slightly over fifty but looked older. Gunder had an accident toward the end of the campaign. During a rapid and perhaps not particularly glorious retreat he slipped on a difficult road, fell and broke his leg, and had to be carried the rest of the way by a strong soldier from Eidskogen[35] – he carried him on his

35. The southernmost township in Hedmark County, located south of Kongsvinger.

back for almost a mile, and the rifle bullets kept whizzing over their heads all along, he maintained.

'But God bless those damn Swedes, always shooting too high!' he said.

Gunder's gun, unfortunately, ended up as Swedish booty.

And so, it appeared, he had been given this position of custodian, or whatever it was, as a sort of military pension.

Håvard wasn't particularly lighthearted at the moment, but at the thought of Gunder Pilterud's wartime exploits he smiled a pale inward smile.

After Gunder was alone with Håvard, he took a closer look at him.

'Good heavens, if it isn't the same Håvard I ran into in 1814!' he said. 'Then you became a corporal and were praised to the skies because you had stabbed and killed a Swede. Times sure have changed!'

He looked at Håvard with that mixture of horror and respect the weak feel toward the stronger, the one who dares to do something dark and dangerous.

'I did hear about that case of yours,' he said, keeping at a safe distance, 'and I couldn't help wondering a bit, because Håvard, you know, is a rare name in these parts – we mostly say Halvor, we do. But that I should meet you again in this way, that . . .'

He couldn't find words to express himself.

'All right, you lead the way then,' he said. 'Through that door, and then along the corridor and down those steep stairs. They are hard on a poor old body who was wounded in the war.'

'A poor old body who was wounded in the war' was his usual way of referring to himself, as Håvard was to discover soon enough. He had long ago forgotten that his enemy that time was a big cow patty, which lay there puffing itself up in the middle of the road, causing him to slip. The leg fracture had become an honorable defect he had incurred in the war, but it made it difficult for him to walk the stairs.

'We have only two other convicts here, besides you,' he said to Håvard when he'd let him into the dark cell. 'One of them is just a lunatic nobody wants to have in the house; the other is a big bull of a man who knocked out all his brother's teeth in a drunken bout last Christmas. They figure he may get several years for it, because his brother hadn't done him any harm, just taken away his girl at a dance.'

It was cold and damp in the dark cell. Getting Gunder to help him, Håvard put on all the winter clothes he had taken along. Still, he constantly felt cold. On reflection, he realized he'd done so from the very moment he had testified for the second time in the courtroom and could tell from the faces of the judge and the co-judges that he was already condemned, finished. Until then he seemed to have thought, They can't be completely insane, can they? It was bad enough as it was – to be chained hand and foot, the shame and the injury. . . . But when he saw their faces after he'd made his second statement, he knew. Sure, that's just how insane they are! It was from then on he started noticing this cold. But not as badly as now, not by a long shot.

'I think I'll have to bring an extra sheepskin for you,' Gunder said. 'This here cell, you know, is awfully cold.'

He got another sheepskin, but it didn't help much. His teeth were chattering and he was cold, he was cold and his teeth were chattering. He wrapped the sheepskins around him, but that didn't help much either.

Gunder Pilterud had a worried look in his eyes whenever he stopped by.

And well he might. The constant cold drained Håvard, and in the end he had difficulty getting up from his bunk.

'You haven't caught pneumonia, have you?' Gunder said.

But Håvard knew it wasn't pneumonia. He had seen people who were sick with that, and who had sometimes died from it. They alternated between feeling hot and cold – their teeth would be chattering from cold, and then they would get hot as an oven. With Håvard it was different – he simply felt cold night and day, all the time.

Locked up as he was, Håvard couldn't know that his case was the daily topic of conversation throughout several parishes. There were sharply divided opinions about this case, and old friends became enemies on account of it.

Gradually Gunder Pilterud understood from the gossip in town that he had a famous convict on his hands and that people disagreed violently on whether he was guilty or innocent. He himself may have been moved at the thought of those heroic days long ago, in 1814, when Håvard became a corporal and he himself got wounded during the retreat. Gunder pulled himself together and spoke to the governor; later he sought an audience with the commandant himself. He explained that the new convict, Håvard Gjermundsen, was anything but well. And besides he sat in the coldest cell of all. Whatever the reason could be, his teeth were chattering all day long, and he couldn't be any warmer at night; for the old sheepskins which had been thrown on top of the bunk were so worn that they gave little more heat than a bunch of rags. Gunder for one believed that this could easily lead to pneumonia, if it hadn't done so already. . . .

He was luckier than he had dared to hope. The commandant of the fortress was an enemy of the judge and a friend of the mill owner. He had just been to a party at the Mill, and he didn't have the slightest doubt: Håvard was innocent, and the Supreme Court would give the judge a thorough dressing down; but that made it important to ensure that Håvard didn't freeze to death or die upon their hands from other causes before the court's decision was handed down. Gunder was ordered to move Håvard to one of the empty offices in the wing; it had a stove and was better in every way. The convict was to get proper porridge and real barley soup as well.

Håvard could once again stretch himself in the blissful warmth of a stove. His chains clanked when he stretched.

But before it got that far, Håvard had been through a kind of crisis.

Some time passed before he understood what was the matter with him. Something was watching him with empty eye sockets from morning till night and then throughout the long night; still, it took him a day or two before he realized he was a prey to sheer, brutal fear of death.

Where is this cold coming from? he thought at first. Some time passed before he understood that it wasn't the winter that was blowing coldly upon him. The cold that penetrated his very bones came from something that was colder than winter. He was gazing down into his own grave, and it was the whiff from that black hole which made his blood run cold.

Little by little he saw that he hadn't really understood anything earlier – not when he sat in the courtroom thinking, This will end badly! not when he saw the death sentence in the faces of the members of the bench, not when he heard the sentence read. The calm he'd shown then, and which had been a surprise to him, had only been a mask. Here in this lonely cell the mask was torn off, and he thought, In one way life was still merciful – I was spared having to show the others how pitiful I was.

But that was what he thought at first, before he felt utterly pitiful.

During the first few days, while he still had some strength, he also thought, If only I had been killed by that bear!

And he thought, If only Rønnau had stabbed me with the knife!

At first he imagined, wishing it with all his might, that a miracle had happened there in the courtroom, that his chains had dropped from his limbs and he stood there, suddenly, with his knife, *the family dagger*, in his hand. Then let each and every one of his enemies have a knife in their hands. Oh! what sport they would have – a brief sport, which could only end in one way, because they were many and he was alone. But he would certainly have left his mark on some of them before it was over, and it was by no means sure that every one would have lived much longer than he.

But no such miracle occurred. Defenseless, chained, he would at some future date stretch out his neck on the block and hear the whistle of the ax, the last thing he would hear in this life – if he would hear it at all. Stretched out for the slaughter like an animal – and after the head was chopped off, his legs might give a couple of twitches before the headless body became still. . . .

How could I have been so stupid that I told the truth? he thought. I should have known that the truth is the last thing people will believe.

His teeth were chattering.

Once he had started to think pitilessly, he couldn't stop. The sentence had to be confirmed by the Supreme Court, but he knew, without a glimmer of hope, that it would be confirmed. When the judges who had seen him and heard him could feel so convinced of his guilt that they condemned him to death, then the Supreme Court, which only got to see the record of the proceedings, was even more certain to do so. He had seen the sharp-nosed face of the court reporter and knew he was his enemy. He had heard what the judge dictated into the record and knew that, in him, he had another enemy.

The two of them would certainly see to it that the record of the proceedings was in order.

What is there about me which makes people believe I am a murderer? he thought. He couldn't give an answer to that; but he had seen that they believed it, all right.

His teeth were chattering as he sat there, wrapped in two sheepskins.

It was bad enough in the daytime. It was even worse at night. When it happened – if it did happen – that he fell asleep for a moment and forgot everything, he would soon stir in his sleep, wake up from the clanking chains, and meet the same ice-cold breath from the all-too-familiar thoughts.

He noticed how this dread, which held him in its grip night and day, little by little drained him of his strength. Bathed in a cold sweat and trembling like an aspen leaf, he didn't even have the strength to sit up in his bunk. He knew it helped to sit up, he could somehow defend himself a little then. But he didn't have the strength for it.

And so it happened – one time, several times – that he experienced what he later considered as the worst humiliation of all during this period. And *that* was a humiliation created by himself – injury compounded by shame, a shame he couldn't even give a name to: at night, trembling from dread, he lay pondering whether there wasn't some shameful or wretched thing he could do which might save this miserable little life of his. Let someone else die, no matter who, only not him. Let Kjersti die, let Tonè die, let his own mother die, as long as he himself could save his life, let *everyone* die but not him. . . .

270

Yet, all along he knew that Tonè *was* dead, and it was he who had killed her. His mother, too, *was* dead. And Kjersti – if he was now willing to betray her to save his own wretched life, it was too late; he could drag her down with him perhaps, but he couldn't save himself.

He knew that he was sinking down into the most abject shame, as though into a bottomless swamp, in harboring these thoughts; but he was so weak and so scared that he didn't even feel the shame as a shame.

The recovery came gradually, and he couldn't have explained to anyone how it came about.

It began with attacks of self-contempt. First in little brief gusts, later as long fits of nausea. In the end the self-contempt appeared simultaneously with his cowardly thoughts. He realized he'd been steeped in a river filled not with water but with stinking slime. He had been to the bottom and now, as he emerged again, he felt covered with slime from top to toe.

That was as far as he'd gotten when Gunder dropped by and took him upstairs to the warm, roomy cell. From then on the recovery went more quickly. But it took its time, several weeks, with relapses, fresh anxiety and fresh self-contempt. When he knew at last that an attack was over, he felt at the same time that he had become a different person, whether better or worse he didn't know, but harder in some way. More pitiless, at least toward himself. Something had been burned out of him – burned out through cold. He knew something he hadn't known before: That is how pitiful I can be – I'd better not forget it.

When he eventually started receiving visitors in the prison – and he did have a few in the course of the spring – the initial mask had been replaced by something he all but believed was his own new, authentic face.

Would it hold up to the end? He didn't know. But he believed he knew how he could strengthen it – and thus shore up whatever worth there might be in him, in spite of everything.

Mr. Paus was the first one to come. He could, after all, visit the condemned in an official capacity. His first visit was a few days before Easter. Håvard was the calmer of the two. Whatever Lise said and whatever he had seen and heard in court, Mr. Paus felt a bit uncertain, and this may have made him speak more like a parson than he otherwise would have done. When he left, Håvard said:

'Thanks for the visit, Reverend. But if your purpose is to convert me to your faith, you don't have to come back again. You and others as learned as you say there is a god, so I guess I'll have to believe it. But he cannot be all-powerful, that I have seen and experienced myself.'

But Mr. Paus did come back, not only once but several times. The first time he said, 'You dismissed me rather brusquely last time, and it was probably my own fault. But I have come back, as you can see. If I didn't, I would have no end of trouble with Lise.'

From then on he and Håvard were able to talk with each other without pretenses. The result was that Håvard told him a little more than what he had said in court. Among other things, he told him about Anders Flateby and added, 'I hadn't expected very much from my neighbors, but from *that* quarter I guess I had expected an ever-so-little piece of testimony.'

By the time summer came around, Mr. Paus could tell Lise, 'You feel convinced that Håvard is innocent. But I know. I also know that one of the things which sustain him is his consciousness of having saved Kjersti's life.'

The same day he wrote a long letter to the Supreme Court, with a postscript by Mr. Thurmann. He also submitted a petition for pardon on Håvard's behalf.

Jon came one day in early May to talk about the spring planting. Without meaning to, he backed up a step as he entered – he thought Håvard had changed so. But soon they sat there talking about the different plots of land as though nothing had happened.

When they were through with that and Jon should have left, he kept sitting there, unable to speak what was on his mind.

'Out with it, Jon!' Håvard said.

It was only that he had greetings from Mons and Goro – . 'Well, from Kjersti too,' he added quickly.

'Thanks. Be good enough to return my greetings. You can say I am doing fine, under the circumstances. Is Kjersti all right?'

'Oh . . .' Jon hesitated. 'I wouldn't say she's very happy.'

'No, I guess not.' Håvard smiled faintly, then grew serious.

'I can tell you one thing, Jon. You don't need to have any suspicion of Kjersti. Kjersti didn't kill Rønnau. Kjersti stood over by the kitchen counter, as I said. And what I related the second time was all true. There happened neither more nor less than what I said.'

'That's good, anyway,' Jon said. And Håvard could tell that he was relieved.

He asked how Høgne Lien was doing.

'Oh, the same as ever. As in the old days, I guess one could say. He sticks to himself again now – walks around and around in his yard.'

Håvard walked over to the traveling bag and came back with a leather purse.

'I have no way of knowing whether Høgne will talk to you, Jon,' he said.

272

'If he does, you can greet him from me and say that I propose you take my place as buyer of Lien Farm. Here you have the thousand dollars. I won't need them now, you know.'

It took some time to persuade Jon, but here it was Håvard whose will was the stronger.

Good Counsel

O ne day in the middle of August the sheriff came riding up through Nordbygda. Part of his errand was to give notice of overdue taxes.

There were some people – even solid farmers – who were always behind in such matters. It was worst of all at Flateby. By now Anders seemed to have gone completely crazy, claiming he was of royal blood and therefore exempt from paying taxes and fees; he would take the matter to court. There he would have Hans Nordby condemned to the forfeit of his house and property at the same time, because he had dealt in lies and tricks.

Foreclosure was imminent at Flateby. But the most important errand the sheriff had this time was to report that the Supreme Court had confirmed the death sentence of Håvard Gjermundsen. The execution was to take place before the end of September, in an appropriate place on the Olstad grounds, where the crime had been committed. This was according to law. More detailed information concerning the date would be announced according to law from the church green in Nordbygda on the last Sunday a service was held there before the execution.

The sheriff knew the sentence by heart and stopped at the three or four biggest farms to report it.

'It will be an ugly way to end the grain harvest,' Hans Nordby said. It was the only thing he said about the big news.

The sheriff had to be home again before evening, so he was in a hurry – at Nordby he could be urged to take only a couple of drinks.

Afterward Hans Nordby and his son, Pål, sat in the bedroom behind the kitchen. Actually, it wasn't called the bedroom anymore now, since the new wife had arrived and the bedroom had been moved to the second floor – it was just as well, for that way the servants heard less of that shrill voice of hers when she complained and carried on before going to bed. The former bedroom was now called *the office*, and Hans got his business done there, though most of the deals were made elsewhere, at parties and such; but he did have a table and a couple of chairs and pen and ink in there, besides the brown writing desk with his contracts and cash.

Pål, who had turned twenty by now, was going to the capital the following day to start a year's training in the office of Baron Rosenkrantz. His father was going with him but would like to give him, in private, a few pieces of good advice to take along.

'It will seem strange to you at first,' he said. 'You'll be far away from home and will be homesick, however unpleasant it may often have been here after we got this troll in the house.'

He never called his wife anything else than 'troll' when he talked to his children and other people he could trust.

'But I have found some very nice lodgings for you, with people I know and who know me.

'You must behave properly, both in the office and in your lodgings. People will notice you because you are your father's son. Be careful in the office – say too little rather than too much, but keep your eyes and ears open. Try to be like the others, then many things will go more easily. I'll have city clothes made for you when we get there.

'In the office you'll meet some people who'll be nice to you – I'm known there, you know – but also, no doubt, a few stuck-up pups. Answer them as little as possible; be *cautious*, as I said, but pay close attention to what they say and do – the day may come when you get your turn.

'Don't ever really trust anyone, but pretend you do when it seems appropriate.

'In your lodgings you should be courteous and quiet-mannered, stand up when older people enter the room, and help elderly women as much as you can. Very few things are more worthwhile than that. Don't say no to a drink – then people will lose patience with you – but watch out that you never get drunk. Better empty your glass when no one can see it. But on that score I don't have any fears for you, since you don't like liquor.' (Hans was wrong on this point, but that is another matter.)

'These are the most important things, the rest we'll talk about tomorrow.'

Hans Nordby had meant to stop here, but Pål had something to ask him.

'What's your opinion about this sentence, Dad?'

Hans Nordby was in no hurry with his answer.

'The Supreme Court has confirmed the sentence,' he said at last. 'It can never be quashed, and as far as I know it is forbidden to find fault with such a sentence. You can get punished for that, I've heard. But if you can keep it to yourself and promise never to mention I told you so, I can tell you, quite frankly, that I think both Håvard and Kjersti are innocent. Håvard didn't have it in him to do something like that, and besides he was more attached to Rønnau than he himself knew. I believe that every word he said in court was true – the reason he kept silent about the pulling of that knife until forced to bring it up was because, as he himself said, he wished to protect Rønnau's good name. The truth, I for one believe, was that Rønnau had lost her common sense toward the end, as far as Kjersti was concerned.

'But she could have taken it easy. For Kjersti, you know, had kept her virginity. That I knew long before the district doctor came with his deposition. You see, I had talked to a couple of women, wise old women, and they can see such things. God only knows how they can see it – whether it is from the eyes, the gait, or whatever; but they can see it. I won't even mention the witch women, they can almost see too much.

'Foolish women are something else again – they see what they *want* to see and nothing else. Well, we have one of those in the house.

'No, Håvard and Kjersti were unlucky, that's a fact. And to be unlucky is the worst thing that can happen to a person.

'Those people on the Supreme Court sit too high, they don't understand farmers.'

'But Dad, that's terrible – that Håvard will be beheaded even though he's innocent.'

'I cannot stick my nose into such things, nor do I want to,' Hans Nordby said. 'The only thing I can tell you is that all of us here at Nordby can thank and praise the Lord that things have taken this turn.'

'But how, Dad?'

Hans Nordby cleared his throat.

'I have told you before that Baron Rosenkrantz can be a strict and difficult man when the wind blows that way. Once I had to give up two hundred dollars which I thought were mine, because he had a different viewpoint and demanded it. Afterward our relations were only so-so for about a year, until I managed to pick up a good bargain for him.

'This happened just before Håvard came up here. And a good thing it was – that he hadn't come yet, I mean. Nobody was supposed to know that there was some trouble between the Baron and me. That was why I went around speaking about *the Baron and I*, until people started laughing behind my back.

'But it turned out well, as I've said.

'Håvard was the only man up this way who could have become dangerous to me. The Baron knows the mill owner – he is a partner in the Mill – and the mill owner had a high opinion of Håvard, excessively high, perhaps. If it had occurred to the Baron, some other time when he was unreasonable, to look around for another man up here, it would've had to be Håvard.

'You ought to know – and I'll teach you more about this when you get

275

older – that there are people it pays to help, and there are people who repay help with ingratitude. One of the most important things in life is to be able to tell the difference between these two kinds of people. Håvard – and Rønnau too – was one of those who remember a favor and become *grateful*, as it's called. Therefore I was always a good neighbor to Håvard – so that he would remember it and decline if he got such an offer.

'But I was always uneasy about him. For suppose I was unlucky some day – not the way Håvard was in the end, but *a little* unlucky, as I was that time when I had to give up those two hundred dollars or, let us say, a bit more unlucky than that. I don't think it will happen, I am wiser now than I used to be – but if I should be really unlucky some day, the offer to Håvard might take such a form that he would almost have to say *yes*.

'I kept thinking about that every day and was as careful as a person can be.

'But now Håvard is out of the running, and we can sit quite safely here at Nordby.'

Pål gazed at his father full of admiration.

'What a wise man you are, Dad,' he said.

Hans Nordby sat on for a while after Pål had taken himself upstairs and to bed.

I am a little wiser than you know, he thought. But there's no point in telling you about it – because you may not be grown-up enough to take it, not yet anyway.

Many of those who thought that Håvard was innocent – and there were quite a few, mostly among women – thought it must be Kerstaffer who'd paid Anton to go lurking among the buildings at Olstad, to report it to the sheriff and appear in court as a witness.

Now, what Kerstaffer had done was difficult to say. Quite possibly, Anton may have picked up a few dollars there. Ten dollars, he himself claimed, when he bargained with Hans about the price. And, little by little, he got ten dollars from up here at Nordby too. But he had to return value for the money.

A wise man will hardly ever tell a direct lie, because it can backfire. But when a lie begins to circulate all by itself, he may help it along – stir up the embers a bit and light a pine stick or two. . . . The gossip about Håvard and Kjersti arose by itself – nobody knew which woman had whispered the first word. But once it had gotten started, Anton was certainly very helpful. And best of all, he believed it all himself.

No liar could compete with someone who believed he spoke the truth.

And no truth could compete with a lie which lots of people liked to believe in.

It was a godsend that Anton's sister had died last year. He lived alone in that filthy house of his, and luckily the path from Nordby up into the home forest went right past. Not a soul knew that Hans Nordby stopped by there every once in a while.

That it was to Nordby and not to Kerstaffer that Anton brought most of what he saw when he was out peeping, nobody knew either.

When he told him about that embrace in the kitchen, Hans asked, 'And then?'

'Well, then they went to their rooms.'

'You're sure of that? You're sure they didn't go together into Håvard's bedroom?'

'Well, now that you say so, I'm not completely sure.'

'I'm not saying anything, one way or another; I wasn't the one standing there, you know. But you aren't sure, you say?'

'No, not quite, but . . .'

'Well, then, we won't talk anymore about it.'

After a couple of more conversations Anton was sure. Sure as sin, too.

They weren't very successful with that bedroom story – Goro was a bit too smart, and then came the district doctor. But a barb remained. And, of course, Hans had nothing whatever to do with it. As far as anyone knew, that is. Not even Anton suspected that.

It didn't cost very much either. Only a dollar now and then. Hans knew very well that if he paid too much, Anton would begin to lie like a trooper, with the end result that nobody would believe a word of what he said. You had to keep a tight rein on him and direct him where he was to go.

It was harder to line up Anders Flateby. But when that baking woman, who was the worst scandalmonger for miles around, came to Nordby and was to go to Flateby afterward, the matter pretty much took care of itself.

You needed a bit of luck, you bet.

To sit there talking with that bag about everything and nothing! A pity things had gone sour between Nordby and Flateby. Håvard had been a poor adviser to me there, unfortunately . . .

Nobody believed in it, of course, except Anders. But that sufficed.

One had to be patient. Sooner or later a solution would turn up.

He had been waiting now for ten long years.

As he walked home over the bare, frozen ground, with moonlight and all, on that evening in November, after he'd been adding up silver and cash down at Olstad, he was thinking, Tomorrow the whole thing will blow up! Tomorrow the sheriff will come and get him.

It took several weeks, though. They probably had to circulate the papers between them first, the judge and the tax collector and the county governor. Perhaps they would take a trip to Christiania, too, so they could make certain that nobody was responsible.

But in the end it was Anton's gossip which tipped the scales. What a strange tramp, that Anton fellow. Once in a while it almost looked as if he thought of himself as the avenging sword of justice, as they said in church. Indeed, at times it had occurred to Hans Nordby that Anton must have lost the bit of common sense he had, that he had become infatuated with Rønnau and had hoped to crawl into bed with her.

But surely, not even Anton could have been *that* stupid.

That beheading, though, was a nasty business. Hans Nordby didn't intend to go and watch it. Instead he would take a trip to the city that day.

A life sentence would have sufficed, he thought. I'm not a wicked person, after all.

Kjersti

*A*fterward nobody could say for sure how it started, who had set it going. Some said it must have been Andrea Nordby, who had used the time while her husband was in the capital with his son. But it had probably started much earlier. Others were of the opinion that it came, first of all, from something this night watcher, Maren Teppen, had said over her cup of coffee while watching over Goro Strøm, who was at death's door. But Maren didn't take part in it – she had been asked to but said no. Still others said it must have been the wife at Flateby, Berte, who had cooked up the beginnings of the whole thing. She was so spiteful she didn't seem to be in her right mind after her husband had gone to wrack and ruin – the sheriff had called to give notice of foreclosure, it was said. But wherever it had come from, it spread like wildfire the moment it was reported that Håvard's death sentence had been confirmed. That was the sixteenth of August. Three days later it was all finished and done with, so the wives in the hamlet didn't waste their time with needless talk that time. . . .

Strange how opinions could change – and so rapidly.

Most of the wives in the hamlet – and far beyond the hamlet too – had been pleased with the sentence when it was first handed down, when the court, as the judge said, found it necessary to make an example of Håvard and sentenced him to death for killing Rønnau. It would be a lesson to the menfolk, the whole lot of them, who blurted out all kinds of things when drunk and probably harbored black thoughts even in broad daylight, while sober. A poor woman who was getting on in years might have to go in constant terror of her life if the law didn't step in with a bang sometimes. And when an outsider like that – though, to be sure, Rønnau was an outsider, too, and hadn't always kept to the straight and narrow, if only half of what was said about her and the mill owner was true. Wasn't it a fact that the mill owner had called on her, not only once but several times, when Håvard was away from home? Then you could imagine the rest. For as everybody knew, nothing was sacred to that fellow – a married man and all. . . .

But that pride goeth before a fall, young Håvard was surely the best proof of. There he had come to this parish from back of beyond and married one of the best farms up here – but it wasn't good enough, it had to be *improved*, everything was to be fixed up, even the dung hole in the cow barn. Berte – the dairymaid as she was called to this very day though she'd been a cotter's wife and had led her husband a dog's life for ages by now – Berte had made a real fool of herself over it, running around and talking about that ten-year-old dung hole in the cow barn. . . . But pride goeth before a fall, as mentioned before. He thought he was a head taller than everyone else, Håvard did. But now, most likely, he would soon be a head shorter, so . . .

These and similar things were said, again and again, during the weeks that followed the first sentence, every time two or three women got together.

But other tunes were heard as well, almost from the very beginning.

What was really going on with this girl, Kjersti? She did get acquitted, true enough, but that was because of the 'state of the evidence.' She'd always been a bit odd and had never mixed with young people her own age. She had much too high an opinion of herself for that, no doubt, being the heir to the Olstad farm and forests. . . .

And as the weeks became months and winter became spring and spring became summer, there were gradual shifts in what was being said and thought.

To be beheaded was certainly no joke. As she said, old Marte Mobråten, 'To lose your head by the ax, that's some punishment, sure is. After all, the Lord has given us only one head.'

There that poor devil was sitting in his dungeon, chained hand and foot, and had only one thing to look forward to – stretching his neck on the block and waiting for the ax to fall. . . .

If the Supreme Court should confirm the sentence, that is.

Then there was the fact that, if the truth were to be told, Håvard hadn't done any harm to any of these women. Quite the contrary, one could say. He had always been pleasant and jovial, and had laughed and joked with them many a time, both at weddings and funerals, as well as at Christmas parties. By comparison, Rønnau was more apt to be stuck-up and proud, if the truth were to be told.

Little by little it appeared that there was scarcely a woman in the whole hamlet who in dead earnest believed that Håvard had done what he had been condemned for. He didn't seem to be that kind of man. Little by little more and more people knew what Jon had been telling everywhere – that in the fall, when the butchering was to take place, Håvard always found a pretext to take to the woods or go to the city. 'I can never bring myself to kill defenseless animals,' he said when Jon once taunted him with this.

No, the fact of the matter was that *if* Håvard had knocked Rønnau against the chimney ledge, then someone or other had first made him go out of his mind. And there were two of them in the kitchen after all, besides Rønnau. . . . And Kjersti, who walked around so quietly and considered herself too good to talk to people, well, she probably had the same thing under her skirt as all of them had. . . .

Men could be bad, for sure, nobody would disagree with that. But if a woman was of the right sort, with a broomstick between her legs on Thursday night, then she equaled ten of the worst fellows you could find in seven parishes.

No, either Kjersti had pounced on this stepmother of hers – and she had no reason to be fond of her, if the truth were to be told – or she had bewitched Håvard so he didn't know what he was doing. As for the doctor, who said she still had her maidenhead – well, a really sly woman could dream up all sorts of weird things before her maidenhead got pricked. . . .

No, *one* thing was quite clear. If there was a murderer at Olstad, it wasn't Håvard, that was for sure. It hadn't escaped anybody that, when this lawyer had driven Kjersti up a corner, like a rat, and the only thing that still had to be done was to squeeze *the confession* itself from her – it was then that Håvard stood up, making his chains ring like harness bells, and blurted out something that got distorted into a confession, just to save that wench, that crafty little witch in the making. . . .

This was about as far as the women had gotten, step by step, and it had all been thoroughly threshed over and over again, until there wasn't a seed left for a birdie in that spike. Then came the report that the Supreme Court had confirmed the death sentence of Håvard Gjermundsen.

By the end of the day the report had spread all over the parish. And, oddly

280

enough, it was rather quiet in the kitchens and the bedrooms that evening. Quite a few must have thought that this was a rather grim business – to behead a man for murder when no one could even be certain it *was* a murder – for each and everyone tacitly agreed that Anton's final testimony was a brazen lie, so much so, in fact, that nobody would give him a job after Jon had chased him from Olstad. But that fellow was hardly going to starve to death very soon, not as long as there were chickens in other people's chicken coops and grain on the pole which he could steal from the neighboring farms.

It was that evening the women started to walk.

They weren't exactly a sight for sore eyes as they wended their way. Most of them had jutting potbellies and chests as flat as a board. Others looked more like a sack of potatoes equipped with two legs to walk on. But all of them had long flat feet which carried them speedily along when they were on an errand for the greater glory of God, like now.

They knew where they could find each other at this time of day and didn't waste time with unnecessary walking. They walked, knowing where they were going and at which time the women were alone. To mix the men up in this, they tacitly agreed, was no use. It was men, after all, that such witches were out to get, warping their sights.

To be sure, here or there a pair of breeches would enter the kitchen as they sat discussing their errand. Then they merely said, 'We were just talking about all the terrible things that have been going on in this nice parish, and with more to come. But we trust the Lord has let it happen for a sign in the sky!'

Whereupon the man usually turned tail and left, remarking to the first person he met, 'I had meant to call it a day, you know. But Olea Årnes is sitting in the kitchen, so I'd better put up with the rain a little longer. For the rain is only wet, but Olea – well, you know Olea!'

The women walked the next day too, and the next. . . .

No, nobody could say for certain who was the first or the most eager. They were quite numerous from the very beginning.

The third day, at dusk – it was a Thursday evening – everything was ready; the message had reached all the right farms and all the right craftsmen's homes by then – they bypassed the cotters. Let the supper dishes stand unwashed if need be; put on your Sunday best and show up outside the cemetery gate.

'We're going to have *a little talk* with Kjersti!' some said.

'Your Sunday best, remember – it's God's judgment we'll be handing down!' others said.

Around eight o'clock the women were all gathered, over thirty altogether.

Andrea Nordby and Berte Flateby, Karen Galterud and Olivia Hagaen, Oleanna Spetalen and Marte Svingen, Tea Mobråten and Kari Spikkerud, Anne Oppi and Olea Årnes, Gorine Putten and Matilde Gørrholen, and many more.

None of the women liked any of the others very much – in fact, if the truth were to be told, everybody felt there couldn't be anything worse than the whole lot of them. But here they were on a higher errand, which was more important than such trifles.

They started walking south along the parish road, toward the private road which turned westward to Olstad. In the slowly falling dusk they suggested a flock of oversized crows legging it down the road. First they walked in silence, a silence that felt like a menace; but then one word led to another, and when they were approaching the turnoff to Olstad, they suggested even more a huge flock of crows on their way to a crows' parliament, all talking at the same time while figuring out what to do with the poor devil sitting in the middle of the circle, alone.

What they had meant to do with Kjersti was never cleared up, because the following day the majority had forgotten most of it, and those who remembered something kept quiet. Perhaps they had meant to tear off her clothes to see if her body bore any marks of the claws of Old Nick after her most recent night at Mount Brocken. . . . Perhaps they had only meant to scratch her up a bit, spoiling her face so that the menfolk wouldn't turn around after her for a while. It is never easy for others to imagine what is going to happen when *righteousness* is abroad. But whatever had been planned or not planned, it was probably mostly forgotten in the heat of the moment as the flock went charging down the Olstad road to the accompaniment of hoarse cries.

There hadn't been any workers at Olstad that day, in the lull betweeen the work seasons. Jon had stopped by briefly at midday. After a quick supper the servant and the maids had set out for a cotter's place by the roadside a little way soouth, where there would be a yard dance in the nice weather. Goro was home alone with Kjersti. Goro had just finished the dishes; Kjersti was in the bedroom, lying prone on top of the bedspread on Håvard's bed. She had removed her shoes and lay with her face buried in the pillow.

Early that afternoon she had noticed that Goro had been crying, and it didn't take her long to force the truth about the death sentence out of her. She had been lying like that since then, without either food or drink.

When Goro heard the yells from up the road, she rushed out to check and got back again to Kjersti as fast as her legs could carry her.

'Run and hide in the barn, Kjersti! A flock of women is coming down the road!'

Something in her voice made Kjersti obey; she sat up and slipped on her shoes.

But fast though she was, the flock of women came on faster. When Kjersti entered the yard, the first women were only thirty or forty yards off and it was too late to go hide anywhere. Kjersti started running down the field.

When the women caught sight of her, their hoarse cries grew louder, and those in the lead, who were the faster ones anyway, increased their speed even further.

But, needless to say, Kjersti was much faster, if only she put her will into it. She could have outrun them by taking the footbridge over to Berg, then outrunning them even more up the hills over there, leading them a dance until they were gasping for breath and lay sprawling by the roadside like empty crow skins, the laughingstocks of the entire parish.

But she didn't do any of that. She just ran straight down the meadow alongside the big rye field. The broad grain poles loomed like an army of goblins in the twilight. Kjersti continued running, down toward the long headland which ended in a precipice out by the lake.

It was after dusk by now; the forest showed black against the pale western sky and the lake lay smooth and still. When Kjersti turned around, as she did a couple of times, the upward-sloping meadow was dark with women in their Sunday best, coursing downhill after her like a broad, black stream. Only a few had any breath left to yell with now, finding it enough of a challenge to keep up with the pack; but she could make out a word or two. *Whore!* she heard, and *Witch!* and *Troll!* and every once in a while a word she wasn't quite sure of, but it sounded like *Ordeal!*

But ahead of the black flock ran two or three women, not so very far behind her. Foremost was Marja Dompen, the carpenter's wife with her long legs and her horse face. She ran like a horse too, with long paces, at a trot, her mouth wide open, though without yelling. Behind her Kjersti could make out Marte Svingen and Olea Årnes.

The faces of these women in the lead had a corpselike pallor in the faint twilight. Without looking any further, Kjersti turned around and ran along the headland, out toward the precipice.

When she'd reached the point, she turned around to look back for the last time. She hadn't been so fast on the last lap, and several women had gained on her. But now as before, the one in the lead was Marja Dompen, who was coming at her with wide-open jaws only thirty to forty feet away. A little farther back someone yelled, *We'll scratch out your eyes!* Another added, *We'll tear every stitch off your back!* And they were joined by a chorus of yells.

People said afterward that the whole thing was very strange – for Kjersti could still have saved herself. A trail went down the steep rock, and as a teenager Kjersti had amused herself by climbing this path, up and down, any number of times, though both Håvard and Rønnau had forbidden her to do so. She could have taken this trail, and not one of the women would have been able to follow her. If she had done that, leaving the women on the edge of the cliff the laughingstocks of everybody, they might even have come to their senses after a while and decided to go home again.

But Kjersti didn't take that trail. She stopped to look behind her until Marja Dompen was only about twenty feet away from her.

We'll scratch out your eyes . . . , she heard coming from farther back. Marja didn't say anything, but as she came charging forward, with wide-open jaws and her hands raised like claws, she was not a pretty sight.

Kjersti let out a single cry, like a winged bird. They weren't sure, but some of them thought she cried, *Håvard!* Then she jumped.

It was a sheer drop of twenty to thirty feet, with a scree of big boulders at the bottom. When the women got to the brink and stood there in a pack looking down, they could see, even in this bat's light, that Kjersti was lying on this rock-strewn slope in a contorted position such as no living person would lie in. Blood, looking black in the twilight, was oozing from her head over the gray rock.

The women stood there, numerous and black, but quiet now. Some were making gasping sounds as they drew their breaths. Some let out their breaths with something like a faint groan. Some withdrew from the brink – you could get dizzy from standing there and looking down. Several pulled back. The hindmost didn't even go all the way to the edge – I wouldn't even set eyes on such an ugly sight! one of them said afterward. They turned around on the spot and walked slowly uphill. The flock dispersed. When it approached the Olstad yard, it wasn't even a flock anymore; they looked like a bunch of women returning from a prayer meeting, each going her own way.

Goro, her face pale as she stood on the porch, ventured to speak to one of the stragglers, who was crying, and learned what had occurred.

The Exercise

H åvard must nonetheless have harbored a kind of hope; he noticed it when the deputy judge came to the jail and read him the Supreme Court decision.

But this hope couldn't have been a strong one. He was over the worst in a couple of days and resumed what he called *his exercise*.

Five days later Mr. Paus paid a call.

Mr. Paus looked somewhat tired; he had had a great many things on his mind lately.

The postscript to the letter Mr. Paus sent to the Supreme Court turned out to be the last official letter from the hand of Mr. Thurmann. He died at the beginning of August, without knowledge of the court's decision. What with the death, the funeral, and everything connected with it, Mr. Paus had his hands full for a whole week. Mrs. Maren Sofie was hit surprisingly hard by her husband's death. Lise, who had loved her father dearly, was inconsolable and full of self-reproach; even Anne Margrethe expressed what Mr. Paus perceived as genuine grief.

One week after the funeral the Supreme Court decision was handed down, and immediately thereafter Mr. Paus received a mild rebuke from the bishop. Though he had undoubtedly acted with the best intentions and, moreover, had come forward with the approval of his rector, still he had allowed himself to be carried away and had violated, to a degree, the obligation of professional secrecy which was incumbent upon every servant of the church when he acted in an official capacity.

It would mean a poorer living when the time came. But Mr. Paus was too busy to think about that. On the fourth day, in the afternoon, Jon came and told him that Kjersti had been chased to her death by the women of the parish. Lise, who had received the report of Håvard's death sentence with a calm that must have been due to a kind of paralysis, oddly enough became quite beside herself when she heard about Kjersti's death. She raved for several hours, pouring out everything that had revolted her recently. She lashed out at the Supreme Court, the judge, whom she called an old thief, Mr. Paus, who had obviously written a poor letter, even her own father. All other men were nothing but targets for her most profound contempt.

Still, the women were the worst – 'this indescribable sex to which I unfortunately belong!' she cried. She wept, screamed, rolled on the floor – Mr. Paus had never before seen her in such a state.

In the end, when her fury was nearly spent, she suddenly made a sort of confession from her own youth; and for several reasons it made quite a strong impression on Mr. Paus.

'And don't you imagine I am any better than the rest!' she said. And then it came:

'Perhaps you thought I was a virgin when you had me? In a way I was, that's true. But in another way I was anything but.

'When I was a young girl, nobody even dreamed that *I* might have any wishes or desires — long-nosed and ugly and lame as I was. But I did. And all my wishes were centered on Håvard. I knew little or nothing, but I made inquiries. I ingratiated myself with our dairymaids, the housemaids, and old washerwomen and got to know quite a lot. And when I lay awake at night while all the others slept, I imagined that Håvard did with me everything I had learned. I knew that Anne Margrethe felt the same way, and I even had suspicions about Mama. Oh, sure, sure! I thought.

'Anne Margrethe was the worst. Oh, how I hated her. She didn't even need him, attractive as she was. She could've had anyone she wanted — well, almost. Anyway, coldhearted from childhood on, she could have managed without anybody. But she was set on having Håvard! Despite the fact that she knew very well how I felt, she had her way and traveled alone to Christiania with him when she went there to get married. Oh, I knew perfectly well what would happen at the posting station, I even knew how she would manage it.[36] And she did manage it — just look at little Andreas! And there I lay at home, tossing in my bed and chewing the sheet. But what Håvard did with her at the posting station was nothing compared to all the things he did with me, long-nosed and lame as I was, in my loneliness at the parsonage.

'Håvard had to die — men admired him, but they envied him even more. And Kjersti had to die — those spiteful women couldn't stand the thought that Håvard had perhaps loved her.

'But what do I have to reproach these others with? Every once in a while during these last months, when I felt most wicked and figured that the sentence might be confirmed — and I knew it would — I would think, In one way it's good! Then no woman will moan with pleasure under him anymore, and now Kjersti will never moan under some other man while thinking about Håvard. . . . Oh, sometimes I am so wicked that the devil himself, it seems to me, is a mere child by comparison.

'And if you want to, now you can banish me from your bed and board and

36. The sexual encounter between Håvard and Anne Margrethe is presented in *The Family Dagger*.

settle down, righteous and exalted, in your solitude. But that is the way I am – part of me anyway every now and then – and sooner or later I had to tell it to someone. And to whom but you, since I can hurt you to boot by my telling it.

'But if you make as though you forgive me or possibly even do so, I can promise you to be a good parson's wife when we get our own place sometime. And I won't ever judge anybody, because I know a little bit about what a human being is like.'

Henrik Paus answered her in a way which now, the day after, somewhat surprised him.

'I don't have to forgive you,' he said. 'Because I recognize in myself everything you have told me.'

That was yesterday evening. They hadn't been able to sleep much – Lise didn't find it easy to quiet down. Today, face to face with Håvard, Mr. Paus thought for a moment in dead earnest about asking his advice. But then he felt ashamed. Håvard had enough to think about without that.

'That letter of mine didn't help any,' Mr. Paus said, slightly embarrassed. And Håvard replied:

'I knew that beforehand.'

Afterward they talked about one thing and another for about half an hour.

Mr. Paus's words to Håvard shortly before he left may, in part, have reflected what he had been through during the last twenty-four hours.

'You die young, Håvard,' he said. 'But it may well be that you've gotten more out of life than many who reach a riper age.'

'I have thought about that,' Håvard said, with his new, calm voice.

And then he added something which surprised Mr. Paus.

'I have told you about Tonè,' he said. 'But I am at peace with her now. I am at peace with Rønnau too, but it isn't quite that simple. I didn't kill Rønnau, that you know. But once in a while I can't help thinking that, in one way or another, without wanting to, I may have caused her death. And so I, too, deserve to die, I guess. I don't know . . .

'But I suppose everybody deserves to die, if the Lord is as strict as some say he is.'

Mr. Paus's answer was the last thing he said during this visit: 'We have agreed not to talk Christianity, as you call it. Or I could tell you that He is both the strictest and the mildest of all.'

When he had left, Håvard thought that actually it was quite pleasant to have Mr. Paus as a visitor. One didn't have to go on with the exercise as long as he was there.

The following day Jon came. He had come part of the way with Mr. Paus yesterday but had stayed overnight at the Mill, where he was to see about a bull calf that Håvard had bespoken.

'It has to do with the grain harvest and the fall plowing,' he told the governor.

Gunder Pilterud stopped him as they walked down the corridor.

'Mr. Paus and I have agreed,' Gunder said in a low voice, 'that we won't let Håvard know that Kjersti is dead. Mr. Paus took the responsibility for that lie,' he said. 'He had a name for it too, which he mentioned, but it was in a foreign tongue.'

'You may rest easy, Gunder,' Jon said. 'It was I who persuaded the parson to keep his mouth shut.'

Jon found Håvard to be the same as the previous time. The change he'd undergone in the prison occurred in early spring.

They finished quickly with everything having to do with the farm.

Then Jon took out a parcel from his pocket.

'Here are the thousand dollars,' he said.

'The thousand dollars?'

Håvard didn't catch on at first, and Jon understood: He's far away now, even if his face doesn't show it.

Then Håvard remembered.

'Didn't Høgne want to sell?'

'I don't know; but I don't think so. I never managed to talk to him. He walks around in circles in his yard again now, even worse than before.'

'You keep those thousand dollars, Jon,' Håvard said. 'I can't think of anybody who's more welcome to them, and some other farm may turn up. Where I go I won't have any use for dollars, you know.'

That was more than Jon could take, and he bawled like a kid for a while.

Then the usual Jon came into his own again.

'I've got a hundred dollars myself,' he said. 'Eleven hundred dollars – I'll be a rich man, won't I! Now I can tell both tax collector and judge to kiss my ass.'

Håvard sat looking at him with a faint smile, the way a grown-up man looks at a child.

Jon remained standing awhile when he was about to leave.

'It must be hard to be sentenced to death, being innocent and all . . . ,' he managed to say at last.

Håvard answered, in a calm voice:

'Yes, it is hard.'

The following day something happened too. Gunder Pilterud came and offered to help Håvard escape.

Gunder knew that Håvard had money with him. They had an agreement – Gunder got a dollar a month for keeping the cell clean, emptying the bucket each day and bringing lukewarm water twice a week so Håvard could wash and shave. It was when he stopped by with the water that he made his proposal.

There was a tannery at the river bend about six miles away. Håvard realized it was the same tannery that Anders Cotter at the parsonage had talked about ten years ago. There Gunder could buy a partnership for a hundred dollars, and he would do it if he could lay his hands on the money – he was tired of the slave labor at the fortress and would like to be a free man.

A hundred dollars – Anders Cotter could have had it for ten; but the prices were rising, that was so.

If Håvard provided the hundred dollars, Gunder could drop by this evening when he made his evening rounds and remove his chains. Then they could pretend that Håvard knocked Gunder down – he'd better punch him in the nose so he would have a nosebleed or something to show for himself. Afterward Håvard only had to lock the door from the outside and take off. Nobody knew him except the governor, and he was never out at that time of day. The gate was unlocked – Gunder locked it only when he was through with his evening rounds. He could leave a sheath knife and a gun with ammunition outside the door. If Håvard nevertheless should meet someone, he could just say he was running an errand for Gunder. There was nobody in this part of the building tonight, so nothing would be discovered until tomorrow morning, and then Håvard would be far away.

But Gunder had to have the money right away, so he could hide it. 'For if they find money on me, they'll get suspicious!' Gunder said, proud of his cunning.

Håvard began to tremble all over and had to sit down.

He knew he had had this plan at the very back of his head – that was the reason he'd taken his money with him. But that was long ago.

Gun and sheath knife, good – an ax he could steal someplace or other. That was all he needed to cope in the Finnskogene Forest throughout the winter, or to the end of his life if he wanted to. Why, it might even be a good life in many ways. . . .

Then came the other thoughts.

They would immediately suspect Gunder, and he would never be able to lie himself out of it. But that was his business, having proposed it himself.

But they would suspect Kjersti too – that she'd provided the money through Jon, perhaps. Jon, of course, could take care of himself; it would be harder for Kjersti. A new trial, with everything unrolled one more time. Kjersti wouldn't be up to it. She might even get the idea of fabricating a confession in order to make them give up their hunt for Håvard.

'No!' he said. 'It would mean living like a hunted animal for the rest of my life, and I don't want to do that. Besides, they would only make Kjersti suffer for it.

'But I might be able to help you with the hundred dollars anyway, when the time comes,' he added comfortingly, seeing how crestfallen Gunder was.

When Gunder had left, Håvard sat motionless for a while. He was still trembling all over. He tried forcibly to repress this tremor, but it refused to stop.

In the end he could see no other remedy than to start his exercise. It was a simple enough exercise – nothing but going through, step by step, what awaited him that last day.

From what he'd heard, such an execution was supposed to take place on the same soil where the crime had been committed. So it had to be at Olstad. He felt pretty sure where exactly, too. This year rye had been grown in the field which everyone still called the waterlogged meadow. There the aftermath would stay green until far into September, and it would probably be sometime in September.

He felt quite certain that this field would be chosen.

He himself would probably be somewhere at Nordby the last night – in the servants' quarters, perhaps. Mr. Paus would keep him company there, and that was good; you could talk to him like to anybody else.

Good that Mr. Thurmann died, he thought suddenly.

But that thought didn't belong to his exercise.

He probably wouldn't get much sleep. When the morning came, they would try to make him eat something, but he doubted he would have much of an appetite. And then they would walk, in a kind of procession he'd heard tell, down the road to Olstad.

Soldiers would've been called up, he'd also heard. Posted around the scaffold in a double row.

He made a guess that he would lie with his head toward the west.

But before it got that far he would stand, with a parson on each side most likely, and hear the sentence read one more time.

Who would show up to watch the spectacle? Many – most of those he knew up there. Kerstaffer Berg surely, if he could stand on his legs.

He thought through all the details. He had done so many times already and would do it many times more. He intended to take note when the day came whether it turned out the way he had imagined or, if it didn't, how it was different. It would help him not to lose his composure.

It was a hard exercise.

But, he thought, many have gone through this exercise before me, and some will go through it after me, too.

A few months afterward, when Gunder Pilterud was working at the tannery, he would often relate the episode when he proposed to Håvard he escape, but Håvard refused on account of Kjersti.

Gunder thought that, if this affair became known and the sheriff came and questioned him about it, all he had to do was to deny everything – for, after all, Håvard didn't escape!

He always ended his story with the same words:

' "They will only make Kjersti suffer for it," Håvard said. And there I stood, knowing that Kjersti was dead! I didn't know what to do. But Mr. Paus had said that we should spare him. And besides I thought that, if I told him about Kjersti, he might just take the gun and go right over and shoot the judge.'

The others got tired of this story in the end – nor did they believe in it very much.

'Cut it out, will you!' they said to him. 'We know it by now.'

The Last Day

*T*he field which had come to be called the waterlogged meadow had been chosen as the scene of the execution. It was now covered from one end to the other with green aftermath. Before the day was over it would be thoroughly trampled down; but it would spring back again. By next summer there would be a meadow thick with clover here.

It was a day in the middle of September, lightly overcast but mild. The summer had been a very warm one, and the potatoes were ripe and could be dug any time; but it wouldn't be done today. People from the entire parish, from even farther away, had decided to take the day off. Plainly, this day was almost like a red-letter day. You couldn't see a man beheaded every day, could you.

The execution was to take place at ten-thirty, it was said. That, you know, was the usual time for church services. But already a couple of hours earlier, droves of people had arrived from far away and settled down on the grassy slope. They helped themselves from the food packs they'd brought along and talked about the crops with people from other groups. If this heat and the nice weather lasted another couple of weeks so people could gather in the grain and the potatoes, then . . . well, perhaps one shouldn't call it a bumper crop till everything was in, but . . .

The scaffold had been erected in the middle of the meadow. It had been slapped together from rough boards and measured eight feet square. It could be mounted in one step. The block, a squared-off beam six feet long, lay at the edge of the scaffold, so that the murderer's head could fall directly on the ground. In the center of the block had been cut a crescent-shaped notch, where the condemned man was to rest his chin. The scaffold was strewn with spruce twigs as at funerals. Here, though, the condemned man was alive, at least when he arrived.

Outside the scaffold, stakes had been driven into the ground to form a big square, and twelve men in the uniform of the Romerike Musketeer Corps patrolled the area, making sure that nobody sat down inside these stakes – the space was reserved for the authorities: the sheriff and the lawyers and the parsons, the executioner and the executioner's assistants, and so forth.[37] One of the soldiers could relate that soon many more soldiers would arrive, three hundred altogether; they had slept in roadside barns during the night. The murderer, Håvard, had been a member of this corps in the 1814 war, even though he was from another part of the country. He had been a brave soldier, it was said, and was brought to the head of the front and made a corporal after he'd killed a Swedish dragoon and taken another captive. Colonel Rosenvinge had remembered him to this very day. And you certainly needed to be brave if you were to go through what awaited Håvard today.

One of the farmers asked this soldier – a big, husky fellow from Eidskogen with reddish hair and lots of brown freckles in his face – if he wasn't nervous because of what he would have to look at today. He said, straightening up, 'So much *courage* comes with this uniform that it takes more than the sight of another man getting killed to knock us over.'

Little by little people – men, women, and children – came drifting in from the hamlet as well as from more remote parts of the parish, and one hour ahead of time the area around the squared-off space was jam-packed with people. A group of boys, from six to seven years and up, had climbed

---

37. Romerike, in Akershus County, lies north and northeast of Oslo; the term is applied particularly to the open, flat areas in this region.

292

some of the big aspens which bordered the north side of the meadow. From there they had a better view, small as they were. An aging man from one of the neighboring parishes was of the opinion that what was going to take place here would be too gruesome a sight for small boys. But a freeholder from Nordbygda called him to order, amiably but firmly, 'There is a lesson for small boys in such a beheading. They will all learn to watch out from childhood on.'

Then came the three hundred soldiers from the Romerike Musketeer Corps, with flying colors, officers, and drummer. They lined up along the outer edge of the square. In an excessively piercing voice, the officer, a captain, commanded:

'Order arms!'

Then the executioner and the two executioner's assistants took up their positions on the scaffold. The executioner was a white-bearded old man. The executioner's ax was wrapped in a black fabric. When he removed it, you could see that the broad blade was wrapped in a thick red cloth. After he had removed that too, it appeared that the blade was protected by a yellow leather sheath. Only when he had loosened that did the broad shiny edge become visible.

It was quiet as in church while, slowly and deliberately, he prepared the ax and leaned it against the railing beside him. The two muscular executioner's assistants had taken up their positions, one at each end of the block.

Then, slowly, step by step, came the small, black-clad group of officials. Two parsons in canonicals – they were the curate, Mr. Paus, and Dean Neumann from the fortress town – further, the governor of the prison at the fortress, the deputy judge from the magistrate's office, the district doctor, and – hindmost – two parish clerks, the ones from the home parish and from the church in Nordbygda.

But two steps ahead of them all, chained hand and foot with clanking irons, walked Håvard, with a sheriff on each side.

Håvard had grown thin and he was very pale, which wasn't so strange – it was a grave moment and, besides, he had been confined to a cell for three-quarters of a year without a ray of sunshine. But he kept himself erect, was freshly washed and shaved, and had put on his Sunday clothes. Afterward it became known that he had stayed in the servants' quarters at Nordby during the night – Nordby himself had gone away, but the agreement had been made in advance. Mr. Paus, the curate, had been with him the first part of the night, but toward morning he had asked to be alone. The two sheriffs took turns keeping watch outside the door. Afterward they could relate that he had slept quietly for a couple of hours toward morning. In the morning he had washed carefully and shaved – the sheriffs removed his chains then but stood guard, because it was said to have happened that a convict cut his throat with the razor.

His holiday clothes and a clean linen shirt had been sent up to Nordby from Olstad, and Håvard dressed as if for a party; but he wouldn't touch food. Nor did he utter a word as they followed the private road to Olstad and farther down toward the scaffold. But he smiled when he saw where the scaffold had been built.

Two steps away from the scaffold the sheriffs stopped, and one of them unlocked the chains. They fell on the ground with a rattling sound. Håvard straightened up and drew a deep breath. He looked calmly about him – it was as though he wanted to impress upon himself all that he saw.

Now the two parsons stepped forward and took up their positions, one on each side of him. But he spoke only to one of them, Mr. Paus, and turned his back on the other.

The tears streamed down Mr. Paus's cheeks, and those who stood nearby heard him say, 'You shall receive amends in heaven, dear Håvard, for all the suffering you must go through today.'

But as far as they could tell, Håvard didn't answer.

Mr. Paus was still talking with Håvard when a man's voice in the crowd yelled, 'We managed to take care of that little whore of yours!'

A thud was heard as the owner of the voice was knocked down.

It became apparent later that it was Little Erik Berg who had yelled, and Amund Moen who had knocked him down – so thoroughly that he lay there till the whole thing was over.

Paus afterward said to Lise:

'Whether Håvard heard it I cannot say for certain. At any rate, you couldn't see the least tremor in his face. I, for one, tend to believe that Håvard at this point no longer perceived earthly voices. In any case I'm certain he didn't catch the perhaps somewhat hasty words I addressed to him. As I have told you, I was absolutely convinced, and still am, that Håvard died an innocent man and that nobody killed Rønnau. He himself looked at this somewhat differently, as I have often enough told you.'

The crowd grew quiet as the deputy judge ascended the scaffold and read the sentence.

After him, Dean Neumann stepped up and said a few words about the avenging hand of the Lord. You could tell that, if he believed anything at all, he believed that Håvard was guilty.

His speech was brief, and Mr. Paus thought that was the best part of it.

294

Now Håvard took a step forward, away from both parsons. He took off his jacket and vest and placed them carefully on the ground. Then he mounted the step to the scaffold and walked over to the executioner. The parsons followed him to the foot of the scaffold. There Mr. Paus threw himself on his knees. It was obvious that this had not been agreed on in advance, for the dean hesitated a moment before he, too, went down on his knees, slowly and ponderously. Neumann was a stout and aging man, and when everything was over Mr. Paus had to help him to his feet again.

Anyway, those who followed everything closely could tell afterward that Mr. Paus may not have intended to fall on his knees either; it almost seemed as though his legs refused to hold him up any longer.

While Mr. Paus was talking to Håvard, the executioner and the executioner's assistants had taken off their jackets and turned up their shirt sleeves.

Coming toward Håvard, the executioner made a sign, and Håvard stepped up to the block. He stood there a moment, drew another breath, and looked out over the lake. One of the executioner's assistants came over to him, pulled his sheath knife, slashed his shirt in the back right down to his waistband, and turned the flaps aside. The point of his knife scratched Håvard's skin so that the blood oozed forth, forming a long red streak. A wave of displeasure passed through the throng. But Håvard bent quietly down and put his head on the block. The captain commanded: 'Present arms!' The executioner, scared, was trembling. The first blow only hit Håvard on the side of his neck. The blood squirted out, but it wasn't death. People could see Håvard clenching his fists; otherwise he lay still.

The next three blows didn't hit Håvard at all, and it became clear to everybody that the executioner was half-blind.

This was a bit more than most of the spectators had asked for. People groaned, and some collapsed. Among those who collapsed were three soldiers – one of them was the red-haired one from Eidskogen. In the direction of the aspens were heard soft smacks as some of the small boys fainted and fell on the ground; others clung to the branches, screamed and wept; but these were only thin boys' voices, and the sound didn't carry far.

At the scaffold Mr. Paus lay prostrate, but he didn't seem to be praying – he was holding his hands over his ears.

The fifth blow severed the head from the body, and the blood spurted from the neck.

Then something happened which many thought was very ugly. Right outside the circle of soldiers stood four witch women, two from Nordbygda and two from the home parish, each with a wooden bowl in her hand. When the head fell, they forced their way in between the soldiers and tried to hold their bowls under the spurt from the jugular. They fell out with one another and started squabbling, but they'd all gotten a bit of blood in their bowls and a considerable amount on their clothes by the time a sergeant and a corporal managed to drive them out of the circle and in among the general public again. This was not done without a good deal of disturbance and considerable chanting of magic charms by the women. But everyone understood why the four women had been so eager – blood from a murderer's neck could heal all sorts of diseases.

Then someone – it was the servant at Olstad, pale and trembling – drove a black horse hitched to a summer sledge into the circle. The horse wasn't from this parish but belonged to the executioner. The two executioner's assistants grabbed the body by the arms and legs and chucked it onto the sledge.

Beside the scaffold lay a long stake, sharpened at both ends. One of the executioner's assistants fetched this stake, stuck Håvard's head onto the thin end and walked out of the circle, the stake raised high so everybody could see the head. A bit of blood oozed from the head down on his hands and arms. He walked up the field to the Olstad road, then followed that road until he reached the crossing at the parish road. There a hole had been dug for the stake. The assistant drove the stake down into the hole so that the head faced the road and trod down the earth around it. The other executioner's assistant came driving up with the body, urging on the horse – 'Gee! Giddy-ap!' He had tucked Håvard's jacket and vest under his arm. When the stake stood firm, the two assistants drove down the parish road toward the graveyard.

The throng was dispersing now that there was nothing more to watch; some of those who had taken a tumble were sitting on the ground. Erik Berg staggered to his feet. He was clasping his jaw with both hands – it seemed something had gone wrong with it. Some of the spectators who wanted to take in everything followed the two assistants.

A grave had been dug just outside the cemetery wall. There they stopped the horse. They stripped Håvard of the rest of his clothes, rolled them all into a bundle, and tied a leather strap around them. Then they threw the headless corpse down into the grave and filled it up again.

The two assistants placed their spades on the summer sledge, turned the horse around, and drove back to Olstad. The spades, too, had been borrowed there.

While this was going on, Mr. Paus had helped Dean Neumann to his feet. It took some time, because the dean, his face bathed in a cold sweat, had gone soft as a jelly and could hardly stand up. He whispered to Mr. Paus, 'You must say something to the congregation – I am not up to it.'

Mr. Paus cast a glance out at the throng, which was already dispersing, and said, 'It's too late.'

He was glad he did that, anyway. In his heart of hearts he formed a hateful, and not very Christian, thought:

They've gotten rid of him at last, so now they can go on living in the same old way for another fifty years!

Thus died Håvard Gjermundsen, farmer at Olstad, a farmer's son from Telemark.

Afterword

T*he Troll Circle* is Sigurd Hoel's most ambitious and complex book. A historical novel whose action is set in the first half of the nineteenth century, it has themes that mirror central ideological conflicts of Hoel's own age. At a deeper level, the story of Håvard Viland probes one of the most intractable questions of all time: Why do attempts at change, social change, so often fail? Hoel's answer takes the form of ritual drama with the thrust of a cultural critique. The narrative encompasses half a dozen fictional genres, including psychological novel, regional tale, novel of marriage, and social novel. Perhaps the term 'novel-tragedy' comes closest to capturing its essential quality.

As the germ of Hoel's story – his childhood discovery of the executioner's block used in the beheading of a convicted murderer in 1833 – grew into a literary project, what chiefly interested him was the 'cycle of old myths' that had formed around the murder, myths containing 'glimpses of an old time' in which the Nordic Middle Ages were still 'vividly alive.'[1] Accordingly, *The Troll Circle* abounds in folklore, superstition, and quaint customs. Hoel, however, treats these and other elements of folk culture in the light of modern mass psychology. Similarly, though the main plot conforms to the time-honored model of a quest, the latter is presented from a psychoanalytic perspective. These contraries manifest a creative tension within the author, between an affinity with the folk and its age-old traditions and a sophisticated analytical intellect schooled in modern science. The novel, considered by Hoel his 'best work,'[2] capped a distinguished career as a literary and cultural critic as well as a writer of fiction.

The Troll Circle (1958) is without precedent in Hoel's fictional oeuvre. The first installment of Håvard's story, *Arvestålet* (The family dagger, 1941), is a romantic tale that pales by comparison. However absorbing as narrative, it lacks a deeper resonance. Nor had Hoel's modern novels, such as *En dag i oktober* (1931; trans. as *One Day in October*, 1932) and *Fjorten dager før frostnettene* (A fortnight before the nights of frost, 1935), alerted the reader to the possibility of a monumental work like *The Troll Circle*. In these novels Hoel had adhered to psychological realism, as he also did subsequently in *Møte ved milepelen* (1947; trans. as *Meeting at the Milestone*, 1951). Like many of Ibsen's male protagonists, the central characters in these novels are ambitious professionals who have failed as human beings, and Hoel's elucidation of the reasons for their failures amounts to a critique of contemporary middle-class culture. Steeped in issues of the moment, these works have obvious features of the period novel.

By contrast, *The Troll Circle* eschews topicality as well as romance while still dealing with social themes, now escalated and generalized: the action of his novel, Hoel writes in a manuscript note, must show 'the general features in men and society that are the same at all times.' The simple milieu and the temporal distance would allow the 'motive forces' of the story to stand out clearly and in depth, revealing the 'interplay' among the elements that shape human destiny in every age, the present included (MS fol.2323:3). This purpose is consistent with the underlying tragic conception. For there to be tragedy with 'real fate' in it, Hoel notes, the novel must not only be true to the period but have an enduring interest (MS fol.2323:2).

The remove from the present gave a powerful fillip to Hoel's imagination, enabling him to achieve unwonted breadth and objectivity in his depiction of character and of everyday life. The character portrayal in *The Troll Circle* has a richness and solidity that can be matched only by *Veien til verdens ende* (The road to the world's end, 1933), Hoel's novel of childhood. Furthermore, as in the latter work, the leisurely pace appropriate to a rural setting made room for genre scenes, inserted stories reminiscent of folktale or legend, and evocations of the Norwegian landscape, the seasons, and ancient folk-ways. These two novels share a poetic dimension which makes them unique in Hoel's production. Significantly, both were the result of many years of gestation.

While the gain in objectivity is crucial to the novel's artistic success, its power would have been considerably less were it not for the author's passionate engagement with his major theme and with the predicament of Håvard, the central character. Started in 1941, during the German occupation of Norway, the book was mostly written at a feverish pace during seven months of continuous work in 1958, leaving Hoel utterly exhausted. In a 1959 interview he said, 'In the final section, where Håvard is beheaded, it was terrible. I felt as though I was laying my own head on the block.'[3] This profound empathy with his hero had deep roots in Hoel's personal experience and political struggle.

Hoel knew, as soon as he decided on a literary career (about 1920), that he would someday write the story of the local murder. In the meantime the image of the young murderer – a freeholder's son who had killed his pregnant sweetheart for reasons of social ambition – metamorphosed into that of a basically good man condemned to death for a crime he didn't commit, ostensibly because he was an outsider. This sea change may be attributed, in part, to the situation in contemporary Europe, where entire ethnic groups were being destroyed because they were different. Moreover, several of Hoel's friends were indicted or persecuted for their convictions: the poet Arnulf Øverland (1889–1968), Wilhelm Reich (1897–1957), and other so-called cultural radicals who had adopted Freudo-Marxism, a utopian doctrine of social transformation and individual liberation.[4] Nor was Hoel himself spared: two of his novels, *Syndere i sommersol* (1927; trans. as *Sinners in Summertime*, 1930) and *One Day in October*, were attacked for their frank treatment of sexuality and other alleged abominations. Thus, the battle of Håvard in *The Troll Circle* – with conformity, religious bigotry, and social inertia – is not unlike the one Hoel himself had fought as a progressive writer and intellectual. In a review of the book, his colleague Sigurd Evensmo aptly called *The Troll Circle* a pessimistic allegory about the fate of the radical in his own time (*Orientering*, December 13, 1958, p.14).

Throughout *The Troll Circle* two opposing themes are evident: the rational drive toward progress and a dark undertow of irrational forces that holds it back. In trying to explain the fear of change, Hoel combines a psychological and a mythic model. Common to both is the journey motif, which Hoel uses frequently as a master image of human life and mental development. It figures prominently in a lecture delivered at Uppsala, Sweden, in 1944,[5] as well as in the notes for a projected book on psychology (MS fol.2364, p.1). At some point of our journey, usually in childhood, Hoel suggests, most of us retreat or make the wrong turn so that we lose our way or go astray. The 'wrong turn' projects the child into a sort of vortex from which the adult finds it difficult to escape. This psychological motif of 'going astray' is so pervasive in *The Troll Circle* that it assumes a mythic quality, as in the beginning of Dante's *Divine Comedy*.

The motif exfoliates from Håvard's favorite ballad about Vilemann and Signe, placing him under a veritable curse of repetition which is envisaged as a special form of fate called nemesis – 'that old transgressions, or what is perceived as transgressions, avenge themselves' (MS fol.2323:3; November 20, 1940). Taking a cue from Wilhelm Reich's character analysis, Hoel emphasizes the crucial role of fear in this process, specifically 'fear of happiness.' Such fear, he postulates, is the underlying cause both of collective inertia and of the individual's 'surrender' to his fate, an attitude which brings about that very 'fate' (MS fol.2323:3). In a subsequent note he states that retribution 'strikes precisely *because one was afraid of happiness*. Retribution . . . strikes the one who . . . seeks happiness but does not dare to seize it for fear of punishment.' This is what is designated in the local dialect as a 'troll circle,' more generally as a 'vicious circle.' Hoel had started his reflections on the projected novel with a question asked by Henrik Wergeland (1808–45): 'Why does humankind progress so slowly?' (1831). He answers it thus: 'The Middle Ages within us. The past within us. The fear within us. Original sin' (MS fol.2323:5; March 14, 1942).

Hoel's definition of 'fate' or 'destiny' links it to ordinary human experience. He notes the 'inexorable, . . . inescapable quality which marks the lives of all people . . . but is occasionally heightened to something terrible, monumental.' Its genesis, Hoel says, is 'the conflict between one's own primitive will to life . . . and all that resists it, outside and within oneself' (MS fol.2323:3). While both these elements are central to Håvard's predicament and character, Håvard's tragedy and the novel's action transcend Hoel's intellectual conception, a possibility he had anticipated. What he hopes for, he notes, is that the action 'will create its own idea, . . . independently of a plan laid in advance' (MS fol.2323:5).

Readers react to Håvard in a variety of ways. Here is a sampling of epithets that have been applied to him: 'an educated, enlightened young man'; 'a lightweight both morally and intellectually,' however 'attractive'; and a man of 'heroic stature.' My own admiration for him is fraught with ambivalence. Able and talented, reasonably experienced and informed, Håvard is endowed with a delicate moral sensibility and an excellent mind. He is high-spirited and courageous, as shown by his wartime exploits, yet genial and companionable; and he is a good husband, father, and neighbor. While not a 'hero' in the conventional sense, he is vastly superior to the average humanity that surrounds him, and his hard-won calm in the face of death could be called 'heroic.' Yet he falls short. It is as though, in depicting Håvard's predicament, his creator has taken a hint from Kafka, whose basic theme, according to Hoel, is that man can never be 'right' before God or 'fate.'[6]

More mundanely, Håvard can never be 'right' before his neighbors, his hired help, or his wife. His new parish, Nordbygda, which introduces itself in the opening chapter as a smugly self-enclosed order immune to outside influence, is a formidable antagonist. Håvard's 'vision' in the woods, sandwiched in between two chapters portraying representative parishioners, appears exceedingly vulnerable. The whole hamlet is typified by Hans Nordby, who lives by the right of the stronger while professing respect for the law. The conning of Sjønne Strøm and the story of Hans's elder brother, Erik – declared insane on the grounds of his religious idealism – foreshadow the possible outcome of Håvard's visionary hopes. Significantly, Erik and Sjønne are both associated with an art motif, namely, playing the fiddle, as is Håvard. The spectral Aeschylean echoes the reader picks up once Håvard has entered the house at Olstad – 'were, will be' – add a fateful ring to the theme of resistance to change. The chapter 'The Dairymaid,' a burlesque version of this theme, marks Håvard's first defeat in trying to carry out his mission.

Still, as the circumstances of his 'vision' show, the greatest obstacle lies within Håvard himself.[7] Meditating on fate after parting from his brother, he reflects that, for fate to acquire meaning, one has to 'control' it and turn it 'where it really did not want to go.' It is the sight of the beggar, with her 'empty' eyes, 'like a deep, dried-out well,' and the nightmarish dream about the reindeer/Tonè that the beggar's eyes bring back to him which call forth the 'dreams, visions, and plans' that suddenly 'gushed forth' within him. These inspired images of 'controlling' fate are clearly a substitution for the uncomfortable thoughts about Tonè's suicide which he has just tried to suppress. The very word 'gushed' (*fosset*) is an echo of the waterfall (*foss*) where Tonè had plunged to her death. Thus, the very energies of Håvard's 'vision' seem generated by guilt. Yet, his self-redemptive project bids fair to make him whole again, for now everything that had seemed 'confused and accidental . . . fell into place, became meaningful.'

Håvard's commitment transcends individualism; like the existentialist project which it resembles it entails a decision for humankind: his goal is to shape a community that will guarantee freedom, dignity, and happiness for all. This might seem a tall order even for a person free of sin or guilt, all the more so for Håvard, whose idealism is tainted by a psychic wound.[8] But the more questionable its basis, the more essential it becomes for Håvard's moral identity. If his hopes are threatened, as happens when he discovers that Rønnau sides with the parish rather than with him, his purpose hardens, and he increases the pressure both on himself and on his cotters. The subsequent revelation of Rønnau's false pregnancy is an even heavier blow, in that, morally speaking, it pulls the rug from under his very presence in Nordbygda and jeopardizes the effective sublimation of his guilt. After the 'child' is no more, his mission gets reified in the drained meadow, now become his 'child.' Thereafter his project is fueled as much by frustrated eros and thwarted desire for fatherhood as by the need to assuage guilt.

The ensuing eruption of violence can best be understood against this background. While due weight must be given to the external factors – mainly the chicaneries masterminded by Kerstaffer Berg and Jon's careless disclosure to the cotters of the master's future hopes – Håvard's staking his all on the drained meadow, the symbol of his mission, is decisive.[9] This becomes quite obvious in Håvard's near killing of Martin. In the following two incidents of violence, the vandalizing of the potato field and the mutilation of the horse, his enemies strike back, driven by thwarted greed and lust.[10] These events, which represent an ominous heightening of the external conflict, bring the action to a preliminary climax, both dramatically and psychologically, as Håvard, in a scene which foreshadows the tragic denouement, edges toward suicide.

How could a man like Håvard, with all his strengths, find himself in such dire straits? One can argue back and forth about his weaknesses, whether excessive compassion and poor judgment or sexual susceptibility and a quick temper – it just does not add up. As Hoel's reflections on tragedy imply, the determining forces refuse to be caught within our ordinary conceptual schemes; they can be conveyed only by myths, legends, and dreams.

An early chapter, 'Rønnau and Håvard,' offers a clue to the fatality that operates in the novel. Lying sleepless in bed, Håvard dreams about wandering in a pathless swamp, being pushed deeper and deeper by something on his back which 'he would have to drag along with him to his dying day.' In a variant on this dream, he finds himself on the church green at home in Telemark, walking around 'in circles, sinking deeper and deeper in sand and mud,' while people stand around looking on. Occasionally he can hear a 'sort of song' in the air: '*Astray* . . . ,' it sang. While this dream relates to Håvard's past life and makes the reader aware of his repressed guilt, it is also oriented to the future, à la Jung. In the chapter entitled 'Omens' in Part Two, Håvard, Kjersti, and Goro discover they are surrounded by a circle of villagers on the church green: a dream has become enactment. Moreover, the word 'astray' in the dream picks up the ballad motif of bewitchment, being put under a spell (Norw. *tatt i berg*; lit., 'taken into the mountain'), turning Rønnau into a kind of mountain troll. Since the destiny of Håvard is preinscribed in the story of his ancestor, the ballad – paraphrased in the chapter 'Greetings from Tonè' – becomes a key element of foreshadowing in the book.

It is the close interweaving of motifs from dreams and folklore in the light of depth psychology which defines the logic of fatality in *The Troll Circle*.[11] The best example of such interweaving is the unconscious transformation of the bear into Rønnau in Håvard's dreams subsequent to his rescue of Kjersti at the summer dairy. The entire episode and its aftermath signify the return of the repressed (with Kjersti stepping into Tonè's place), a development that has been prepared for by the collapse of Håvard's sense of mission. Simultaneously, Håvard's situation acquires a deeper, paradigmatic dimension from the bear episode, echoing as it does ancient lore about maidens rescued from dragons or ogres; the exploit brings Håvard instant notoriety, making him a folk hero overnight. Moreover, the mention of church bells in the text alludes to the ballad of Vilemann and Signe, in which the hero, after the spell is lifted, falls in love with and marries the sister he has just liberated; he recognizes her only at the sound of the church bells years later, with disastrous consequences.

The recurrent dream not only 'interprets' the situation of crisis that exists with Rønnau's persistent abuse of Kjersti, but – like the previous dream commented – casts ominous shadows upon the future: Rønnau's death and Håvard's possible implication in it. It contains all the Freudian elements, including an unavowable wish, namely, that Rønnau disappear so as to make room for Håvard's love of Kjersti. Being placed within the context of an ancestral legend whose outcome is known to the reader, the dream seems doubly fateful. Håvard's emotional quandary is sufficiently demonstrated by his having to imagine making love to Kjersti in order to respond to Rønnau's increasing sexual demands. Though he understands he is in a bad way – intuitively he perceives these dreams as a warning – his attempt at self-understanding through a review of his past is to no avail. Håvard senses that all that has happened to him constitutes a 'single strange web with some pattern or other, which he glimpsed a little of but not all. He felt that if he could see the whole pattern, he might be able to turn his fate around.' Instead of relying on a sense-making *project*, Håvard at this point hopes that sheer *understanding* – of the past – will 'turn' his fate. But before he can accomplish the seemingly superhuman task of seeing the 'whole' pattern, the machinery of justice has started grinding.

Throughout his life, despite his reputed rationalism, Sigurd Hoel was a seeker after faith. In his next to last novel, *Ved foten av Babels tårn* (At the foot of the Tower of Babel, 1956), he writes: 'The gods are dead . . . and people are running around like stray dogs.'[12] In his manuscript notes the gods figure as Christianity, Marxism, and psychoanalysis (MS fol.2327:1; May 25, 1953). Similarly, the hero of *The Troll Circle* seeks a global meaning to his life, striving to avoid mere contingency or fortuitousness on the one hand, predestination and fatalism on the other. His visionary project, a syncretistic blend of secular Christianity, utopianism, and democratic liberalism, sustains Håvard for a while, but eventually his faith wanes and he faces the horror of pure materialism ('The Passing Years'). The return of the repressed in the bear-killing episode goes to show that mere material success is not a viable human option: the moral vacuum that it entails must somehow be filled. Without a justifying faith that invests his life with meaning, Håvard falls prey to chthonic forces. The more palatable, somewhat romantic possibility that Kjersti's love might generate a new faith is not seriously considered. Toward the end, judging by Håvard's refusal to save his life when opportunity offers, he seems to have chosen another way out.

Faced with imminent death and seeing all his former rationalizations crumble, Håvard can find peace only through an irrational philosophy of expiation. In this new interpretation, the events of his life are linked by a chain of blood guilt, from the moment he killed a Swedish soldier during the war to the death of Rønnau, for which he also now seems to assume responsibility. While this expiatory metaphysic, which is reminiscent of Schiller's and Dostoyevsky's redemptive tragedy, is a noble attempt at a religious theodicy and enables Håvard to meet his end with heroic dignity, he has, in fact, adopted an all-too-familiar moral fatalism. In terms of sense-making, Håvard's new attitude represents the entrenchment of his sporadic temptation to read events or words as signs or omens. Thus he hears the house at Olstad or the dead Tonè 'speak' to him, and he fears the watchful 'eye' of God invoked by his neighbors after the bear-killing episode. It seems that, however enlightened Håvard is, he cannot avoid being influenced by the received ideas of his time – a character trait which justifies the aesthetic of fate tragedy that underlies the novel's form. Håvard's spiritual conflict, which has always been present, is resolved by a quasi-religious faith that vindicates his sick conscience. This neat explanatory model, however, seems to be undercut by other aspects of the narrative. In the process the text of *The Troll Circle* opens up to interpretive indeterminacy.

For though the logic of Håvard's new perception is understandable, the reader will not necessarily accept it. And the novel suggests other readings which do not square with a simple pattern of retribution. Thus, Hans Nordby sees Håvard's life as determined by bad luck, or evil chance, reducing Håvard's story to a tragedy of circumstance; however, it is that same Nordby whose intrigues against Håvard have left little to chance. Another reading would be based on the classic concept that character is fate – 'character' denoting not only Håvard's moral flaws or errors but his good traits as well, chiefly a courageous, uncompromising and, yes, noble nature, notwithstanding the suspect psychic roots of these qualities. Håvard's honesty and compassion, and his vision of a new society, eventually invite his destruction, or so it appears. But however valid they may seem, each in its way, none of these readings does full justice to Hoel's complex implementation of his concept of tragedy. We are left, then, with an interlocking network of conflicting forces, in which fortuitous circumstance, individual and collective evil, and personal weakness and nobility work together in producing tragedy.

At a deeper level the text can be read as ritual drama. Håvard, admired by women and envied by men, *must* die, like Christ, in order that the people of Nordbygda, as Reverend Paus says in his parting words, 'can go on living in the same old way for another fifty years!' There is an indirect allusion to Jesus in Håvard's thought of Nicodemus. Moreover, he is clearly a scapegoat figure, one upon whom the community projects its cardinal sins, incestuous sex and murder. Finally, both the trial and the execution contain distinctively ritual elements.[13] The execution, with its aspect of evil epiphany, is a quasi-religious occasion, taking place at the 'usual time for church services.' One is led to suspect that the ritual tragedy is ultimately traceable to a brutally repressive society, necessitating periodic eruptions of near-paranoid aggression to safeguard the very social order which provokes them.

The complexity of *The Troll Circle* is also evident from Hoel's use of foils, so widespread that one might speak of an aesthetic form designed by analogy. This analogical structure, so brilliantly used by Shakespeare in *Henry IV, Part 1* and in *Hamlet*, is exemplified in narrative by Dostoyevsky's polyphonic novel. A great many characters in *The Troll Circle* echo themes central to Håvard's story, while others find themselves in similar predicaments but deal with them differently. The noted analogues may be tragic, pathetic, or grotesque. Mention has been made of Erik Nordby, incarcerated in Kerstaffer Berg's basement for life on account of his zeal for social reform. Høgne Lien, whose entire life is reduced to tracing increasingly narrowing circles in his own yard, offers a grotesque parody of Håvard's tragic inability to put his past behind him. By contrast to these figures, who are losers, Jon the Hunter and Amund Moen play Fortinbras to Håvard's Hamlet. Jon, indifferent to society as well as to morality, has what it takes to succeed, namely, luck: Håvard's downfall is *his* big break – ironic though it may be, because Jon *loves* Håvard. Amund Moen, tough, fearless, and unscrupulous, is accused of killing his wife – who dies under suspicious circumstances – but avoids being indicted, marries the woman he loves, and gets an heir, in ironic contrast to Håvard's fate. The mill owner and Hans Nordby, linked with Håvard through an actual and an imagined relationship with Rønnau, respectively, are shrewd, practical men with, seemingly, a good deal of sympathy for him. The mill owner, ruled by prudence and common sense, avoids the trap into which Håvard falls and is a happily married man, and a father. And Nordby, whose greed, lust for power, and meanness of spirit make him an epitome of the local ethos, is Håvard's near-villainous antithesis.

These parallels and contrasts produce a bewilderingly ambiguous impression and serve as a warning against easy syntheses and generalizations in interpreting the book. At the same time the resulting incongruities turn the novel into a trenchant analysis of the workings of society by projecting Håvard's tragic nobility against the commonplace virtues and repellent vices of the community that eventually destroys him.

With its multilayered structure and interpretive indeterminacy, *The Troll Circle* can be said to embody the ironic-tragic mode so characteristic of twentieth-century fictional narrative. Because of Hoel's juxtaposition of the hero's subjective fate with multiple perspectives upon it, mythic, sociological, and psychoanalytic, the novel poses a considerable challenge both to critics and readers, a challenge that I, for one, have found worthwhile accepting.

Port Jefferson, New York, August, 1990

NOTES

1. 'Da Sigurd Hoel fant bøddelens blokk' (When S. H. found the executioner's block), *Frisprog*, October 25, 1958; MS fol.2323:5 in the Department of Manuscripts, the University Library, Oslo. For a report on the murder, see *Indlandsposten*, September 2, 3, and 4, 1935; MS fol.2323:1.

2. Birger Christoffersen, 'Møte med Sigurd Hoel' (A meeting with Sigurd Hoel), *Stockholms-Tidningen*, June 9, 1959. The reviewers seem to have shared this view, and a Danish critic proceeded to nominate Hoel for the Nobel Prize in literature.

3. Ibid.

4. The extent to which Hoel was preoccupied with the situation of Reich, who spent most of his working life as an exile in various countries, is shown by the existence of an outline for a novel, 'The Refugee,' among Hoel's papers at the University Library in Oslo (MS fol.2365:8).

5. 'Dybdepsykologi og diktning' (Depth-psychology and literature), in Sigurd Hoel, *Essays i utvalg* (Selected essays), ed. Nils Lie (Oslo: Gyldendal, 1977), p.79.

6. Sigurd Hoel, *50 gule* (Fifty yellow [books]) (Oslo: Gyldendal, 1939), p.177.

7. For a more extensive interpretation of *The Troll Circle*, see Sverre Lyngstad, *Sigurd Hoel's Fiction: Cultural Criticism and Tragic Vision* (Westport, Conn.: Greenwood Press, 1984), pp.127–57.

8. See *The Scarlet Letter* (in Nathaniel Hawthorne, *Novels* [New York: Library of America, 1983], pp.344–45), where Hester's parting message is that a person who wants to change society must not be 'stained with sin, bowed down with shame, or even burdened with a life-long sorrow.'

9. The fact that Håvard is beheaded in this meadow causes the latter to be subsumed under the symbol of the troll circle. The tragic irony of the situation seems to echo the conclusion to Goethe's *Faust*, where the sounds that Faust perceives do not, as he imagines, stem from work on his great drainage project but from the digging of his grave. See Goethe's *Faust*, Part Two, Act V, Sc.: Great Forecourt of the Castle.

10. These acts of criminal mischief are based in part on information Hoel received

from his elder brother, Olav, in 1942, relating the latter's experiences with his own neighbors in the 1920s (MS fol.2323:1).

11. The key to Hoel's practice in this respect may be C. G. Jung's conception of the archetypes, as well as his theory that myth and folklore are expressions of the unconscious psyche. See Tutta Laukholm, 'Folkelig tradisjonsstoff i Sigurd Hoels forfatterskap' (Traditional folk material in S. H.'s literary work). Thesis, University of Oslo, 1968, pp.1, 24, 74, and passim.

12. *Samlede romaner og fortellinger* (Oslo: Gyldendal, 1950–58; Collected novels and stories), XI, 153.

13. In *The Stranger*, by Albert Camus, also stemming from the period of the German Occupation, Meursault refers to his imminent execution as an 'implacable ritual' (trans. Matthew Ward [New York: Vintage, 1988], p.109). Both Hoel and Camus depict miscarriages of justice arising from profound societal imperatives.

Selected Bibliography

WORKS BY SIGURD HOEL
Translations

'Christmas Eve.' *The Archer* 2 (Jan. 1928): 27–36. Included in the story cycle *Ingenting* (Nothing; 1929) under the title 'Sne' (Snow).

Meeting at the Milestone. Translated by Evelyn Ramsden. London: Secker & Warburg, 1951.

'The Murderer.' Translated by Janet Garton. In *Slaves of Love and Other Norwegian Short Stories*, edited by James McFarlane, 136–43. Oxford: Oxford University Press, 1982. Originally published as 'Morderen,' in *Prinsessen på glassberget* (The princess on the glass mountain). Oslo: Gyldendal, 1939.

One Day in October. Translated by Sølvi and Richard Bateson. New York: Coward-McCann, 1932.

Sinners in Summertime. Translated by Elizabeth Sprigge and Claude Napier. New York: Coward-McCann, 1930.

'The World.' *The Norseman* 8 (May–June 1950): 198–202. Translated from 'Verden,' in *Veien til verdens ende*, 1933.

Other Works: A Selection

All works listed in this section have been published by Gyldendal Norsk Forlag in Oslo.

Arvestålet (The family dagger). 1941.

De siste 51 gule (The last 51 yellow [books]). 1959. Prefaces to Den gule serie (The Yellow Series), a library of contemporary novels in translation that Hoel edited at Gyldendal Norsk Forlag.

Essays i utvalg (Selected essays). Edited by Nils Lie. 1962.

Ettertanker: Etterlatte essays og artikler (Afterthoughts: Posthumous essays and articles). Edited by and with a foreword by Leif Longum. 1980.

50 gule (50 yellow [books]). 1939. Prefaces to the first fifty books in the Yellow Series.

Fjorten dager før frostnettene (A fortnight before the nights of frost). 1935.

Ingenting (Nothing). 1929. A story cycle.

Mellom barken og veden (Between the bark and the wood). 1952. Essays on politics and culture.

Samlede romaner og fortellinger (Collected novels and stories), with a fore-word by Sigurd Hoel. 12 vols. 1950–58. The standard edition of Hoel's collected fiction.

Stevnemøte med glemte år (Rendezvous with forgotten years). 1954.

Syvstjernen (The seven-pointed star). 1924.

Tanker i mørketid (Thoughts in a dark time). 1945. Essays on Nazism.

Tanker om norsk diktning (Thoughts about Norwegian literature). 1955. Chiefly reviews.

Ved foten av Babels tårn (At the foot of the Tower of Babel). 1956.

Veien vi går (The road we walk). 1922. Stories.

Veien til verdens ende (The road to the world's end). 1933.

CRITICISM

Beyer, Harald. *A History of Norwegian Literature*. Translated and edited by Einar Haugen. New York: New York University Press, 1956.

Brostrøm, Torben. 'Den onde sirkel' (The vicious circle). *Vindrosen* 6, no.2 (1959): 160–62.

Hannevik, Arne. 'Kjærligheten og trollringen – noen grunnmotiver i Sigurd Hoels diktning' (Love and the troll circle – some central themes in Sigurd Hoel's work). *Ord och Bild* 70 (1961): 89–95.

Jensen, Brikt, ed. *Sigurd Hoel om seg selv* (Sigurd Hoel about himself). Oslo: Den norske Bokklubben, 1981.

Longum, Leif. *Drømmen om det frie menneske. Norsk kulturradikalisme og mellomkrigstidens radikale trekløver: Hoel, Krog, Øverland* (The dream of the free individual: Norwegian cultural radicalism and the radical triumvirate between the wars – Hoel, Krog, Øverland). Oslo: Universitetsforlaget, 1986.

Lyngstad, Sverre. 'Sigurd Hoel and American Literature.' *Edda* 84, no.2 (1984): 193–204.

———. 'Sigurd Hoel: The Literary Critic.' *Scandinavica* 22, no.2 (1983): 141–58.

———. *Sigurd Hoel's Fiction: Cultural Criticism and Tragic Vision*. Westport, Conn.: Greenwood Press, 1984.

Mylius, Johan E. de. *Sigurd Hoel – befrieren i fugleham* (Sigurd Hoel: Bewitched liberator). Odense: Universitetsforlaget, 1972.

Nøstdal, Kjell. 'Sigurd Hoel's *Trollringen*: Ein analyse av nokre aspekt ved verket' (Sigurd Hoel's *The Troll Circle*: An analysis of some aspects of the work). Thesis, University of Bergen, 1970.

Tvinnereim, Audun. *Risens hjerte – en studie i Sigurd Hoels forfatterskap* (The giant's heart: A study of Sigurd Hoel's literary work). Oslo: Gyldendal, 1977.

Ytreberg, Stein. 'Om pessimisme og optimisme hos Sigurd Hoel' (On pessimism and optimism in Sigurd Hoel). *Edda* 65 (1965): 315–24.

Other volumes in the series Modern
Scandinavian Literature in Translation include:

The text was set in Linotype Galliard
by Tseng Information systems
The book was designed by Dika Eckersley